Nobody Lives Forever

RANDOM HOUSE NEW YORK

Nobody Lives Forever

Edna Buchanan

All rights reserved under International and Pan-American
Copyright Conventions. Published in the United States by
Random House, Inc., New York, and simultaneously in Canada
by Random House of Canada Limited, Toronto.

Library of Congress Cataloging-in-Publication Data

Buchanan, Edna.
Nobody lives forever/Edna Buchanan.
p. cm.
ISBN 0-394-57551-2
I. Title.
PS3552.U324N63   1990
813'.54—dc20   89-42775

Manufactured in the United States of America

9 8 7 6 5 4 3 2

FIRST EDITION

Book design by Carole Lowenstein

For my mom, who read me my first story

Man that is born of a woman is of few days,
and full of trouble.

JOB 14.1

ACKNOWLEDGMENTS

For their support, friendship and inspiration, I am indebted to Dr. Joseph Davis, D. P. Hughes, Sergeant Gerald Green, Major Mike Gonzalez, Lieutenant Edward Carberry, Joel Hirschhorn, Rose Klayman, the Reverend Garth Thompson, Sergeant Christine Echroll, Walter Wilson, Mike Baxter, David Thornburgh, Officer Lori Nadelman and the library staff at *The Miami Herald*.

Special thanks to Michael Congdon, my agent and good friend, for his guidance.

And to Peter Osnos, my editor, Mitchell Ivers, Amy Roberts and all the people at Random House.

Nobody Lives Forever

PROLOGUE

*I*t was the night of the full moon over Miami. The shooting started early.

A short-tempered motorist brandished his gun to scare strangers who cut him off in traffic. The strangers, undercover cops chasing a robber, assumed he was an accomplice and shot him five times.

An exasperated housewife ended a noisy quarrel with her spouse by firing her pistol out a window. The bullet killed their next-door neighbor.

A man roused from a sound sleep by a pounding at his door believed he was about to be burglarized. Again. He opened fire with his shotgun and blasted the intruder. Then he remembered, his wife was expecting the Avon lady.

A taxi driver struggled with a robber for his gun. He won, saved by his bulletproof vest, but his out-of-control taxicab skidded into a pickup truck that slammed into a light pole that toppled onto a house and left twelve square blocks in the dark.

A deranged high school teacher shinnied up a power pole, flung his clothes at passersby and demanded six million dollars from the police, who tried to coax him down. When a fire department aerial truck arrived with a fifty-foot ladder, he scrambled higher and grasped a hot wire. "He did a spiral on the way down," a fire chief solemnly told a TV news crew.

Carloads of men, shouting in Spanish and armed with MAC 10 machine pistols, fought a running gun battle along the Sunshine Turnpike. The survivors refused to speak to police.

Rival crack cocaine dealers settled a Liberty City turf dispute with sawed-off shotguns, and the embattled staff of an often-robbed fast-food chicken emporium exchanged shots Wild West style with bandits who got away.

Cuban gangs stomped Puerto Ricans, American blacks fought Haitians, and Anglo rednecks warred with blacks and Latins. A jogger with a knife in his belt and rape on his mind slowed his pace to watch a young woman unload groceries from her car in a quiet residential neighborhood. And at Miami International Airport, José López-Gómez, a visitor from Colombia, cleared customs and anxiously sought a taxi. Glistening with perspiration, he felt feverish and was beginning to experience abdominal cramps.

Somebody got careless in a blighted neighborhood miles away. The mistake proved fatal. Sparks from a free-base pipe ignited a barrel of solvent used to manufacture crack cocaine. The drug house exploded with a blast that raised the roof, rocked the area and shattered windows blocks away. The force of the explosion and the scattered rain of debris caused J. L. Sly to pause in his practice of kung fu feints and postures. He gazed skyward for a moment, then resumed his silent combat with the eerie shadows that spilled across his Overtown street corner.

This was the full moon city police dread most, scaling a sultry summer sky on a Friday. Passions soared with the temperature and the sweltering evening rapidly escalated into one of those nights that overwork the cops, emergency room personnel, and the chamber of commerce. Dead bodies began to stack up. So did calls for help.

Homicide detectives on the afternoon shift stayed on overtime. The midnight crew was called in early.

*L*aurel Trevelyn found herself at home alone again. The quiet residential street was drenched in moonlight, reflections off the bay and hidden terrors. She paced tearfully, becoming more and more agitated, frightened and furious. She knew she was losing control. She knew that bad things happened when she was left alone in the night.

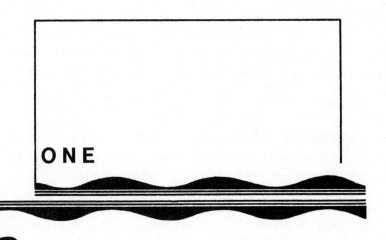

ONE

*S*tepping into the night left him breathless, as if slipping into a black well. Alex loved the welcoming whispers high in the palm trees and the radiant energy released by pavement still warm to the touch at midnight. Darkness gave him a sense of freedom and excitement. The strictures of the day were gone, the eager and prying eyes closed.

His steps, though cautious, were brisk as the rage and pain ebbed and fell away like a discarded garment. He breathed the soft and tender night air deeply, his senses more acute, skin tingling. Across the water, a dog barked, then whimpered. The smell of freshly mowed St. Augustine and the scent of night-blooming jasmine mingled in a languid breeze off Biscayne Bay.

The black sky was thick with charcoal-colored clouds scudding fast across the bright full face of the moon. He crossed an unfenced yard, carefully skirted a newly planted vegetable garden and bent slightly to pass beneath a nearly invisible plastic clothesline stretching east to west. Prowlers or Peeping Toms chased on dark nights sometimes run full tilt into Adam's apple–high clotheslines. What a bummer, he thought, to wind up gasping on the ground as somebody's pit bull tears into your shin.

He hugged the shadows, cutting quietly through hushed yards perfumed and shaded by heavily laden grapefruit and orange trees. Flutters from a color television screen bounced rainbows off the second-story windows of a stately old Spanish-style home as he passed by. A heavy metal mailbox mounted on a pole stood lonely sentinel at the gate, while inside, David Letterman or a late-night movie flickered with imitations of life.

Television—it made him laugh. The only turn-on left in so many bedrooms. How many millions of people sleep clinging to their remote-control channel selectors and dreaming full-color beer and new car commercials?

He wanted to shout, "Wake up! It's me, Alex! This is real life out here!"

Instead, he picked his pace up to a trot, across the damp lawn and narrow street to a sprawling ranch house. No traffic streamed along the two-lane causeway at this hour, no headlights. He alone, confident and surefooted, sailing solo through a sea of night. A gull joined him, wheeling and chuckling above, then swooped out across the velvet bay. A big jet winked its landing lights through the treetops and rumbled west toward Miami International Airport. At ground level, bright eyes glowed knowingly, watching. A stealthy striped cat broke its gaze and vanished into a stand of Australian pines.

The house stood quiet, without lights. The muscles in his stomach and throat constricted simultaneously as he stepped soundlessly up the stairs. A split second of uncertainty, then his gloved fingers pushed deftly at the screen, just above the latch. Already loose, the wire mesh tore easily from the weathered wooden frame. Reach in, push up the lock button, lift the hook from the hasp. The screen door swung open with a squeak that brought beads of moisture to his upper lip and accelerated his pulse. The inner door was protected by only a simple push-button lock. He slipped a charge card from the pocket of his jeans, slid it between door and frame and worked it down behind the lock. At an angle, in the groove, pull it back. His hands were steady. The push button popped with a dull click. He carefully replaced the card in his pocket and inched the door open slowly, wincing at the creaks and groans of the hinges.

Silence. He stepped inside, closing the door very gently behind him. Straining to see in the dark, he inhaled kitchen smells of coffee and greasy cooking. A sudden scrabbling sound and a slow, guttural growl from beneath the table froze him in his tracks, and he nearly cried out. He'd forgotten the damn dog. Sad faced and shorthaired, the buff-colored mongrel stood stiff legged, a snarl rumbling in his throat.

"Bosco," he whispered hoarsely. "Hello, Bosco. Here, boy." Reassured, the dog cocked his head to one side and blinked in puzzlement. "Come here, Bosco!" Bosco took a few hesitant steps, claws clicking on the polished floor, then slumped heavily to one side. The old dog rolled onto his back, four feet pawing the air, tail thunking the tile. He offered his stomach for scratching. Alex looked speculative, then stopped and roughly rubbed the furry belly. The dog was his. When he straightened up, the animal scrambled to his feet and shambled alongside, tail awag, an eager accomplice. Snuffling in the stillness, he led the way into the dining room, the metal tags on his collar faintly clinking. He would point the way to the family silver if he could, Alex thought, if that were what I was after.

His penlight stabbed the darkness. A shiny palmetto bug, routed from cookie crumbs and empty, milk-stained glasses, skittered from the table in flight. Alex moved down a hallway, ever so softly, heart pounding. The door to a child's room stood open. A teenage daughter sighed heavily in her sleep and tossed fitfully, one knee drawn up, the sheet kicked away as he watched. His shadow fell across the lovely throat that would bruise so easily and the tangled hair that glowed softly in the moonlight. He fingered the cold steel blade of the hunting knife in his belt as he watched. Inhaling deep breaths, suspended in time and motion, as if in a dream, he waited until she was settled and lying quiet once more. Then he moved on, shivering with excitement.

He heard the snores before stepping across the doorsill into the master bedroom. The woman's bloated body hogged the center of the bed, lying on her back, huge breasts spilling out of the shapeless nightgown. Her open mouth emitted piggy sounds and saliva that pooled in one corner. The man slept naked. He had lost the bedclothes to the woman, who in her noisy slumber grasped them greedily to her body. He lay on his stomach at the edge of the bed, palms flat, fingers slightly curled, as though hanging on in desperation. His skin looked hard and smooth in the semilight slanting through draped windows. Dark curly hair covered his back. Alex stared curiously, imagining them awake and active, in sex. He found his intrusion into their home, the intimacy of their bedroom, exhilarating. He savored a delicious sense of power and omniscience. He had heard that many rapists experience the same elation, enjoying the violation of a victim's most personal and private space.

He plucked a ring from the cluttered dresser top as the wind swept a cloud away from the surface of the moon and silvered the room. Eyes startled him, shining from the beveled mirror, staring straight into his own. He failed to recognize at first their alert, expectant expression. He had last glimpsed that vibrant face in a photograph, bathed in a sudden splash of light and frozen in time. His throat caught with sudden emotion, as though unexpectedly seeing a loved one long absent.

He stared unblinking into his own reflection.

A snorting, rooting sound from the woman on the bed set him back to business. A delicate cameo gleamed in the frail light, and he snatched it off a nightstand. Conscious of every footfall on the carpeted floor, he lifted the woman's scuffed tote bag from a chair, slid out the French purse, overstuffed like its owner, and removed the bills. He scooped up a pair of pale gold earrings and then rifled the man's trousers, hung on the back of another chair. Only two singles in his billfold. Poor schmuck, Alex thought, and took them.

One more long, fantasy-fueled look at the lovely teenager, sleeping so prettily, then he padded swiftly through the house, back the way he'd come. Nearly home free, a piece of cake. Moving too quickly, he stumbled into a dining-room chair. Clutching at the back to catch his balance, he staggered heavily against it. It bumped the table, and something—a glass—toppled onto its side and rolled.

He tried to catch it, but it fell to the floor, shattering the stillness. Fear filled his throat. Creaking and thrashing sounds came from the bedroom. His muscles twitched as he fought the impulse for headlong flight.

"Bad dog!" The woman's voice was raspy with sleep and anger. "Bad dog! Lie down!" The animal whined and crawled back beneath the kitchen table where he lay watching, moist eyes baleful. The bedsprings creaked heavily again, then sank slowly into silence. Alex clung to the back of the chair, sucking in deep breaths. The house fell quiet. He waited motionless for five minutes, ten. Time, he thought. He was always cheated and had to fight for time. He never had enough. Now it moved so slowly in the dark. The heart-shaped face of the tender teenager smiled shyly from a silver frame on the mantel above the fake fireplace—sheltered, indulged, untouched. His anger surging, he listened to a dining-room clock tick away the seconds until it was safe to leave. The dog's tail thumped the floor hopefully as he passed.

"Watchdog, come here!" The dog heeded the whispered command and stood up, grinning in that silly way mutts do. Alex smiled back, stooped and reached out his left hand. With the right, he drew the knife. Head down, as though bashful, the animal padded dutifully forward. The blade was razor-sharp. It was easy. He kept the fingers of his left hand tightly wrapped around the dog's muzzle until the twitching and the quivering stopped. Alex stood up slowly, being careful where he stepped, and wiped the bloody blade across the dimpled face of the teenager in the framed photo. The smeared mustache effect almost made him laugh. At the door, Alex turned to watch the widening stain still creeping across the yellow tiled floor. Satisfied, he stepped out into the dark well of night. The street was quiet and unlit, except for the sound of an electric bug killer zapping mosquitoes on somebody's patio and the cream-color glow of the big moon. He was hot and excited and very pleased.

It was better, far better than he had thought it would be.

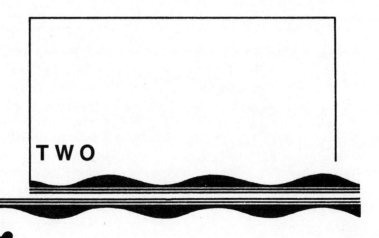

TWO

*T*he digital alarm read 4:18 A.M. when Rob Thorne awoke. He had been dreaming he was Officer Thorne, snappy in dark blue, rolling from his patrol car, diving for cover, under fire, emerging heroic, lives saved, just like the cops on television, just like Rick, the cop who lived next door. Admirers were crowding, reaching to shake his hand. The chief stood by, smiling, with a medal . . . Rob lay there for a moment, sorry to be awake. Then the rising and falling sound of a burglar alarm pierced his consciousness. Dogs were barking.

Was it a prowler? He slid from between the cool sheets and padded to his bedroom window. He cranked open the jalousies to hear the night sounds above the hum of the air conditioner. The commotion seemed to be coming from a distance, perhaps the next island. Wind or heat lightning often triggers home and car alarms. The keening sounds carry across the water. He rubbed the back of his neck sleepily and wondered if anybody had called the police.

Then he saw it. At first he thought his eyes were playing tricks on him. But no. A slim, dark figure silhouetted, standing motionless next to some trees. He blinked, then strained to see, but it was gone. Changing position, he moved closer to the screen. There it was, near the rock garden next door. Something stealthy, moving closer to Rick's house.

Laurel Trevelyn, Rick's new girlfriend, was home alone. The windows were dark, Rick's car absent from the driveway. A tip-off to a prowler—an invitation. Rob turned quickly toward the phone, bashing a bare toe painfully on the night table in his haste. Hobbling, he reached for the receiver to call Laurel, but he could not see to look up the number and did not want to switch on a light. Somebody was lurking down there in the dark. Laurel was alone, and Rick had asked him to look out for her.

Rob pulled on a pair of cutoffs, snatched a baseball bat from the corner of his room and flew barefoot to the rescue. What a good thing it was that he had *not* gone with Rick, he thought as he ran down the stairs. Just a few hours ago he had been disappointed. He had become a police buff, clamoring constantly to ride along as an observer with Rick and his partner, Jim Ransom, on the midnight shift in homicide. Both detectives had tried to discourage him.

"Shake your family tree, kid. If no Julios fall out, forget it," Jim had said. "A name like Thorne gives you chances of zilch and zero, thanks to some federal judge and affirmative action. They're promoting nothing but Latinos, blacks and women. You're young, you're smart, stay in school. Find something with a future."

But he had persisted, asking to join them that very night, a Friday, with no classes in the morning. Rick had stopped him midstride. "Listen, kid, I need a favor. There's been a prowler in the neighborhood. Keep an eye on things, will you? Watch out for Laurel until I get a chance to beef up security around here. Okay?"

"Sure, sure, Rick." Though disappointed, Rob was secretly pleased to be trusted with the assignment. Now he was elated. Had he gone, he would have missed this. He had been trying to impress Laurel since the day she had moved in, lithe and graceful in cutoff blue jeans, long legs tanned, her hair tawny and sun streaked. He had even fantasized about what might happen if she and Rick ever split. The way Rick goes through women, who knows, he thought. She is closer to my age than his.

He burst out the back door, taking a deep breath as the warm air enveloped him. Blinking in the dark, he sprinted toward the rock garden, holding the bat in front of him, clutched in both fists, ready to swing. The fleeting shadow moved quickly now. "Halt!" he shouted. "Stop right there!"

Moving faster, the figure crashed through a hedge, plunging into the shrubbery on the far side of the house. Rob heard the footfalls now, somebody running hard through a small grove of orange and grapefruit trees next to the Singer home. Adrenaline pumped through his veins as he took off in pursuit. He knew he would have no trouble overtaking his quarry. He was fast and in good shape and knew the neighborhood like no prowler could. Thrilled, he felt this was what it must be like to be a cop. There was no doubt in his mind now about his future.

Ahead, the runner hesitated, blocked by a six-foot fence of unfinished lumber. Realizing that the pursuer was gaining, the shadowy figure turned and dashed toward the bay. Rob quickly changed direction. He had the prowler trapped between him and the water. Too bad Rick could not see him now.

The moonlight exposed a flash of pale skin and movement in a dark mass of sea grapes at the edge of the bay. "Come out of there, you bastard!" He lunged and caught a shoulder, but in a frenzy of thrashing, the prowler wrenched away.

There was scrabbling among branches close to the ground. Rob grasped a kicking foot by the ankle, and they grappled in the dark. "Hell, you're just a kid," he said, in disgust and disappointment. He stepped back and shouted a warning.

"Come out, or I'll shoot." He had no gun, but it sounded good. He liked the timbre, the authority in his voice. Stepping forward, he raised the bat to his shoulder, swinging it like a shotgun at the prowler. The branches parted in bright moonlight. Rob's mouth dropped open, his eyes widening in surprise. The sound was like a clap of thunder. A bullet caught him square in the chest, knocking him off his feet.

Thrashing and small snorting sounds telegraphed the short-circuitry of his nervous system. Then they faded, until the moon's reflection was the only light left in his wide-open eyes.

THREE

*P*rowlers are low priority, usually gone by the time police arrive. Patrol Officer Mary Ellen Dustin hoped this one would not be. She did not mind getting all sweaty in a foot chase—or involved in an arrest and its time-consuming paperwork. Probably some dicky waver, she thought. Men—fed up with them and the current sad state of her love life, she would almost enjoy catching some peeper with his pants down. Oddly enough, the call was right on Rick's block, a few doors away from the very man who had left her with the blues. She floored it, holding back on lights and siren. If a prowler was lurking and she did not nail him, it would not be her fault. This was her last night on patrol before transferring back to homicide. Maybe she could end it by presenting Rick with his very own neighborhood flasher.

She was just half a mile away when the dispatcher reported possible gunfire at her destination. Shit, she thought, uptight homeowners shooting at shadows. Miamians are so well armed that police officers must always assume that everybody has a gun, including the victims, the witnesses, passersby and, of course, the perpetrators.

She flicked on the siren, hoping they would all hear it and throw down their weapons. No need for a noiseless approach now.

Lights shone from several houses on the block. Officer Dustin saw no one as she stopped in front of the address where the call had originated. She unsnapped her holster, then saw a middle-aged woman in a nightgown running across a lawn toward her. She was screaming. Oh Lord, Officer Dustin thought, somebody's been hit. Dammit!

*H*omicide Sergeant Rick Barrish and Detective Jim Ransom were looking for a man who had run a footrace for life and won, sprinting out the front door of the drug house an instant before it exploded. Somebody else, not quite as fast on his feet, was dead, still buried in the smoldering wreckage.

The detectives swung by Woody's all-night grocery and snack bar to shoot the breeze with whoever was out and about in Overtown at that hour.

J. L. Sly was holding forth on the street corner outside, his coffee-black skin aglisten in the heat. Despite record-breaking temperatures, he wore an immaculate white sport coat and crimson trousers over a short, spare frame that moved with a fluid, almost catlike grace. Oozing confidence and good cheer, he eased inside to join them.

"My man!" he greeted Rick. They exchanged a high five, then Sly dropped into a crouch, a martial arts position. His slender hands sliced and swept the air in swift circular motions. "What under the full moon brings my friends to this black hole between heaven and earth?"

"Business," Jim said, his tone officious. "You heard the crack house blew up, right?"

"Thunder and sorrow." Sly intoned the words, speaking them slowly and nodding solemnly. "I am quick to seek knowledge that I was not born possessing."

Jim looked pained. "I am quick to kick ass when somebody jerks me around."

"Words of wisdom soar higher, on stronger wings than words of war," J.L. informed him. He turned to Rick, with a flourish. "Your friend does not reach out to embrace the sparrow with the folded wing, the symbol of inner peace."

"Nope. He's never been accused of it," Rick said, grinning. "How goes it, J.L.? You aren't terrorizing Overtown with your kung fu, are you?"

Sly danced lightly around the far larger detectives, feinting and dodging. "I am not certain if I am a man dreaming that I am a butterfly or a butterfly dreaming I am a man."

"Just don't get your ass in trouble with that stuff." Rick's deep-set gray eyes glowed against his bronzed cheeks, his tone was good-humored and friendly. He lowered his voice. "We would like to talk to the individual who bailed out just before the roof went up."

Sly stepped closer, speaking softly. "Street name Blinky, usually present at the Nairobi Stereophonic Diner."

"Thanks, buddy."

"Like a drifting cloud—I ask for nothing. I want nothing."

"You'll get nothing from me," Jim muttered. His jowls bore a dark stubble. Burly and built like an aging linebacker, he wore the prisonlike pallor of a man who sleeps by day and works at night.

Sly smiled sweetly at the glowering detective. "A log that floats in the water forever will never become a crocodile."

"What the hell?" said Jim, but Sly was already outside, melting into a late-night crowd that parted respectfully before him.

"J.L.'s okay," Rick said, grinning.

"Sure, except he's walking around using up oxygen that some useful creature could be breathing."

*7*he store's fluorescent lights interfered with reception on Rick's walkie, a handheld police radio. Static was breaking up a machine-gun-fast exchange of transmissions. He stepped closer to the door, coffee cup in one hand, the other holding the radio to his ear to hear the action.

A 330—a shooting—with a possible 45—a death—on the island, in his neighborhood.

Rick drove. Jim clung to the dashboard and worked the radio, trying to glean more from dispatch. The first uniform was at the scene. "That's Dusty's unit," Jim said with a sidelong glance at Rick. Fire rescue was also present. The shooting victim was a young white male, apparently dead at the scene. That was all.

"Sounds like one of the neighbors popped your prowler. Saves us the trouble. We can chalk up one for our side. Street justice, my favorite: swift and sure." Jim grinned at the thought, even as hot coffee slopped over his fingers from the Styrofoam cup he struggled to steady.

The ten-minute drive took less than five. Rick's usual commute home was short and scenic. Life on San Remo, one of the residential islands clustered between Miami and Miami Beach, gave him the best of two worlds, a small, quiet neighborhood with tree-lined suburban streets, just four miles of bridge and blue water from downtown Miami's metropolitan skyline and modern police headquarters. The security and tranquillity had become important when he and Laurel had decided to play house. Their whirlwind romance had surprised his friends, who had doubted that at age thirty-six he would ever relinquish the life of a high-performance ladies' man. They were still taking bets. Dusty had been the most recent of a long line-up of women loved and left.

Rick hoped Jim was right about the shooting. He almost believed it until he swung the unmarked car into his own driveway and heard the screams.

They did not come from Laurel. His searching eyes quickly found her, alone on the outer rim of chaos, huddled barefoot on a small stone bench six feet from their front door, knees drawn up, head down, her hair wet. His long legs covered the distance in a few quick strides. "You okay, babe?" He pulled her close in a hug. She did not resist or respond. "What the hell happened?"

She raised amber eyes blank with shock and bewilderment, her face pale and sickly under her suntan. "I don't know what happened," she whispered. She resembled a lost child about to cry. "It's Rob." She gestured toward the Thorne home, her hand trembling.

"Oh, shit." Rick squeezed her shoulder, then stepped toward the source of the screams, his heart sinking. The dead boy's mother was struggling to escape the restraining arms of her husband and a police officer. Blood stained the front of her nightdress. Her flailing arms reached out to her son.

A paramedic turned away from the corpse, caught Rick's eye and shook his head. "No way, Sarge. Nothing we could do."

"He was gone when I got here, Rick." Mary Ellen Dustin swallowed the feelings that still surfaced when she saw him. "I thought I felt a faint, thready pulse for a few seconds." She shrugged hopelessly. "Maybe it was wishful thinking. He's so young. I would have called the squad anyway. You know"— she lifted her eyes toward the mother—"more for her, than him."

Rick nodded. "What have you got so far, Dusty?"

"Several people heard the shot." She sounded professional and impassive. "As you know, the victim lives two houses north of the scene. Somebody called in a prowler report. I was en route when another caller reported shouts and running. Apparently the victim came out with a baseball bat to try to stop somebody and walked right into it. Nobody here saw what happened, or the shooter. We've got no weapon, no description. Nobody heard a car. The offender may still be in the area. I secured the scene and set up a perimeter."

Laurel appeared next to them, wearing bedroom slippers and clutching a pink wrapper around her. In the pulsing red and blue lights from half a dozen patrol cars, her blond hair streaming, she looked about sixteen years old.

"Step back please, miss . . ." Dusty's voice trailed off as Rick folded a comforting arm around Laurel's shoulders.

He introduced them.

Dusty smiled and said hello. So this is the one, she thought bleakly. Of course—the perfect cheerleader: fresh and young and beautiful, even with no makeup, in the middle of a lousy night.

"Sorry, I should have realized, Laurel." Dusty stared. "Your hair is wet."

"I—I was in the shower when it happened."

"At this hour?" Dusty looked at her quizzically.

"The dead boy is our next-door neighbor," Laurel crooned softly, then buried her face in Rick's shoulder and wept.

"I know." Dusty continued to watch Laurel, her eyes curious, until Rick impatiently signaled her to continue her preliminary report. She had little more. "I got here within five minutes. It looks like he took one square in the chest."

"See if the bridge tender saw anything suspicious, coming or going, call the

ME, get K-9, and request the lab unit with the high-intensity lights." Rick scanned the neighborhood with new eyes. "It's black as hell out here," he announced, as though seeing it for the first time. The lack of traffic and the feeble glow of the charming, widely spaced, old-fashioned street lamps had always been appealing, compared to the relentless orange glare from the sodium-vapor anticrime lights downtown. He had never before scrutinized the street where he had grown up through the clinical eyes of a homicide detective evaluating a crime scene.

"I already asked, the lights are in use," Dusty said.

"Then get a fire truck and the chopper. There are lots of places to hide around here," Rick snapped. "Nobody comes on or off the island unless they live here. No sightseers. Check out anybody walking on the causeway and anything that looks out of place in the neighborhood. Check the cab companies for pickups in the vicinity."

Two other uniforms swiftly cordoned off the area with yellow crime-scene tape. Rick stepped inside, focusing his flashlight on the baseball bat beside the body. If the bat or the grass beneath it was bloodstained, it might mean the kid had connected, they might be looking for an injured suspect. It would be something.

But there was nothing. He examined the body briefly, struggling to block images of the gap-toothed tyke who had trailed him and other big boys around the neighborhood, the clowning teenager with a mouth full of metal and a growing fascination for police work, the kid eager to be a cop like him. The shoeless, shirtless corpse sprawled toes-up on the grassy lawn resembled none of those memories, but Rick knew this would remain his clearest, most painful recollection, the one that would haunt him—forever. His face grim, he walked to the rescue van where the parents clung to each other. The man stared at Rick, hope fading in his eyes.

Rick had spoken to survivors, next of kin, hundreds of times. It never gets easier, he thought, only more difficult. They had never been his next-door neighbors before.

"Helen. Dan." He stepped directly in front of them, deliberately blocking their view of the body, forcing them to focus on him. "It's true. Robbie was shot, and he's dead. There was nothing anybody could do to save him. We don't know who did it yet, but I assure you we will do whatever it takes to find out. You know I'm your friend. You can count on me now more than ever."

The woman moaned.

"Time is important here," Rick told them. "I want you to be strong, to put your grief aside, so you can help us to do the right thing."

"What can we do?" the father asked in a monotone.

"Do you know what Robbie saw?"

"We didn't even know he went out." The father's voice was flat and hollow.

"What was he doing out here?" the mother asked, her voice rising. "What was he doing? What was he doing?"

Rick knew. The knowledge tasted bitter in his mouth. The kid would have been safer in a police car with him than home asleep in his own bed. If only he had stayed there, safe in his own bed.

*N*eighbors helped the parents back into their home. Rick walked calmly to the car, wheeled and slammed his right fist into a treetrunk. He welcomed the pain.

"Damn palm trees. That one was asking for it." Jim loomed behind him, matter-of-fact and down-to-earth. "It looks like there was a little wrestling match. Let's get the lab to try to lift prints off the body."

A long shot, but it had worked before. In two of the partners' prior cases a killer's fingerprints had successfully been lifted from the skin of a victim. A rapist who had killed a young girl had left a thumbprint on her ankle. The technique is most successful on women because their skin surfaces are smoother and less hairy. In the second case, however, an identifiable finger-print was found on the forearm of a man who had struggled with his killer.

"We've got people canvassing. So far nobody heard a car or a boat take off. I asked for a printout of all the burglars who work the islands and the beach."

"What if this isn't a burglary, Jim?"

"Then unless we get lucky, we've got a real whodunit. But what else could it be? Who else but a burglar would be sneaking around here at four A.M.? Damn shame, Rick. He was a good kid. He woulda made a helluva cop." Jim shook his head. He found little to admire in life anymore, but he had liked the young man, whose eager and intelligent interest had flattered him. The aging detective nodded toward the Thorne home, now ablaze with lights. "He the only kid?"

"Yep, the one and only. I was in high school when he was born. I watched him grow up. When my folks retired and moved to Saint Pete, I moved back into the house. Then I bought it from them. Such a nice quiet neighborhood." He smiled bitterly.

"Life is a fuck sandwich," Jim said. "It's the goddamn full moon," he grumbled. "Full moon—it never fails. When we get the sumbitch who did this, he's mine. This one deserves to get blown away on sight."

"Yeah," Rick said, "but he probably won't be."

"You know damn well what'll happen, Rick. Struggle, in the dark—you watch, they'll say it's no death penalty case. Betcha they'll drop it to second degree. Worse yet, it'll turn out to be some little prick who gets a free ride cuz he's a juvenile. Not if I can get him in my sights first."

Like some of the uniforms sweeping the bayfront on both sides of the island, Jim held a long pump-action Remington twelve-gauge shotgun at his side.

Rick sighed. Jim bellyached and blustered constantly about the system and its flaws. He always talked street justice. Tonight he was in no mood to listen. "Put that back in the car. I have enough to worry about without a loose cannon as a partner."

"Miami is Dodge City these days." Jim brandished the weapon, thick fist wrapped around the wooden stock in a caress. The long barrel reflected a lethal glow in the dim light. "What we need is a little street justice, or maybe we should call it poetic justice. What's wrong with that?"

"Nothing, except it's against the law—and makes you as bad as they are. Why risk your neck and your career for some puke? It's not worth being a martyr. Put that in the car and let's get to work."

The detectives stripped off their jackets and loosened their ties. Rob Thorne appeared almost peaceful, bathed in sudden bursts of flashbulb brilliance: the star of the show, the center of attraction. Camera lenses misted over in the soft, moist heat as explosions of light, and the muttering of men at work created an almost-surreal tableau. Overhead, the shadowy fronds of a towering royal palm seemed to catch the clouds that roiled across the innocent full face of the moon.

Police and technicians paused to greet a new arrival. Bob Lansing, a round and genial bespectacled man, always introduced himself as the only doctor in town who made house calls. Of course, he explained, all of his patients were dead.

"Let's see how this young fellow got this way," Lansing, a county medical examiner, said cheerfully. As he shifted the body slightly, the small, harmless-looking bullet hole brimmed and overflowed with blood that spilled and streaked Rob's chest.

Lansing scrutinized the limp arms, then lifted each foot to inspect the soles for clues to their final steps. He and Rick rolled the body over together. No wounds in the back, but there was something, a small hard lump, protruding just below the left shoulder blade. Bullets slow down as they travel through a human body. The skin often stretches like elastic, yielding to the impact and capturing the spent projectile just beneath the surface.

"Ahh," the doctor said. "Want the bullet?" The autopsy would not be performed until midmorning. Detectives might find it useful to know the bullet's caliber now.

"Anything we can get," Rick said.

"Anybody got a penknife?" the doctor asked casually. Detectives and uniforms who did knew better than to respond, all except for newly arrived Patrol Officer Terry Lou Mitchell, eager to help. The doctor admired the keen blade of her knife, then used it to smoothly open a one-inch incision. The wound gurgled loudly, bubbling blood, as he probed with a gloved finger.

The doctor held up the slug as though it were the prize from a cereal box. The bullet was a .38-caliber, in good condition. They eased Rob over onto his back. The wound continued to sputter and hiss with a ghastly sound as air from a punctured lung escaped the chest cavity.

Smiling in gratitude, the doctor placed the bloodstained knife in the palm of his smeared rubber glove and offered it back to its owner. The sturdy young woman had used the red Swiss Army knife to peel fruit for her daily cottage-cheese lunches. "I don't think I need it anymore," she said quietly and turned away.

"You pick up more stuff that way," Jim whispered to the doctor, who winked.

*7*hroughout the rest of the night, Rick's kitchen served as unofficial command post for those whose working lives revolve around violent death. For some weary technicians, it was their fifth major crime scene of the night. Laurel appeared numb, her dazed expression changing only to wince as if in pain at the throb of the police chopper passing low overhead, again and again. First with a fiercely brilliant searchlight and then with the first rosy blush of dawn, the crew scanned the neighborhood and its rooftops. Fleeing killers will often fling a murder weapon up onto a building.

A family on the other side of the island found their dead dog just after dawn. Huddled in a neighbor's kitchen, so that crime-scene technicians could work uninterrupted, they learned that the intruder who prowled their home might also be a killer.

"I could have been raped and murdered in my own bed!" Sandra Corley announced grimly. The big woman wore a shapeless housecoat and scuffs.

Larry Corley looked pale and shaken. "Our kids were asleep in their rooms, Rick. It coulda been one of them, or us. We never heard a thing. We lost some jewelry, a little cash and a cameo that belonged to Sandy's mother."

"No gun? You're not missing a gun?"

"Never owned one, Rick. I may get one now. I never dreamed this could happen here on the island."

"Bosco didn't bark his brains out?"

"That's the hell of it," Larry said, shaking his head. "You know Bosco. Our kids grew up with him. He was harmless. Nobody had to kill that dog to keep him quiet. We never heard a whimper, not a thing."

"We should have got rid of that damn mutt a long time ago," Sandra announced, sipping noisily from a coffee mug. She wiped her mouth with the back of her hand. "What did he do when we needed a watchdog?"

"He watched," Larry said. There was no humor in his smile.

"I think that's right," Rick said grimly. "It looks like it wasn't done to keep him quiet. There was a lot of blood . . ."

"Tell me about it," Sandra snapped. "Did you see my floor?"

"But we didn't find a trace anywhere else in the house. Whoever did it apparently did the dog on the way out, just for the hell of it."

"That's it!" Her voice was raspy. "I want a Doberman named Killer—today."

"How old is Lacey now?"

"Thirteen." The father and Rick exchanged wary glances.

"Boyfriends?"

"Not yet."

"You sure?"

"Christ, Rick, she's in the eighth grade."

"Anybody bothering her, following her, calling?"

Sandra's eyes looked frightened instead of angry for the first time. "She's going to her grandmother's in Vermont—tomorrow, *if* we can't arrange to send her today."

"You think some psycho is . . ." the father's voice trailed off.

"Doubtful," Rick said. "We just have to cover all the bases. Problems with anybody lately? On the job, in the neighborhood, in the family?" They shook their heads.

The weeping children, Lacey and her eight-year-old brother, mourning their dog, were little help.

Despite a high crime rate in the city, there had been few problems on the island. A knife had been used at one scene, a gun at the other. Yet what were the odds of two violent criminals choosing to roam the same peaceful island on the same night? The other recent prowler complaints had been minor, nuisance-type calls, reports of sounds and shadows in the night. These two cases have to be part of one isolated incident involving one offender, Rick thought. A prowler, pursued and panicky, pulling the trigger in the dark. Murder among strangers, the most difficult homicide to solve.

Back at the command post, Rick was surprised to see Laurel bustling around the kitchen, pouring steaming coffee brewed from beans she had ground herself, fixing sandwiches and sliding ashtrays beneath the cigarettes of preoccupied smokers as they filled out their paperwork and completed diagrams. Good girl, he thought fondly, relieved by her show of resilience. He regretted her exposure to this, the ugly side of his job. Part of the charm that had initially attracted him was her naïveté about his work. Investigating violent death is so consuming a task that the lines between personal and professional life become blurred. The two comingle until no private place is left untouched. Unlike Dusty and the other women in and out of his life in recent years, Laurel understood little about police work, even less about death. He liked that. Her innocence touched him, stirring emotions he thought were long lost to the cruel brutality of the streets. She thrilled to the crackling excitement of the seventeen-channel police scanner he kept at home, and the job-related war stories she continually coaxed from him. He knew that. But he had been in control, keeping their time together in an isolated compartment, untainted by the job. The daily pain and sordid secrets were his own. Now she had seen violent death on their doorstep. It could have happened anywhere. He cursed the fact that it had happened here.

Spontaneous, moody and unpredictable, she was barely grown up. He did not want her to become callous and accustomed, as he was, to trouble and death. How would this change her?

Her fair hair had been wild, whipping like a banner in the wind, when he first saw her. She was a triple traffic violator who did not give a damn about his authority.

He had been on the outs with the captain, which was not unusual. Rick had thought he had a sure shot at solving an old homicide by traveling to Seattle to talk to a suspect who now lived there. The budget was tight, as always. Cash and manpower were in short supply. The captain had called the expense unjustified and denied the trip request. Rick was furious. The two men had clashed, and as a result, he had been temporarily transferred to motors. He had worked days, riding a big Kawasaki 1000, telling himself he was better off writing tickets, escorting funerals and stopping speeders. The hours were regular, but it got old fast.

Speeding thirty miles an hour over the legal limit in her open white MGB convertible, Laurel had changed lanes abruptly, causing another motorist to swerve off the road. She swung into a wide U-turn, bounced across a flower bed on the median and ignored Rick's flashing light and siren. He had to chase her for four miles. Pulled over, she pouted. Then they made eye contact, and she had trouble suppressing a smile as he lectured her sternly.

He studied her license. She told him he was too serious.

"Smile!" she told him. "You can do it. It's not that difficult. Come on," she coaxed. "Life's not all that bad."

She stared boldly at the sandy hair that curled from under his helmet, the motor squad's lightning-bolt insignia on his shirt, and the lean and muscular six-foot three-inch frame in the tapered trousers and shiny leather boots. "Hey, Bootsie," she said. "Lighten up."

He found it difficult to keep from smiling. But he managed. Too bad about her date of birth, he thought. He snapped the ticket book shut abruptly and handed back her driver's license. "I'm going to let you go with just a warning this time, miss. But you're headed for trouble if you don't pay more attention to your driving. This could have earned you half a dozen points against your license. You know what that would do to your insurance rates? But more important, I'd hate to have to be the one to tell your parents their daughter had been badly injured, or worse, in a traffic accident."

Her eyes were wide and full of mirth. "You mean I'm not under arrest?"

She tucked the license into her wallet among half a dozen credit cards and glowed up at him, eyes apple-green under blond bangs. "Why don't you teach me to drive? Show me what you're talking about, Bootsie."

Spoiled brat, he thought. Her eyes were flecked with amber, the look in them was blatant. She was outrageous.

He dug a quarter out of his pocket, handed her his card, flipped her the coin and smiled. "I never back down from a challenge. Give me a call when you're eighteen." He kicked over the Kawasaki and roared off, leaving her in the dust.

She was funny. She was also beautiful. Rick knew a lot of beautiful women, Dusty among them. But there was something else, something about this one. He thought about it that night as he drank a beer at the Southwind. Later he thought he spotted her little sports car once or twice on the expressway.

It was a total surprise six months later when, back in homicide, on a bad night in a world full of dead people, live troublemakers and mean dogs, a call was transferred to him from motors.

It was her birthday.

FOUR

*W*hen everyone left, Harriet, the homemaker in Laurel, took charge. She shut down the central air conditioner and threw open all the windows. She soaked a thick bath towel in the sink, wrung it out and swung it around the room to cleanse and circulate the air befouled by cigar and cigarette smoke. Then she scrubbed every square inch of kitchen surface with Lysol. The guest bathroom was next. She hoped that the police technician with the greasy skin and bad complexion had not used it, but she was afraid he had. She had always been fussy about bathrooms, haunted by bad dreams and memories of one that had been full of blood.

She hand-polished the ceramic tile floor. No mops, no applicators. She crouched on her only concession, a thick plastic kneeling pad, wearing a small smile as she scrubbed. She was sorting out and savoring every compliment on her coffee, her thriving houseplants and her home-baked muffins. Energized and elated, she was not at all tired. She loved this room—the kitchen was the heartbeat of this home, her home now.

The shining floor bore no resemblance to the raw floorboards of the first kitchen she remembered. She would never forget its dank, smelly icebox, the pitted porcelain sink, the empty shelves lined with dust. She remembered balancing on a wobbly chair to stir thin oatmeal before she was tall enough to reach the burners on the cheap stove. She rubbed harder, as if to scour that first kitchen out of her memory. Elbow grease—that's what her father had always demanded. "Elbow grease!" he would bellow. He wanted her to do every-thing—everything. She remembered his big soft stomach and his sickening smell. She remembered him coming into her room at night when she was alone in the dark. That son of a bitch.

Odd that she could remember so little about her real mother now. Only the sharply thin naked limbs, sprawled ungainly in the tub. And of course the blood.

Harriet got to her feet, kneading the small of her back with her rubber-gloved fingers, and reached again for the can of Lysol. She depressed the nozzle, spraying a diffuse stream of disinfectant across the room and then stopped to survey her domain. She regarded it with satisfaction, this kitchen with both a hooded gas stove and a microwave oven, with its gleaming stainless-steel twin sinks. When Rick's parents had retired, they had remodeled the kitchen to enhance the value of the house they planned to sell. Then their bachelor son had decided he wanted his childhood home, the place where he had grown up. He did no cooking, so the kitchen had never been used when they had moved in. Left up to Laurel, Harriet thought, it would still be that way. But Harriet loved it and used it all: the spacious cabinets in pale pickled oak with state-of-the-art slide-out shelves, the white Corian countertops and the lazy Susan in the corner—perfect, light, bright and immaculate, the way she would always keep it. She had arranged her cookbooks on a shelf above the spice rack next to the philodendron with the shining leaves, polished daily with mayonnaise. Her Cuisinart, the crock pot that had belonged to Rick's mother and his four-slice toaster were lined up like soldiers at attention. All their appliances and kitchenware irrevocably mingled together—forever.

Harriet loved the house, the plants, the garden, but most of all she loved this room where copper-bottomed cookware glowed warmly from hangers on the wall. This was even more modern than the adopted parents' kitchen and far better because it was hers. Being here meant everything to Harriet, which was why the shooting and Rob's death, so close by, frightened and angered her. She did not mind the others so much, but she was furious at Alex. She wished she could stop him from coming out and doing these things. He was careless. He was stupid. Rushing into the shower, leaving Laurel with wet hair when the police arrived. And that policewoman had noticed. You can lose everything so quickly, Harriet thought, even your life. One mistake and it can all be gone. Achieving what is most dear to you and then holding on to it is never easy.

Harriet promised herself that she would do whatever she had to.

FIVE

*T*he first twenty-four hours, the most crucial in a homicide investigation, led the detectives nowhere. Dead ends, blind alleyways—the lab found no prints and little physical evidence. Ballistics matched no other outstanding cases. Dusty volunteered to stay on and help work the Thorne case, though she would not officially rejoin Rick's team until the first, which was Sunday. "Appreciate it, but catch some rest while you can," he told her. "By then we'll need somebody fresh. There's not much you could do now anyway. We've got nothing."

Divers had spent the daylight hours since the murder plumbing the waters around the islands and the causeway, on the theory that the fleeing killer might have deep-sixed the gun. They found tin cans, junk and old tools.

A police chopper crew patrolling the bay spotted something else—another corpse. The find created a flurry of excitement. Hopes were that the killer had botched his getaway and drowned trying to swim from the murder scene, or that his car had plunged off the side of the bridge.

"We don't get that lucky," Jim said glumly. "Things never come wrapped up that neatly."

He was right. The uniforms who got there first radioed that the body, floating facedown in the mangroves at the edge of a small uninhabited island, appeared to have been submerged too long to be linked to the murder on San Remo.

Nonetheless, Barrish and Ransom boarded a police boat at the mouth of the Miami River. "Just what we need. I hate this." Ransom looked pained. The twenty-five-foot patrol boat sliced through the water, a damp breeze lifting the thinning hair Jim had carefully combed to cover his bald spot. "If I wanted to go to sea, I'da joined the Coast Guard. I know I'm gonna be sick."

"You think about it too much, Jim," Rick shouted over the noise of the twin engines. "I've seen you go green just standing on the dock. Relax. Enjoy it. Look at that." The late summer sunset was spectacular, the western sky and the mirrorlike water aflame with blood-scarlet color.

Jim shook his head and glared accusingly at the darkening eastern edge of the world, where the bay already gleamed silver. "It wuz the goddamn full moon," he muttered. "Full moon. It happens every time."

"I tell you Rick, twenty-seven years is enough. I shudda bailed out a long time ago. I don't know why I waited this long. My back is killing me from lifting too damn many dead bodies. The job is getting worse, not better. Always on call, the fucking hours, you don't eat right, you don't sleep right, you don't go to the bathroom right. . . . The public doesn't give a shit. Now with all these damn Cubans . . ."

The swarthy young patrolman at the helm, a native of Camagüey Province, swerved smack into a swell, throwing Ransom off balance. The heavyset detective lurched across the deck and clung to a rail. "Son of a bitch," he muttered.

The corpse floated facedown where the mangroves and the roots meet, awash in crystal-clear water over white sand. The mottled skin on his naked body looked gray. Several patrolmen stood by, along with a crime lab photographer. Ransom unfolded a polypropylene body bag. Rick stripped off shoes and socks, rolled up his trouser legs and stepped gingerly into the shallows for a better look. Bay water lapped gently around his ankles, cool and soothing. Wiggling his toes, he sighed, inhaling a deep breath. Then he sniffed again. The body did not have the usual unmistakable odor. It smelled more like an old septic tank.

Ransom lit a cheap cigar. He usually did at scenes where a body was no longer fresh. Rick always said it was difficult to discern which was worse, the stench of death or Jim's big stogie.

Rick and the young marine patrolman pulled on rubber gloves, dragged the dead man clear of the roots, counted to three and rolled him over. The body had obviously been in the water for some time, yet sea life had done little damage, even to the eyes and face. The usually voracious fish and crabs had found this corpse unappetizing for some reason.

Rick hunkered down to scrutinize the body, then looked up with a wry half smile. "We lucked out, Jimbo. There is a God, after all."

"What the hell?" Ransom lumbered closer, aching back and queasy stomach forgotten. "Just what we don't need," he mourned. "Another whodunit. We'll never get to go home."

A fact of death is that the more sudden it comes, the longer it takes to sort out the facts and clean up the mess.

"What does that look like to you?" Rick asked. A half-inch hole gaped at the left of the man's navel, just below the ribs.

Jim stared in the fast-fading light. "Like about a .45-caliber." He frowned at Rick's positive expression.

"Only if the killer screwed it in. Look closer." The young Cuban cop stood openmouthed. Uniforms closed in around the body.

"Son of a bitch," Ransom said, squinting. "You're right." The hole in the man's body was ringed by thread marks. "What do you wanna bet that it's that damn Morningdale Mortuary again?"

"This is no homicide. The guy's been embalmed," Rick told the others, as he rocked back on his heels, elbows resting on his knees. He used a pencil as a pointer. "See here, no bullet made that hole, it was a trocar, an undertaker's tool. It's attached to a pump that sucks out the body fluids. Embalming solution is forced in. Then they plug it up. The plug is obviously missing."

"But what's he doing out here, Sarge?" The young officer looked bewildered. "How come they didn't bury him?"

"They did," Ransom said. "At sea. Probably . . . six, eight months ago. That damn Morningdale is still screwing up. Six months sitting in saltwater, on the bottom, the casket falls apart around him and he just pops up."

"I'm surprised nobody spotted him before now," Rick said. Shadows and reflections off the water dappled his tanned face. "They must have missed the Gulf Stream when they dropped him in, otherwise he would have gone north. He must have floated back in south of Fisher Island, between Stiltsville and the reefs and Soldier Key, completely across the bay."

"Like a homin' pigeon," Jim said, forming the words around the cigar still clenched between his teeth. "This guy's done some cruising."

"Caskets," Rick told the rookie, "are built to be put in the ground, that's the problem." In a proper sea burial, the casket is weighted, holes drilled in the top and the lid secured with strapping iron. Tricky business, just uncommon enough to baffle the inexperienced help at some funeral homes.

On the way back to the dock, Rick entertained the young marine officer with the story of another Miami funeral home's maiden attempt at a sea burial. Mourners had sung a farewell hymn as the casket was slid over the side of their hired vessel into the Atlantic, a mile east of Government Cut. It had not sunk. The box had bobbed about on a choppy sea until the lid came off. Waves had wafted the body up and out. Wind and current had carried the corpse, dapper in a dark blue suit and a tie, into the lanes used by big cruise ships out of the port of Miami, and into the path of the *Song of Norway.* In response to a cry of "man overboard!" hundreds of Caribbean-bound tourists had rushed to the rails to watch the crew launch a lifeboat.

.   .   .

$\mathcal{T}$hat evening the detectives interviewed a number of young Rob Thorne's shocked school chums, baseball teammates and a few tearful girls he had dated. Chances were remote that anything in young Thorne's life-style had led to his murder, but the investigators had nothing else and intended to leave no avenue unexplored. Rob Thorne was clean, or seemed to be. So was the Corley family. It had seemed depressingly clear from the start that the shooting had stemmed from a random encounter in the dark.

"Whatta we do now, bro?" Jim said, as they wearily compared notes back in the office that night. He tossed a half-eaten slice of pizza back into the box. "Christ, this stuff is lousy. You can't tell where the pizza ends and the cardboard begins. Why the hell do we order from them?"

"Because they deliver at three A.M., and they won't take any money from cops." The low-pitched voice came from Detective Sergeant Rudy Dominguez in the next cubicle.

"They must be trying to kill us," Jim grumbled.

"It must be bad if *you* won't eat it," Rick said. "It looks like the only thing left for us to do is finish the paperwork, beat the bushes one more time, talk to all the snitches and then beg. I'll see the parents in the morning. I think they want to post a reward, and I won't discourage them. We can appeal to the public for information, dangle the reward money, sit by the phone and hope somebody drops a dime on us."

"I sure as hell hope we come up with something, because if this one takes us years to solve, buddy boy, I ain't gonna be here. I ain't waiting around." Jim worked the phones while Rick talked to a reporter from *The Morning News.* One of the unwritten rules of their partnership was that Rick was point man with the press.

Quotable, photogenic and personable, he felt at ease with reporters and rarely shot himself in the foot. They flocked around him at major crime scenes, usually ignoring Jim, who liked it that way. He often said that if the best reporter in town was on fire, he wouldn't piss on him, or her, to put it out.

His attitude stemmed from an unfortunate incident following the rescue of a housewife abducted from a shopping center parking lot. A reporter—female —had asked if the victim was injured. "Nope," Jim had said. "She wasn't hurt. She just got raped."

He was quoted. What had begun as a positive news story ended in a public relations disaster. A storm of outrage boiled up among local feminists. One group named Jim as the Male Chauvinist Pig of the Month. The chief was furious once somebody explained to him why the statement was offensive. He issued a written reprimand. Jim had been sentenced to three months of sensitivity training, on his own time. The entire experience had taught him one important lesson: Never trust a reporter. "Burn me once, it's your fault. Burn me twice, it's my fault"—that was his philosophy when it came to the media.

Hunched behind his desk in the glare of the electric-orange office partitions, his face settled slowly into a squinty-eyed scowl. Somebody in charge had decreed that bright international orange panels were de rigueur when the new ten-million-dollar police station was built. The panels offered a semblance of privacy to the hyper, the hysterical, the homicidal and the distraught as they were interviewed by detectives.

Jim believed that the blinding orange agitated half-crazed suspects and caused even docile witnesses to grow irritable and argumentative. The color made his head throb, especially when he was short on sleep. Peering through reading glasses, he riffled through his telephone calls. "Oh shit," he said. The message in his hand was brief and to the point: *"I'm being poisoned again."*

The full moon brought them all out of the woodwork. Terrance McGee worked in the downtown public library and was periodically convinced he was being poisoned. Whenever he suffered a bellyache or an upset stomach, or thought that his coffee, soft drink or burger had a peculiar taste or that his urine was not the right color, he was sure that *they* were at it again. Who *they* were or why they wanted to kill him was never precisely clear. Sometimes he suspected coworkers, other times perfect strangers. Occasionally it was the CIA. Sometimes it was Castro's agents.

He was fortyish, never married and a pain in the ass. The overworked detectives had long ago agreed that they were the only people on earth with a real motive to kill McGee.

Hoping to defuse his fixation and wash him out of their hair, they had agreed to analyze the contents of a sugar bowl he swore had been poisoned by a mysterious someone who had slipped into his apartment undetected. The crime lab report had reached Jim's desk. He scanned it and dialed McGee's number. It rang four times, then someone carefully lifted the receiver but said nothing. Faint but rapid breathing could be heard at the other end of the line. "McGee! This is Detective Ransom, Miami Homicide."

"Don't hang up, Detective! I'm here! I'm here! I didn't know who it was."

"You don't find out unless you say hello," Jim growled.

"There was another attempt this morning. It was in my . . ." The intensity in McGee's voice left him almost breathless.

"I've got news," Jim interrupted.

"The lab report?"

"Sure thing."

"Should we discuss it over the telephone?"

"I don't see why not. I have the results before me. That stuff *will* kill you, McGee. It was one hundred percent sugar granules. You got to lay off that sugar, it's bad stuff."

"You mean they didn't find anything?" McGee was incredulous.

"Nada."

. "But how do you explain the chills, the sweats, the runs?"

"Maybe you were coming down with a bug, it's been going around. But read my lips, nobody wants to poison you. Get off that kick, and get a life."

"But—"

"No buts, *nobody* wants to kill you. It should be a load off your mind. Now forget it."

"Thank you, thank you, Detective." McGee sounded unconvinced by the clean bill of health.

Jim hoped this would be the last they heard from him, but he was doubtful. The man's paranoia seemed cyclical. Sometimes he was quiet for months. When he did resurface, fearful and full of conspiracy theories, it seemed always to be when the detectives were at their busiest. "Why," Jim would patiently ask, "would all these people go to all this trouble? Why would anybody care enough to break into *your* apartment and poison *your* sugar bowl? What makes *you* so special?"

Instead of seeing the logic, McGee's eyes would smolder with new intensity. "I have no idea, Detective, that's why I need your help, before it's too late."

Rick insisted there was no point in trying to reason with McGee. "It's all real to him," he said. "There is no logic in craziness."

McGee called again ten minutes later. A secretary took the message, and Jim shuffled it to the bottom of the stack. Then, the corners of his pale lips curved into a sly smile. He decided to leave it for Dusty. She would be in tonight. Let her deal with him, he thought.

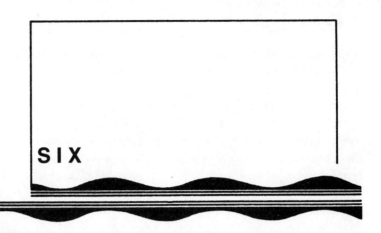

SIX

*A*lex heard what Harriet was thinking as she scrubbed herself in the shower. He hated to be criticized. He emerged furious, stalked into the dining room and turned up the volume on the police scanner, trying to drown out the clamor from the others. *Not my fault*, he thought. *That dumb asshole! If that kid had stayed where he belonged, none of it would have happened. What the hell was he trying to do? Be a hero? Well, look at what all that macho shit got him. Dead. He deserved it for not minding his own damn business.*

Roughing me up, bellowing that he had a gun. Stupid bastard left me no choice. Better to waste a jerk like that anyway.

He sat drumming his fingers on the table, his face softening as little Jennifer began to sob. She could not find her blankie, and Alex had frightened her by firing the gun. She hated guns. She wanted to go play with Benjie, the little boy next door. She cried more when Alex told her she could only come out to play with Benjie when they baby-sat for him.

The tears dried as Marilyn came out, prowling the room, sulking as usual and puffing a cigarette. She sat down at Laurel's dressing table and carefully outlined her apple-green eyes with mascara and pencil. Then she doused herself with cheap perfume and painted her fingernails blood-red, a shade she knew Laurel would hate. All the while she bitched and complained about not getting enough sex. She knew the others were listening. All but Laurel, who could not hear any of them.

Marilyn was pissed off at Alex for blowing away the nice-looking young Thorne kid just as she was getting to know him. She was also pissed at that fat-ass Sandy Corley, who had caught her out in the driveway earlier, flirting with Larry. He had stopped by to chat while walking their new Doberman, but Sandy had rudely interrupted their tête-à-tête and steered him home.

Chagrined, he had marched along docilely. He probably would not be allowed out again for a month, Marilyn had thought angrily. *Pussy-whipped, that's what he is. Pussy-whipped.* She had even said it aloud, hoping they overheard.

When Marilyn's nails were dry, she filled out an order form for a leather G-string pictured in a Frederick's of Hollywood catalogue. Then she strutted over to the kitchen cabinet in her four-inch stiletto heels, hips swaying provocatively, and downed two slugs of bourbon. "If nothing else," she said, hips slung to one side, tossing back her long hair, "it makes life easier to take in this damn monastery."

Marilyn might be a slut, Alex thought from his place down in the tunnel that joined their minds, *but she was not so difficult to deal with. At least he could reason with her. Sometimes they even thought alike. In fact, at times, like now, she was not bad to have around.* Even though she didn't particularly like kids, Marilyn had fixed Jennifer a cup of hot chocolate with marshmallows, fished her blankie out of the clothes dryer and promised that she could watch cartoons on TV in the morning. *Marilyn was a good ol' girl most of the time, not like that homemaker.* Harriet had raged unmercifully, calling Alex stupid and sloppy. "You'll ruin it for all of us!" she cried.

Who is she to talk, he thought, *that bitch, with all the shit she pulls.*

Jennifer came back, her mouth still chocolate-stained, clutching her blankie, sucking her thumb and whining. That did it. He was fed up. He burst back out, using his growing strength. "You cunts think about nothing but yourselves!" He smashed his right fist into his palm, put on his clothes and stormed out.

That near disaster the other night was awkward, he thought, *but think how awkward it turned out to be for the Thorne kid.* He suppressed a chuckle, determined not to let one slipup stop him. He was growing stronger and feeling better about himself all the time. Temporarily, however, Alex knew he had to use extreme caution. *The others were right, it could have been a goddamn catastrophe. If he could only get rid of them all for good, especially that bitch Harriet. And Laurel, who could cause all of them real problems when she panicked, which she always did when she realized she was losing time. Stupid and hysterical, she had no idea what was going on. Occasionally one of the others came in handy when he got in a tight spot, but their nagging and complaining frosted his ass. Somebody was going to pay,* he swore, *for all of it. What about his pain, all his lost time? He had to find a way.*

He drove within the speed limit and was careful to signal properly. It wouldn't do to be stopped. That could ruin his plans. The moonlight was radiant and the night air was wonderful, soft and warm. He sighed. *The days always took so long to die.*

The convenience store was one he had visited before, some time ago. There *would be more cash on hand now, since they had started selling Florida lottery tickets. He felt like a winner tonight. It was time to act.*

The store glowed in the dark, jutting out of a small strip shopping center. Closed shops, a shoe repair and a take-out pizza joint slumbered on either side. The front entrance was guarded only by pay phones and trash receptacles. Nobody browsing in the racks of magazines. The only customer strolled out with a six-pack. Alex pulled on his cap, adjusted his shades and stepped boldly through the front door into the light, heart swelling with excitement. He could see anyone approaching through the big plate-glass storefront. Of course, that meant they could see him, too, so he had to be quick.

The thin, dark man behind the counter—flanked by the frozen slush machine and the sausage sticks—was Pakistani.

"Is late at night for sunglasses," he said. Alex smiled and showed him the gun. The cold metal was far more eloquent than words.

Alex enjoyed the man's stricken expression. His brown eyes were wet and enormous, his body twitched. Alex gestured impatiently toward the cash register. Frightened, the man abruptly reached for something below the counter. Alex squeezed the trigger. He did so without thinking. The clerk sank to his knees, then crumpled over onto his side, his body jerking and convulsing. Alex peered over the counter to see what the man had reached for. A paper bag, to hold the money.

Too late. Now, more trouble. It is harder than ever to make a living in Miami, he thought. He never intended to hurt anyone. Shit just happens.

He emptied the cash drawer and eagerly stuffed a handful of lottery tickets into his jeans. Humming, as though a casual shopper, he strolled by the case of ready-made sandwiches and chocolate chip cookies, through the door and out to his car. What was that song running through his mind? Very catchy, a show tune—"If They Could See Me Now"—that was it. He did a little dance step, eased himself into the front seat and drove away. He couldn't help but smile. Wouldn't the next customer be surprised? He wished he could stay for the excitement.

What had happened was not his fault, Alex told himself. The counterman made a bad move. This case would not generate as big a deal as the next-door neighbor of a hotshot homicide detective, but it would keep the cops on their toes. Nothing like keeping the cops on their toes.

They say these things become easier with experience. They're right, he thought. Pawing through the bills and the coins on the front seat with one hand, he fingered the lottery tickets. A huge smile spread across his face, and he broke up, into high-pitched laughter. Hey, asshole, he asked himself, what are you going to do if you have the winning ticket?

SEVEN

*T*he city stayed busy. Detectives Dominguez and Mack Thomas went out to investigate a shooting at an all-night convenience store. Rick and Jim eventually quit to catch some sleep. But Jim did not go directly home. He glanced at his watch and saw that he would be able to make it on time after all.

*R*ed-eyed from lack of sleep, his suit rumpled, but stepping lightly for a man of his size and state of weariness, Jim slipped quietly into his usual rear pew. Sunday morning services had always been a soothing contrast, a little R and R for the spirit after the chaos of Saturday night life and death in Miami. The serenity and beauty, the traditional words and music and the good and decent people around him, they salved his soul.

He and Molly had been married in this church, almost thirty years ago. Happy memories still dwelt there, even though the place was no longer sanctuary. Over the years the city and its inhabitants had changed. The church had been invaded repeatedly by thieves who stole everything from Baby Jesus, snatched from his crèche at Christmas time, to the baptismal font and the vestments.

As bad, if not worse, were the street people and mental cases whose faithful attendance might have been admirable, had they been lucid. Their only contribution was chaos. You never know, he thought, watching an elderly, shabbily dressed woman. He had been to many scenes where survivors of the depression had died alone, often malnourished, under circumstances of abject poverty, with a small fortune, their hoarded life savings, stuffed in a shoebox or a mattress. They had refused to trust banks, or spend their nest eggs, no matter what.

The usual crazies were present in full force today, including the one who always spent the moments of silent meditation rummaging noisily through her crinkly shopping bags. A bearded young man, the picture of health, always coughed continually through the sermon—nonstop. During the fellowship hour in the adjacent social hall later, he would never cough. Not once. He did talk, at length and eagerly. He did know his scripture. That's the hell of it, Jim thought. They always know their scripture.

A painfully thin woman, wrinkled and snaggletoothed, always insisted on sitting way up in front, then swiveled in her pew, scowling, grimacing and occasionally giving the finger to innocent worshipers seated behind her. A raspy-voiced man, dirty, agitated and unable to sit still, bobbed up and down, shuffled in and out, mumbling all the while, genuflecting constantly. Sometimes he simply dropped to his knees in the center aisle.

The church was under seige and struggling to survive, yet the ushers were forced to hold on to the collection plates, rather than pass them, to prevent some of these characters from helping themselves. Had they been well-heeled contributors, Jim reasoned, they could be tolerated as eccentrics. But as things stood, the church definitely needed a bouncer.

He had volunteered. He would have relished the job. The patient and good-natured pastor had politely declined his offer without an explanation. Board members agreed that a problem existed but rejected his second suggestion, that the ushers, all men of retirement age, be equipped with Mace.

He realized that his impatience and anger at these people was probably not by-the-book Christian. Still another example, he thought, of how going by the book no longer works.

The deranged chorus was in rare form this morning. In the good old days, he reflected, he had put people in jail for less. More evidence that America's misfits and criminals now own more rights than the law-abiding, long-suffering taxpayers. Go by the book, turn the other cheek, and they overwhelm you.

He was uncertain anymore if there was a damn God or not. He could not help but doubt it much of the time, on the job. But something always brought him back to this place, with its old and worn wooden pews. Perhaps it was habit, or the memories. He used to consider the church his only lifeline to sanity in a world gone mad. Now he was not so sure. But without this, he had nothing left to believe in.

So he still came, and sometimes lingered in the walled courtyard. The coral rock enclosed a garden with trees, flowering shrubs and a carillon that sometimes played "Amazing Grace," his favorite hymn. Maybe this place reminded him of Pennsylvania and the Sunday school he had attended as a child.

He was seventeen when he learned that nobody lives forever. He had lied about his age to land the job. He told them he was eighteen. Fresh out of high school, young, strong and eager. His second week there the world exploded in his face.

They were working on experimental airplane fuel at the Apex Gunpowder Plant, an eight-mile-square building barricaded inside a horseshoe-shaped mountain. Explosions were not unusual. The plant had been built with the blasts in mind. The constant concussions would pop out the wooden frames of windows that were plastic-coated screens, instead of glass. Both doors and windows were linked to steep chutes, safety slides for the employees. They were taught to land on their feet, running for the metal rings that hung about forty feet from each exit. When a man grabbed the ring, high-pressure jets of water would tear the clothes off his body. He would be left naked, but not burned.

All the workers wore fire-resistant work suits. The day it happened, Jim saw some burned down to their belt loops.

The blast erupted in a solvent recovery building that was always wet and considered safe. Twenty-five two-story tanks were each surrounded by thick red-brick walls. Each tank held ten thousand pounds of smokeless powder.

The explosion pulverized the bricks into red dust. Men tried to escape by fleeing up the sides of the mountain, but fire and heat overtook them.

Sixty people were killed and hundreds hurt. Jim was coated with red dust but not seriously injured. He ran back to help other survivors. None of the late-model cars parked near the blast site would start. Pressure from the blast had collapsed the hollow copper floats inside their carburetors. Older cars with cork floats were unaffected. Jim loaded injured men into his Ford jalopy and careened to the nearest hospital, back and forth several times. He lost his eldest brother, his father and his best friend. Dozens of young men he had gone to school with were among the dead. He believed later that all he saw that day helped prepare him for police work and for investigating murder in Miami. Nothing he saw now ever bothered him, he said, nothing ever happened that he had not already seen as a teenager or later as a Marine at Panmunjon.

He was stoic, even on the day Molly announced she was leaving.

He was certain she would change her mind, but she did not. So he simply decided that when he retired he would return home to Pennsylvania, where she had resettled, and reclaim her. He had no doubt that it would happen until their married daughter in Orlando telephoned with the news that Molly had remarried.

Rick was the closest thing Jim had to family life now. He had trained Rick as a rookie, seen him promoted to sergeant and was content to work for him. For years Jim had avoided promotional exams because promotion always meant a transfer and he liked nothing better than being a homicide detective.

His plan was to wait until retirement loomed and then push for promotion. Rank, even a sergeant's stripes, would bring a bigger pension. But he had delayed too long. Who could have foreseen that South Florida, the city and the department, would change so much? Few Anglo males would ever again win promotion no matter how high they scored on exams.

No matter. He and Rick were a good team. Despite widely diverse backgrounds, they had clicked from day one. Rick was accustomed to being a star, a stranger to hard times. A native son, born in Miami, an only child, all-state quarterback at Beach High, football scholarship to the University of Florida, he was always spoiled—by his mother, his teachers and eager cheerleaders of all ages. He reverted to beach bum after college, spent a year as a sun-bronzed lifeguard, then joined the department, disappointing his father, who had hoped to hand him the family business, a small chain of appliance stores. Women loved him. Men liked him. He was a hell of a detective. Rick and Jim worked well together, achieving a nearly 90 percent clearance rate on their cases, a major accomplishment in an era of difficult-to-solve drug murders.

Jim felt vaguely uneasy about Dusty rejoining their team. She was good, probably the best female detective he had ever seen, and he more than liked her, but he still yearned for the good old days before affirmative action and the women's movement. Female cops are fine in their place, he always said, as long as that place is the juvenile bureau or the shoplifting detail. Who wants a woman to back you up in a brawl or a riot? And in homicide, detectives spend most of their waking hours with their team partners—how can you relax when one of those partners is a woman? Sex is always present, especially with a woman as good-looking as Dusty. He was always uncomfortably conscious of a woman's presence, although he noticed that it was not that way for most of the new generation of young cops. He knew Dusty had had the hots for Rick. She probably still did, and the heat had once generated both ways. Jim had actually felt more comfortable when Rick was screwing Dusty. At least everybody knew where he, or she, stood.

When that romance was in full flower, Jim and Rick still went fishing a few times a month, still hit their favorite spot for a couple of cool ones at least twice a week, still followed the fortunes of the Miami Dolphins and still talked incessantly about their cases. On duty, off duty, city time, their time, it all blurred together. They lived the job, solved a lot of cases and enjoyed themselves. Then along came Laurel. At first Jim was convinced that it was just the transient attraction of a new face and a firm young body. He never really believed it was serious until the day Rick borrowed his pickup to move Laurel's belongings into his house. Rick seemed happy—so far. Love is what counts, until it ends, and end it will, Jim thought. That's what love does. Nobody lives forever, nobody loves forever.

He drove from the church to a Beach deli for a rare roast beef on rye and a side order of cole slaw to go. In the small kitchen of his condo apartment, he dumped the cardboard dish of slaw over the roast beef, slapped the lid back on the sandwich, popped a cold beer from the refrigerator, sat down at the table and opened his Sunday newspaper. Rob Thorne smiled at him from a photograph on the local page, under a headline that read PROWLER SLAYS COLLEGE BASEBALL PLAYER.

The story quoted a police spokesman, who said the usual: "An arrest is imminent."

"That asshole must know something we don't," Jim said, swallowing another swig of beer. "I wish it was that easy."

He sighed, took off his shoes, peeled off his socks, dropped them in the clothes hamper and yawned. Then he padded barefoot to the window, drew the blackout drapes to shut out the sun as it climbed a brilliant sky, turned the control on the air conditioner up to high, took off his clothes and went to bed.

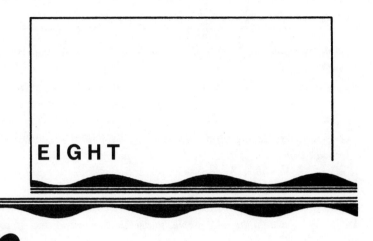

EIGHT

*L*aurel impatiently checked the time. The kitchen wall clock was shaped like a coffeepot, a percolator with a little light bubbling at the top. It said ten o'clock. Rick was not home yet. Where is he, she thought, biting her lip. She hated the stress of constantly being left alone, she could not endure it, she thought, staring out the window. She was afraid that strange things would take place, that frightening forces would engulf her again, that it was already happening. Her posture changed subtly, her spine straightened, her chin lifted. Her eyes faded to a paler shade, more gray now than green, and her mouth settled into a no-nonsense, matter-of-fact expression.

*H*arriet emerged, took a deep breath, glanced around the room, tied an apron around her waist and went briskly to work. She scalded half a dozen plump ripe tomatoes, removed the skins and began to mince parsley for the sauce.

A gray kitten the color of blue smoke skittered across her kitchen floor in madcap pursuit of sunbeams and shadows. The creature belonged to Benjie, the three-year-old son of the Singers next door. How annoying. Harriet continued her tasks. The spoiled brat is far too young to own a kitten. They always say, she thought, that no one really owns a cat. Sure enough, this one would not stay at home. How did the animal escape Benjie's grubby paws and get into her house anyway? Most likely through Chuckles's kitty door in the garage. It was burden enough putting up with Chuckles, the Siamese. He was crouched under a chair, watching the kitten intently, his tail twitching.

She diced the tomatoes. Fascinated by the sound and her movements, the kitten scrambled quick as lightning to the top of a stepstool used to reach the high shelves in the pantry. From that vantage point the leap to the cutting board was merely kitten's play.

"I'm warning you," she said pleasantly, as she sliced fresh mushrooms. *"Don't do it, kitty."*

She raised her head to listen as Rick's car crunched into the driveway. The mischievous kitten batted the countertop with a tentative blue-gray paw. Harriet paused for a moment to watch as the kitten plunked itself down prettily on the stool's top step, gazing up at her, golden eyes unblinking, expecting to be admired. When she moved the knife it pounced, all four feet landing like feathers on the immaculate white countertop.

Sighing, Harriet lay down her knife as the kitten scampered closer to inspect the cutting board. The pink nose quivered. Harriet selected the thin-bladed filet knife, sliding it from the solid maple storage block slowly, as though unsheathing a sword. Holding it delicately, she admired its balance and the way it fit so well into her hand. Top-grade cutlery with surgically sharp stainless-steel blades and triple-riveted solid maple handles. Outside, a car door slammed, and in her mind's eye she saw Rick walk across the lawn and stoop to pick up the morning newspaper.

"Kitty," she whispered, hissing softly through her teeth. Intrigued, the animal abandoned its fascination with the cutting board and turned its attention to her. The knife pierced its chest easily. Harriet was a bit surprised that it took so little force to slide it in cleanly, nearly to the hilt, impaling the creature like an ice cream on a stick. The breastbone must be just soft cartilage in a kitten that young, she thought. And of course the knife was scalpel-sharp. All of her tools and equipment were well maintained. *"I warned you,"* she whispered cheerfully, withdrawing the knife. *"This is my kitchen."*

She heard the clang of the garbage can lid at the side of the house and scowled. What was Rick doing? Irritated, she hoped he was not placing anything that was not neatly wrapped or bagged into her heavy-duty, double-weight aluminum garbage can.

*T*he morning sky glowed as blue as any paradise. The neighborhood seemed safe and still once more. The heavy scent of summer flowers hung on the hushed air, and a small flotilla of bright sails bobbed on a turquoise bay. Weekend sailors were out in force. Rick picked up the newspaper, which was rolled inside a plastic bag, and stood, legs apart, in the middle of his velvet-green lawn. The grass grew so fast this time of year, you could almost hear its radiant energy, the faint humming of photosynthesis, busy breeding, germinating and sprouting, a never-ending life process accelerated by the heat and moisture of the season. The morning was so splendidly alive that it seemed death did not exist and the night of the murder had never happened. The only trace was a length of yellow crime-scene tape that hung limply from the slim trunk of a frangipani tree. Rick untied it, rolled the tape tightly and dropped it into the new heavy-duty aluminum garbage can Laurel had bought recently. As he did he thought he heard the grinding rumble of the garbage disposal in the kitchen. He did not disturb the Thornes, hoping they were still sleeping, though he doubted it. Had he something to tell them, he might have done it now, but there was nothing. Facing the bereaved parents would be easier after some food and a few hours' sleep.

The house was quiet when he opened the front door. Laurel appeared to be still asleep, facedown, hugging her lace-edged pillow. He unbuttoned his shirt and sat gently on the edge of the bed, making an effort not to wake her.

"Good morning, Sergeant." She rolled over, flinging the bedclothes aside with abandon. The slim, sensuous body was naked. He noticed her flowered cotton nightgown crumpled on the carpet. She must have heard his car. "I assume this is a raid," she said.

"Hot damn." Rick grinned. She was in one of those wild and crazy seductive moods. He was delighted, despite his exhaustion. Nothing chases the ghost of a sad and frustrating case and soothes numb weariness into a relaxed warmth faster than good sex.

"It's inspection time, Sergeant. I want to see your weapon." Her small hands, like darting birds, were busy with his zipper and the swelling behind it.

"Jesus, I love it when you're like this," he whispered. "You're so crazy. You drive me nuts." He fumbled with his shirt.

"No, no, leave it on," she murmured, her voice low and husky. "Just take off your pants. I like it this way."

Her fine, soft hair billowed over the pillow. Her body was stretched out, taut and lithe, nipples on the small, firm breasts hard and pointed, her arms reached out to him. Golden shafts of morning light found their way through the leafy bower outside the window and played shadow games across her smooth skin. She was chuckling softly, her lips ripe and swollen.

"Get your handcuffs," she demanded, her eyes apple green and brazen. "Let me show you how I handle a prisoner."

Clumsy in his eagerness, he stumbled to the dresser, one bare leg free, the other dragging his trousers and boxer shorts. He found the cuffs, kicked off his trousers, left them in the middle of the floor and returned to her.

*D*uring their fun and games, she astonished him by easily slipping free of the cuffs. "How do you do that?" he murmured. "I've only seen a few escape artists who could pull that off. I had to chase them," he recalled dolefully.

"Muscle control." Her eyes were bold. "It helps me do a lot of things extraordinarily well, don't you agree?"

He grinned lazily and yawned. "For sure." His voice was drowsy. She grew very quiet, eyes shadowed in the filtered light. She did not move, nor did her eyes change when he gently kissed her. "Maybe I'm lucky you're not always like this. I don't know if an old man like me could hack it."

He asked her to wake him at five in the afternoon, then rolled over and drifted into sleep without seeing that his request caused her discomfort. Laurel sat up and stared hard at the clock, her brow furrowed. Rick was asleep. The entire day stretched before her.

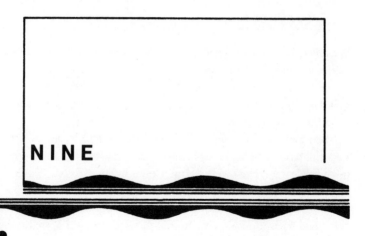

NINE

*T*erry Lou Mitchell encountered Mary Ellen Dustin in the ladies' locker room at the fitness center. "I met Rick's new significant other at that homicide scene on the island," she said teasingly.

"It's a damn shame," Dusty said, her voice cool. "He was a nice kid."

"I must say, I was impressed by Miss Teenage America. All tan and sleek—and young."

"Maybe that's the attraction," Dusty said wryly. "It's the first time I ever got dumped for a younger woman. I'm not even thirty yet." She swept her thick, shining blond hair back, away from the high cheekbones and strong face, and fastened it with a plastic clip.

"She looks a little like you, you notice? Like your kid sister or your younger cousin. I was surprised."

"Not as surprised as I was."

"Who knows what evil lurks in the hearts of men? Not me. See ya out there. I'm gonna try the treadmill for a while."

The center was located in a renovated bayfront hotel and offered discount memberships to police officers and their families, another perk of the job. Rows of Nautilus machines resembled medieval instruments of torture, with their straps, stirrups and gleaming metal. Treadmills, weights, rowing machines, exercise bikes and the men and women using them were reflected everywhere in mirrored walls. What had been a ballroom was now lined with ballet barres, carpeted in pale green and also mirrored for classes in aerobic dance, Jazzercise and total conditioning. Aqua-aerobics took place, weather permitting, in an Olympic-size pool overlooking the bay and the city skyline.

Nearly naked, seated on a bench in front of a row of lockers, Dusty was pulling on her tights when she saw Laurel, just three feet away. Her first reaction was to wince, wondering if the conversation had been overheard. To her relief, Laurel, wearing a white leotard and adjusting her pink headband, looked as startled as she was. Both smiled after an awkward moment. "Hi, Laurel!" Dusty sang out the greeting as she got to her feet. "Thank God for spandex," she said, patting her hip. "It hides a multitude of sins, or at least pulls them all together."

"You have nothing to worry about." Laurel looked uncomfortably at the rosy, full-blown and bouncing breasts Dusty was stuffing unselfconsciously into her black leotard. Her own were mere buds by comparison. "I didn't know you were a member."

"No choice, since the cop shop's group medical refuses to pay for liposuction. And what do you *mean*, nothing to worry about?" She finished tying a shoelace. "I always wanted dimples, but not in my thighs, which, unfortunately, is where they have appeared. Time to fight the war against cellulite! Let's go!" She reached into her locker for a set of red hand weights, then slammed the door.

She smiled and tossed a casual arm around Laurel's shoulder. Laurel quickly stepped away, out of reach, a reflex she seemed to instantly regret. "Here." She snatched two towels off a stack still warm from the dryer. "Take one."

"Sure." Dusty took the towel, hesitated, then followed Laurel out into the big mirrored room. She had wanted to ask if there was any progress in the Thorne case but swallowed the impulse. Rick probably did not talk shop with Laurel anyway. What *did* they have in common? Rick might still be working if they had come up with some good leads. Where is he, she wondered. Home in his bed? Alone? His long lean body warm with sleep? If he is, and I lived there, she thought, I wouldn't be here. Was the unmistakable glow Laurel wore, unenhanced by makeup, the aftermath of sex or simply the bloom of youth? She sighed. Her instinct was to be pleasant but not too friendly. She did not want Laurel to sense her feelings.

In another time, another life, she might have reached out to Terry Lou, or even to Laurel, as a friend. They obviously had something in common, the same taste in men, or at least one man. But friends no longer came easily, casually for her. When Dusty had chosen Miami for a fresh start, she had deliberately severed all old ties, leaving them behind, with everything that was painful. Hoping to become a brand-new woman, without a past, she kept no relationships and after five years had made little effort to cultivate new ones. She had dropped the barriers only once—unfortunately. With Rick, all things had seemed possible. She had been convinced for a time that her life would be rich and full, but, she told herself, she should have known better. Some shadows never fade.

Most of the center's aerobics instructors were women. But today it was Barry, a high-energy young man who wore a ponytail, headband and stretch tights that left little to the imagination. Dusty was pleased. Barry liked the music loud. She deliberately chose a spot in front of a powerful stereo speaker. The booming music would blast all thoughts out of her mind. She liked not having to think about her life, the intricacies of her job or the cruelty of the streets, to simply let the beat of the music fill her mind and body.

Nearly two dozen women and three or four men stood waiting, about to begin. Poised on a raised and carpeted platform at the front of the room, Barry smiled fondly at his own multiple reflections in the mirrors. He always seemed about to laugh, like a man keeping an exuberant secret. Hands flat on the floor, his muscular legs apart, he led them into warm-up stretches that made the friendly bulge in his tights even more difficult to ignore. Jogging and jumping into a high-impact routine, he bellowed gruff commands at the spoiled housewives with flabby thighs. "Move it! Pull in that stomach! Breathe!" They snickered and ate it up, making it clear that no one but Barry ever talked to them that way. Skin glistening, he inhaled deeply. His long hair was wet and curling, his body all strength and sinew. What a motivator and what a great ass, Dusty thought, ignoring the cramp in her right calf as she followed his movements. The music overwhelmed and washed over her as she concentrated only on her breathing and her accelerated heart rate. There was a distraction: Laurel, across the room, dancing vigorously in front of a mirror, oblivious, big eyes riveted, as if fascinated by her own image. Laurel's changing expressions were oddly disturbing. Dusty looked away, but her eyes drifted back, drawn by something puzzling that she could not quite fathom.

The pace eventually slowed to a jog, and the class cooled down and went to the floor for push-ups. Barry's T-shirt was so saturated that huge drops of perspiration dripped from the midline of his chest, disappearing into the pale green carpet. Drop after drop, in rhythm to the throbbing beat of the music. Dusty wondered how it would feel to have those warm wet drops splash onto her bare breasts. Too bad this man would never know how much she liked to see him sweat and how much she admired his ass. She hoped fervently that he was not gay. Perish the thought.

Those who had not already dropped out and escaped to the showers rolled onto their backs, for buttocks tucks.

"Your back stays glued to the floor. Contract those abdominals," Barry demanded. "Squeeze those buns!" He watched the sweaty, writhing bodies, his half-smile wicked. "Come *on*, ladies! A pelvic thrust. I *know* you know how to do that. Like trying to pick up a grape with your cheeks."

The class broke, and Dusty headed to the locker room. Laurel lagged behind. The mirrored wall offered Dusty one last reflection. Laurel and Barry, heads together, laughing. Dusty was startled by Laurel's body language, hips slung to one side, her back arched.

. . .

*D*usty lathered her hair and stood in the shower longer than usual, eyes closed. By the time she wrapped a towel around her head and another around her trim waist, she was alone.

She was not due to report to homicide until eleven P.M., but energized and eager to start, she decided to go to the station that afternoon. She had no other plans, and the Sunday atmosphere at headquarters was relaxed. The brass rarely make personal appearances on weekends. The troops can usually carry out their jobs free from meddling, interfering, second-guessing or ego trips by politicians or commanders impressed by their own authority. For a self-starter who really wants to work, it is the best time. She could clean out her locker, move her belongings to homicide, read the supplemental reports on all the team's active cases and check out new leads in the Thorne homicide, all before Rick and Jim arrived.

A traffic light stopped her at an Overtown intersection a few blocks north of headquarters. A young black man stood at the crosswalk, wearing a neatly pressed suit the color of an Easter egg. His two-toned shoes had been buffed to a high shine, and he was carrying a baby. The big-eyed tot in his arms, no more than a year old, wore sky-blue, from his cap down to little blue leather shoes neatly laced. Smiling, Dusty waved the man in the gaudy lavender suit across in front of her. He was a high stepper, conscious of his attire and that of the immaculately dressed child in his arms, definitely an individual en route to an important destination, somebody with a place to go.

The image touched her, freezing her smile as she watched them. Stricken by a yearning as vague as it was painful, she longed to be . . . what? A part of something or somebody else? To spend the week eagerly anticipating Sundays and holidays? To dress up, as the man and little child had, to join friends and family at a place fragrant with home cooking and alive with hugs and laughter? A place where people love you and welcome you back—no matter what.

Hell, she thought, I dumped all that a long time ago, or it dumped me. How long had it been since a Sunday or even a holiday meant anything more to her than work or the mundane tasks of everyday living?

The blues closed in, and she fought back fiercely, shaking off the sudden loneliness literally, tossing her shining hair from side to side like the beauties in shampoo commercials. Come on! She told herself. What *is* this, the Norman Rockwell Syndrome? Feeling sorry for yourself, or what? Are you nuts? "What the hell *is* a normal life?" she asked aloud. She'd learned her lessons the hard way. Watch what you wish for, she thought. You might just get it.

Always wanting more can lead to disaster. Learn to be happy with what you've got. So she'd had Rick, for a short time, and dreamed life would be different. But it was not and never would be. She was elated to be working with him again. He had been a positive presence in her life for more than five years, since he came to lecture her police academy class on homicide investigation. Long-legged and sandy-haired, earnest, with a face that would still look boyish at fifty, he obviously cared about the job and about people. That was the big difference between him and most other cops, the big difference between him and most other men. Respect, friendship and camaraderie will be enough, she thought. Hell, the man will probably spend more waking hours with me than with this cheerleader he's involved with. Wait until Laurel finds out about the schedule, the overtime, all the demands of the job. She buoyed herself with the thought. Rick and I will still be close—but, she told herself, it will never be the same. She's the one he goes home to.

Salvation, she had learned in the past, is to work hard at something important, to become lost in something so difficult and all-consuming that it becomes your armor, a shield against the rest of the world and what it can do to you. Work is ultimately rewarding. Dedication is admirable. Only she would know it was actually self-defense.

She wheeled her sporty red Datsun into the police parking lot, tires squealing on the blacktop. The most important thing I can do now, she told herself, is to help catch the son of a bitch who killed the Thorne kid. That would be rewarding.

She thanked God for her job, took her service revolver out of the glove compartment, slipped it into her oversized purse and walked tall into the big building.

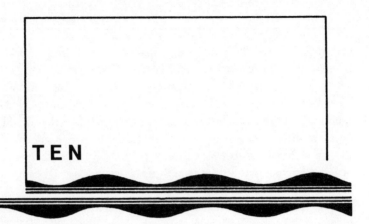

TEN

*C*ooking breakfast at five P.M. is an unnatural act, Laurel thought. She plucked a wisp of gray fluff from the drain in the stainless-steel sink, studied it closely and looked puzzled. Nothing was right anymore, and she was scared. She had been coping and doing well, happy for the first time, convinced that nothing frightening would ever stalk her life again. Rick was wonderful, so strong and protective. But then he had switched back to the midnight shift, leaving her alone. Their young neighbor had been killed in the dark, practically on their own lawn, and now this gloriously good-looking policewoman and her big boobs seemed to be in the picture.

Cops who work together are like family. She knew that. Once Laurel had accepted Jim, along with his endless gripes and complaints, she had found he was not as threatening as he appeared. In fact he was really sort of a big, bluff teddy bear. Jim was important to Rick, so Laurel made Jim important to her, but Dusty was another matter. She was beautiful, and she and Rick shared an air of easy intimacy. The relationship was probably rooted in nothing more than shared police experiences, Laurel told herself. But this woman will now spend the long nights with Rick. While I wait here, alone and afraid, they will share meals and jokes, laughter and anger, danger and triumph. I'm shut out, she thought, and losing time again. This always happened when she was pressured. And why did she feel under pressure? Was she simply insecure, or was she jealous with good reason? All she knew was that she must *not* be left alone in the dark.

She watched, slightly queasy, as Rick wolfed down the scrambled eggs, marmalade and hot bread. She wore pale lipstick that matched the satiny pink ribbon holding back her long hair. "If you could just go on days we could live like normal people for a while," she began.

Rick gazed fondly, through bloodshot eyes, at this soft-eyed and tender young woman, so unlike his voracious bedmate hours earlier. "Years ago I never thought I'd get used to midnights, either. But if you work homicide and want results, it's the only shift to work. It's simply a matter of adjusting your body clock, sweetheart. It takes a little time."

"It's just that I've always been a day person. And after Rob . . ." Her voice faded to a whisper. "It's so awful."

He put down his half-empty glass of orange juice. "What happened is another strong reason for me to stay on nights," he said, his voice still husky from sleep. "We have to solve this one. And don't worry"—he reached for her hand—"all that stuff about the killer returning to the scene . . . it's bullshit in this kind of case. The guy who did it ran like a thief. He's not coming back. Even so, I did ask one of the guys who moonlights as a locksmith to come by tomorrow and beef up security. And my next day off, we'll go out to the range again. I want you to practice with my off-duty gun."

"You know I'm afraid of guns," she murmured.

"You won't be once you're more confident. You've got to know how to use it. You did great last time." His words were firm and almost fatherly. "There's nothing to be scared of. And you'll get used to these hours. Look," he said, arching a wicked eyebrow, "at what a swell morning we had."

She looked up, puzzled, then carefully finished buttering a piece of toast. She placed it before him like an offering.

"What do you mean?"

"What do you think I mean? You already forgot our little fun and games? Lady, you really know how to shoot a guy down."

He looked wounded.

"I just wasn't sure," she whispered, and quickly turned to fill his coffee cup. She was actually blushing.

He caught her hand as she moved toward the stove. "Let me get your coffee," she protested.

He buried his face in her apron and planted a kiss where her crotch would be. "Ahhh," he said. "I thought I smelled something good."

"It must be the spaghetti sauce," she said. "I think I'll freeze some." She hurried into the kitchen, leaving him shaking his head and grinning.

The doorbell rang. "I hope to hell it's not the Thornes." He winced with dread at the thought. "I have to go by there later."

Laurel opened the door to Dusty, all business, clutching a file folder. "The lieutenant asked me to drop this off since I was doing some more canvassing over here anyway."

"Come on in," Rick called.

She stepped inside, looking slightly uncertain. "I can only stay a minute. Thought you'd be up by now."

"Anything?"

"Nope, just a press release for you to sign and something for you to tell the parents. Rob's baseball team and some of the other student groups at the university are collecting donations to boost the reward fund if the family's initial offer brings no results. If the money isn't needed, they plan to establish a memorial scholarship."

Laurel had left the door ajar. Now it was inching open. "Hello?" It was Beth Singer, from next door. She wore battered tennis shoes, tan walking shorts and a peach-color blouse.

She apologized for barging in. Her eyes, dark with concern, widened with interest when she saw Dusty, then smiled to acknowledge her. "I know you've all got a lot on your minds, with the investigation and all, but Benjie is beside himself."

"Sit. And don't mind me," Rick said, rubbing the stubble on his cheek. "I just got up, haven't shaved yet. Have a cup of coffee. You too, Dusty."

"I would love some," Beth said, sighing and shaking her auburn hair. "I spent half the day next door with the Thornes. What a nightmare. The other half I have spent beating the bushes."

"What is young Benjamin's dilemma?" Rick asked.

"We have a state of emergency," Beth said flatly. "Boo Boo Kitty is missing, and Benjie is bawling his eyes out. We've looked everywhere for the little bugger, and I don't know how I'll get that kid to go to bed tonight unless we find her."

"I haven't seen her. What about you, Laurel?"

"Not since yesterday." She poured Beth's coffee, slopping some into the saucer. "I'm so clumsy," she apologized, blotting it awkwardly with a napkin.

Rick sipped his, then stared into the cup. "Is this instant?"

Laurel nodded, her face flushed.

"What happened to the fancy contraption that grinds up the beans and spits out the coffee?"

"I'm sorry. It won't work."

"It's okay, babe, I drink worse stuff on the job all the time. I'm just spoiled rotten. What's the matter with the machine?"

She shrugged helplessly. "I can't get it open to put the beans in."

Dusty bounced energetically out of her chair and into the kitchen, uninvited. "Let me look at it, I'm pretty good with these things." She swiftly examined the machine. "Here," she said, simply sliding open the little panel. "There's nothing wrong with it. The beans go in here, the filter there, the water there, and the coffee comes out here. Voilà."

"Of course." Laurel looked flustered. "I just forgot how the darn thing works."

"When all else fails, read the instructions," Rick said. Laurel seemed so disconcerted that Beth threw both arms around her in a warm hug. "It's been a rough weekend. It's a wonder any of us are still sane," she said, sitting down again across from Rick. "I know I won't be if Boo Boo Kitty does not bring her furry little ass home."

"Someone must have picked her up last night," Laurel said.

Beth shook her head. "She was here this morning. She and Benjie were playing in the backyard. I was hoping she had wandered in here."

"Bet she doesn't miss a meal," Rick said heartily. "Cats know how to take care of themselves. She'll come back. Chuckles is almost fifteen years old, and he has never missed a meal."

"Yeah, Chuckles was your mom's cat," Beth said smiling.

"He came with the house," Rick said. "Mom thought he'd have trouble adjusting to condo living. I built his pet door in the garage when he was the size of Boo Boo."

"Tell your folks I asked for them next time you talk to 'em. I'm gonna go check across the street," Beth said. "If Boo Boo Kitty shows her face, puh-leeze call me."

"What does she look like? I'll keep an eye out too, as long as I'm in the neighborhood anyway." Dusty pushed her chair back from the table and stood up, altered instantly from friendly feminine coffee-klatsch demeanor to the no-nonsense body language of somebody accustomed to taking control: alert, back straight, feet slightly apart and planted firmly. Rick watched. He could not help recalling that he liked her reverse transformation better, from tough cop, a cool professional, to woman, warm and seductive, wet and willing. Wonder Woman to sex kitten. He had always found it a turn-on.

"Appreciate it. Small, pale gray, fluffy. Thanks for the coffee." Beth winked at Laurel, who looked ill.

ELEVEN

None of the messages waiting at headquarters related to the murder of Rob Thorne; it was as though the killer had appeared out of nowhere, then melted back into the muggy night. The reward might generate some tips. The parents had offered five thousand dollars for information leading to the killer's arrest and conviction. They were willing to make it more, but Rick advised against starting high. If the facts were out there, the people most likely to have them would turn in their mothers for a lot less than five thousand dollars.

The fund-raising effort by the student groups touched Rick. It made the dead boy's parents cry.

Dominguez and Thomas were still working the convenience-store shooting. The next case would go to Rick's team. There was no hiatus. He and Jim went to records to pull a printout of recently paroled burglars to check out in the Thorne case. They were only gone for fifteen minutes. By the time they got back, it was their turn. A stranger was dead.

Dusty looked up brightly from her desk. She wore deep blue, the same shade as her eyes. "We've got one holding," she said briskly. "Went down about ten minutes ago. Some kind of a fight down in the Hole, one dead, the perp is being held at the scene by uniform."

"Shooting?" Rick said coolly, picking up his walkie.

"Nope," she said. "No weapons involved, apparently. Just a beating."

"Let's go."

Dusty punched the elevator button. "And *who* is Terrance McGee? He says he has found new evidence. Are you really investigating attempts to poison him? Why didn't you fill me in?"

"A wacko," Jim said. "Paranoid."

"Really? I just spent a half an hour on the telephone with the man."

"Now he's got somebody new to talk to," Jim said gleefully.

"And he sounded so sincere," Dusty said, as the doors slid open and they stepped inside.

"They always do," Jim said.

"Ain't *that* the truth?" The doors whooshed closed.

*7*he Hole is inner city, a tough Overtown neighborhood of dilapidated apartments, thriving crack houses and all-night bars. The disgruntled suspect was locked in the back of a cage car. "Sly!" Dusty called out in surprise. Gone were the graceful and fluid movements. He waved awkwardly. His hands were cuffed at the wrists.

When he saw that no one in the slightly unruly crowd was watching, that all eyes were glued to the covered corpse sprawled on the pavement, he furtively shook his head. "I didn't do it," he mouthed frantically from behind the glass.

"It's J.L. Sly," she said aloud, in her precise, deadpan delivery. "And he says he didn't do it."

Jim grunted. "That's what they all say."

"We warned him about that kung fu crap," Rick muttered. "Let's see what we have." He stepped over the yellow crime-scene tape, lifted the paper sheet, did a double take and whistled. The dead man was a well-built Latin, nearly twice J.L.'s size. His only apparent injury was a small, slightly bloody cut on the forehead.

"What have you got?" Rick asked a young cop. He was a rookie who snapped to attention, all spit and polish.

"Sir, the two individuals in question apparently participated in some type of altercation. The alleged perpetrator, a local resident who is well known for his expertise in the science of martial arts, struck the victim a single blow, causing his demise, sir."

"Is that the head injury?"

"No, sir. The laceration to the front of the victim's head appears to have been sustained when it made contact with the pavement, sir. He was apparently already deceased at that point in time."

"I wish you would speak English," Rick sighed.

"Beg your pardon, sir?"

"Never mind. Good job, Officer."

"What *are* they teaching them in the academy these days?" Dusty asked softly. She stood on the opposite side of the dead man. "Big fellow, isn't he? J.L. must be good to waste him."

"Everybody knows his reputation, I wonder why this guy didn't back off."

"Maybe he's new in town."

The crowd had become increasingly raucous. "Okay," Dusty shouted. "Back on the sidewalk, everybody! You, too. You know you can't block the street. You heard me!" The crowd scattered before her like a flock of pigeons.

Jim watched. Her ability to control ghetto crowds always impressed him. Young blacks will often obediently follow orders from a woman, while the same orders from a man would create a confrontation. There is nothing macho about decking a woman, he thought, or maybe it's the matriarchal society they live in. So many young blacks are raised by mothers and grandmothers, women accustomed to being listened to, women who have to be tough to survive and bring up their children alone in bad neighborhoods.

"Okay, now, listen up," Dusty shouted. "If you saw what happened, step right over here so I can write down your name. Those of you who didn't see anything, stay behind that yellow rope, or better yet, go on about your business."

The witnesses were eager. The victim had burst into the corner bar, belligerent and disoriented, screaming in Spanish. He appeared to be under the influence and scuffled violently with several patrons. He eluded their grasp and ran out the door, smack into J. L. Sly. The crowd watched J.L. posture and pose as he warned the stranger to back off and behave himself. But J.L.'s sudden crouches and shrill king fu cries were no deterrent. Instead, the big man kept coming. Wild and roaring, he forced J.L. into a corner, his back to the wall. Excited, the crowd pressed in for a closer look. The moment of truth came—and went. J.L. hesitated. Disappointed doubters catcalled. The big man lunged forward for the kill. At last J.L. hit him. The blow missed his opponent's head by a mile and glanced off a burly bicep. No matter. The big man dropped like a rock and never moved again. The stunned crowd fell back, whispering "Kung fu" and respectfully murmuring J.L.'s name.

J.L. appeared dazed himself. He simply stood there, staring down at his crumpled victim until police arrived.

The detectives sent the dead man to the morgue and took J.L. to headquarters. Stoic as they drove through the awed crowd of spectators, he managed a clenched-fist salute for a few acquaintances who pressed their faces against the car windows and shouted his name.

He was an entirely different man in the interrogation room, slumped woefully, crumpled in a wooden chair, hands still cuffed.

"Killed the guy with one blow," Jim said, nodding approval. "You don't have just a reputation anymore, J.L. You rate legend in your own time. But most likely you will never get to enjoy the status because, speaking of time, you will probably never see daylight again."

"You're not going to charge me, are you?" Panic cracked his voice. He searched each face, his eyes wild. "I barely touched him."

"J.L.," Dusty said gently, "the man is dead. He didn't commit suicide."

"Come on, guys, I helped you out *beaucoup* times."

"I know, we're friends," Rick conceded. "We warned you. But did you listen? You think this makes us happy? We're going to have to charge you with second-degree murder."

"It was an accident!" J.L. screamed.

"Martial arts training makes your hands lethal weapons. You've said so yourself a thousand times. You didn't have to duke it out with the man, you could have run, or walked away. The fact that you iced the guy with one blow makes it obvious you knew what you were doing. I'm sorry," Rick said, nodding at Dusty.

"Now, J.L.," she said, "I believe the officers at the scene advised you of your rights, but we want to do it again, and we want you to initial every paragraph."

"It's not true!" J.L. wailed. "Take these off," he whimpered, rattling the handcuffs and holding up his wrists.

"I don't know about that," Dusty said. She looked at Rick, then back at J.L., who was now sobbing as tears skidded down his face. "As ludicrous as it seems, since he *did* just kill a man with his bare hands, I am inclined to take them off."

Rick sighed and nodded, then dug in his pocket for the key. "Behave yourself, will you, J.L.?"

The man nodded, rubbing his wrists and sulking. "Thanks, Miss Dustin. I have a confession to make. A good example for wise men to follow . . ."

"Okay, but the form first."

J.L. listened and scrawled his initials after every paragraph. "Now?" he whispered, still sniffling.

Dusty nodded and handed him a tissue. He blew his nose loudly, wiped his eyes and began.

His confession was not precisely what they expected.

"Look at me," he demanded. "I'm five feet, four inches tall, with lifts in my shoes. I weigh a hundred and twenty pounds. I never grew."

The detectives looked puzzled.

"Neither did Michael J. Fox, J.L. We want to know about what happened tonight—" Dusty said, clearing her throat.

"I'm coming to that. I'm coming to that. Look at the neighborhood where I grew up. You know it's survival, survival of the fittest. And I was never *fit.* I couldn't do no sports. I didn't have no brothers and sisters to stand up for me. I was sickly when I was a child. In school nobody wanted me on no team. Other kids picked on me, knocked me down and took my stuff."

"The fight tonight, J.L."

"I'm getting to it. I'm getting to it! Give me a chance!"

"Okay, okay."

"I never did much but stay to home, sitting in front of the TV—and then one day it changed my whole life. I saw a show about kung fu. It came on every week, stories about a man who was taught the ancient art, a man who brought harmony and got respect. He could protect people and right wrongs. Like Sir Galahad."

Dusty's right eyebrow raised slightly at the image.

"So you learned kung fu," Jim said impatiently.

"No." J.L. looked genuinely surprised at the suggestion. "Where would I learn that? I saw the movements of the great circle and learned how to scream from watching the TV show. I practiced a lot. I practiced all the time," he said softly, "in front of mirrors by myself.

"When my mama died I took her home, back up to Georgia. I promised her I would. Then I stayed up there for a while visiting my cousins and relatives. Day after I come back, I had on my new suit, the one I bought for the funeral, and a bunch of jitterbugs in Overtown decided to take it away from me. It wouldn't even have fit any of them. It was just sport to them.

"I don't know why I did it. But I had been practicing my moves and my yells so much, it just happened. They got scared and backed off. I told them I learned it from an oriental man, a master I met while I was away. I got respect. I could walk down any street, anytime. Everybody believed it, because I was good. I was really good. I never had to put a hurt on anybody. Although," he stared at the floor, his voice dropping, "I might have told them I did. I said that's why I came back, cuz I hurt a man real bad and the law was after me."

"But it wasn't true?" Rick said.

"That's right, it was show. It was all show. But everybody believed it. People looked up to me. I could stop barroom fights. I could make bullies back down and stop beating on their women. I could be a hero. All I had to do was walk in and move like this." He got to his feet and slipped into a crouch, his dark hands moving in menacing circles.

"Sit down," Rick said, absently rubbing his temple as though his head ached. "You're saying you never really learned it?"

"That's right," J.L. said, sliding gracefully into his chair.

"Then what happened tonight?" Dusty asked.

"That's what I'm trying to tell you," he said earnestly. "Nothing. That's exactly what happened. Nothing. That crazy man was about to kill me. I knew I was about to die. But everybody was watching, and he wouldn't back off, so I finally took a chop at his head, but I missed. I barely touched his arm. Let me show you."

He reached over and lightly tapped the side of his hand on Rick's upper arm.

"Watch it." Jim's big hand instinctively went to the .38 in his leather shoulder holster.

"It's okay," Rick said, holding his arm up, as if to demonstrate that it was still intact. He shook his head in disbelief.

"So if that was all that happened, how did you drop the guy?" Jim said.

"He just fell down."

"Just fell down and died. Well, that's novel," Jim said.

"If, and I emphasize that word," Rick said, "*if* you're telling the truth, it had to be just a lucky punch. You got pumped up and hit him harder than you thought. With your reputation, it's going to be an uphill battle for you to convince a prosecutor that it's manslaughter, not homicide."

"Manslaughter? I barely touched him. I know I didn't hurt the man!"

"Nobody shot him," Jim said. "Nobody knifed him. I didn't see an arrow in his back. You hit him and he's dead."

"We have to book you," Rick said.

"You're really going to put me in jail? I don't believe it. I—I've never been to jail. It's not right. Sergeant, Miss Dustin?" His eyes moved from face to face in search of a friend.

Dusty looked away, staring uncomfortably at the arrest form on the table in front of her.

Rick ignored his pleading gaze and summoned a uniform who stepped in and motioned for J.L. to get to his feet and accompany him to the booking desk. "I didn't do it!" he insisted.

"Watch him," Jim told the officer. "His hands are lethal weapons."

"That's not true!" J.L. said. "I may have been wrong to fake it, but everybody has to be a hero sometime." The officer snapped a new set of cuffs around his wrists and steered him out the door, still protesting.

"Everybody has to be a hero sometime! Everybody has . . ." J.L.'s mournful wails echoed off the cold walls of the empty hallway until cut off by the elevator doors as they closed.

Rick, Dusty and Jim sat in the sudden silence without speaking for a moment. Dusty finally said it softly, as if to herself. "Everybody has to be a hero sometime."

TWELVE

The weekend death toll mounted. So did the paperwork. Miriam Kelton, night investigator at the Dade County Medical Examiner's office, grabbed a quick sandwich and nibbled it at her desk.

She buzzed the morgue for Lester, one of the attendants. "They're bringing in another one," she said, swallowing a small bite of ham and cheese on rye bread, "a traffic dispute."

Dr. Lansing popped out of his office. It had been a long hard night, and he had already vowed to never ever be stuck again with weekend duty during the full moon.

"What's cooking?"

Miriam had the sweet face and curly perm of a grandmother who would look more at home baking cookies. She clucked and shook her head at each day's new collection of corpses as though they were errant children. She compiled the case histories and efficiently completed the voluminous paperwork the rascals generated. In stern, maternal fashion, she also handled the grief-stricken, angry and/or crazed next of kin who arrived to claim their dead. Paid a pittance by the county, she was worth her weight in gold.

More exasperated than weary, she peered up from behind the stack of multicolor folders: red for murder victims, green for suicides, blue for traffic fatalities and orange for the still-unclassified casualties of life in Miami, the riddles yet to be unraveled.

"Well, a relative of that Latin fellow has been driving me crazy, calling every five minutes wanting the body released."

"Which Latin is that?"

"That Juan Doe killed in a street fight in Overtown by that martial arts expert. He has been identified," she said, waving a red folder, "as José López-

Gómez. And the family wants the body. They don't want an autopsy, but I told them it's required and they'll just have to wait."

Lansing, still wearing a bloodstained lab coat, took the file. As he thumbed through the papers inside, he absently picked up the remaining half of Miriam's sandwich, took a bite and chewed thoughtfully as he read.

"We know very little about him," Miriam said. "He had a very high body temperature when they brought him in, even though he'd been dead for several hours by the time he got here."

The phone bleeped. Miriam answered and rolled her eyes at Lansing. "López-Gómez," she whispered. "I'm sorry," she said into the phone. "I went over this with you before, sir. We can't just send your brother to the funeral home. There must be a post to legally establish the cause of death . . ."

As Miriam listened to the man's protests, Lansing opened the door to the morgue and its odors, none of them pleasant, then stopped and gestured, offering to return her sandwich. "No, no," she waved him off, "you finish it. I wasn't hungry anyway." She covered the mouthpiece with one hand, "Don't forget, Doctor, they still want you out at the scene of that traffic dispute. They last called about twenty minutes ago, you should get over there.

"I'm sorry, señor," she spoke into the telephone as the doctor departed. "We understand how you feel, but that is the law in this country. These things must be handled according to the law."

*W*hen their shift ended the three detectives went directly to the Metro Justice Building for court. They joined the cops, crooks, witnesses and victims, prosecutors and probation officers, defense lawyers and do-gooders, courtroom observers, reporters and ne'er-do-wells, all in various stages of impatience, apprehension and agitation, all trying at the same time to push past the metal detectors guarding the entrance.

Dusty attended a bond hearing for J.L. Jim and Rick were due at a pre-trial hearing in one of their homicide cases. A little girl had stepped off a yellow school bus half a block from home. She never got there. Five days later she was found in a toolshed behind a vacant house three miles away. The condition of her body made it impossible to determine whether she had been raped. But she was nude, her clothing and school books missing. She was ten years old.

From a nearby dumpster, the detectives had fished a pair of bloodstained trousers stamped in the waistband with the name of the linen company that supplied them to an industrial cleaning firm. Rick and Jim traced the trousers to a man named Harry Roper. The little girl had stepped off the school bus at 3:25 P.M. Roper had been ejected from a bar a block and a half away at 3:00 P.M. the same day. He had a history of sex offenses.

The evidence was all circumstantial, but taken in for a statement, Roper broke down, cried and confessed. He never meant to hurt her, he said, he simply could not control himself when he drank.

As the detectives sat in a crowded courtroom waiting for the judge to take the bench, a tall, well-tailored figure conferred conspicuously with a court reporter. His dark hair and glossy fingernails were perfectly sculptured. Not a crease marred the lines of his well-cut Armani suit, and his custom-made shoes gleamed as if the soft leather were caressed nightly by somebody hired to do the job. Norman Sloat exuded success and confidence, along with a restless air of repressed energy and aggression.

"Wonder what the hell he's doing here?" Rick said quietly. "Hope it's not our case."

"Doesn't matter, it's open and shut," Jim said and yawned.

"Nothing is open and shut with Sloat."

The lawyer's talent for publicity and for freeing his clients bordered on legerdemain. For one major murder trial, he had retained a professional astrologer to assist in jury selection. The voir dire sounded like singles' bar dialogue. Each potential juror was asked his or her sign, to be charted for compatibility with the defendant's horoscope. The press loved it.

The bar association did not, vowing to nail Sloat this time for failing to adequately represent his client. The effort was quickly dropped, however, after members of the jury, all water signs, unanimously agreed, in record time, to acquit. Who could argue with success? Not the bar association.

Sloat drove a big Mercedes, wore nine-hundred-dollar Italian suits and was on a first-name basis with every news anchor and editor in town. The flamboyant defense attorney loved money, but he loved something else even more. If a case was destined for the front page, the financial status of the accused notwithstanding, Norman Sloat would be there.

The lawyer snapped a cheery little salute to the two detectives, then nodded at several reporters in the spectator section. When corrections officers herded in the prisoners and Sloat shook hands with Roper, Rick felt the hair on the back of his neck begin to tingle.

The judge called the calendar, and Sloat rose to announce his presence for Roper. He approached the bench and moved to have Roper's confession thrown out as evidence. Pausing for theatrical effect, then smiling benignly, Sloat outlined the grounds for his motion.

His client had been advised of his Miranda rights by the detectives, "present here today," he acknowledged, gesturing toward them, diamond pinky ring winking. However, Roper had been unable to comprehend those rights because he had been drinking. "My client is addicted to alcohol, your honor. He has a low tolerance to it and a history of poor judgment when he is drinking. The detectives had already examined his prior record. Yet they picked him up *at* a bar, knowing the man cannot hold his alcohol, advised him of his rights and *then* proceeded to take his statement, knowing full well the man was *incapable* of making a rational decision at the time. It was incumbent upon them to wait, overnight if necessary, until such time as he was sober, alert and in full command of his faculties before having him make serious legal decisions that could affect the course of his entire life."

Ignoring objections, the judge allowed Sloat to introduce Roper's arrest report and the detectives' depositions, relating that they had found him at a bar, along with doctors' affidavits stating that Roper's alcoholism was involuntary because he was addicted and therefore not responsible for his actions.

Defeat already lurked in the young prosecutor's eyes. He argued that the defendant's statement was the heart of his case.

Sloat stood waiting behind the defense table, smiling expectantly and rubbing his polished palms together.

The judge supressed the confession.

Jim shot out of his seat, his face red. "Your honor, the man confessed to murdering a little girl!"

"I am clearly aware of the gravity of the charge," the judge said solemnly, speaking slowly, one eye on the reporters who were scribbling furiously. "Had you been there at the time, I presume you would have followed the correct procedures to ensure that the defendant fully comprehended his Miranda rights."

"Your honor." The prosecutor stepped in front of the detectives, signaling them to sit down. "We have no choice but to nolle prosse."

The defendant raised his head for the first time, looked around and blinked. Unsure of what was happening, he tugged at his lawyer's sleeve for an explanation. Sloat slapped his fingers away as though flicking a speck of lint from his immaculate cuff.

The judge peered down at Roper, told him he was free to go, called a recess and left the bench.

Rick closed his eyes for a moment. The parents of the murdered child had attended every hearing until this routine pretrial motion. They had all expected Roper to plead guilty if he could negotiate a deal to escape the death penalty. Free to go—what would Rick tell the family? This was one of those gut-wrenching times that he hated the job.

He stepped into the crowded corridor. Jim had slammed out ahead of him and was pacing in a fury. Dusty came striding down the hall to join them. She was smiling. Then she saw their faces.

"What happened? You boys look like somebody took your ice cream and cake away." Scalding TV lights suddenly flooded the hallway, and Dusty followed her partners' eyes to an alcove where Sloat was holding court for the press. "Uh oh," she said.

A reporter started toward them. "Let's get out of here," Rick said. He took their arms and hustled Dusty and Jim into the elevator. "I think I need a drink."

"At ten o'clock in the morning?" She gave him a sidelong glance. "Sounds good to me."

THIRTEEN

*T*he detectives settled at a wooden table in the dimly lit back room of the nearly empty Southwind Bar and Grill. Rick and Jim drank Jack Daniel's like people in pain swallowing their medicine and hoping for quick relief. Dusty sipped a glass of chilled wine.

Rick called from a pay phone to tell Laurel a case had gone awry in court and he was delayed.

Dusty watched him speaking intimately into the telephone, then leaned across the table, her voice a near whisper. "Jim, what do you really think of Laurel? There's something strange about her. . . . She's just not right for Rick."

"Your problem is that you think *you* are." His pale eyes were cynical.

She looked wistful. "My personal feelings have nothing to do with this. You're his friend too. Neither one of us wants to see him hurt. She's not the sweet little thing she seems to be."

"Oho!" His eyebrows raised over the rim of his glass. "Forget the wine, I'll order you a saucer of milk."

"I'm serious."

"So am I."

"You should have seen her at the fitness center the other day, really coming on to Barry. The way she looked . . ."

"The guy with the ponytail? I thought he was gay." Jim scowled.

"You're impossible."

"Hell hath no fury . . ." He grinned.

*T*he jukebox in the background made it obvious that Rick was not calling home from the Justice Building. "Where are you?" Laurel asked.

"We're grabbing a bite to eat downtown," he said. "Our case took a wrong turn in court. We have some things to go over."

"Who are you with?"

"Jim and Dusty."

"Oh." Laurel sounded thoughtful.

"I should be there in a couple of hours."

"You need to get some sleep. Are you all right?"

"Sure. See you later, sweets."

*M*iriam Kelton looked up from her desk at the medical examiner's office. The man wore a chauffeur's cap. "We are here to pick up the body," he announced politely. He glanced casually at a slip of paper that he drew from his pocket. "José López-Gómez." Miriam looked puzzled. "Do you have a release signed by the doctor?" she said, reaching for the paper.

"*Sí,*" he said, and drew a machine pistol from under his dark jacket. "Where is he?"

The two attendants, Lester and Sam, dropped their jaws and raised their hands as the stranger prodded a protesting Miriam into the morgue with his pistol. "I don't know who's who back here," she told him in the high-pitched peevish tone usually reserved for a misbehaving grandchild. "I just handle the paperwork."

A short, horse-faced man had joined the gunman. He too was armed. The man in the chauffeur's cap signaled to him, jerking his head toward the covered gurneys in the autopsy room, referred to as the Pit by those who labor there. The second man stalked through the rows, jerking back paper sheets to expose naked bodies.

The barrel of his own gun aimed at the ceiling, he twisted his neck to peer into the face of a dark-complected corpse. "*No es el,*" he called, snatching the flimsy sheet off another. He stared somberly into the face of an elderly woman. She resembled his grandmother. He crossed himself with his free hand and devoutly rolled his eyes toward heaven. A shotgun victim was next, a man who had already been autopsied.

"*¡Dios mío!*" the gunman muttered softly, then stopped to scrutinize the corpse more closely, a look of recognition spreading across his face. "Hey, I know him, it's Pepe!" He reached for the tag that hung from the dead man's big toe, stared at the name printed there and nodded. "*¿Que pasa, Pepe?*" He turned to his companion. "*Es Pepe.*"

"*¿Pepe?*" The first man looked interested, craned his neck, then muttered a curse. "*¡Apurate! ¡Apurate!* Hurry up!"

"*¿Adónde? ¿Adónde?*" said the shorter man, shrugging his shoulders. He swung open the door to another small room. It emitted cold air that smelled sour, like a refrigerator in which something has spoiled. Bodies were stacked three deep.

The man in the cap brandished the gun. *"¿Adónde?* Where? Where?"

Miriam exchanged glances with the morgue attendant named Lester, a middle-aged black man. Her snippy look said that this situation had gone just about far enough. "Outside," she snapped. "The one you want must be in the trailer. Outside."

They all stepped out a side door onto the loading dock, as the shorter man swiveled his head back toward the last corpse he had uncovered. *"Adiós, Pepe,"* he said softly.

A huge refrigerated trailer purred out in the warm, damp parking lot. When Miami broke all records for homicide in 1981, the county had been forced to lease a refrigerated Burger King trailer to store the overflow of bodies.

The shorter man scrambled up the breakaway stairs and disappeared into the trailer. He reappeared in the doorway minutes later, looking pleased, "He's here. *Completo."*

The other man grinned.

"Where are his clothes?" the short man asked Miriam.

"I have no idea," she pouted. He jerked the gun at her again. "I assume the police property bureau has them."

Before locking her and the two morgue attendants in the refrigerated trailer, the gunmen forced Lester to strip off his baggy surgical greens. Awkwardly, like dressing a huge doll or department store dummy, they tugged and pulled the shirt and pants onto the empty-eyed corpse. Then hurriedly, as though he were a sick friend, they walked him to their car. His bony bare feet and the tag on his toe dragged in the dust.

Dr. Lansing returned ninety minutes later. He was humming and thinking about going home. Since the office had not beeped him for some time, life must have quieted down in the big city. He thought he heard rapping sounds from the trailer as he parked in his slot near the front door and walked into the office. Must be something to do with the refrigeration system, he thought. Only dead people in there. He hoped fervently that the noise was not a sign of mechanical breakdown. That could be unpleasant. The temperature was eighty-seven degrees and climbing.

Then he saw that the phone lines were all lit up and bleeping. Nobody was manning the front office. Or the Pit. He was alone in the morgue.

*J*im raged on about the failing system, lawyers who were sharks, weak-kneed judges and deviate child killers.

"Here's to the new obscene word: *addiction.*" He raised his glass.

Rick and Dusty joined him, raising theirs morosely.

"They call alcohol an addiction, and now the surgeon general says even smoking is an addiction. How convenient—they just can't help themselves," he said, his last three words taking on the whine of a pleading defendant. "It's all bullshit! Every asshole in jail says he couldn't help it, and his lawyer uses it as an excuse to get him off. Whatever happened to good old basic responsibility for your life and your own actions?"

"What can we do about Roper?" Dusty asked, her arms folded on the table.

"Unless we find a witness or some hard physical evidence, nothing. We can't refile the charges," Rick said bleakly. "It was all circumstantial. The confession is what cinched it, or so we thought."

"He walked." Jim drained his glass and slammed it down on the table so hard that Dusty winced. "Nobody's got the manpower to tail him night and day. We just have to hope no other little girl crosses his path when he's in the mood. I've had it just about up to here with the system, with this job, with this town. Roper was as sober as you and me when we advised him and took his statement."

"Maybe more so, at this point." Rick stared into the bottom of his empty glass. "He really was," he said, answering the question in Dusty's eyes. "We were so careful."

"I'm gonna see if I can get us some sandwiches," Jim muttered, struggling to his feet.

"You don't get mad, you get hungry," Dusty said, smiling.

"Very funny," Jim said, and strode toward the bar, leaving Dusty and Rick alone at the table.

She smiled and raised her wineglass. "Like old times, Rick."

"Yeah." His smile was lukewarm, thinking about Sloat.

"Trouble at home?" she said.

"Nah, Laurel is okay. She understands."

"I wish I did." Dusty slipped out of the severe navy-blue blazer she had worn to court. Her white blouse looked soft and gauzy.

Slow down, Rick cautioned himself, a couple of more drinks and you'll want to rest your head on it.

He took a mental step back, to refocus on Dusty from a polite distance. "So, how is life treating you, kid? Everything okay?"

She studied her glass in the uncertain light. "Sure."

"So what's happening? Who are you seeing these days?"

"Nobody, actually."

"Come on," he coaxed, "you can tell it straight to me. We're old buddies."

She looked up, an odd light in her eyes. "I thought we were a helluva lot more than that."

"What brought this on?" He glanced toward the bar to see where Jim had gone, then sipped his drink, avoiding her gaze. "Sure, we've got some history, good times I won't forget, but you know how tight I am with Laurel." Suddenly he grinned. "Do you know, that woman actually irons my shorts? What a housekeeper! Almost too good. She's got my saucer in the dishwasher before I can set my coffee cup down." He shook his head. "If I hadn't met her . . . Dusty, there is something so exciting, so different about that girl . . ." He trailed off and found himself wanting to go home.

"Different isn't always better, Rick. I never thought that what we had was such a casual affair." Her voice was soft. "It was damn serious to me." Tears glistened in her wide blue eyes.

"Kid, we're just having a bad day." Rick looked uncomfortable. "Some damn headline-hungry lawyer has fucked up our case, a killer is walking the streets, we're all tired . . ."

"Remember what we used to do to forget when things went sour on the job?" She looked directly into his eyes. "You never outlive your past, Rick."

He gazed back this time, remembering. "Listen," he said, lowering his voice. "Playing house with Laurel doesn't mean I'm dead. I think about you. Who could forget what you're like?"

"I don't *believe* you. You're living with another woman and . . ." She chewed her lower lip.

He looked puzzled. He had thought that was what she wanted to hear.

"Believe it or not, Rick, I haven't . . . indulged, since you and I . . . I just don't have the heart. I guess I thought we were really going somewhere. I cared."

"You're sure that's not the wine talking? Abstinence is hard to believe in a woman as warm and affectionate as you are."

She looked exasperated. "Why do men, especially cops, always think sex is a necessity of life? I am not a slut," she said bitterly. "Believe it or not."

"I would never have wanted you if you were." His voice was defensive.

"I'm sure you're very flattered," she said miserably.

"How was I to know? You never said anything about us."

"Actions speak louder. I thought you knew. And what could I have said? And when? It hardly seemed appropriate when you suddenly started talking about Laurel. The next thing I knew she was moving in with you. That was obviously not the right time to broach the subject."

"I'm sorry." He was silent for a moment, then spoke as though thinking aloud. "You always seemed sort of distant, secretive. I assumed it was some guy who either really burned you or was gonna surface one of these days, out of your wicked past."

She looked up, her face white. "What do you mean, my wicked past?"

"Just an expression."

"My past is not what we're talking about here," she said sharply. The tears were gone, replaced by something else. He thought he saw fear in her eyes, but the lighting was lousy and he was well into his third drink.

She was sliding her arms into her jacket. "Cold?" he said, and reached out to help.

She shrugged him off and got to her feet. "I have a lot to do today."

Jim loomed up behind her. "Coming through," he said. He juggled three grilled cheese sandwiches on paper plates. "You don't know how hard it was to get these before the kitchen opens at noon. I almost had to pistol-whip the manager."

He placed them lovingly on the table, as one of their pagers began its urgent high-frequency beep. They stared at each other, stricken. "Oh, no!" they chorused, each reaching for his or her beeper. It was Rick's. He separated a quarter from the change on the table and trekked back to the telephone.

Dusty sighed and sat down, reaching unenthusiastically for one of the sandwiches. Her face felt hot. Jim threw her a sharp, questioning look. She slid the plate in front of her. "Thanks," she said. "I think I'm feeling the wine. If we have to go back in, I better eat one of these first. Yecch! Why'd you let 'em put so much butter on it?"

"Just like a woman," he said, his mouth full. "Always complaining."

Rick returned with the news. "We've got a call at the ME office."

"Christ," said Dusty, wrinkling her nose, putting down her sandwich and wiping her mouth with a paper napkin. "Why do they need us? We're off."

"Yeah, but they say it relates to one of our cases."

"Figures," Jim said, wrapping the remaining half of his sandwich in a napkin and tucking it in his pocket. "Let's pick up some coffee on the way."

7he front door to the medical examiner's office was locked.

"We've been robbed!" Miriam announced as she swung it open.

"What did they take?" Jim said, digging out his gold-rimmed reading glasses and opening a small notebook.

"José López-Gómez." Dr. Lansing sat at a desk looking glum.

Lester, still wearing only a T-shirt and jockey shorts, sneezed—several times. Miriam was furious. "I told the doctors we needed better security. I warned them. Listen to that," she said, as Lester sneezed again. "We could have caught our death in there."

"They took a stiff?" Jim said, slapping shut his notebook and staring in disbelief.

"And locked us in the trailer."

"With thirty-seven dead folks," growled Lester, sniffing loudly.

"Thirty-six now," Miriam corrected.

"Who was it? What did they look like?" Dusty said.

"It was his brother," Miriam said, her tone accusing. "He'd been calling for hours. He said the family didn't want an autopsy."

"Who is this missing stiff?" Jim said.

"Case number 89-1582," Dr. Lansing said, and handed over the red folder. "José López-Gómez, white Latin male, age twenty-seven. Died after a single blow from a martial arts expert outside a bar in Overtown. Arrived with a temperature of 107. He hadn't been posted yet, but I'd say he's a possible OD."

"Brother my ass," Rick said. He and Jim exchanged glances.

"Maybe J. L. Sly is not so deadly after all," Dusty said. "Had López-Gómez just come through customs?"

The doctor shrugged. "Don't know where he was before the fatal episode."

"Think he's a body packer?" Jim asked.

"Wouldn't surprise me," Lansing replied.

"If so, Doc, somebody else is probably doing your autopsy for you, right now," Jim said. He opened his notebook again, trying not to smile as Miriam gazed at him balefully. "How do we classify this, Rick? An abduction? Possession of a stolen stiff?"

The detectives drove back to Overtown. A uniform who patrolled the area had learned that the man was registered at a nearby motel. He had signed in a few hours before his fatal encounter. José López-Gómez had looked fine then, the manager said, though in retrospect he did seem a bit preoccupied. Rick asked him to show them the dead man's room. It was a shambles, drapes and shower curtain pulled down, a lamp and a chair overturned. They found some laxatives and an enema bag in the bathroom. No sign that they had produced the desired results.

A boarding pass lay among the other papers on the night table. He had arrived in Miami aboard an Avianca flight from Bogotá, Colombia, two hours before check-in at the motel.

It seemed clear to the detectives that López-Gómez had succeeded in smuggling cocaine into the country in balloons or condoms, or whatever drug-stuffed little packets he had swallowed. But they must have leaked—at least one did. The drug had paralyzed his intestines and the contraband had stalled, stopped dead in his gut, a fortune in cocaine he could not retrieve. It had killed him. The people he worked for must have realized something had gone wrong, that he was dead. "I guess they decided to get the stash back before the ME found it during the autopsy," Rick said.

"Oh, lawdy," Jim said. "I'm glad it ain't me looking for that surprise package."

Rick nodded. "Messy job. I reckon we'll find him."

"With our luck, we probably will. I hate it when people who aren't doctors start cutting on bodies." Jim sighed out loud and shook his head. "What a town. Even the dead aren't safe in Miami."

FOURTEEN

*R*ick knew the house next door would haunt him until he arrested Rob Thorne's killer. Before going home, he checked to see what tips had come in. Not a call, nothing from the street at all, even with the promise of a reward. Strange. He had to make more time to work on the case. But even with all the time in the world, what would he do? Where would he start? The killer has to be the prowler who stalked the Corley home, he thought. What we need is a break, just one lead.

He had hoped to shower and change before Laurel saw him. Rick was always meticulous about his appearance and grooming, conscious of certain niceties most people never need consider. He was not certain that he smelled like the morgue but suspected he did. There was no way to avoid her.

She sat in the breakfast nook, writing a letter, blush-color stationery on the table top in front of her.

"Are you hungry?" The look in her amber eyes was one he had not seen before.

"Nah, not right now. I thought I'd shower and just get some sleep."

"You're not here or you're asleep." She sighed and twisted the cap on her pen. "Nice day?" Her voice had a peculiar lilt. It sounded artificial.

"No. Not at all. It's been a bummer so far." He felt wary, sensing that his day was not about to improve. "Writing your folks?"

"I miss them. I wish they hadn't moved to Orlando."

"Seems like everybody who retires around here bails out of Miami. Beats me why."

"Did you and Dusty have a nice lunch?"

Something in her voice made it all fall into place. Rick blinked. Then he began to explain—too much.

"We were trying to figure out what to do about our case in court today.

Norman Sloat pulled one out of a hat and our child killer walked. Then, a few minutes after I called you, we got sent out on an investigation. I just came from there."

Laurel nodded slowly, her expression said she was not buying it. "I know you and Dusty slept together, Rick."

"Not today!" He said it quickly, without thinking.

"I knew it!" Her face was pink. "With a thousand cops in the whole damn department, why is she suddenly assigned to work with you? On the midnight shift, which somehow now extends . . ." she studied the kitchen clock, a queer expression on her face, looked away, then turned to stare at it again, as if astonished ". . . to three o'clock in the afternoon?"

She fled into the living room without waiting for an answer. He was torn between going after her and taking a hot shower, which he wanted very much. He followed as far as the doorway and tried to sound reasonable. "It's all part of the job, hon, going to court in the A.M. and getting called out when there's a development in one of your cases."

"You and Dusty had an affair." She stated it solemnly as though announcing the six o'clock news.

"A long time ago, nothing serious, before I met you."

"You really cared for each other?"

"Nah," he said, then hesitated. "It might have been more serious on her part, but I didn't know it at the time."

"When did you find that out?"

"She mentioned it today. I never realized."

Laurel sank down on the pale, flowered sofa, small hands clasped in front of her, her chin quivering. "Is that why you insist on working nights, to be with her?"

"Of course not." Rick massaged his forehead with the palm of his hand. "She's a good detective, a good person. The job is all we have in common." His voice was tired.

"How long have you known her? Was she ever married?"

"She came from someplace in Iowa. I met her a couple of years ago when she was first transferred to the detective bureau. I don't think she's been married. She doesn't talk a lot about herself. We worked together. One thing led to another. It ended when you and I got serious."

"You were still sleeping with her when we met?"

Rick disliked the interrogation, but he did not want to appear evasive. "Yeah, I guess so."

"When was the last time?"

"I don't remember. Meeting you blew my mind." He flashed his most winning boyish grin and stepped toward her, placing his hands on her soft shoulders.

"What's that smell?" she said, grimacing.

He sighed. "It's not another woman's perfume."

She looked intense. "Why didn't you tell me about you and Dusty before?"

"It was no big deal. We'll probably run into a lot of women I've known. Believe it or not, I had a life before we met. Most of them are very nice women, and they all know that you are special. I never moved any of them in here. Just you.

"A lot of cops' girlfriends have to cope with ex-wives, ex-in-laws, ex-out-laws and his and her kids by ex-marriages. All we're dealing with here is something as nonthreatening as a partner on the job. It's nothing, sweetheart."

"You've had her in our home. You see her every day. Someday your life could depend on your partner, you say that yourself. How can you trust somebody you jilted? Somebody you threw over? Don't you think she's hurt and angry?"

"Nope. She's a professional, a grown-up, a good woman."

"And I'm not?" Tears coursed down her cheeks and she looked like she was beginning to hyperventilate.

"This is getting us exactly nowhere," he said, exasperated. "I'm taking a shower."

*H*e stood under needles of water as hot as he could stand, then twisted the faucet until it was ice-cold. Hell, everybody else was punishing him, he might as well do it to himself. The house was quiet when he stepped out of the shower. He walked naked to the bedroom, peeled back the sheet and settled into bed with a sigh. His thoughts were a jumble of Dusty's and Laurel's tears, Latino body snatchers, a homicidal child molester on the loose and the mystery of who killed Rob Thorne.

He should get up, he thought, to find Laurel and talk to her. But what if it wound up in a bigger argument? Better to cut his losses now, get some rest and give her a chance to cool off. He thought he heard a sound in the hall. Uh oh, he thought, bracing for an angry onslaught. He opened his eyes. Laurel was peeping around the door frame, her blond bangs tousled into bad-girl curls. She tiptoed into the room with exaggerated small steps and a mischievous expression. She wore pink baby dolls he had never seen before and clutched a battered teddy bear and a small bedraggled blanket.

"Hi, Daddy," she cooed in a little-girl voice. She ran and jumped onto the bed, giggling. He opened his arms.

"Laurel . . ."

"My name isn't Laurel," she lisped. "It's Jennifer." Her right thumb was in her mouth, and she sucked it loudly, peering coyly at him from under her tangled bangs. She pouted prettily for a moment, then began to playfully explore his naked body under the sheet as her pink tongue flicked across her lips.

"Okay, little girl, wild child. It's Jennifer," he said, relieved and pleased at this turn of events. This girl knew games he had never played before.

"Teddy wants to kiss it," she said in her baby voice, and pressed the staring face of the stuffed bear against his private parts. "Now Jennifer wants to kiss it."

Rick leaned back on his pillow and closed his eyes, but not for long.

Her kinky role playing was wonderful and so exciting. Her body seemed almost like a child's. In a slightly disturbing, wonderfully guilty way, it almost made him know what it was like to be a child molester.

Later they shared more forbidden goodies, chocolate chip cookies and milk in bed. She curled up and went to sleep next to him, with Teddy in the middle. Unsolved crimes and jumbled thoughts drained from his mind, Rick drifted off to sleep. He awoke at nine that night feeling refreshed, recharged and strong enough to go back out and fight the world. He awoke Laurel and Teddy with kisses and breakfast in bed. Slow to awaken, she seemed dazed and confused, still unable to adjust to his backward schedule, he realized.

When the phone rang, he was glad it was not Dusty.

"I just got a call and I'm going in early," Jim said. "I thought you might want to do the same. It looks like we've got a suspect in the Thorne case."

"Hallelujah! See you there shortly, pal." Oh, yeah, Rick thought, it looked like Laurel-Jennifer and Teddy had changed his luck.

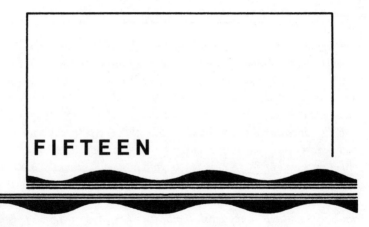

FIFTEEN

*A*lex cruised along tree-shaded Brickell Avenue, where the bold shapes
and colors of Arquitectónica architecture sweep the dark sky. The buildings
resemble giant whimsical Tinker Toys, bursting with life, big bucks and commerce by day. By night it is a different and peaceful world. No high-crime lights
here either. He turned due east, across the Rickenbacker Causeway, the car
windows open, the salt breeze bracing. A damn shame to be forced so far afield,
he thought. But he had promised Harriet he would do nothing illegal in their
own neighborhood again. The cops were all over the islands anyway, with their
watch orders and beefed-up patrols. He stayed on top of their every move,
amused by their efforts. He would not have minded playing a little more cat
and mouse, but he would not really miss it or mind the inconvenience tonight.
He was fond of Key Biscayne anyway.

During the day, especially on weekends, traffic was bumper to bumper,
wall-to-wall used cars, huge tie-ups. Everybody headed for places to play, the
Seaquarium, the marine stadium, the beach, the marina, and Cape Florida,
where the old lighthouse still stands. And Miami drivers always find a way, he
thought, to make the jam-ups worse. They slow down to a crawl just to watch
some poor slob change a tire. If there is a wreck, forget it. They will abandon
their cars in traffic to run and watch.

On weekends, at the beachfront barbecue pits, black, Latin and redneck
teenage gangs engage in hand-to-hand combat. They wield clubs and knives,
and sometimes guns. But late on a soft summer weeknight like this one, there
is little movement across the broad bridge, only motorists headed home late
from the Key's few nice bars and restaurants and, of course, the occasional lovers
parked among the trees down near the water.

He swung into the customer parking lot of a big waterfront restaurant that
features white-glove service, tropical rum drinks and fancy dinners. The place

was still open, and he sat quietly, watching. Inside, the lights were soft and the music mellow, a romantic place to dine. A narrow wooden bridge stretched from the entrance to the parking area, across a pond with ducks. The landscaping was lavish, red passionflowers with their spidery tendrils, birds of paradise and—palm trees.

Palms are making a comeback, he thought. The place known for palm trees and beaches had had little of either for a while. Lethal yellowing disease had killed nearly all of South Florida's picture-postcard coconut palms, and Miami Beach had eroded away to a twelve-foot strip of sand at high tide. But a blight-resistant palm had finally been developed and the federal government had spent millions to replenish the beach. They had dredged shells and coral rock from the ocean floor, pulverized the mixture and dumped it ashore. The result is not as fine as sand and will occasionally cut your feet. But spread it out into a big broad beach, and the tourists, they don't know the difference. They see a wide beach and palm trees and think Mother Nature did it. Just bring your cash and credit cards, Alex thought. There is one born every minute.

He watched a couple emerge from the restaurant. Holding hands, smiling, bellies full. What's next? he thought. The man was a big guy, a horny bastard too, shoving her up against his car, making sure he got his money's worth before they even got out of the parking lot. All giggles, she's loving it. Good times tonight. Alex was almost tempted to join them.

Nothing is more fun or thrilling, he thought, than watching people who don't know you can see them. They act natural for a change, he told himself, instead of being such goddamn hypocrites and phonies. He still thought about that house on the island, the pretty girl asleep, never knowing he was in her room with the power in him to do any damn thing he pleased. Nobody could have stopped him. Now, that was a turn-on.

A flash of blond hair caught his eye, inside, at a table. For an instant it looked like the bitch. His stomach tightened, filled with fury, a sensation like ice cubes pressed against his groin. He knew, of course, that it could not be, that it was not her. Yet his eyes were riveted now, straining the distance. They left their table, moving toward the entrance. He would soon see. She wore white, her light hair pushed up in swirls. Dangling earrings dancing in the light. The man held the door. Alex sat frozen in the warm night air, his hand pressed against the cold metal weight of the gun in his belt.

She stepped out into the night smells and shadows. She was taller, a little heavier. It was not the bitch, but he despised her anyway, for the resemblance. Look how she holds her head and turns to him, Alex thought. He's nothing, a dark-haired, middle-aged man with a little paunch under a good suit.

Nice car. They climb right in, no monkey business. The man jams the key directly into the ignition, and they are moving. I could run them off the road, *he thought. I could do anything I choose to them, but what is there to gain? Something had to make it worth the effort. He sat quietly, to think and to soak in the warm wet sea of night. There are so many more stars in the sky out here, he thought. Out in the Glades, far from the city lights, you can see even more. He wondered what the Indians still out there did on nights like this? What they thought. It would be nice to smoke a little dope or have a drink, he thought. It was that kind of night. He was sure that was what some of the kids parked down by the beach were doing.*

He decided to see, and started the engine. The dark narrow street to the beach seemed carved out of jungle that overwhelmed both sides of the roadway and mingled in the tree tops overhead. It was like driving through a dense green tunnel. What a place to get lost in, he thought, if you like scorpions and snakes. What a place to leave something you don't want found. He would have to remember that.

He stopped at the edge of the beach and decided to walk along the tree line, where an occasional car was parked. He placed his keys up on the back wheel, where he could snatch them quickly for immediate departure should that become necessary. At the edge of the paved parking lot his running shoes crunched on scattered fragments of shattered glass bottles—within sight of a trash bin. He hated that. The slobs think it a treat to smash their Coors and Corona bottles on the pavement. The goddamn pigs—he would relish rubbing their faces in it. Some people are really disgusting, he thought.

It felt good to stretch his legs and stroll in the night breezes off the water. There were lights on the horizon, it looked like a freighter. The downtown skyline glittered in the distance. It was quiet, except for the sounds of the crickets and sea birds. Then laughter from down on the sand. A couple on a blanket. On the Fourth of July the beach had been blanket-to-blanket people who had come to watch the fireworks. The holiday fireworks had ended weeks ago. This couple was busy working on their own.

He stepped quietly, as close as he could, then crouched to watch. They were teenagers. She was demurring and then giggling, every step of the way. He was undaunted, working diligently on removing her clothes. Her bra was unfastened, her breasts exposed. It was a tug-of-war. Every time he lifted her blouse, she giggled and pulled it back down. She made other sounds when he nibbled her nipples. Now the blouse was off, in one swift motion, over her head. Amazing, in the bright light from the stars you could even see the bikini lines where her suntan ended. They had a bottle of wine. Alex noted that the kid was imaginative enough to trickle some over her breasts and lick it off. Loud smacking and sucking sounds. Both were laughing and squirming around a lot. Nothing is nicer than a hard teenage body, Alex thought. The boy's shirt was open, then off. A good-looking, muscular boy, like that dumb Thorne kid who'd tried to stop him on the island. The girl hesitated, trying to sit up, asking the time. The boy lied. She relaxed and went back to tonguing his ear and nudging his groin with her bare knee. His hands were busy, busy. Her skirt was down around her ankles. Little bikini panties—was he really trying to remove them with his teeth? What a kid, Alex thought.

Things were moving a lot faster now. Hey, didn't anybody tell these kids about safe sex? What is this? Alex was having such a good time, vicarious as it might be, that without thinking, he laughed. He stifled it with the hand that was not on his crotch, but too late.

He was only a dozen feet away and the breeze, blowing in their direction, carried his little snorting sound.

"Mario!" Sudden panic was in her voice. "Somebody's there!"

Mario rolled over, looking dazed, and saw Alex. "Son of a bitch!" he said. The words set off a frantic thrashing and a scrambling that Alex found comical, like a cartoon. Arms, legs and for an instant, a round white bottom shining pale in the dancing lights from sky and water. They were pulling on clothes so fast that the wine bottle was kicked over and gurgling in the sand. He saw the kid reach for it and grasp the bottle like a weapon.

Time to leave. Alex had been so engrossed that it took him a moment to get his bearings and remember exactly where he had left the car. "Who is it, who is it?" Alex heard her say, some of the words muffled as she pulled her blouse down over her head. She sounded scared.

"Son of a bitch," the boy said again. Alex could scarcely blame him. The boy hopped around for a second, got his other leg in his trousers, pulled the zipper and flew in his direction.

Alex had bolted like a jackrabbit, but after the initial spurt he had settled down to a steady jog, watching, waiting to see what the boy would do. He had really hoped the kid would not be dumb enough to try to chase him.

But he did, clutching the bottle in his hand and yelling. "Hey, sicko, want a good look? Come on back here! I've got something to show you."

They both ran, beneath the stars in the dark, the warm sand under their feet. Alex was panting and perspiring, more out of excitement than fear. The kid was fast. Alex knew he was in good shape, but the boy seemed to be gaining, probably propelled by frustration and anger and the need to show off for his little girlfriend, who was calling, "Mario, don't leave me here! Dammit, Mario! Come back!"

Her voice was quavering and moving now, like she was running too. Swell, Alex thought, both of them. He would have to shoot them both. Sex and death—they were so much alike. He never thought of one without the other. He concentrated on his breathing and scanned the empty beach for trouble as *he ran. If other people heard the commotion and called the cops, he could have a problem. There is only one way off the Key by car. In emergencies, Alex thought, the cops radio ahead and the bridge tender raises the fucking thing. Then nobody leaves the island until they know what the hell is going on and find whoever they're looking for.*

He remembered the parking lot and quit beelining for his car, veering off, ducking under some low-hanging vines and pounding onto the pavement. He could hear the kid behind him, breathing even harder than the huffing and puffing he had been doing on his beach blanket. Alex darted into the lot, across the broken bottles, the boy close behind him. He heard the cry of pain, turned, saw him hopping, and then he was down. He had run right onto the glass with both bare feet. Alex jogged back to the car, exhilarated.

He snatched the waiting keys off the back tire and slid into the driver's seat. "Mario, where are you?" It was the girl. These two never give up, Alex thought. She was running right toward the car. He flipped on the key and floored it. The wheels spun in the sand, but the car did not move. He had hit it too hard, the back tires spun, whined and dug themselves deeper into the loose sand. Christ! The girl looked uncertain now, but was still coming, head-on. "Mario? Is that you? Don't leave me."

The engine roared and the tires turned crazily in the sand with a sickening, zizzing sound. Cars get stuck out here all the time and need tow trucks to pull them out, Alex thought. How would he explain this to AAA? How would he explain this to Mario, who was most likely limping in his direction at that very moment?

He tried to remember the proper technique. The girl, her dark hair tangled, was still trotting determinedly in his direction. Despite his situation, he managed to note that though she was wearing her blouse and skirt she had never put her bra back on. He wondered about the bikini pants, then reversed gears and gently gave it the gas, using a little more control, turning the wheel. The car jumped back, then lurched forward as he hit the horn and the lights. She was right in front of him. The lights blinded her. Her eyes were big, her mouth open, but he could not hear the scream. At the last moment she threw her hands out in front of her. He cut the wheel hard and the car whomped her to one side, off the right front fender. It was a soft thud of a sound, like hitting a big rag doll. It was no high-speed impact. He looked back as he cut the lights and headed toward the main road. She was up on all fours, swaying, probably not hurt bad, but too dazed to even try to read his license tag.

It worked out just fine, he thought, flicking his headlights back on and pulling cautiously onto the causeway. It was nice to use smarts, instead of the cold steel of a gun or a knife. And it had worked out especially well for the teenagers.

They would never forget him—or this night. They almost had sex, and they almost died—sex and death. Of course they would never know how close they came. He wondered how they would explain what happened at the beach to their families. He hoped he had taught them a lesson.

Smiling to himself, he switched on some easy-listening music as he drove up onto the expressway and headed home.

SIXTEEN

*T*he man was slim and blue-eyed. Sipping coffee and enjoying a sandwich, he looked at home in the stark and heartless interrogation room, like somebody's visiting kid brother. He had confessed to the rape of a teenage schoolgirl attacked at knifepoint in her own bed. He had been caught in the act. Simmons, a detective in the sexual battery unit, took his statement and began to question him about other unsolved cases.

The young man glowed at the attention. He liked to boast and play word games. His mention of San Remo Island and a pretty girl who lived there had sent Simmons to the telephone to suggest that the man might be a suspect in a more serious crime. By the time the detectives in the Thorne homicide arrived, the man had confessed to another rape.

The suspect studied Rick and Jim curiously when Simmons asked if he would mind them joining the discussion.

"Why not?" he shrugged. A court reporter, a chubby, wavy-haired young woman whose impassive face reflected nothing, took down every word, her graceful fingers moving nimbly.

"We were talking about the victim last month, near Morningside Park . . ." Simmons said.

"Yeah, a stuck-up, tight-ass little number," the suspect said, eyes hooded behind his cigarette smoke, watching to see how the new arrivals would take the remark. Rick and Jim showed no reaction. He had tried to speak to her twice, he said, from his moving car as she walked on the street near her home. She had ignored him. She found him impossible to ignore when he tickled her throat with the blade of his knife at three A.M. in her own bed.

"How did you get into the house that time?" Simmons asked.

"Sliding-glass door." He slouched down in his chair, long legs stretched out in front of him. "Love those sliding glass doors. Nothing to it."

Rick saw the subtle glint of confirmation in Simmons's eyes. That was how the rapist had entered the house.

He explained that he knew the right bedroom because he had watched her at night.

"Once I saw her at the Omni Mall and followed her home. A couple of other times I just parked down near the Boulevard and walked the neighborhood."

"Were you ever challenged?" Simmons asked. "Did anybody ever stop and question what you were doing there?"

"Nah, I was wearing shorts, jogging shoes, headband, the works, so if I get stopped by the cops, I'm just getting my workout." He looked pleased. "I don't carry ID. If some cop stops me, I give a phony name and address. No way he can check. That way, if something comes up later, no cop even has my name. No law against jogging, and joggers don't usually carry wallets."

His eyes sought approval for his cleverness. "Hey, if it hadn't been for that gung ho neighbor butting in the other night, I'd still be out there and you guys wouldn't have a clue."

"Probably so," Simmons said mildly.

At the mention of the neighbor, Rick and Jim had exchanged brief glances. "He a friend of yours?" the suspect asked.

"No, never met the man," Rick said.

"He's the neighborhood block captain for Crime Watch," Simmons explained. "A Vietnam vet."

"A crazy son of a bitch, running around with that shotgun," the suspect said, shaking his head. "Somebody ought to do something about that guy."

"You ever carry a gun?" Rick said quietly.

"Nah, they do nothing but get you in trouble. You don't need 'em," he said. "I took a few, when I found them in houses, but I got rid of them right away, sold 'em."

"Who was buying?"

"A guy named Manny, down on Southwest Sixth Street and Second Avenue."

"Does he have a business address, or were these street deals?"

"A business, he's got a little shop."

"One thing I'm curious about," Rick said. "This all happened not far from the Boulevard, where hookers, all shapes, all sizes, all ages, parade up and down day and night. You could have had a hooker with no problem, so why did you go to all this time and trouble and run the risk?"

The suspect's stare was incredulous. "I never paid for sex in my life!" He was obviously indignant at the suggestion. "You ever take a good look at most of those hookers? They're dogs. You don't know what the hell kind of diseases they've got, or if they're gonna set you up to get robbed. I wouldn't have nothing to do with them, man. Besides," he gave a leering grin, "it's more interesting this way. You know what I mean."

He stubbed his cigarette out in the ashtray. "How about sending out for some cheeseburgers?"

"That can be arranged," Simmons said agreeably. "The officers did advise you of your constitutional rights at the time of your arrest?"

"Yeah, so did you, twice." He seemed impatient.

"Well, let's go over it one more time."

Jim stirred in his chair. Rick shot a warning glance at him. "Got to make a pit stop," Jim said, and got up to go to the john.

"While you're out there, maybe you can order the cheeseburgers," the rapist said cheerfully. "I'll take two, medium well, with catsup and pickles on the side. And, eh, a couple of Classic Cokes."

Jim stared at the man. The room fell silent, all eyes focused on him. "Medium well, catsup and pickles on the side," he repeated. "A couple of Classic Cokes."

He shambled out of the room, telling himself that any man about to cop out to an unsolved homicide should have all the cheeseburgers he can eat.

He rejoined them a short time later, his broad face carefully arranged into what he hoped was an amiable expression. He watched the wavy-haired, chubby-cheeked court reporter. Neither she nor the suspect seemed at all uncomfortable at her presence, Jim thought, so why was he?

"So you've raped two or three of them," Simmons was saying in a casual fashion.

The suspect put down his fresh cup of coffee, paused and looked slyly at his questioners. "Try adding a zero to that number," he said. "You'll be a lot closer."

"Twenty or thirty?" Rick said, looking impressed. "All here in Miami?"

"That's for me to know and you to find out. You're the detectives." The suspect seemed amused by his attempt at wit. "Got any more cigarettes?"

Simmons slowly shoved a pack of Marlboros across the scarred wooden table top.

The rapist tapped the pack, slid out a smoke and waited for the attentive detective to light it for him. He let them chew awhile on his latest revelation. He would have preferred not being caught, but now that he was, he enjoyed the recognition, the attention and the break from the dismal jailhouse routine.

Talking to the detectives entitled him to special food, special privileges and a celebrity of sorts. He intended to milk it for as long as he could.

"So you know Morningside, the Roads section, Allapattah, and you've been over there around the causeway islands?" Simmons said casually.

"Yeah, I been over to San Remo, nice neighborhood."

Rick felt a chill in his stomach, thinking of Laurel, alone at night. His face remained frozen in a half-smile. Rapport with the rapist was important.

"Did you assault anybody over there?" Simmons asked.

"Nah, I just looked around."

"What brought you there?"

"Some broad, a little dark-haired girl, nice ass. I saw her in a bookstore at the mall a couple times. She was driving one of those small Japanese cars. I followed her over to the island, thought she lived there, but I guess she was just visiting. I went by a few times after that. No sign of her car and she wasn't around, just an older couple."

"How could you tell she wasn't there?"

"Parked up by the causeway and walked around in my jogging clothes."

"Which side of the island was that?"

"The south side, a pink house with some kind of birdbath out front on the lawn."

Christie, Rick thought. He knew her, knew the house. She'd grown up on the island, too, like Rob Thorne. She was in college at Gainesville, probably in summer session now. Smart as a whip, determined to get through in three years. He'd last seen her home at spring break.

"When was that?" Simmons said.

"I don't know, months ago, maybe April."

"When were you on the island last?" Simmons said.

"That was it. Maybe I rode by one more time in June to see if her car was there, but it wasn't."

Thank God, Rick thought, his face revealing nothing.

Simmons nodded slightly to Rick, handing the interview over to him at that point.

"What about last week?" he asked the rapist. "Say Friday night, Saturday morning. You went over to the island that night too, didn't you?"

"San Remo? Nope." The rapist lit another cigarette and watched the blue smoke as he slowly exhaled. "Haven't been in that neighborhood for a couple of months." He looked amused. "Why, some broad say I been there?"

"You weren't walking around? On the north side of the island that night, maybe four or four-fifteen A.M.? Carrying a gun?"

Something changed in the rapist's eyes. He glanced over at Simmons. The rape squad detective was leaning back in his chair listening intently and did not seem about to speak up for him.

"What is it with you guys? This is straight arrow. I haven't been over there in months. I got no reason to lie." He looked at Simmons again. "You been telling me what a good memory I got. If I'd been there, I'd remember. And I told you before, I got nothing to do with guns. Don't like them."

"Come on, pal," Jim said. "You've been pretty up front until now. Why not tell us about the shooting?"

"Shooting!" The rapist shot out of his chair so fast that it fell over backwards. "What the fuck you talking about?"

Rick ignored the outburst. "You were prowling the island," he said calmly, "looking for a victim, you got chased by a neighbor and you shot him."

"Why don't you just tell us about it?" Jim said soothingly. "Maybe it wasn't your fault. He was a big guy. Did he come at you out of the dark? Maybe it wasn't homicide, maybe it was self-defense."

"Homicide!" The rapist's eyes swept the faces of the detectives so fast that it looked like his head was spinning. "I don't believe you guys! I didn't kill nobody. You hear me?" He jabbed a forefinger. "No guns, no shooting. You ain't pinning nothing like that on me. No way!"

He snatched his nearly empty Styrofoam coffee cup off the table and hurled it to the floor. "No way! Goddamnit!"

The detectives sat quietly. Drops of splattered coffee rolled slowly down the wall, leaving dun-colored trails on the drab off-white paint.

"I ought to make you clean that up. I guess you don't want your cheeseburgers now, either," Jim said sadly.

"What day was it? Friday night, Saturday morning? I've got an alibi. You can check it out!" he raged, his face reddening, the muscles taut in his neck and jaw.

"What did you do with the gun?" Rick asked. "Sell it to Manny? Or drop it in the bay?"

"What alibi?"

Simmons looked earnest, still maintaining the good-guy posture.

"You tell them! Didn't I give you the truth about everything!"

"That's right," Simmons said. "As far as I'm concerned, you've been very open and truthful. If you do have an alibi, we can check it out. No problem."

"Well, you do that!" The rapist uprighted his chair, sat down sullenly and lit a cigarette. "My mom and stepfather own a bungalow down in the Keys. She doesn't drive, and he had a stroke so he can't. Every Friday night after rush hour, I pick them up, and sometimes a couple of their neighbors, and drive them down there. We come back late Sunday night."

Jim snorted. "Your folks would say anything to back you up. What about witnesses from the real world?"

The rapist looked smug. He was calmer now and thinking clearly. "Well, my stepfather would not lie for me since I am not exactly his favorite person.

Then there are their neighbors, a nice Christian couple who would not lie for anybody, but how about," he paused, "the cops?"

Eyes glittery, he gazed at them one by one to see if he had their full attention. He did.

"If you recall," he said slowly and distinctly, "the U.S. Border Patrol put up a roadblock at Florida City last weekend and stopped every motherfucking car."

Rick nodded. The drastic attempt by the government to block the endless flow of illegal drugs and aliens had made controversial headlines. Weekend traffic was tied up for hours. Cars overheated in ninety-degree weather. Motorists were infuriated, and the groundswell of outrage had caused Key West citizens to launch a movement to secede from the United States and form their own republic.

"You still coulda made it back in time," Jim said.

The rapist shook his head and looked sorry for him.

"When we finally got through the jam-up, I tried to make up for lost time."

"And?" Rick said.

The rapist paused for effect. "I guess I was driving too fast. On the Seven Mile Bridge. A trooper pulled me over for speeding. I was mad as hell—in fact, he'll probably tell you I gave him a hard time—but now I see he did me a favor. He is the man who's gonna get you two assholes off of my case."

A muscle in Jim's right cheek began to twitch.

"You have the citation he wrote?" Rick asked.

"Sure. You'll find the ticket in my car, in the glove box." He turned to Simmons. "If you don't mind, I don't want to talk to those two anymore."

"Sure," Simmons said. He nodded at Rick and Jim, who stood up to leave. "I'll be right back," he said, and walked outside the room with them.

"Don't forget the cheeseburgers," the rapist called after them.

"Catsup and pickles on the side," Jim muttered.

"And two Classic Cokes!" the rapist sang out.

"I'll get the inventory on his car," Simmons offered. "It was towed after he was arrested."

"Good," Rick said. "If there is a ticket, we need the time and the date. If they match his story, we need to talk to the trooper, ask him to confirm by describing this guy."

"He could be blowing smoke," Jim said, "about this ticket shit. Or it could be the wrong date."

"I hope so, he looks good," Rick said. "A burglar, a prowler. A rapist with a rap sheet. He steals guns, likes to tippy-toe around in the dark, and he admits to being in the neighborhood at some time."

"I better get back in there," Simmons said. "I've got a lot of other cases to talk to him about. I hope he's not too spooked." He looked skeptically at Jim. "You really order his cheeseburgers?"

"Certainly. A uniform is on his way in with them. Oh darn," he said, over his shoulder, as they walked away, "I forgot the catsup and the pickles, and the two Classic Cokes."

To Rick, he said, "Too bad it wasn't me with a shotgun who caught that piece a shit in the act, instead of the Crime Watch captain."

Dusty looked up, her smile eager. "How did it go? Is he our man?"

"Could be." Rick was surprised that Dusty could appear so vibrant on so little sleep. "He's looking good but claims an alibi. If it checks out, we're back to square one."

"Please, God, let it be him," Jim said fervently, rolling his eyes toward heaven.

"Amen," Rick said.

Dusty's eyes softened when she looked at him. Jim sighed. Rick has got to be one crazy son of a bitch, he thought. Laurel may be a beautiful girl, but this one is all woman.

Rick was on the phone, scribbling an address. He turned to them, his expression resigned. "The good news is, they found López-Gómez. The bad news is, we were right. He's already been autopsied—by an amateur."

"Awwww. They don't need us," Jim said. "He's stolen property. Can't robbery or missing persons handle it?"

"Yeah," Dusty said. "We already sent him to the morgue once. It's somebody else's turn."

Rick shook his head. "He belongs to us."

SEVENTEEN

The body snatchers had used a Ginzu knife, the one advertised by fast-talking pitchmen on late-night television commercials. Their surgical theater was in a cheap motel room west of the airport. The bathroom was now a Salvador Dali nightmare—in surreal greens, reds, browns and purples. Rummaging through López-Gómez's intestines had proved far more difficult than expected.

A middle-aged maid made the discovery. She quit her job on the spot, saying she was leaving Miami for good.

Dr. Lansing was already there, in high dudgeon. "They didn't even know enough to clamp off the abdominal aorta," he grumbled in greeting. "Look at this mess!"

The amateur pathologists had begun their treasure hunt with José López-Gómez reclining in the bathtub, his upper body elevated. Their first mistake, they discovered, after severing the big artery along the backbone, the one the size of a garden hose. The blood in the upper part of the body quickly flooded the area they were most eager to explore.

"They had to tear out his entire digestive tract and search through twenty-six feet of intestine," Lansing said.

"It smells to bejesus," Jim said, pulling his handkerchief out of his pocket.

"It could have been worse," Rick said, noting that the air conditioner was set on high.

"What is that?" asked Dusty. "It looks like a burn. How do you suppose this happened?" A section of plastic shower curtain had shriveled, and there was a scorch mark on the wall over the tub.

Dr. Lansing smiled approval. "You know, it's really good to have you back aboard, Detective Dustin. I was about to point that out. This is extremely interesting." He looked enthusiastic. "I think I can tell you something about one of the men who made this mess."

"And what might that be, Doc?" Jim's voice was muffled by the handkerchief pressed over his nostrils.

"You're looking for a man who could be minus his mustache, eyelashes and eyebrows. See the distended bowels. We all know from experience during autopsies about the enclosed gases that build up." The group nodded unhappily. "They're a mixture of methane and other gases. If you light a match or a cigarette lighter as the bowel is punctured and the gas escapes—you get a beautiful blue flame."

Lansing leaned over the tub and what was in it. "Look at this!" he said triumphantly. The item he retrieved and held high in his gloved hand was a cigar, the end bitten off.

"You mean a flaming fart took off somebody's eyebrows?" Jim said.

"Yep. Every time he cut to take out a bag, here came this puff of gas. It was okay until he lit his cigar. Maybe he just wanted a smoke, maybe it was to mask the odor. Whichever, it was like opening a propane container and lighting a match—one big *whoosh,* like a flamethrower. He'd have singed his face, hair, the whole thing. I'll show you," Lansing said eagerly. "Anybody have a cigarette lighter?"

Nobody moved. They were alone in the room. The uniforms, usually eager to crowd into any air-conditioned crime scene, had elected to wait outside on this one.

Lansing studied each solemn detective in turn, then shrugged and turned back to the tub.

"Did they get the cocaine?" Rick asked.

"Looks like they did," the doctor said. "See where the stomach and intestine is all inflamed? That looks like a ruptured condom. It probably killed him."

"Let us know when you're sure," Rick said. "If so, that could get our man Sly off the hook. No telling how many bags there were. But they must have thought it was worth it, to go to all this trouble."

"I bet they didn't think so any more by the time they were through," Dusty said. "I'll let the hospitals know to be on the lookout for a Latin male with singed whiskers and a distinct aroma."

*T*he nervous motel manager was convinced that the occupant of room 109 had fallen victim to a gruesome murder. "He was already dead when he arrived," Jim told him. "Trust me."

The man who had signed the register and his companion matched the description of the gunmen at the morgue. But one would look different now. The room was registered to José López-Gómez. "Cute," Jim said. "For a stiff, he really gets around."

Jim slammed the door of the wagon after López-Gómez was slid inside, zipped into a polypropylene body bag. "This is getting to be a habit," he told Lansing. "Try to hang on to him this time."

EIGHTEEN

*D*usty was assigned to distribute the police artist's drawings of the two Latin body snatchers to hospital emergency rooms. "One must have flash burns and may be missing his eyelashes, eyebrows," Rick said. "See if you can come up with an ID. Try all the Latin clinics too."

"That'll take days," she said.

"Try to get it done tonight," he said grinning. "Then go home. You don't need to come back in, unless you hit paydirt."

"What an incentive. Bye, guys." She picked up the manila envelope with the pictures and took off.

From his desk, immediately behind Rick's, Jim was scowling at another detective, his feet up on his desk, chatting on the telephone, just out of earshot. "Wonder what the good goddamn he's up to now," Jim muttered. "That guy has covered up more shit than a cat. It's amazing he's still around. You can't trust him."

"What do you think about Dusty, Jim? Can I trust her?" Rick swiveled his chair around to face his partner. His face was serious.

Jim looked perplexed. "You're the man who should know, bro. You got some reason not to trust her?"

"Not exactly. But I thought our working together would be no problem. Now I find she apparently took our . . . relationship more seriously than I thought. She got a little weepy the other day."

"At the Southwind." Jim nodded.

Rick leaned forward and lowered his voice, although no one else was close by. "Laurel knows, and she's a little jealous that we're working together."

Jim looked puzzled. "How'd she find out about you and Dusty?"

"I told her."

"Oh swell, there's not enough trouble in this world, you like to create a little more for yourself, huh? Jeez, when it comes to policemen and sex, the heat from their balls travels up to their brains and turns them to shit."

"Give me a break, Jim. She picked up on it somehow and asked point-blank. I'm not gonna lie to her."

"She woulda put it together anyway," Jim conceded. "Women can smell it on each other when they have the hots for the same guy. Dusty always had eyes for you, probably always will." His pale eyes looked wistful.

"Remember back when Dusty first joined the department? We didn't know her yet, but you couldn't miss her. There was scuttlebutt about some situation she was involved in before she came to Miami. You remember what the scoop was?"

"They talk about every broad that joins the department. I don't listen to station-house gossip, unlike most cops."

"You don't think she'd do anything to upset Laurel, you know, woman scorned shit?"

"Hot pants have no conscience," Jim said, leaning back in his creaky chair. "But on the other hand, Dusty is a champ as far as I can see. And if it's a mandate that we gotta have a woman in here, I sure want her and not somebody like Foster, who couldn't find her ass with both hands if she was sitting on it. You know she takes off her bra when she thinks it's too hot in her patrol car. Or Tierney, who wouldn't know if it was day or night without her police radio—all she's conscientious about is the shade of her lipstick and what her hairdo looks like.

"Or even that good-looking redhead in forty sector—a real sweetheart, but if a stranger so much as said 'Boo!' she'd go into cardiac arrest. There's places for women, Rick—police work ain't one of them. If we have to have a woman partner, we're damn lucky it's Dusty. I warned you when you first started screwing around with her that you shouldn't shit where you eat. Everything that goes around comes around."

"Thanks, pal. I could have lived without the lecture." Rick frowned. "You're right, I guess. A lot has happened lately, and Laurel is sort of moody and changeable. I never know what to expect with her. She still has some growing up to do."

"Told you that, too," Jim said, shifting his gaze over Rick's shoulder. "Uh oh, here comes trouble."

Mack Thomas ambled toward their desks.

"Looks like he ate the canary."

"Well, I see you finally put that bum Sly right where he belongs," Mack said. He removed the cigar from his mouth and looked pleased. "So the king of kung fu has got his ass in a sling this time."

"Maybe, maybe not," Jim said. "We're waiting on word from the ME."

Thomas parked himself on the edge of Rick's desk. "I've got some news. Your neighbor, the Thorne kid. Wuz that his name?"

Suddenly attentive, Rick kicked an empty desk chair in Thomas's direction.

"Remember my Pakistani convenience-store clerk blown away in a holdup that is still unsolved?"

"Yeah."

"Well, ballistics now informs me that the .38-caliber bullet that nailed him came from the same gun that wasted your neighbor." He waved a yellow copy of the lab report.

Jim was on his feet and took it from Mack's hand. "When didja get this?" he said accusingly, staring at the date.

"It came to my attention yesterday."

"Why the hell didn't you tell us right away?"

Mack extended his palm, stiff fingers vertical, as if to deflect the arrows of instant outrage. "I've been very busy with grieving relatives," he said, "and it momentarily slipped my mind. But no problem. Time is of no essence. We've got nothing, no witnesses, no suspects, no leads, same as you have in your case—zero."

"I want to see the file," Rick said briskly. "Everything you've got."

"Likewise," Mack said. "We've got to catch this guy. He's leaving too many dead bodies in our jurisdiction."

"We do have a suspect," Jim said. He turned to Rick. "What about our rapist?"

Rick dialed the rape squad.

"Just about to call you," Simmons said. "I got the ticket from the wrecker service that towed his car. The time and the date are as he told us. The trooper confirms it. He remembers the guy, says he had a bad attitude. If it wasn't for the old folks he had with him, he probably would have arrested him. He's sorry now that he didn't. Sorry, Rick. I know this guy is going to cop out to some other rapes, but it looks like he's not the man in your homicide."

"Thanks, that's okay, Dave. It was a good try. Appreciate it."

"Son of a bitch," Jim said bitterly.

"We've got nothing," Rick said. "Except now we know it was no isolated incident. This guy is trigger-happy."

Picking up his walkie Jim held it close to his ear. "Maybe we do have something," he said. "Sounds like another convenience-store shooting just went down."

. . .

*T*he hospital emergency room was a beacon of light in a sleeping city of darkness. Rick and Jim burst through the automatic doors, men in a hurry. The wounded clerk was alive.

A passing patrolman had heard the shot, seen the man with the gun flee the store and drawn down on him. The robber had dropped his gun and surrendered.

It was a good catch, worthy of officer-of-the-month honors, Rick thought, but disappointing nonetheless. The robber's gun was an automatic, .22-caliber, and his getaway car had been stolen in Atlanta, where he had escaped from police custody twenty-four hours earlier.

The clerk, a young black man robbed seven times in as many months, was fed up and tried to wrestle the gun away from the holdup man. He did not believe the weapon was real. It was. The clerk was lucky. The bullet had entered and exited his left thigh, inflicting a painful wound but no major damage.

They talked to him briefly in the ER. "It was small," he said, wincing in pain, his face wet with tears and perspiration. "I thought for sure the damn thing was a toy. I'm probably in real trouble now. Company policy is never to resist a robbery. I hope I don't lose my job over this."

The detectives stopped at the nurse's station to talk to the officer writing the report.

"Can you believe that?" Jim said. "The poor guy gets shot and has to worry about getting canned cuz he objected to getting robbed for the umpteenth time. They oughta give him a bonus for balls."

"They're worried about liability," Rick said. "They'd rather give up the few bucks in the till than see somebody get hurt and file a claim."

"Yeah," Jim groused. "If the robber got injured, he probably woulda sued— and collected. I'm telling ya, Rick, I gotta bail outta this line of work."

The nurse in charge returned to her station, and Rick flashed the boyish grin that was second nature. "How goes it, Aileen?"

"Good, now that you're here. Have you come to take me away from all this? At last?"

"Not this time. My roommate won't let me."

"That's right. I forgot. How is domestic bliss?"

"I'm not sure yet, I'll let you know."

"What else is on your mind?"

"These two guys." He placed the likenesses of the two Colombians on the desk. "Did Dusty come in earlier with these?"

"Detective Dustin? Haven't seen her tonight—or them. What are you looking for, a bullet wound?"

"No, one of them may have flash burns on his face."

"Leave the copies, we'll let you know if they show up."

A teenage girl was weeping noisily in a wheelchair behind Rick. Her clothes were torn, there was a small cut on her forehead and her lower lip and knees were bloodied. "What happened to her?" Jim asked the nurse.

"Some sort of run-in with a car. Her boyfriend is over there having slivers of glass dug out of his feet. Must have been quite a date. Remind you of anything?" She smiled coyly at Rick.

"Hey, they weren't all that bad," he said. "Were they?"

The dark-haired young man she had indicated lay facedown on an examining table in a nearby cubicle, partially concealed by a privacy curtain. A doctor seemed to be working diligently on the bottoms of his feet. Officer Terry Lou Mitchell stood at the head of the table, eyes narrowed, her expression dubious. She was shooting questions at the patient and filling out a report.

Her face lit up when she saw Rick, and she stepped out from behind the curtain. Just then the automatic doors whispered open, and four people surged inside. They were a middle-aged couple, a youth about twenty, and a young girl who strongly resembled the bruised teenager in the wheelchair.

The girl in the wheelchair began to wail. "Mami, Mami!" She opened her arms as her mother and sister rushed to her. The father and the brother looked around, spitting curses in Spanish, saw the young man on the examining table and charged.

"Uh oh," Jim said.

Officer Mitchell stopped them, waving them back as though directing traffic. "Your daughter's okay. It's not his fault. They both got hurt," she said. "He is being treated right now. Let the doctor do his work."

Reluctantly, the two men joined the women, still angrily muttering invectives over their shoulders.

"What the hell happened?" Rick asked Mitchell.

"Who knows?" She spoke quietly, out of the corner of her mouth. "They're ticked that the kid kept their sixteen-year-old darling out way after curfew and she wound up getting hurt. They were out partying on the beach at Key Biscayne, a little beach blanket bingo. Doing a little drinking, I think, if that's all they were doing. He claims he cut his feet up while chasing off some intruder. She says she got scared, ran after them and got bumped by a mystery car whose driver didn't stop.

"She has no car description, no tag number." She looked skeptical. "God only knows what really happened out there. They probably aren't sure themselves and wouldn't tell if they did. You know how kids are."

"Yeah," Rick said, "having been one myself." He turned away, eager to go back to the station to read Mack's file on the convenience-store murder. With any luck, it would help them find a killer who apparently never left a witness.

NINETEEN

*A*lex now saw what the big attraction was. The place was not just a gym, it was a fucking fantasy factory. The dudes in the Nautilus room flexing and straining on gleaming metal machines were pumping up their imaginations as well as their bodies. He watched their eyes, riveted to the mirrors, staring at their own images. He felt certain they saw Rocky or Rambo instead. And the women, prancing about in their pricey exercise togs, stretching, bending, entranced by their own reflections, had to be envisioning themselves as Bob Fosse dancers. Oh yeah, he saw exactly what he had been missing, skimpy little leotards stretched taut across throbbing pudenda. Hints of pubic hair curling around those narrow little all-cotton crotches. That perspiration could be so provocative, depending on who wore it and where it dripped, had never occurred to him before.

Today was an event, the first time he had been out here. It would not be the last, he decided. Aside from a few flabby fannies hit hard by gravity, the specimens were incredible. All the limber bodies, the deep breathing, the muscle control, the protruding nipples. The girls who work the hardest at this, he thought, are the ones who need it the least. The instructors were something to see. Barry, wearing a knowing grin and tights that looked painted on, and the women, tan and beautiful, supple and well toned, running and dancing. Alex didn't know which one was more of a turn-on, the little Latin girl who made up her face like she was about to step on stage at Vegas, squealing like a baby pig during her high kicks and hip tosses, or this one, Tawny Marie, apparently the chief instructor.

What a body! She looked as strong and sleek as a panther, and as agile, with the discipline of a marine drill instructor. Her voice was warm, throaty and full of vitality, urging everybody to push just a little harder. Sounds like a Lamaze class, he thought. Looking at her, he knew what he would like to push. Lithe and muscular, her long dark hair streaming, she looked like a wild Indian. She can attack my wagon train any time, he thought. He imagined what she would be like; all that strength, endurance and control. The possibility made him even more breathless than trying to keep up with her. Damn, he thought. He could find out where she lived. Pay her a little surprise visit. Take some private instruction, or give some. He loved it. This had become more fascinating than his initial reason for coming out here, which was to see what the bitch was up to now.

He kept trying not to watch her; seeing her filled him with such fury that he lost his train of thought and messed up his footwork. It would not do to crash clumsily into anybody during the aerobics. Damn, he thought, Aerobics III. Survivors of this class deserve a purple heart. All this was supposed to be good for the cardiovascular system. He hoped the effort was worth it.

Before he emerged to join the class, he had watched Laurel and Dusty in the same room. So aware of each other, yet unaware of him. Careful to ignore each other, he thought, when they were really curious as hell and sisters under the skin. How stupid they both were, to be taken in by the same man.

It had been difficult, almost impossible, not to stare at them in the mirrored room. They were everywhere he looked. Hundreds of them, rows of those same insipid faces and pale hair. The rage they sparked had made him dizzy. Taking a deep breath, he had tried to think clearly and coolly as their images surrounded him, a hundred, a thousand mirror reflections.

Dusty and Laurel share one consolation, he thought. When together in the same room, each knows that the other is not with Rick at the moment. He smiled. It probably never occurs to them to wonder what other cow he is with at this very moment. That man would screw a snake if he could hold onto it.

Cops are not exactly famous for their monogamy, Alex thought. He wondered at the endless supply of women eager to lie down for a good-looking cop like Rick. Is it his penis or his gun that attracts them? Definitely not his brains. Maybe they're simply fascinated by death and danger. That must be why lowly flatfoots on the beat have as many eager groupies as rock guitar players who make big bucks, he concluded. They love it. Guns, the symbols of sex and death, do attract women.

He looked at Dusty, thinking she probably sleeps with her piece. This woman loves guns so much, he thought, maybe he could use one to show her a few tricks she might like. She was getting down and into it now, exhaling hard through her round pink circle of a mouth. The woman has got a great set of lungs, he thought. They seemed about to pop out of her leotard. He liked those damp spots, those circles of sweat, one growing at the small of her back, the other spreading between her breasts. The muscle definition in her calves and her shoulders might be called sexy by some men. He thought it a bit much. These *women were rugged. He would love to see some two-bit street thief try to put the snatch on one of their purses. The punk could be in for a nasty shock.*

Trying not to think about Laurel was impossible. Thoughts of her body filled him with instant outrage and anger. He wanted to rip her apart, to tear out the bloody organ that Rick loves in every woman and then watch her die. Sex, then death. He wanted to see the look on her face when she knew. Somehow he had to let her know he was there. He could not resist. Maybe a little love note. That would get her attention and stir up the pot a bit.

The class was winding down. Thank God, he thought. Tawny Marie must be trying to kill us all. He would return the favor some night when she least expected it. She was not even winded. What a woman. They should send her on a mission to rescue the hostages, he thought. She would bring them back, and pity the poor soul who got in her way.

They went to mats on the floor, just in time, Alex decided. When he tried, he could see them both, flat on their backs, legs apart—their favorite position, the stupid twats, grinding and bouncing their hips up and down. Dusty's face was flushed from exertion and concentration. Laurel's was pink but peaceful, as if in a coffin.

Maybe a little note would do the trick, set events in motion.

He wanted to scare the hell out of her before she died.

TWENTY

Scrawled in red ballpoint pen on the back of a membership form, the note had been slipped into her canvas Jane Fonda gym bag. Laurel kept her driver's license and car keys in the same pocket.

I AM GOING TO KILL YOU, BITCH.

The large letters at the bottom leaped out at her first. The writer had pressed so hard that the pen tore the paper.

> *I hope you are reading this in front of your locker. The one with the picture of you and the asshole taped inside.*

Her eyes rose to the photo on the open door beside her. She and Rick at the beach on the fourth of July, playing and laughing as he dragged her toward the surf.

> *This time you're not going to fuck anybody. I am going to fuck you. Beating the shit out of you will be just the start. When they lay you out at the morgue even the doctors will wonder who could do this to another human being. Imagine what it will be like on that cold slab at the morgue with your eyes bulged out, bruises all over your tits and blood coming out of your pussy. I am looking forward to it so much that I had trouble keeping it in my pants when I saw your bouncing little ass in class today. Soon.*

The signature was a single initial: *A.*

She spun around to see if anyone was watching. No one, except Dusty, emerging from the shower room, looking relaxed, wrapped in a towel, her hair wet. She looked startled at Laurel's intent expression, then smiled. Laurel whirled and rushed out as Dusty stared after her.

She pounded the gas pedal, roared into the driveway, scattering gravel, and burst through the front door. Her entrance sent Chuckles, the usually imperturbable Siamese, slinking to safety under a chair. Laurel's hand trembled as she showed the note to Rick.

"Damn," he said sleepily. "Who the hell . . . ?"

"You're the detective," she said, pacing the floor quietly in her Reeboks and gnawing a thumbnail. She looked frightened. "First Rob, now this."

"What's going on over there? Are there other complaints?"

She shrugged and shook her head.

"Damn," he said again, rubbed his eyes and reached for a pair of Levi's. "Let's go find out." He drove. She sat quietly, her body tense, her lips pressed tightly together.

"This happens to good-looking women all the time," he said to comfort her. "But," he grumbled, "I don't like it happening to you. Some smart ass is gonna get burned when I catch up with him."

They met Dusty, just leaving the fitness center, gym bag slung over her shoulder. Her hair, still wet, was combed straight back. She looked strong and beautiful in a white Police Olympics T-shirt and shorts. "Rick! Are you finally going to exercise those bones? This I have got to see."

"What did you make of this?" He gestured with the note in his hand.

She looked puzzled, and he turned to Laurel.

"You showed it to Dusty?"

"No, I didn't." Her voice was low, as she shook her head. She had discerned a trace of impatience in his voice. "I didn't show it to anybody."

Dusty scanned it and rolled her eyes. "Where did you find this, on your car?"

"No," Laurel said coldly. "In my gym bag."

"Hummph," Dusty said thoughtfully, and reread it. She studied Laurel, her expression hard to read. "Any skirmishes lately with the man at the front desk or the guys in the parking lot? Did you shoot down somebody who made a pass? Another member, an instructor?"

There was nothing, Laurel said.

"You hear any other complaints from the women here?" Rick asked.

Dusty shook her head. So did Mark Hamilton, manager of the club. A short, stocky man who looked anything but fit, he sat behind a big desk in the center of his narrow, all-white, Danish modern office. He chewed his lower lip and screwed his face into a scowl as he perused the note. "There's been nothing like this," he said. "And we've got no new staff on payroll." He got to his feet and squeezed by his visitors, patting his protruding belly as he excused himself. "This place keeps me too busy to get any exercise myself," he said sheepishly, and called in Tawny Marie.

She pranced into the room like a long-legged thoroughbred entering the winner's circle. A white togalike minidress covered her bright leotard and shiny tights. Her long hair was pulled back and held by a butterfly clip. Her glowing skin bore no trace of cosmetics, and her smile was toothpaste-ad perfect.

"Where have you been working out, Rick? You're a total stranger here lately." She glanced at the other faces in the room and then back at his. "Is this business?" Her warm brown eyes grew larger as she read the note.

"Boo, hiss," she said, wrinkling her nose. "Sicko alert."

Rick explained. "It isn't just obscene," he concluded. "Because of my job and the fact that we have a recent unsolved homicide in our neighborhood, I have to take this seriously. Especially since nobody else seems to be a target. I'd be more comfortable if this freak had a scattergun approach and everybody here had little love notes in their gym bags. That's why I want to know who did it, and why. It shouldn't be too hard to figure out. It had to be somebody in your class this morning. That narrows it down to one of the guys in that group . . ." His voice trailed off as Tawny Marie and Dusty exchanged glances.

"There were no men in that class, Rick," Tawny Marie said.

*R*ick was irritated during the drive home when Laurel pointedly asked how he happened to know Tawny Marie. He played dumb, his voice casual. "Strictly from the center, sweetheart. I helped organize arrangements to have the guys train there for the Police Olympics. She coordinated it at that end. Did a good job."

"Did you ever take her out?"

His eyes closed in a moment of exasperation. "Nope," he lied, recalling his conversation with Jim. "I think I bought her a drink once . . ."

"Did you . . . ?"

"No way."

Neither spoke again until they rolled into the white gravel driveway and the shade of the canvas carport. "You have any ideas about the note, hon? I felt kind of stupid. Why didn't you mention that you were in an all-girl class?"

"I didn't remember that there were no men." She sounded vague and looked confused.

"Have you seen anybody acting strange, giving you the eye?"

She turned to him. "You mean you haven't figured it out yet?" Bewilderment no longer clouded the green-gold eyes. They were gray, with granitelike certainty. Her voice was razor sharp and crisp with conviction. "You *are* the detective." She studied him boldly, her chin held at an arrogant angle.

"I wish everybody'd stop saying that," he said ruefully, only half joking.

"I know who did it. I know who's trying to scare me."

"Good," he said. "Now we're getting somewhere." He shifted the car into park, left the engine running to keep cold air blasting from the air conditioner, and half turned toward her on the leather seat, looking expectant. "Who, babe?"

"The only person in that class who knows me and has anything against me." She paused for a moment. "Dusty."

"You mean you think she . . . oh, come *on*! She wouldn't do a thing like that, babe. Count on it. You can take that to the bank. You can't really believe that."

"I don't want to, but I do," she said emphatically. "You always talk about motives and opportunity. Nobody else has a motive. She certainly had the opportunity. She was right there."

"That's ludicrous," he said sharply, and switched off the ignition. "A lot of weirdos out there see somebody and don't even need a reason. Or they know I'm a cop."

Her face remained closed.

"Why?" he asked. "She wouldn't do something that stupid. She's a police officer, for God's sake, and a friend."

"Not my friend. She's jealous of me because this is my home now." The voice was slightly louder and higher-pitched.

"I never heard anything more off the wall. She's my partner, we work together," he said flatly, as though that were the bottom line. He opened his door to the moist summer heat that overwhelmed the car in seconds, clasping them both in its breathless embrace.

She still sat, looking petulant. He walked around, crunched open her door and rested his left hand gently on the back of her neck. "Come on, babe, there's gotta be some other answer."

She stepped out, glancing up into his eyes with a small smile. "I'll fix you an omelette. Then I really have to get busy. I need to do the baking and then start work on the garden."

He stood staring after her, his hands on his hips, then shook his head and followed her slowly into the house.

*R*ick thought the accusation forgotten, but that night at the station he could not help but notice that one of the three pens always clipped to the outside pocket of Dusty's big soft leather handbag was missing. He saw only two. Was the missing pen red? He tried to recall. If the note was a bizarre practical joke that had backfired, he thought, she would be smart enough to toss the pen. He was annoyed at himself for even considering such a possibility. More serious was the possibility that the note might somehow be linked to the Thorne murder.

The homicide file Mack Thomas had compiled in the convenience-store killing of the Pakistani clerk had finally arrived on Rick's desk. The contents were disappointing.

"There's nothing in here," Jim said, disgusted, shaking an empty manila envelope marked "Evidence."

"They didn't even interview the guy who worked on the victim's night off, to see if anybody had been hanging around or if there had been any arguments or unreported holdup attempts. I don't believe this guy. I've seen misdemeanor investigations that were more thorough than this fucking first-degree murder case."

*7*he wind pounded like frantic fists on the windows. Stormy weather was always more fierce on the bay islands. Laurel slammed doors and sobbed out loud. Alone, she thought only she could hear. There were clothes in her closet that she could not remember buying, in styles she would never wear, shapeless cotton housedresses and a leather miniskirt, too many events she did not remember, puzzles she could not explain, gaps in time, missing hours. She had tried to call a dozen times during the past two weeks. Something had always stopped her. Now she managed to dial the number.

"Mother?" She could barely speak the word, her voice breaking.

"What is it, Laurel?" The voice echoed trepidation.

"It's happening again. I can't remember. I'm losing time." The hand that held the telephone was trembling.

There was silence.

"Mother?"

"Are you sure?" The voice sounded resigned and weary.

"Of course I'm sure!"

"What does Rick say?"

"He doesn't know!" Shrill and hysterical, she was crying now.

"You must try to stay calm, Laurel. Don't let yourself get upset. You know that makes it worse. Perhaps," the tone was hopeful, "since Rick doesn't know, it's not serious this time."

"It *is* serious. Terrible things are happening. I'm going crazy," she moaned, rocking back and forth in her chair.

"Don't use that word, Laurel. Never. Especially not to Rick. Try to stay strong and catch hold of yourself. How bad is it?"

"I'm not sure, but I'm scared. Shall I tell Rick?"

The voice was uncertain. "I don't think it wise. Do you?"

"He'll hate me, and I don't want to lose him."

"Well then, I wouldn't. If you were married . . ."

"We're not! What am I going to do?"

"Your father is not all that well. To be truthful, I'm not in the best of health either. It would be a real hardship for us to come down there now, but," she sighed, "I'll tell him, and we'll try to come soon."

"Soon, mother. Please! I'm sorry."

"So am I." The older woman sounded exhausted. "We thought you were happy."

"I was, then all these things started happening, like before, only worse." Laurel said good-bye, put her head down and sobbed.

The tears slowly subsided.

*S*everal *minutes later Alex lifted his head and dialed the same number. Laurel's mother answered on the second ring. He told her to butt out and mind her own goddamn business. "Just stay up there, outta our hair. Got me?"*

Harriet called again, a few minutes later. She cheerily explained to Mrs. Trevelyn that everything was just fine and that there was no point in a visit now.

"If you're truly certain that you don't need us . . ." There was hesitation, but obvious relief in the worn-out voice.

Harriet reassured her, saying a pleasant good-bye. Then she called a conference with the others. Laurel's precarious state of mind could adversely affect them all. "She's becoming unhinged. She realizes she's losing more and more time. We must try to confuse her as little as possible."

"So what? I could care less." Marilyn snapped her gum and crossed her legs. "After all we've done for her."

"It's for our own good," Harriet persisted. "If she becomes any more frightened, she'll have those meddling parents down on our necks, or she'll go crying to Rick that she's nuts. Either way, we wind up back at the shrink, Rick will dump her and we'll lose this house."

"That son of a bitch better not try anything funny," Alex said malevolently. He paced the room. "I didn't like that fucking doctor either."

"She wouldn't even have Rick if it wasn't for me," Marilyn said, flaunting the fact. "I was the one who met him."

"Only because I was driving the car." Alex jabbed a thumb to his chest, full of his own importance. "Don't forget that."

"Yeah, but the minute you heard the siren, you took off and left me in the driver's seat," Marilyn said. "I was the one he liked. I'm the one who called him. Laurel never even met him until we were already out on a date." She smirked. "I wish I could have seen her face when she suddenly found herself

feeding Rick oysters in a restaurant and couldn't remember how she got there."

"It's a good thing he thinks she's cute when she's embarrassed and confused," Harriet said. "That's another thing, if you get yourself in a jam in the future, Alex, I really think you should see it through and not leave it to one of us to handle."

"Well, it worked that time, didn't it? Although maybe you're right, I should of stayed out and shot his ass right off that motorcycle. Then we wouldn't be stuck with that bastard. And," his voice rose, "who the hell are you to talk? What about you leaving Laurel in the kitchen with that fancy coffeepot she couldn't figure out? You're the one who's supposed to take care of all that stuff."

"I thought it amusing." Harriet giggled. "It's about time that dumb klutz learned to use it. She takes all the credit for what I do, and she can't even boil water."

"But you're the one who keeps harping that we should quit spooking her."

"That's right. But you're the one who'll ruin it for all of us if you don't stop. That note you sent Laurel was really stupid."

"Stupid? What about you? You dumb bitch. Was it cool what you did with the kitten? You coulda blown it yourself. Rick was right outside. Laurel almost picked up on the cat hair in the sink. The damn animal lived right next door."

"So did Rob Thorne! And the filthy little creature was going to mess up my kitchen!" Harriet shrieked. "You know I will not stand for that!"

Jennifer began to wail. "See what you've done now," Harriet raged. "You woke up the little one."

Marilyn began to buff her nails and complain that she was not getting enough action from Rick because he was never home.

"I'm lucky he's not, or I'd never get out," Alex said. "There you go again, just thinking about yourselves."

"At least somebody here thinks," Harriet hissed from deep in the tunnel. "What were you going to do if the Thorne kid, or that boy on the beach, caught you? Kiss them on the lips? Or leave one of us out there to deal with it?"

"Leave it alone. I handled it, didn't I?"

"Sure, in your usual cavalier fashion, just like your little visit to the Corleys. If I hadn't found the jewelry you stole strewn around the bedroom. . . . Can't you ever put anything away? What if Laurel or Rick found it?"

"She wouldn't have known what the hell it was," he sneered. "We all know the broad is no rocket scientist."

"Rick would have. We'd all be in trouble."

"Speaking of trouble, Marilyn has got to stay away from Barry at the fitness center. He'll think he's talking to her and say something that blows Laurel's mind. It's too dangerous. Plus he knows Dusty. That fucking bitch has got to go!"

"Christ, I have little enough sex life as it is!" Marilyn wailed. "I was just getting to know that young stud next door, and you blew him away! My personal life is my business."

"Like hell it is," Alex said. "Your business is our business. Besides, Barry's gay."

"He is not!" screamed Marilyn.

"You're right about Dusty," Harriet said thoughtfully. "She and Rick are out there screwing around together somewhere right now. What if he decided to dump Laurel for her? Dusty has got to go."

"For once," Alex said happily, "we agree on something."

*W*ind punished the trees outside the station, and the air was thick with the threat of rain, though none had fallen as predicted. The weathermen were wrong as usual.

"They got all that radar, barometers and shit and they ain't never right," Jim said. "Put me in a high-rise building downtown, looking out the window with a pair of binoculars, and I can tell ya what weather is coming. Unencumbered by science, I could do a better job than those half-ass jokers any day of the week."

A tropical depression was stalled in the Caribbean and weathermen were watching to see if it died at sea or churned up enough energy to give birth to Hurricane Armando, the first of the season. The detectives were still griping about the gaps in Mack's scant reports when they were dispatched on their first call of the night, a possible jumper at Jackson Memorial, the big county hospital.

They left the unmarked Plymouth on the emergency room ramp and met Aileen at the door. Usually unflappable, she looked harried.

"It's the sixth floor." She waved them toward a waiting elevator held open by an orderly.

"Who the hell is he?"

"A patient." She handed Rick the chart. "Old guy. Albert Klonsky. In for tests, a little heart, a little emphysema, a little depressed . . ."

"Obviously," he said, his deep-set gray eyes meeting hers for a flick of an instant.

Her mouth crimped slightly with the suspicion of a smile. "Bring 'em back alive," she said, flashing a thumbs-up as the doors slid closed between them.

*R*ick grasped the sill and leaned out as the others moved away from the open window. The old man's callused feet groped, inching along the ledge, toes curled as if to grasp the weathered concrete. The wind howled through the canyons of hospital complex, ruffling his sparse hair and whipping the hospital gown around his bony knees. Chin muscles taut, his eyes bulged as he tried to see the open window without turning his head.

"Kill the walkies," Rick murmured to those behind him. To the open air, out in the night, he said, "Hi, Al, Albert Klonsky." He kept his voice pleasant, his expression earnest. "Stay right where you are, and try not to move." Cars looked small six stories down. A blaring horn sounded like the cry of a soaring bird. The man on the ledge stood rigid, rolled his eyes at Rick, took a deep breath and sidestepped further away. He looked resigned, as though it would be no big deal to take a step forward and ride the wind.

"Leave me alone." The voice came thin and cracked, a wail from a distant echo chamber.

"Nothing is that bad, Pop. We all have our beefs and problems. It's never too late."

Tears streaked the old man's cheeks and the too-thin shoulders hunched forward slightly like those of a high diver ready to leave the board.

"Hold it, Al." Eyes tight on the old man, as if they could hold him in place, Rick shrugged off his tan sports jacket. He handed it to Jim, along with his gun. "I'm going out there," he said softly, loosening his tie.

"Whadda you, crazy? You nuts?" Jim whispered hoarsely.

"I'm afraid the old guy's gonna go."

Dusty hissed through her teeth, her radio to her ear. "Rick," she said, her voice an urgent whisper. "Wait for fire, they're going to set up the life pack."

"How long?"

"ETA is fifteen minutes."

"Too long. It takes another five to set up the air bag. This guy won't wait."

"For God's sake . . ."

He stepped out of his Florsheims and the window, onto the cold narrow strip of concrete. Wind buffeted his body, stronger than he had expected. It sounded like the ocean in his ears.

"I'm not coming out after you," Jim warned, in a low mutter. "You know I can't stand heights."

Rick pressed all of his 170 pounds hard against the face of the building and did not look down. He inched slowly along the ledge.

"What are you doing? Don't come any closer!"

"Albert, this is scary." Rick's shoulder blades were jammed hard against the cold concrete. He had not been afraid to step out there quickly; now he regretted it. Was that the pattern of his entire life? He remembered he was wearing his favorite shirt, the one he had worn the day he passed the sergeant's exam. He hoped he would not ruin it, or worse. The damp and penetrating cold iced his spine, reminding him of something. Eight years old—an uncle in Vermont showing him how to leave the imprint of angels on a field of white, lying in the snow, his arms spread-eagled, gazing into a chalk-color sky and a pale and tired sun that radiated no warmth. He was certain that it could not be the same fierce sphere that sizzled sidewalks in Miami, where the sun was a promise of life in a city by the sea exploding in verdant splendor, where trees never stood barren, where the landscape was forever green and alive. Now it was dark and his back was cold and drenched in perspiration, despite the wind that droned and hummed through the surrounding maze of buildings.

Wings flapped nearby—a pigeon, startling them both.

"Don't come closer!" the desperate voice croaked.

"I have to," he said, knowing he did not. This certainly was in no job description or departmental manual. Police brass would surely criticize this, as they do anything outside of textbook behavior. Sometimes you have to go with your gut feeling. Sometimes it's wrong.

The old man stared. "I wanna die," he whimpered.

"You'll feel different in the morning. Everything always looks better once the sun comes up."

"No. Leave me alone."

"You know what somebody looks like when they fall or jump from this height? The skull shatters, it splits open like an egg."

The old man seemed unshaken.

"What if you change your mind on the way down? After it's too late? What if you don't get killed, just crippled, and you have to live with that?"

The man in the flimsy hospital gown fixed watery eyes on a dark and misty horizon. Rick slipped his handcuffs from his belt and snapped one around his right wrist. He reached out slowly and clicked the other ring around the old man's hairy left wrist, next to his plastic hospital bracelet. At the sound, the old man swayed slightly, as though about to fall or leap.

Rick shuddered and held his breath. "Hold it. Take it easy."

He heard muffled curses and frantic radio transmission from the room behind him.

"What'd you do that for?" the old man said.

Rick breathed again, heart pounding. "I don't know," he said honestly. "But I do know one thing, I don't have the key with me. Wherever we go now, buddy, it's you and me."

"Why?" The old man arched his neck, and they made eye contact for the first time. "You could get killed. You shouldn't have come out here. I want to die."

"Well, I don't. And I don't believe you really do, either. Anybody you want to talk to? We can get them here fast."

"Nobody who cares." His shriveled face puckered in self-pity and his eyes leaked tears. The wind lashed at their knees, flapping his hospital gown like a sheet on a clothesline.

"I care, Al. I have somebody who cares for me. I think you do too."

The old man tried to wipe his runny nose on the sleeve of his hospital gown, but the handcuff caught his arm in midair.

"Let's go back inside, have a cup of coffee and talk about it."

"I can't." The old man quaked. "My legs are numb. I . . . I'm dizzy."

Jesus Christ, Rick thought, not now. Down below, police cars, flashing lights. The fire department's yellow life pack was out there somewhere, on the way, mounted like a giant Mattel toy atop a speeding fire rescue truck. Rick had seen firefighters leap like stuntmen into the big cushiony yellow balloon five stories below during training exercises. He remembered feeling a strong sense of relief that he was not a fireman.

The wind seemed stronger now, a high note sounding in his head. His handcuffed wrist jerked as the old man teetered. Rick braced, trying to hold him taut, back against the building, with his cuffed hand. "Take deep breaths and let them out slow. Slow. Now take a couple of small steps this way. Small ones. Careful. I'll help you balance."

"I'm scared," the old man whimpered.

"So am I, Al. You have to help me out. I'm thirty-six years old. I'm gonna get married. Her name is Laurel. We're about to set the date. I forgot to tell you about that."

"Tying the knot?"

"That's right. I love her, Al, and she needs me. Help me get to go on the honeymoon. Come on, now, little steps. Sidestep. Sidestep. One, two. One, two. That's it. Our own chorus line—but no high kicks, Al." The bare feet crab-stepped, then faltered. The old man stared at the gathering traffic and upturned faces in the pools of light below.

"You think they got TV cameras down there?"

"Nah, reporters would be yelling 'jump.' Let's not give anybody a thrill. You married, Al?"

"Why do you think I'm out here?"

"Atta boy. You still got your sense of humor, you're okay. Let's go back inside where it's warm. Just a couple more steps."

"I can't. How can we get back in the window?"

"We got out, we can get in. Don't sweat it." Rick reached the window, grasping the inside frame with his left hand, as the old man minced cautiously toward him. "Okay, Al. Put one foot back inside. Careful now. Somebody will help you. I'll follow you in."

Rick glimpsed Jim's nearly bald head at the window, heard heavy breathing and realized it was his own.

The old man extended his bare foot. The wrinkled sole, black with grime, groped uncertainly in the air for a moment. Jim caught it solidly by the ankle. Dusty reached up and wrapped her arms around the old man's waist. A smattering of applause and cheers rose from the police, fire and hospital personnel gathered below. Jim and Dusty were slowly lowering him into the room when the old man suddenly flailed both arms. The cuffs yanked Rick's right arm and his feet flew out from under him.

He spun in midair, clawing at the sill with his free hand. The sounds below turned to a something like a sigh, then shouts of alarm.

Dusty, Jim and a uniform clung to the old man, who bellowed as his shoulder wrenched out of the socket and his feet shot toward the ceiling. The grunts and gasps sounded like a wrestling match as they grappled to hold onto the frail body. "Don't let go!" Dusty panted.

"Somebody get a rope!" Jim yelled. "A sheet, anything!" People milled in confusion and panic at the door behind them.

The old man screamed as the cuff bit into his wrist with all the force of Rick's weight at the other end.

Rick saw dark sky and the sheer, clifflike facade of the building. His legs climbed empty space, feet searching for something solid that was not there.

The pain in his right arm was excruciating. His left hand slipped from the sill, but Jim caught his wrist. A good solid catch. Rick heard the sound, flesh on flesh, like a slap.

Two men were holding on to Al. Dusty took Rick's right arm above the elbow with both hands, and she and Jim heaved together. Rick hurtled over the sill and everybody fell to the floor in a panting, cursing, tangled heap.

Tears shone in Dusty's eyes, but she never cried.

"You son of a bitch." Jim got to his feet, growling. "Don't you ever do that again." His voice was tough, but his hands shook and he sat down heavily on the narrow hospital bed.

Dusty bit her lip and winced at the pulpy purple flesh around Rick's right wrist as she unlocked the cuffs. "Okay," she said lightly, trying to sound piqued. "I give up, what were you trying to do out there? Give everybody a major coronary?" The tremor in her voice gave her away.

Albert was rolled swiftly away, strapped to a gurney, moaning and grasping his injured shoulder. Rick still sat on the floor, looking dazed. A hospital orderly and Dusty tried to help him stand. He shook them off and got up slowly on his own. "Oh, no." He looked down at his clothes. "I ruined my good shirt."

. . .

$\mathcal{D}$ usty held Rick's coat and gun while Aileen cut away the remainder of the shirt in the emergency room, preparing to take him to X ray. "Like old times, isn't it?" the nurse said cheerfully. "Remember the time you fell off your motorcycle?"

"I didn't fall off," he protested, gingerly examining his wrist. "It skidded on a patch of oil when I was chasing a suspect in a stolen car."

"Sure," she said. "And the time you fell off the DuPont Building?"

"I knew there was some reason I didn't like heights," he remembered. "I didn't fall off. The fire escape broke under me while I was chasing a suspect."

"Sure. And remember this one?" Smiling, she tickled an old crescent-shaped scar an inch below his collarbone.

"I always wondered about that one," Dusty said, without thinking. "How did it happen?"

"Knife," Aileen said, raising an eyebrow. "That was the time he finally caught a suspect he was chasing."

"That'll teach him," Dusty said. The two women exchanged knowing glances, acknowledging what each had shared with this man.

"You're ganging up," Rick complained. He rubbed his forearm and winced, oblivious to the moment. "Nobody's even read me my rights."

$\mathcal{S}$ o how come you never broke this wedding shit to me?" Jim demanded as they climbed into the car. "Setting the date, huh? You shoot your mouth off to a stranger, but your partners are the last to know?"

"I would have said anything to keep that old man from showing me his trick high-diving act." Rick looked sheepish. His arm, not broken, rested in a sling. "I just wanted to connect with him."

"Sounds like wishful thinking to me," Jim said.

"You never know," Rick said cheerfully. "Maybe it's not such a bad idea."

Dusty, in the back seat, said nothing.

TWENTY-ONE

*R*ick's injury frightened Laurel to tears, but she quickly snapped back and coped well, filling the house with cut flowers, morning glories, sea lavender and scarlet sage from the yard. Their fragrances mingled with mouth-watering aromas from the kitchen. She cosseted and babied him, announcing that her special egg custard would cure any hurt. It slid down his throat silky smooth, sweet and creamy.

He thought he was sated until a primitive drumbeat began to throb from the stereo speakers. She paraded proudly and seductively into the bedroom in four-inch-high stiletto heels he had never seen her wear before. Her lips and fingernails gleamed blood-red and she no longer seemed shy and modest, as she often was, about exposing her breasts. In fact, she had rubbed the nipples with something that glistened. All she wore with the spike heels was a yellow hibiscus behind her left ear and a pair of his boxer shorts—and something clinking beneath the shorts, a surprise. A St. Valentine's Day joke, a novelty gift to her when they were first dating—a chain-and-metal chastity belt. Medieval knights supposedly had locked their ladies into such contraptions before riding off to the crusades. Vicious little metal teeth ringing the opening were designed to inflict severe damage to any member daring to enter. He had felt guilty at the time because the gift embarrassed her. She didn't even seem to know what it was for. Now she did.

Role-playing again. God, he loved it. Swinging her hips, calling herself Marilyn, teasing him unmercifully into finding the hidden key. She was even hot to play sex games with his gun. He took it from her as she moistened the barrel.

"Oh, no, you don't," he warned. "This is no plaything. Too many people get hurt in games with these. I go to too many scenes where 'unloaded' guns went off."

She curled her blood-red lips and pouted. He grinned. "It would be too embarrassing to explain how the family jewels got shot off," he told her.

She giggled. "We could unload it."

"Christ, it's loaded? I thought you already emptied it." The discovery nearly cost him his erection, but not quite. She tossed her bright hair back over her naked shoulders and wet her lips. "I thought you liked living dangerously."

"What a wacky broad, I love it," he said, unloading the gun. He slid the weapon under the bed and dropped the bullets onto the carpet beside it. "Come here, you," he said, reaching for her. "I'll show you how dangerous I can be."

*H*e awoke and saw that the room had been straightened as he slept. He heard the whirring of the juicer, smelled sausage and coffee and padded barefoot into the kitchen. She was already dressed, wearing an eyelet-trimmed apron and mixing batter. It struck him that she had even changed her nail color since last night. "I squeezed the orange juice," she said, smiling. "Ready for waffles?"

"Do you know what an amazing woman you are?" He nuzzled her warm neck. It smelled like vanilla.

He sat at the table, drank juice and coffee and repeated the lies he'd used to lure Albert back from the ledge. She turned from the mixing bowl and studied his face, her expression grave. "Were you putting the old man on, Rick, or do you really have marriage on your mind?"

The coffee was excellent, the sun streamed in the windows and the room around him glowed. A good day to be alive. "Jim said it sounded like wishful thinking."

She smiled and resumed mixing, holding his eyes in her gaze. "Is it?"

He had come close to being killed out on that ledge, though he would never admit it aloud. Cheating death stirs certain emotions about life.

"I do want kids," he said matter-of-factly. "Christ, some of the guys my age already have teenagers . . ."

Her gasp interrupted. She had scorched her fingers on the waffle iron. She looked dazed, then examined her blistering skin. "I'll get some butter," she said, wincing.

"Wait, didn't you say the other day that aloe is best for burns? I thought you put some in the refrigerator. Didn't you, babe?"

No answer. Instead, she was staring at the kitchen clock, the ersatz coffee-pot perking away, high on the wall above the sink. "That must be fast," she whispered.

"Nope." He consulted his watch. "Right on the button. Keeps perfect time." He found the aloe, wrapped and neatly labeled, in the vegetable storage bin next to the avocados and summer squash. He sliced a chunk from the fleshy leaf and smeared her fingers with the sticky juice. The burn did not appear serious, but it must be painful, he thought. Her eyes were misty.

"Nothing I said, was it?" he teased. She looked wary, as though she had no idea what he was talking about. "I mention wedding bells and kids and you put your hand in the waffle iron. I guess it's a better sign than if you stuck your head in the oven."

"Oh, Rick!" She threw herself into his arms and hugged him tight, voice quaking with emotion. "I think we should get married right away. I need you so much." She was crying.

"Hold on," he said, startled. "We don't want to do anything hasty. All I mean is that it's probably time to start thinking about where this relationship is headed." He kissed the burned fingers. "Feel better, babe?" She nodded and said nothing. She looked pale. Small wonder, he thought. They certainly had not slept much. She seemed withdrawn, almost frightened. She should take some time to get used to the idea. Actually, he thought, so should he. He now felt a bit scared himself. How the heck did this happen? Somehow he had stepped in it without intending to, almost committing before knowing he was ready. He was usually more cautious. He felt uneasy without knowing why.

Her moods, both dark and light, came and went like quicksilver. A hour later she was bustling in the kitchen again, humming as she worked.

TWENTY-TWO

She insisted on shaving Rick the next day in deference to his injured arm, still stiff and sore. "You don't need your good right arm as long as you have me," she said.

"You sure you know how to do this?"

"Of course," she said confidently. She wiped her hands on her apron and tucked the towel around his neck like a bib. "I shaved my father a few times after he got shaky and couldn't do it himself—and he survived."

She sat Rick on a low kitchen stool near the sink, his face wrapped in a hot towel. Perched on a higher stool behind him, she was able to wrap her bare legs around his middle as she worked.

He had brought his shaving cream and safety razor in from the master bathroom, but she ignored them. A straightedge razor and a natural bristle shaving brush with a marble handle were laid out on one of her thirsty 100 percent cotton kitchen towels next to a steaming hot bowl of water.

"Where'd you get them?"

"I've used them before. I'm old-fashioned. I think they do the best job."

He relaxed against her soft body and let her play the role of barber as she brushed warm lather onto his face. He enjoyed being babied. "I hope that thing is sharp enough."

"I keep everything very sharp." Delicately, she picked up the razor. "There's nothing worse than a dull blade."

He closed his eyes as she began on the right side of his face, stroking against the stubble. She seemed to know what she was doing.

"You know, Rick," she said, as she skimmed the blade clean on the edge of the bowl. "I think we need a fence, a privacy fence, between our yard and the Singers."

"Why?" he grunted, trying not to move.

She went on carefully scraping his upper lip. "I know that Ben and Beth are your friends. But as the poet says, good fences make good neighbors."

He grunted questioningly again.

"Before their cat disappeared, it was always sniffing around over here. Now they're talking about a *puppy* for Benjie. The boy won't even stay in his own yard." She sounded exasperated. "He's tramped through my impatiens, and I found a toy shovel in my herb garden. We don't tolerate anybody mucking about in what we work so hard to grow. He has no business over here unin-vited." The razor rang against the rim of the bowl with the clear sound of a small bell.

"He's just a little kid, honey. How much damage can he do? Someday my kids will be playing in the yard, and it won't make much difference." He felt her legs tighten around his midsection. "I thought you liked Benjie. He's just doing what kids do, babe. They mess up, spit up, break things." He grinned until he felt the blade on his face again.

She tilted his chin up firmly and drew the razor along his throat. Her legs clasped him so tightly, knees wedged into his ribs, ankles locked around his solar plexus, that he was uncomfortable. He had never realized how muscular her legs were. This was not such a good idea after all. "Easy," he muttered from between his teeth, wanting to stand up and escape, but afraid to make a sudden move with the blade still at his throat.

"We only want the fence to protect our home," she hissed.

He could not see her face but definitely did not like the sound of her voice. This was no time for her to pick a fight about a fence. He reached up to stay the hand with the razor, and the blade caught him, just under the chin.

"Oh," she said. "I told you not to move."

She sighed and put the razor down. "Look at that."

He reached up and got blood on his fingers. Relaxing her grip, she slid off her stool and brought him a wet towel.

"Dammit," he said.

"You shouldn't have moved. I told you not to. Here, it's all right," she said soothingly. "Poor Rick."

It was not bad, but it did bleed. Pressing the towel to his chin, he went to the bathroom for a styptic pencil.

"Careful," she called after him, concern in her voice. "Don't get blood on the carpet or the good towels."

*R*ick's team was in line for the next whodunit, a murder without a suspect or a smoking gun. The call came an hour later, summoning them in early. His arm ached and his chin still oozed blood, but he disliked missing the start of an investigation. He swallowed four aspirins and drove to the station.

The weather was schizty and windswept. White caps danced on the water as he crossed the causeway. The ominous sky suddenly brightened until the glare off the surface of the bay was blinding. He flipped down the sun visor and struggled with his sore arm, to angle his Ray Bans out of the glove compartment. Moments after he put them on, the vast expanses of sky and water faded fast, from radiant blue to turbulent shades of gray. He yanked off the sunglasses and tossed them onto the seat beside him.

Miami's weather was so changeable, from moment to moment, "like some people," he muttered.

They held a tumultuous discussion in the kitchen. All were agitated, and it quickly became chaotic. Harriet was eager for Laurel to become a bride. Then the house would truly belong to them. Free-spirited Marilyn refused to consider the prospect of being tied down. Both violently opposed a baby in the house. Laurel had thrown away her birth control pills that morning, but Marilyn had fished them out of the trash. She had swallowed two to make sure, determined to be a sensation in her string bikini during the season. Harriet vowed that no brat would live to track up her home and dig in her flower beds. Benjie was annoying enough. In fact, something was definitely going to have to be done about him.

A blessed event was certainly no part of Alex's agenda. He fumed that it was just like that bitch Laurel to think only of herself and her happiness. He had always hated her and her easy life, lived at the expense of all of them.

Little Jennifer alone loved the idea of a baby. The prospect of having someone to play with delighted her, but she was hopelessly outnumbered.

"Listen," Alex told them, "marriage may not be such a bad idea."

"I am no housewife, and I'm not gonna be one!" Marilyn shrieked.

"Be sensible," Harriet urged her. "If we marry Rick, we get to keep this house, with my kitchen, my garden and the new microwave."

"How would you like to get rid of Rick, and still keep it all?"

Alex had their attention.

"The other night, up on that ledge. Rick mighta bought it, right? Cops get killed on the job. Happens all the time. It got me thinking. What if Rick gets married and then gets himself killed on the job? You know there's a civic group in Miami that pays off mortgages for cops' widows? Free and clear. There's also big cash death benefits and a lifetime pension. Nice, huh? Hey, cops get killed. It's a fact of life. It would be my pleasure. But," he cautioned Harriet, who was

paying rapt attention, "don't try to pull any funny stuff here. It has to happen on duty."

"You won't be content until I have no sex life at all," Marilyn whined.

"Listen, listen to me," Alex soothed. "Rick gets blown away, you can have all the dates you want."

"Even Barry?"

"Sure," Alex said. "But I tell ya, you're wasting your time. The guy's gotta be gay."

Marilyn tossed her head in disgust, then considered the prospect. "I do look good in black."

Jennifer began to wail. "I like Rick, and I don't like guns. I wanna play wif Benjie."

"Now you've made her cry again," Harriet said. "I hope you're all happy. You know Rick does make a mess around here, and he never helps with the housework. Once he's gone, I could have the fence built and order the new drapes I want, the French illusion sheers. But what about Laurel? She'd come unglued, she could be a problem."

"Right," Alex said. "But you can see she's getting weaker. Soon we can get rid of her too."

"Be careful," Harriet warned.

"I'm working on it," he said. "Don't worry about it. In the meantime I've got a plan, a way we can score some big bucks until the death benefits roll in."

"Now you're talking. I'll drink to that," Marilyn said. She sashayed over to the cabinet, took out a bottle of Rick's bourbon and poured herself a double.

*L*aurel found herself alone in the kitchen moments later, a strange taste on her lips. The bourbon bottle was out on the counter, and she wondered how it got there. It was not like Rick to have a drink before going to work. Then she looked at the wall clock. She had last checked the time a few minutes ago, yet, according to the clock, more than two hours had elapsed.

Sobbing in the bathroom, she was frantically scrubbing her freshly painted blood-red nails with polish remover when Marilyn came out, pulled on her leather miniskirt and went to find out the truth about Barry.

TWENTY-THREE

*T*his whodunit was also a whoisit. A woman found on the bank of a drainage ditch that bordered a high-density apartment complex just off the expressway.

The unexpected event had blossomed into a block party of sorts. Hordes of gawkers had obstructed and backed up traffic at the start of rush hour. The excitement of a real-live murder had lured the crowds, who in turn attracted the hot dog, cold drink, balloon and ice cream vendors.

Jim drove, but not even the blue flasher on the dash or his badge displayed out the window in a burly fist helped gain them access to the scene. The street and even neighboring lawns were cluttered with cars parked every which way, abandoned by drivers who feared missing something. "Start ticketing these illegally parked cars," Jim told a uniformed officer who was trying vainly to divert traffic as horns blared and tempers frayed.

"But some of them belong to reporters," protested the officer, who was red-faced and wore half moons of perspiration under his armpits.

"Good," Jim growled. "Write them first."

"Swell, so that's the mood we're in today," Rick said. "You know that nobody screams louder than reporters when they get tickets."

Jim smiled at the thought. He scanned the eager faces in the crowd. They turned toward the detectives as one, looking expectant. "What are we?" he asked. "The entertainment committee?"

He locked the car and winked at Dusty. "Let's pay our respects to the guest of honor."

The corpse was covered by a sheet, a real one, more substantial than the usual flimsy paper shroud. The uniformed sergeant, beefy and middle-aged, with a lot of mileage on him, looked smug. He smiled at the detectives. They recognized it instantly as a bad sign. He peeled back the sheet for them, curling his wrists as though unveiling a work of art.

The dead woman's clothes were tasteful and looked expensive. Her well-manicured fingernails and toenails glowed with glossy mocha lacquer. She wore gold and emeralds on her right ring finger, and diamonds and gold on her left pinky finger.

Her head was missing.

No one spoke for a moment. There were whoops of excitement from the crowd and the clicks of Instamatic cameras. Some adults were actually holding small children high on their shoulders so they could see. "Well," Jim said to the sergeant. "Where is it?"

"Ya got me, Jim," the sergeant said. "Doesn't seem to be here."

"Shit. I was afraid you were gonna say that."

Spectators hung precariously from the upper balconies of the nearby apartment complex. "Cover her," Rick said quietly. The sergeant pulled the sheet back over the corpse as onlookers shouted in protest.

"Lovely crowd," Dusty said. "Why us?"

"We must live right," Rick said.

"There's more people out here than were at the fucking fourth of July parade," Jim said.

"We have to look at her," Dusty said softly. "We get paid to do it. But some of them even brought their kids. Look at their faces." The people pressing forward, straining at the yellow crime scene tape, wore leers and grins, their eyes glittered with excitement. Dusty turned away and watched a silver airliner climb the clouds east of Miami International Airport.

"So we don't have a face or teeth to compare with dental records, but she's still got her prints, clothes, jewelry, a lot of other identifying points," Rick said. He was thinking aloud, his tone detached, the way he always reacted to death in its most grotesque forms. The more gruesome the scene, the more business-like he always became, as though official procedures, rules and routine were shields against emotion, madness and death. "Why would they take the head?"

"Religious rite. Santería?" Dusty said.

"They usually steal the parts they need from a cemetery," Jim said. "It's a lot less risky than murder."

"Some psycho," Dusty said flatly.

"Probably," Rick said. "Where do you think it is, Jim?"

"I dunno. We better have the divers check the canal and then the rock pits around here. Maybe somebody wanted a souvenir. Hope it's not on his mantelpiece in this weather. I can tell you one thing, I'm betting it turns up."

"Yeah," Dusty said bleakly, as though not happily anticipating the discovery.

"I can't see any other obvious trauma," Rick said, lifting a corner of the sheet with his good left hand. "It's not a clean cut. Do you think an alligator . . ."

"Makes sense," Dusty said. "If she got hit on the head or had a bullet wound, the gator would go for the blood. I don't know if we've had any sightings lately this far east."

"So if she was shot, our bullet could be in some gator's belly . . ." said Jim.

The intense afternoon sun suddenly slid out from behind threatening clouds. The detectives, standing in the glare, simultaneously became aware of something hurled, a spherical shadow arcing across the ground before their eyes, a round object soaring high over the corpse. Mouths open, heads raised, they stared into the blinding brilliance of the sun, their eyes following the flight. A running boy about eleven or twelve years of age caught the thing in his arms and sprinted across the adjacent field, shouting with glee, a half-dozen other boys in hot pursuit.

The detectives' eyes teared, blinked and focused hard on the object clutched in the boy's arms. A soccer ball.

"I need a drink," Jim said.

"Maybe I'm going crazy," Dusty said.

"No," Rick said. "It's not us, it's Miami."

*A*t the morgue, Dr. Lansing pronounced the decapitation sloppy, but definitely not the work of an alligator or any other form of Florida wildlife.

"It's probably romantic," Dusty theorized.

"Why so?" Rick asked.

"Hey," Dusty said, checking the labels in the dead woman's clothes. "You know how love is."

Rick silently watched her copy designer and manufacturer names into her notebook. When she'd flipped it open he had glimpsed some of the earlier notations, in red ink.

"I was just going to call you guys, to confirm what we thought," Dr. Lansing was saying, "about your suspect. In the Overtown kung fu case."

"He is a current resident of the Graybar Hotel," Jim said.

"Charged with?"

"Homicide."

"You can forget that." The doctor wiped his hands on his lab coat and removed his eyeglasses. He held them up to the light and squinted at the lenses. Dusty, who was standing closest to him, saw they were spattered with tiny specks of blood and bone particles.

"Anybody have a handkerchief?" he asked.

No one answered. The doctor shrugged, rubbed the glasses on his coat and carefully put them back on his face. "We were right. Cocaine or, you might say, a leaking condom killed the man. No trauma, except for the fall following the fatal episode."

"Do tell," Jim said. "What the hell."

"He sure didn't act like a dying man," Dusty said. "He was about to beat our suspect's brains out."

"His behavior had all the earmarks of cocaine psychosis," the doctor said.

"Looks like we've got us a valuable confidential informant again." Rick looked pleased.

"If he will even divulge to us the time of day," Dusty said. "Remember, he's sitting in jail, not at all thrilled that he ever was your CI."

"He'll get over it. He likes us," Jim said reassuringly.

*7*he captain wanted them back at the station ASAP to respond to media requests for interviews about the headless corpse.

"First things first," Rick said.

At the Dade County Jail, he arranged to have J. L. Sly's personal belongings processed for release.

J.L. shuffled into the interview room, a defeated man, wearing the look of a whipped puppy. If he had had a tail, it would have been between his legs.

He sat without a word, gazing at them reproachfully.

"How have they treated you, J.L.?" Rick was smiling. So was Dusty. Even Jim's gruff features were arranged into something that looked moderately friendly.

"What a happy group," J.L. said morosely. "Have you found some other crimes to charge me with, more nails in my coffin?"

"No way," Rick told him. "Good news. We just talked to the state attorney, and all charges are being dropped. You're free to check out of this hotel and go. You didn't kill him."

J.L.'s eyelids dropped to half-mast, as though digesting the news. He picked at the dirty ashtray on the table between them with a fingernail. "Free to go? Right now?"

The detectives all nodded and said he was.

"No charges?"

"No charges," Rick said.

"I didn't kill him?"

"Nope, it was just like you said. You never hurt him."

"You're lucky that we're your buddies and we looked into it," Jim said.

J.L.'s liquid eyes were guarded.

"Who did kill him?" he asked, almost casually.

"Nobody," Rick told him. "He OD'ed on cocaine. He was a mule and had a gutfull. It leaked into his system and proved fatal."

J.L. sprang to his feet in a light and graceful movement. Even in shapeless jail clothes, he suddenly seemed a taller and more powerful man than the prisoner who had slunk into the room minutes earlier. Flexing his knees tentatively, he sidestepped into the familiar crouch. His eyes narrowed, his hands rotated, slowly at first, then more aggressively, in a series of challenging circles.

He paused to regard the still seated detectives. "Cocaine?" he asked.

"That's right," Rick said. "An OD."

"We're still looking for a couple of Colombians who put the snatch on the corpse to get the stash back," Jim said. "One of 'em should have flash burns on his face."

A corrections officer in a brown uniform arrived to escort the prisoner downstairs to the release desk.

J.L. swaggered to the door, then turned back to the detectives, his expression earnest. "Don't tell anybody about the OD. Okay?"

"Let's go," said the bored guard.

J.L. regarded the upstart for a moment, head high, nostrils flaring, then dismissed him with, "Even a man who is a bit slow may locate the light and become truly one with nature."

"What the hell is that supposed to mean?" Jim asked irritably as the door clanged closed behind them.

"I think he made it up," Dusty said.

"He shudda been a reporter. I know a newspaper where he could get a job."

"Speaking of which, we have to go make a press release," Rick said.

There was little to tell the reporters. The dead woman was fair-skinned, middle-aged—probably in her early forties—and dressed in expensive designer clothes, size ten. About five feet four inches tall, she weighed approximately 135 pounds and had probably died earlier in the day. Cause of death uncertain. The motive did not appear to be robbery since the killer had not removed her rings or an expensive gold watch. Her description matched no recent missing persons report. Anyone with a clue to her identity was asked to call the police. Her head was still missing.

The story was at the top of the evening news, and the department was flooded with calls. Instead of quickly identifying the dead woman, as the detectives had hoped, the coverage generated a flood of calls from cranks, psychics with visions, armchair detectives and people who thought she could be a long-lost friend or relative. Miamians possess more than their share of unusual fantasies. Hundreds of them, their overactive imaginations fueled by tricks of light and shadow, happy hour or a few snorts, saw mysterious packages they suspected might contain the missing head. One man swore he'd seen his neighbor's pit bull burying a suspicious object in his backyard. They all called the police.

The usual bomb scares plummeted, head sightings soared and pranksters ran riot. A top-rated radio station offered a prize to the caller who most accurately predicted when and where the victim's head would be found. The contestant who came closest would win tickets for two on a weekend murder mystery cruise sailing out of the port of Miami.

"This is sick," Jim said between phone calls. "I can remember when Miami was normal like any other town."

"So can I, Jimbo," Rick said wistfully. "You know, when I was a kid you could go hear all the great black jazz musicians at the clubs in Overtown without the locals trying to do a tap dance on your face. You used to be able to drive down Collins Avenue, eyeball the big estates on the ocean—and actually see the water."

"That was before the concrete canyon, before they ruined it," Jim said. "If you didn't know the ocean was there, you would never guess it now. You were lucky."

"Yeah," Dusty joined in. "I wish I had grown up here."

"Where *are* you from?" Rick asked.

"Midwest," she said, turning back to the telephone.

"I knew that. Iowa, right? But where?" he persisted.

"Small town." She began dialing.

"What's the name of it?"

But she was already speaking into the phone.

"Here's one for you, kid," Jim said, sliding her a phone message from the stack they had split. "Your new boyfriend."

It was from Terrance McGee.

"They've been having lots of nice long talks," Jim said. He winked at Rick, who was looking thoughtful, then snorted and blew his nose loudly. "Damn, I think my allergies are kicking up again. I bet those were fucking melaleuca trees out at that scene."

Dusty was chatting with an elderly woman who had called earlier to offer her help. The woman was certain she had once seen a television show in which a headless body had been discovered. It might have been *Kojak,* or maybe *Magnum.* She suggested that police check with the network to see how the TV detectives had solved it. Dusty thanked her for the suggestion. When she put down the telephone, she glanced at the message from Terrance McGee, sighed, slipped it to the bottom of the stack and went on to answer the next call.

"It's odd," Rick said. "That we haven't heard from this woman's family. She looks like somebody who would be missed, unless she's a visitor who just arrived."

"Or maybe her nearest and dearest, the one who would logically be reporting her missing, is the one who did it," Dusty said. "I wish there had been engraving in her jewelry. I think everybody who wears a watch or a ring ought to have their initials engraved inside." She pretended to pout. "It should be compulsory."

"Why stop at initials?" Jim growled from his desk. "It should be their entire name, address and Social Security number."

"Yeah, along with a list of all their known enemies," Dusty said.

"And the name and phone number of the next of kin," Jim said. "It would make our lives easier."

"I think it would also be very nice," Dusty said, "if they had their prior rap sheet, if any, tattooed to their inner thighs, along with . . ."

"I think it's time we go get something to eat," Rick said. "You two are getting punchy."

"You buying?" Jim muffled a sneeze.

"Nope."

"What the hell, let's go anyway," Dusty said.

They squeezed into a booth at the Star Dust diner on Biscayne Boulevard. Dusty ordered a club sandwich and iced tea, Jim, the pork chop with mashed potatoes and Rick, the homemade meat loaf. He asked for macaroni and cheese on the side instead of mashed potatoes. A smiling red-haired waitress obligingly took their order and disappeared into the kitchen.

"Did you see that?" Dusty told Jim. "That waitress would beat up on anybody else. Look at the menu. It says no substitutions, but our sergeant is soooo cute, and his arm is in a sling too. What a spoiled brat. He always has his way."

"Nice work if you can get it," Rick said, looking cocky. "I know Sheila. I've been coming in here for a long time."

Dusty rolled her eyes. "Now it's Sheila, the redheaded waitress. See what I mean?"

A baby in the booth directly across from them began to howl. The parents glanced around, embarrassed, as he continued to scream, red-faced with anger.

"He's got a temper," Dusty said, smiling.

"I wonder if he's the same one," Jim said, his voice nasal, his eyes watering.

"Who?" Rick asked.

"The screaming baby," Jim croaked. "It's always there, at every restaurant, at every movie you pay six bucks to see. Whatever happened to baby-sitters? Don't people hire them anymore?"

"They're probably a working couple who drag the kid everywhere because they feel guilty," Rick said. "I won't make that mistake when I have kids."

"You've obviously given the matter some thought," Dusty said quietly. "Hey, I've been meaning to ask you all day. What happened to your chin?"

"Yeah, looks like some headhunter was after yours," Jim said.

"Shaving cut." He looked sheepish and fingered the wound.

"You ought to have Laurel shave you until your arm is better," Dusty offered.

"That's an idea," he mumbled unenthusiastically.

The pint-sized tyrant in the next booth waved pudgy fists and screamed louder. "To hell with 'Say No to Drugs,' " Jim said, glaring. "They oughta make it 'Say No to Babies.' Ban the baby!"

"I'll drink to that," Dusty said, raising her water glass. Her tone was playful, but her eyes were sad.

*R*ick finished his coffee first and went to the telephone. Shortly after the body was found, a check revealed that the headless woman had never been fingerprinted in Dade County. He dialed records, hoping a search through the National Crime Information Center had borne fruit. As usual, a clerk put him on hold.

"Maybe they've got something," Dusty said hopefully.

Jim grunted and put down his coffee cup.

"Jim, I'm worried about him. Don't you think Rick's moving way too fast with Laurel? There is something strange about her. And that note, do you . . ."

Jim glowered for a long moment before interrupting. "I'm telling you again. Start that shit, Dusty, start getting bitchy and putting her down, you lose him as a friend and you don't ever work for him again. Hell, that's the problem working with women. They just can't help being jealous and catty."

"It's not that, Jim, I swear." Her blue eyes were earnest. "I admit I may be jealous. But that has nothing to do with it. She's strange. I think she wrote that sick note to herself. Not only that . . . I think she may have dumped her next-door neighbor's pet kitten in the bay. You should have seen the look on her face when she was asked if she'd seen it. I think she's a sick chick."

"Sure, and she's the Tylenol killer and did away with Cock Robin too. Forget it," he said gruffly. "She's a nice kid. You just didn't like getting dumped. Nobody does. But it happens to the best of us. If something is wrong with that broad, let Rick find it out all by himself. He's a big boy. Don't look for trouble, Dusty. That's all you'll get."

"I'm serious." She sighed and stared out the window at passing traffic.

"So am I. She's a kid, that's all. You forget what it's like to be that young. She makes him happy. At least somebody around here is happy."

They looked up expectantly as Rick rejoined them. "We did not get lucky," he said, sliding into the booth. "The FBI had nothing."

"Look," Dusty said. "If the labels she was wearing were bought in South Florida, chances are she shopped Neiman-Marcus in Bal Harbour. The shopping center is open late tonight. How about if I go up and canvass?"

"You just want to go shopping," Jim accused.

"Till I drop," she said. "But not tonight. Would you rather I go to the autopsy while you go to Neiman's and Saks and describe her ensemble to the buyers?"

Jim and Rick quickly agreed that Dusty would canvass the shopping center. Rick would attend the postmortem and Jim would enlist recruits to handle the phones.

TWENTY-FOUR

*T*his is my favorite season, Alex thought, pleasant weather with a hint of danger. Unpredictable storms, all with the potential to grow into killer hurricanes, lurking out at sea, and something in the air, a crackling energy and tension. Miami is actually cooler and more comfortable in late summer than most places in the nation. The city's highest recorded temperature is ninety-eight, and refreshing breezes constantly sweep in off the sea.

Yes, this was the best place to be, Alex thought, and tonight he would drastically alter their life-style. It was time to do a little shopping, shopping for dollars. Money makes everything easier, including justice.

He drove north on Miami Beach, sharing the long and winding ribbon of Collins Avenue with the off-season tourists in their rental cars. They all streamed along in the shadow of the big high-rise condominium towers and the old-time hotels that look like pink castles out of a dream, left over from the days when a new luxury hotel opened every year, before builders got greedy and began to clutter the landscape with condominiums. It might be a blessing if that storm in the Caribbean whips up into a monster hurricane, Alex thought. A direct hit is what we need to clean up this town—instant urban renewal. It happened once.

The big one in 1926 was Alex's favorite chapter in Miami history. Nobody then knew about hurricanes or the eye of the storm. When the eye passes over, wind and rain die down, followed by a stillness as calm as death. The sun emerges in a sky of balmy blue. They did not know then that the other half of the storm was yet to come. People thought it was all over, and many decided to go off to see the damage in Miami Beach. Miamians loved eyeballing disaster even in 1926. The survivors piled into their Model Ts, packed up the kids and the grandmas and chugged out onto the wooden causeway, the only bridge to the Beach. It was bumper to bumper with sightseers when the second half of the killer storm struck. The rusted hulks of old Fords and the bones of their passengers are scattered there still, on the sandy bottom of Biscayne Bay between Miami and the Beach.

Some people learn everything the hard way, Alex thought. The water, the weather and this city can be deceptive. The placid eye of the storm, the sun-dappled bay with its soaring seabirds, the lush evergreen city they all look so inviting, so sunny and innocent but they can be killers at heart. Like some people. Look at me, he thought.

Too bad about Barry. He could have sworn the guy was gay. Well, Marilyn could go on a shopping spree after tonight. That would make it up to her. She and Barry had really been cozy when Alex came out and spoiled their fun. He probably did over-react, he thought. A matter of pride and machismo. But he was not sorry. Nobody will be allowed to spoil things before Rick marries the girl. The errand, to deposit a little package—"the Best of Barry," Alex chuckled—with the scorpions and the snakes in the dense jungle growth near the beach on Key Biscayne, did delay him, but now he was making up for lost time. He liked staying busy.

The shopping center. Posh city, stores with no price tags in the windows. Banks of colorful flower beds, topiary, tinkling fountains, brambles of bougainvillea peeking from huge hanging baskets, lavish landscaping with prices to match, outdoor cafés where they charge $4.50 for a cup of coffee, Gucci and Saks and Neiman Marcus. No bargain basements here. Alex knew the place well. There had been a misunderstanding some time ago. "I'm back," he announced, to no one in particular. "You won't catch me shoplifting. This time I walk away with everything you've got." The parking lot attendants dress in red and white uniforms with helmets, like Bahamian police. It pissed Alex off that they charge for parking. He thought it outrageous to pay admission to spend money. What a rip-off.

It would not be advisable for him to park in the lot anyway. It was not his style to wait for some old geezer in a pith helmet to lift the exit arm and allow him to drive out should he have to leave in a hurry. That would not do at all. He was an impatient person. By necessity. The nice little street in adjacent Bay Harbor Islands, right behind the shopping center, better served his purpose. Must remember to feed the meter. The little things are the ones that trip people up, he thought. One must always appear law-abiding, like the average good citizen. Deception again, the name of the game. No wonder he identified so well with this fun city and wanted a life here. It had not been much of a life so far, but it was getting better—fast. He was the strongest and becoming even stronger all the time.

The shopping center, double-decked no less, with its exclusive shops, was like a showboat of light and color on a river of darkness. Across four lanes of Collins

Avenue stood elegant old hotels and swank condominiums, set back from the street, regally facing the sea. Behind the center are curved and quiet small-town streets with houses and apartments owned mostly by winter visitors. This was not exactly the height of the tourist season. At this hour, just past twilight, no one walked the street and motorists were preoccupied, headed north toward Golden Beach and Hollywood or into the front parking lot of the center, where they stopped to be issued time-stamped tickets by the old geezers.

The covered, double-decked rear parking lot was shadowy and less than half full. Nobody around. It was almost time if the men he was waiting for arrived on schedule. Speak of the devil. The neatly painted red truck was precisely on time. This was it. Nothing could stop him now. The driver parked at an angle near the far back door of an exclusive shop. The courier stepped out, smiling at something the driver had said. Not even in uniform, carrying no gun. More discreet, less attention-getting, that was their thinking. Sounded dumb to Alex. The courier looked casual, a well-built guy about twenty-seven, striding alone to the back of the store, around the sweeping curve of a building, punching a button, speaking into an intercom and stepping into an elevator.

In approximately twelve minutes, he would emerge carrying a bank bag swollen by the day's receipts. When he stepped, alone, off the elevator, Alex would be waiting. He had to take him before the man moved back into his driver's line of vision. It was chancy, but Alex was fast. The courier had to give up the money and be back on that elevator, dead or alive, when the door slid closed. It would not open again unless activated by security personnel upstairs. The elevator would rise to the third-floor office, and by the time the victim reported what happened, Alex should be out the other side of the parking garage and back to his car. The waiting truck driver would not become suspicious or impatient until the troops came barreling off that elevator. It should take a good five minutes before that happened. Local police would be rolling by then. They would probably block both auto exits and the Bay Harbor Causeway west to Miami. By that time Alex should be driving south, already in the next police jurisdiction, the town of Surfside, which was just four blocks away. That little municipality, which has its own police department, is just eight blocks long and less than a mile wide from the bay to the sea. Nine blocks and three traffic lights later, Alex would be rolling through Miami Beach police jurisdiction. Since their radios operate on totally different frequencies, they would remain unaware of any crime unless and until the local cops here made a point of notifying them. So many cops, so many departments, so little communication. That is what he always heard them say.

If the fellow gave him a hard time or refused to give up the money, that would be another story. If he had to use the gun, the driver might hear the shot, even in his air-conditioned truck with the motor running. If so, he might think it just *a backfire. With all the echoes in the parking garage and the elevator, he would not be sure where it came from. Drivers have orders not to leave their trucks. But what if he was curious, curious enough to step out and investigate? People don't always follow orders. The driver was armed. He could be a problem. Alex decided he would worry about that if it happened. Maybe it wouldn't.*

Waiting alone in the dark, he felt cool and confident. His heart beat faster and his skin tingled, but those were not unpleasant sensations. He reminded himself not to run, but to walk briskly. The money would go right into the folded shopping bag under his arm. He could dump the checks and the change later. The countdown was on. Four minutes to go. He assumed his post in the shadow of a concrete urn flowing with philodendron, just two steps from the elevator door. The weight of the gun was comforting. The knife was also in his belt. It would be quieter, if he was forced to use a weapon, but a blade could be messy and dangerous. If you fail to hit somebody just right, in a vital spot, they are sometimes more angry than hurt. Even when you do hit them just right, it often takes a long time for them to stop what they are doing and fall down. It was not like he had a hell of a lot of time here. The gun was his favorite, the trusty old .38-caliber revolver. So nice and impersonal. Solve all your problems with the twitch of a finger. Never even get your hands dirty. It will stop somebody, get them permanently off your case without even mussing a hair or rumpling your clothes. Guns command respect and usually make people quite agreeable, even eager, to do exactly as you wish. He would not dare to try and pull this off without a gun.

Two minutes and counting. The air was so still behind the shopping center, where buildings blocked the wind from the sea and the rumble of big air-conditioning units drowned out the roar of the ocean. He hated not seeing a big, open expanse of sky. He could glimpse only a strip of starless velvet from where he waited. Deep cerulean with steel gray clouds burgeoning on the horizon. We may see rain yet tonight, he thought. He must remember to drive carefully, the streets are very treacherous when rain first begins to fall. Mix a little water with the coating of oil and dust on the surface and the blacktop becomes slick enough for cars to hydroplane, sailing out of control off the road or into oncoming lanes. This would be very poor timing for a little fender bender. No, that would not do at all. No off-the-wall slipups. He re-membered the story Rick had told of the bank robber who locked himself out of his getaway car. How embarrassing. And the street kid who stole a car loaded with loot, stranding a greedy burglar who had re-entered the house for more. To say nothing of the dope dealer who stopped to use a pay phone— they always use pay phones—and turned to see his Mercedes, loaded with cocaine and $120,000 in cash, driven away by a sixteen-year-old car thief. The victim did not report it, of course, and the cops were totally unaware until the

Liberty City kid, a ghetto high school dropout, came to their attention by paying cash to buy motorcycles for all his friends. He was probably fortunate that the cops found him first. Rick always brought home such wonderful stories. Alex would miss them, he thought, after Rick was dead.

One minute and counting. Here it comes! He could hear the automatic doors opening, then closing, with a clang that made his heart lurch. The grinding of the elevator as it descended. This was it. A deep breath, pull down the cap, pull out the gun. This guy better deliver if he wants to go home tonight. Open sesame. The courier stood dead center, legs slightly apart, eyes straight ahead, the moneybag under his left arm, supported on the bottom by his right hand.

He blinked, his eyes not yet adjusted, as Alex stepped forward out of the shadows. "Hey!" he said, and took a step back. Alex planted himself between the doors to block their closing. The muzzle of the gun was leveled at the man's heart. Alex gestured for him to hand over the bag. He hesitated. Alex cocked the gun. The dull metallic click made an impression. The man's mouth opened, but he swallowed the words. His gray eyes were speculative, darting behind Alex, who did not like that. It made his finger tighten on the trigger. The man saw it and raised his right palm slowly, in a staying gesture. Alex liked the scared look in the eyes, now totally focused on him as they well should be.

He gestured quickly, impatiently with the gun. The man gave up the money-bag. It was heavier than Alex expected, and he grasped it in a strong grip, then stepped back, smiling, releasing the doors. At the final instant, he realized the man was making a move. He saw it in his face, the grimness in his eyes and the tensing of the muscles in his jaw. The man lunged for the control panel. Alex thought it was to keep the doors from closing, but it was an alarm bell. The man's thumb was on it, and it was damn loud. Son of a bitch! As the doors glided closed, Alex fired two shots. The sound of the damn bell was unnerving, and the moving doors kept narrowing his target. The man inside had hurled himself to the left, so that even at such close range Alex missed. He saw the slugs slam into the elevator's back paneling.

Shit! Shouts behind him. Where the hell did he come from? A uniformed security guard. Not one of the old codgers, but a young one, wearing a holster. He was walking fast, now running, approaching from the direction Alex had planned to take. He was fumbling as he moved, unsnapping the holster. The damn bell was still ringing loud enough to wake the dead. The elevator was moving. The courier inside was already yelling for somebody to call the cops. That son of a bitch, Alex thought. He should have killed him. He never should have given him the chance to pull this shit. When that elevator spits him out on the third floor, he will come back down, with reinforcements.

The damn security guard and his gun blocked the escape route. Alex couldn't run the other way, past the truck. The driver was armed and mobile and had a two-way radio. No way Alex could outrun a truck. The security guard had a radio too, strapped to his belt. There was no place to run, except toward him. The guard hesitated, apparently afraid to shoot first, uncertain of what exactly was happening. "Halt, stay right there!" he shouted. He was about a hundred feet away. I'll shoot his damn ass off, Alex thought.

He fired the first shot. The guard looked surprised. He stopped running so suddenly that he staggered forward a few steps, but he was not hit. Dammit, Alex thought. He dived behind a parked car. He could not see the guard, but he heard him babbling into his radio, and he heard the fucking truck start up. The elevator behind him had stopped on the third floor. In a matter of moments it would be on its way back down. He had to be out of here. Most armed security guards have had a little firearms training, but not much, unless they are ex-cops. It is hard as hell to hit a moving target. Running for it was his best bet. Here we go! From the corner of his eye he saw the headlights of the truck. He ran like hell, the moneybag in one hand, the gun in the other, charging the car where the security guard was hiding. He pounded right by him, running and shooting, heading for cover behind the next row of parked cars. He could smell the gunpowder and see the flash as he fired. Sure enough, the guard was too busy wincing, ducking, hiding his head and trying to crawl under the car to shoot back. It won't take him long, though, Alex thought. Here it comes, he's firing, one, two, three. The dumb shit was shooting right into the roof of the parking garage, concrete chips flying everywhere. Alex ran low along the row of parked cars between them, heading west. His own car seemed so far away, and if they saw it, got the tag number, he was fucked.

He had fired four, two left before he had to reload. The way the guard was popping them off, if he had a standard revolver, which he probably did, and no second gun, which he probably didn't, he would have to stop to reload soon. It sounded like he was killing a lot of parked cars. Sounded like he hit some-body's gas tank or radiator, something was splashing, running out all over the place. What the hell! Who the hell are they? A whole herd of people, seven or eight of them, civilians, shoppers, stampeding around the corner of the building, rushing toward him. These damn Miamians, they are so accustomed to crime and violence that when they hear shots, they run, not in the opposite direction like normal people, but to go see. They're crazy, he thought. The security guard waved his arms, yelling at them to get back and giving Alex a good chance to get off another shot at him. Now the shoppers were all scream-ing, pushing, shoving and stampeding back around the corner for cover. That's more like it, Alex thought. These people are crazy.

He had to stop to catch his breath. It would give him a chance to dump some of the change that was making the moneybag so heavy. Something was coming his way, something wet, rivulets from a big, dark, widening puddle. Sure *enough, gasoline. Somebody had had a full tank. Fire could be his ticket out of there. Fire could distract most of them long enough for him to get out of the garage, across the sloping, landscaped lawn and back to his car on the next street. He'd flick his Bic and make a run for it.*

Good thing he was careful and jumped back, it caught with a whomp that could have singed his ears. Now, feet, do your stuff, he thought. The fire leaped between him and the guard and the elevator. The smoke, with no place to escape fast, would start stacking up in this garage. Nobody would see him running now. New arrivals would rivet on the fire. With any luck, he'd be out of there in a few seconds. He just had to run down the empty exposed traffic lane and out the far side. Damn! The truck was coming, bouncing over the speed bumps and accelerating. The guy had his arm out the window, holding his gun. Who does he think he is, Wyatt Earp?

Oh, shit, the truck was gaining on him. He couldn't make it. Bullets would just bounce off that fucking truck. He would have to dump the money. That's what the driver wants, the damn moneybag. That's his whole gig, Alex thought, he'll give up on me if I throw down the bag. He'll know he can't wait and come back for it later. In a shopping center full of Miamians, with cops and firemen running every which way? He wouldn't find two nickels when he got back.

Shit, all this effort. For nothing. Here goes. He pulled open the top of the bag and gave it a nice little heave, so it plopped into the splash of headlights behind him, then ran like hell. He heard the brakes squealing. Sirens, probably cops and firemen, coming from every direction. Down the slope. Glad he wore his running shoes. Out onto the street. Walk calmly. Can't stop huffing and puffing. Take a deep breath. Take off the cap, stuff the scarf.

He saw his car waiting halfway down the block and fought to keep his knees from wobbling. What was this? A woman, a senior citizen, walking a little dog on a leash.

She must live around here, he thought, not carrying a handbag. The dog is all perky and prancy. What is this shit? She had seen him and was coming across the street. She wore glasses and a wrapper, with what looked like a nightgown underneath.

"Good evening."

"Hi, there," he said, staying out of the light from the street lamp. What else could he do?

"What happened? What's all the excitement at the shopping center?"

She was eager. Her eyes lit up. Will these people ever quit? His knees shook, he wanted to run but couldn't. Don't blow it now, he thought, willing his voice to sound casual, with no trace of a tremor. He stopped, cocked his head to one side and said: "It's some sort of fire, I think."

"I hope no one's hurt," she said, then looked back at him expectantly. "Do you live here?"

"No, just visiting." He started to move away. She picked up the little dog. He could swear they looked alike, with their bright eyes, floppy ears and graying muzzles. Their eyes were drifting back to the confusion and mounting noise at the shopping center. Good, he thought. He really did not want to strike up a friendship or have to shoot her and the mutt and bring down more grief on himself. But he sure as hell didn't want her to see where he went, which car was his.

"I think you can see the whole thing from the top of the little rise there. It looks down into the parking lot."

"Oh. Thank you. Come, Pookie." She set the dog down on all fours and the two trotted toward the sirens.

Alex lost no time retrieving the key from the back tire and gently rolling the car around the block, heading south, doing some deep breathing. He was shaky. This was the closest he had come to disaster yet. It was one thing to shoot people, it was something else to have them shoot back. These damn people just don't take crime seriously enough, he thought. That's the problem, they are so inured to it, or maybe just so fed up with it, that they don't follow orders, even from somebody behind a gun. Everybody wants to fight. The only answer is to shoot them. It was damn sure what he should have done this time. A Surfside police car, racing to the scene. A hook and ladder, siren screaming, careening toward the center. How the hell would they get that thing into the parking garage? Alex pulled over to the side and stopped. Every good citizen knows an emergency vehicle has the right of way. Well, he was walking away from this one without a dime, but at least he was walking away. This was a setback, but just a minor one. It should have worked.

It's them, Alex thought. It's their fault. They constantly interfere with my thinking and my plans, he told himself. He was furious. They dragged him down like stones. It was clear to him now, he would have to settle his score with them first. Everything would be better once they were put to rest. Permanently.

TWENTY-FIVE

*J*im's wet sneezes erupted half a dozen times as he arrived at the station. His eyes were itchy, red-rimmed and nearly closed. His head ached. He cursed the man, whoever he was, who had conceived the brilliant idea of importing melaleuca trees from Australia to Florida at the turn of the century. People called it the paper bark tree because of its corklike peeling bark. Its brushy snowy white flowers soon made it a favorite ornamental. It was a bonanza, a money tree—for allergists. Not even a native, the melaleuca has caused untold miseries, Jim thought resentfully, like so many other nonnatives who never belonged in Florida, or the United States of America, in the first place.

The only recruits eager to help answer phone calls from the public barely spoke English or were too dumb, in his opinion, to discern whether they were talking to a crank, a helpful citizen with a legitimate tip or public enemy number one. They were useless, he thought, but he assigned the best of what had to be the world's worst academy class to help.

When Jim plodded into the detective bureau, a routinely unnoticed event, he was greeted with suspect joviality. Mack Thomas led the pack, ambling by his desk to comment, "Working hard, eh, Jim, I hear you're really trying to get a head.

"A head," he repeated, when he saw no reaction. "Get it?" he said, laughing at his own joke. Jim wheezed, fumbled for his handkerchief and realized he had left it in the car. Snorting to keep his nose from dripping, he foraged through Dusty's desk for a box of Kleenex. He found it in a bottom drawer. Good Girl Scout, he thought, always prepared. She usually handed them, solemnly and without comment, to weeping survivors or remorseful suspects. Despite the pastel-colored flowers printed on the cardboard box, he carried it to his desk, ignored the other detectives who hovered like vultures and blew his nose, vigorously.

"Don't take it so hard, Jimbo. You'll get some head one of these days," a robbery detective quipped, amid raucous laughter.

"Another broad who keeps losing her head," said another.

"I heard she had a good head on her shoulders," Mack said. "Did you hear the one about the headhunter who . . ."

Jim pushed back his chair and lumbered to the locker room. His clogged sinuses felt solid. He was sure he had stashed a bottle of nasal spray in his locker after an attack of the melaleuca, night-blooming jasmine or whatever had made his head feel like a lead balloon the last time.

First he took a leak, pulled up his zipper, washed his hands and frowned into the mirror over the sink. He looked terrible, nose red, eyes puffy. He had to get some relief before taking on the most promising among the stack of messages that had grown alarmingly since that afternoon. What did somebody want with the damn fool woman's head anyway, he thought irritably? Maybe some sort of weird religion? Enough of them had shown up in Miami since the influx from the south. Voodoo rituals, Santería rites, people sacrificing animals, stealing bones out of graveyards. There was a cult, he recalled, that had done some beheadings back in the seventies, but they had done it to each other, to members of their own sect who had become disenchanted and wanted out, not to expensively dressed middle-aged white women. He hoped it was not the start of some new trend and wondered why they always seemed to start in Miami. He hoped Rick was learning something valuable at the autopsy. He dried his hands, dropped the paper towel into the wastebasket and stepped into the adjacent locker room, fishing in his pocket for his keys.

He was alone. The room was stuffy, and more gloomy than usual. It was windowless, and the single overhead fluorescent bulb had apparently burned out. The only light was what little spilled through the doorway from the john, and that was blocked by the tall rows of metal lockers. He found his and fumbled, trying to unlock it in the semidarkness. The flimsy metal door seemed stuck. Annoyed, he rattled it, then yanked it hard.

It sprang open. Something round and hairy rolled off the shelf above his head and fell toward him out of the shadows. A red mouth wore a grotesque grimace. The eyes stared without seeing. Jim hurled himself back, slamming against the lockers behind him, his heart pounding. The thing hit the floor with a thud, bounced a few inches, rolled, then lay still.

Gasping for breath, his heart galloping in his chest like a runaway horse, he hesitated, looked around, took a small step closer, leaned over and squinted at the ugly thing. "Son of a bitch," he muttered, still breathing hard, and kicked at it with all his might. His toe did not connect dead center and the effort threw him so off balance that he nearly fell. The thing scuttled along the floor until it bumped against another wall of lockers and stopped dead.

"Those motherfuckers!" he croaked. He felt like he had swallowed his Adam's apple. "Cops!"

He washed his face, composed himself and strolled back into the office, delicately carrying the object by some of its long hairs. Surveying the room, he noted which detectives were struggling to keep straight faces. "Very clever," he announced, and placed the disgusting thing on top of his desk. "Okay," he bellowed, hands on his hips, "whose smart ass idea was this?"

He had always wondered why tourists ever bought these revolting souvenirs, Indian faces with seashell ears, big eyes and grinning red lips painted on hairy brown coconuts. He knew why somebody had bought this one.

"It didn't faze me," Jim lied, as they ringed his desk. He lowered his voice. "But what we gotta do is get it into the women's locker room. They'll shit."

Mack had casually lifted one of the perpetually ringing telephones that was being ignored. "Hey, it's Rick," he said. Jim punched the lighted button and picked up.

Rick sounded tense. "Did you hear about Bal Harbour?"

"Naw, what?"

"They're working some kind of running gun battle, fire and maybe an explosion—at the shopping center."

"Christ, that's where Dusty went. Have you heard from her?"

"Nope, and I can't raise her on the air."

"Shit. Maybe she walked into something. You know if any cops are involved?"

"Don't know. It's all pretty sketchy, it just went down. One of their detectives was here on a natural, and they called him out on a three. Pick me up ASAP and let's get over there. I'm worried about her."

"Look out the window, that's me pulling into the parking lot." Jim shrugged into his jacket. He had never found the nasal spray, but he could live without it. Striding past Dusty's desk, he glanced around, saw no one watching and slipped the coconut, face up, into her bottom drawer, where the Kleenex box had been.

*7*hey cut through traffic, taking a three signal, using the blue flasher on the dashboard and clearing intersections with the siren. Dusty still did not respond to her radio, despite their repeated tries. "That's not like her. Christ, I hope she's okay," Rick said. His voice sounded strained.

"Maybe the batteries died, or it got dropped."

"She could have lost it in a chase."

Jim cursed and weaved around motorists who failed to yield to siren and lights, while Rick filled him in on the postmortem. There was little to tell. Their headless Jane Doe had an old appendix scar, which might help to identify her, and Dr. Lansing had estimated her age at between forty-five and fifty.

*F*ire trucks still labored at the scene and the shopping center looked surreal, roped off and illuminated by moving red and blue lights. It swarmed with police. The detectives flashed their badges and asked for the person in charge as they scanned the scene for a glimpse of Dusty's blond hair.

The Bal Harbour chief, a heavyset man in his sixties, was both cagey and curious. "Don't you fellas have enough crime to keep you busy on your own side'a the bay?"

"One of my detectives was up here investigating a city homicide, we can't raise her on the air and when we heard what you had working we thought she might be involved," Rick said.

The chief paused for a long moment, then spoke with deliberate slowness. "It is customary to notify the local department when you're conducting an investigation in our jurisdiction." He paused again. "I don't remember any such notification from your detective." He sighed audibly.

"Detective Dustin was only canvassing," Rick said. "She was trying to identify a homicide victim by her clothing."

The chief's eyes flickered with interest. "You mean the woman who lost her head? That your case?"

"Unfortunately," Rick said.

The chief looked amused. "Why do you think somebody wanted it?"

"Good question. We'll know better once we have her identified."

"You have reason to think she might be one of our local residents?" he said. "We've got no missing persons at the moment."

"Nah, it was just a long shot, that she might have bought her clothes here. You haven't seen our detective? Tall, good-looking blonde, about thirty."

Without taking his eyes off the newcomers, the chief called over his shoulder to some of his men in uniform. "Anybody seen a lady detective from the city?"

There was no answer, just expressionless stares from suspicious small-town cops, who obviously considered the crime scene their domain. "If she was here," the chief drawled, "it looks like she beat feet when the fireworks started. Maybe she didn't want to get involved." He guffawed. A few of his men joined in.

"Then I guess she wasn't here." Jim's raspy voice was sandpaper on steel. He hated these petty territorial disputes that arose every time they stepped over the damn city limits. The smoke made his runny eyes smart even more. He pinched the bridge of his nose and tried to breathe.

"What happened here?" Rick asked, looking around and ignoring the chief's last remark.

"A robber tried to stick up the armored car courier as he came out a back elevator with the day's receipts from Farnsworth and Company. Almost pulled it off, but a private security guard who works for the center stumbled onto it. They exchanged some gunfire, a few cars got hit, one of them in the gas tank, and a fire started. A couple of cars burned."

Rick's looked intense, his brow furrowed. "Was the courier in plainclothes or uniform?"

"Plainclothes. They just started, how'd you happen to know about that?"

"A countywide bulletin. It was read at roll call recently. Security at some of the more exclusive stores and shops decided it would be safer and more discreet if the armored car personnel who made pickups at their establishments were not in uniform."

"Guess somebody knew that," the chief said thoughtfully.

"The subject get away?"

"Yep, but not before dropping the moneybag. The cash is being tallied up now, but it looks like full recovery, about $60,000. Didn't get a dime."

"Any description?"

"White, young, windbreaker, blue jeans, baseball cap and shades, dangerous as hell, runs like a rabbit."

"Car description?"

"Nope."

"Prints?"

"The moneybag was pawed over by the armored car driver who picked it up and half a dozen security people and store personnel."

"Too bad," Rick said. "What kind of gun, what caliber did he use?"

"Revolver. The courier thought it looked like a snub nose, a .38, like a detective special." His eyes narrowed as he looked first at Rick, then at Jim. "The lab guys are digging slugs out of cars and the elevator panels now. We don't have much a this here," the chief said, his face placid. "We run a quiet community, some people with more money than God spend their winters here. We keep an eye on their homes and their yachts for them. They like to keep a low profile, and so do we. This kind of thing is more up your alley, over that side'a the bay. Any ideas?"

"I won't be surprised if it is one of our bad guys, somebody known to us," Rick acknowledged, ignoring the inference. "I'll talk to robbery, see if it sounds like anybody they know, and ask the lab to match ballistics on our open cases, see if we pull a match."

The chief nodded, his face serious. "This was bad, but it could have been a lot worse. We could've had some people dead, including innocent bystanders." He paused for a moment. "Wonder whatever happened to your lady detective?"

"That is something I'd like to know," Rick said, "and something I intend to find out. Let us know if we can help, Chief." The two men shook hands.

"That prick," Jim muttered as they walked back to their car. "That lardass and his little fiefdom. He couldn't find his way home if they took down the street signs. Did you hear that crack about Dusty? And a detective special?"

"Hell, what can we expect with more than thirty Miami cops indicted in the past couple of years, one of them still on the FBI most wanted list? The guy doesn't know us, doesn't know if he can trust us. And where the hell *is* Detective Dustin?"

Jim snorted and blew his nose again for a long time. "Good question," he sniffed. "Here's a pay phone, why not try her at home?"

Rick shrugged, fed the phone and dialed Dusty's number. He did not have to look it up. It rang twice, then Dusty's voice on the line: "I'm not available at the moment," she said coolly, her tone measured, "but I'll be very disappointed if you don't leave a message when you hear the tone." Rick waited, kept listening, then hung up. He checked his watch.

"She's there," he said, relieved.

"Why didn't you talk to her?"

"The answering machine was on," Rick said.

"So how do you know she's there?"

"You know people who use the machine to screen calls but can't resist sneaking it off the hook to hear who's on the other end? She's always been one of them. She picked up. I heard the extra click and a clock chime in the background. It was the correct time." He was suddenly angry. "Son of a bitch. What is going on with that woman? Why would she go the hell home when she's working? Why won't she answer her radio? She had us killing ourselves, running on a three and winding up embarrassed because we thought she might have walked into a situation and got herself hurt."

"Maybe she's getting screwed on city time," Jim said thoughtfully. "Who is she . . ."

"I wouldn't know," Rick said curtly. "To hear her tell it, nobody."

"Not with that body," Jim said. "Somebody's tapping that. We know it ain't you, right?" He cut questioning eyes at Rick.

"Damn right," Rick said.

"Then why do you sound just a little bit jealous?"

Rick shrugged impatiently and shook his head. "Some habits are hard to break."

"You gonna write her up for this?"

"Damn straight. I'm her supervisor. I couldn't ignore it if I wanted to. But first I want to hear her story, find out what the hell's going on."

They got into the car and Jim switched on the ignition.

"This thing that happened up here tonight. It's weird, Jim. Something's not right. I've got a gut feeling about it."

When they walked into the station, Dusty was at her desk, prim and proper, manning the telephone. She avoided Rick's glare.

The first time she cradled the receiver, he jerked a thumb toward a glass cage. "We need to talk, Detective."

Jim watched from his desk as she reluctantly followed him, like a misbehaving schoolgirl being marched to the principal's office. He thought a moment, then removed the coconut from Dusty's desk drawer and dropped it in the wastepaper basket. He replaced the cardboard box of Kleenex after stuffing a fistful into his jacket pocket. She'll need it, he told himself. He hated it when women cried. He sighed. The last thing Dusty needed now was a practical joke, much as he would have enjoyed it. He liked to banter with her and tease. She reminded him of Molly, feisty and full of personality. He yearned to be the one to comfort her, but Dusty would never turn to him, he thought. He was no young stud or ladies' man like Rick.

He shuffled through the phone messages and sighed again as he saw two from Terrance McGee. Fortunately they were for Dusty. One bore the scribbled notation: "He says everything okay now."

Jim raised an eyebrow. Thank God for small favors, he thought. McGee doesn't think he's being poisoned anymore. Dusty's chats with the man might actually be doing him some good. He hoped Rick would not be rough on her. God knows, he thought, we all have times when we are not where we are officially supposed to be. The job constantly intrudes on your life, so if your life occasionally intrudes on the job and no harm done, what's the big deal? It was just her bad luck to be caught. Who could foresee that a gun battle would go down in the damn shopping center she was supposed to be canvassing?

He glanced curiously into the glass-enclosed office. Rick had closed the door and assumed the position of authority, behind the desk. Dusty sat in a straight-backed chair in front of him. Jim saw with satisfaction that she was not crying—yet. Hang in there, kid, he thought, silently cheering her on until overcome by a paroxysm of sneezes.

*W*hat the hell is going on with you?" Rick said heatedly. "You've always been dependable, reliable. What is this shit?"

"Okay, so I wasn't at the shopping center. I"—she hesitated, her voice weary—"I'm having a bad day, and I needed a break. I was wrong. Write me up, give me a suspension, do what you have to do." Her eyes looked past him, focusing on the darkness outside the single window.

"Where were you?" he demanded.

She seemed reluctant to answer. He waited.

"I headed toward Bal Harbour, but I felt down, depressed, turned off the radio and just drove. Stayed on the expressway, picked up the turnpike and drove. At Palm Beach, I turned around and came back."

"You took the city car outside the county without permission?"

She nodded, with a sigh.

"Oh swell. What then?"

"I stopped at my place, realized I had to get my shit together and so I came back in. On the way I heard about what happened up at the shopping center. If I'd been where I was supposed to be, I might have stopped it. I'm sorry."

"You seemed fine at the diner." Rick studied her more closely. Pissed off at Laurel after his close shave that morning, he had found himself comparing her to Dusty. As exciting as all the quirkiness and role playing could be, there was something to be said for constancy. At least he always knew where Dusty was coming from. His concern on the way to the shopping center had made him realize that he did take her for granted. Though he saw her every day, he had not really looked at her lately. And she was worth looking at. She was wearing her hair different, a little longer and more wavy. Her knees were suntanned. She always did have the best knees in the station. She stared back, her eyes soft and sad.

"It's personal, Sergeant."

"Hey, cut out the 'sergeant' shit. It's me you're talking to. Listen," he gestured casually. "If you were off playing a little kissy-face somewhere, hell, we've all been there."

Her mouth tightened and a flush crept across her cheekbones. She leaned back in the chair, threw one leg over the other and fumed.

"I don't mind telling you, I envy the new guy." He was watching her carefully.

"There is no guy," she said, her foot swinging impatiently, "since you."

To his surprise, he felt relief. He *was* jealous. Dusty and he had shared a life he and Laurel never could. Just as he could never picture Dusty as the perfect housewife, bustling around a kitchen, wearing an apron instead of a gun.

"I love it when you get mad. You turn me on," he teased.

"I don't *believe* you," she chided, her tone exasperated. She glared at the ceiling. "Look. It's the first time I've done anything like this . . ."

He shifted his chair slightly for a better view of her long legs, his gaze settling on the curved instep and the smooth line of her calf. "There's something else I need to know. The night I asked you to drop the composites of those Colombian body snatchers on the ERs and the clinics . . . did you?"

"I papered every clinic in town with them, Sergeant."

"I thought you'd go to the county ER first. Makes sense. Yet when Jim and I swung by there that night to talk to the wounded store clerk, you hadn't been there."

"I figured those guys would go to a Spanish-speaking clinic first. When I heard you and Jim take a signal at the ER, I knew you'd think of it, so I scratched it off my itinerary."

Satisfied, Rick rubbed his palm across his face. "You want to go talk to Doc Feigleman?"

"The department shrink?" She put both feet on the floor and drew her spine up straight in her chair. Her voice and her expression shared indignance. "Look, I'm having a couple of bad days—everybody's entitled."

"I don't want you to ever think you can take advantage of our past relationship," he said quietly.

"I'm not taking advantage of it!" she said angrily, her perfect teeth gnawing her rosy lower lip.

"Well then," he said, "with that settled, you want to get together later . . . for a drink?"

Silently she searched his face and found the answer. "You're serious."

"Never more so." His eyes were fixed on hers.

She let out her breath, stood up abruptly and strode to the door. Her hand on the knob, she turned, "You would be better than the shrink. Probably do me more good." Her voice was shaky.

"Guaranteed for what ails you."

"You are so bad," she said, "and I love it."

"Your place okay? Let's keep it low-profile," he said quietly. "I don't even want Jim to know."

She nodded and glanced out at the detective bureau.

He cleared his throat and looked around sternly. "Well, Detective, I guess that's enough of a tongue-lashing, so to speak. For now." He grinned. "We'll finish this later. I'll bring the wine."

"Right, Sergeant," she said briskly.

She marched out of the office, chin up. Jim admired the fact that there were no tears, though her hands were trembling. Hell of a girl, he thought.

After an hour, Rick told her to take comp time and go home early. Jim caught the look they exchanged. She was glowing. Oh, shit, he thought.

"Cover me, Jimbo," Rick said thirty minutes later. "Raise me if you really need me. Otherwise I probably won't be back tonight. There's something I have to take care of."

"At Pigeon Plum?"

"I didn't say that."

Jim shrugged. "Didja find out what was bugging Dusty?"

"It was nothing major. Dusty'll be okay," he said, the sheen in his eyes an admission.

"If Laurel calls?"

"I'm out at a scene."

Jim sighed, part envy, part concern. These young guys never learn. "I hope you know what the hell you're doing, pal."

Rick did not hear. A man in a hurry, he was already on the elevator, punching the down button.

Jim picked up the ringing telephone on Rick's desk not a quarter of an hour later and wished he hadn't. "Hi, Laurel." He tried to sound casual and friendly. "Naw, he's not here right now. I think he's out at a scene. Well, I stayed here to finish up some paperwork."

She asked when Rick would be in the office. "He's pretty tied up out there. He may not be back tonight. You'll probably see him before I do. If he checks in, I'll tell him you called. Everything all right?"

She said it was and hung up.

A few minutes later, the middle-aged secretary took a call for Dusty. "I think she's off, let me check." She put her hand over the receiver and called to Jim. "Is Dusty coming back tonight?"

He shook his head and she told the caller, "No, she's gone home."

Jim turned in his chair. "Who was that looking for Dusty?"

"Don't know," she said. "Didn't leave a name."

"Voice familiar?"

"Maybe." She looked puzzled.

"Man or woman?"

"It was hard to tell."

He shook his head in disgust and turned back to his work.

*A*lex *hung up the telephone. Personally, he didn't give a shit, but it was important to know just exactly what the son of a bitch was up to now. Laurel had been disturbed when Rick was unreachable. Frightened and lonely as usual, she had wanted to hear him reassure her that he would be home soon. When she became agitated, Harriet had surfaced, suspicious and anxious to know where the hell Dusty was and whether this was a threat to their household. Marilyn was furious if there was even a remote possibility that Rick was having*

*sex with anyone else. Jennifer simply sniveled because it frightened her when
the others got worked up. Harriet suggested that Alex call headquarters and ask
for Dusty. The fact that Dusty and Rick were both gone for the evening and
Alex could discern no mention of a homicide scene on the scanner heightened
Harriet's suspicions. Flipping open the leather-covered address book next to the
telephone, she found D, for Dustin, and dialed the number.*

*Dusty answered on the first ring, eager and throaty, not the voice of a woman
planning to sleep alone. She said hello twice. Harriet hung up. The address was
1560 Pigeon Plum Circle, in the Grove. Alex agreed to go check it out.*

*R*ick parked discreetly across the street, the rear end of the car in shadow
so the official city tag would not stand out like a sore thumb to anyone passing
by. He wavered between growing excitement and guilt. It seemed so long since
he had been with her. That he was doing this astonished him, yet at this
moment he could not imagine being anywhere else. Despite Laurel's spontaneous and creative sexuality and all her homemaking skills, he had yielded to
something stronger, his powerful need for a woman who shared his fears and
frustrations, someone who understood as he did the tragedy and black come-
dies played out on Miami's mean streets of night. Wanting her so much
created a deeper inner conflict. He had always resisted serious relationships
with women who also lived on the cutting edge of pain. Seeing the dark side
of life and death somehow damaged people in his eyes. He could not remember when he had first begun to believe that they were no longer whole, that
the cruelty of the job made them damaged goods. His mother was a single-
minded homemaker whose life revolved around making his father happy. He
wanted that too. Young, sheltered and protected, with no career ambitions,
Laurel had seemed perfect. He must be crazy, he thought, torn by conflicting
emotions. None of it made sense. But he knew that what he wanted and
needed right now was waiting for him inside, between a pair of long legs.

He rang the doorbell and felt his trousers swell with his erection.

She opened the door immediately, the dim light behind her glowing in her
blond hair. She wore something long and black and lacy that took his breath
away. His throat ached when he looked at her. "Hi, blue eyes."

She moved right into his arms like she belonged there.

"I'm so glad to see you," she whispered.

He was taking off his jacket. She took the bottle. "Asti Spumante, you
remembered."

"I remember everything." He was loosening his tie. "That's why I'm here."

"I'll get the glasses." She turned in the doorway. "Did you just call?"

"No, why?"

"Had a hang-up."

"Humph. I bet it was Jim, unless you have somebody else checking up on you." He raised an eyebrow.

"Jim?"

"Yeah, I think he's already onto us. You can't slip anything past that guy. He's too sharp."

He turned down the volume on the walkie so that they could just make out the calls, stood it on the coffee table and sat in a rose-color armchair. "What are you doing?" she laughed, a glass in each hand.

He was taking off his shoes.

"Mister Romance, huh?"

He looked embarrassed. "We might not have much time. I'm still on call if anything happens."

She stood in front of him, smiling softly, her face sweet. "It's all right," she said. "Whatever time we have. It's enough."

He popped the push-up cork on the bottle. It flew somewhere behind the sofa. Her laugh had a giddy ring to it.

"Why don't we drink this in the other room?"

"The kitchen?" she said brightly.

"No, you gorgeous idiot. The room with the bed."

"Sounds good to me."

"Careful," he cautioned in the bedroom doorway. "Don't get any makeup on my shirt."

"Sure," she said wistfully, and unbuttoned it for him.

It felt good, really good to lie naked on her bed, a glass of wine in one hand, the other under his head, and watch the long black lace gown slip off her creamy shoulders and drop like spilled ink around her feet.

"Something this good can't be bad," he whispered in her ear.

"I thought we'd never be this way again. I'm so happy you're here."

Her mouth and her breath tasted sweet. He raised his head from them suddenly. "What was that?"

Her voice was thick with passion. "Must be stray cats out there at the garbage pail."

"Don't move," he said, kissing her throat. "I'll be right back." He stood naked in the moonlight for a moment, looking out. The only view was the alley behind her townhouse and a small shed for the garbage cans. He saw nothing else. Turning back, he looked at her, the moonlight on her body, then drew the drapes and hurried back to her open arms. With any luck, they would have until dawn.

TWENTY-SIX

The news burst out of ballistics with the force of a shotgun blast the following afternoon. The bullets dug out of a fire-singed Eldorado parked behind the Bal Harbour Shopping Center and the elevator used by the courier had been shot from the same gun that had killed Rob Thorne and the Pakistani convenience-store clerk.

The day was full of revelations. As the team assembled early, more news developed. The headless woman had a tentative name, Jonina Vandermay. The well-to-do widow had been reported missing by her accountant. He had telephoned her swank Sunset Island home when she failed to appear for a scheduled appointment. The Jamaican housekeeper informed him that Mrs. Vandermay had not come home for two nights. Though the unexplained absence was entirely out of character, the housekeeper had not notified authorities for several reasons. Her employer was a troublesome woman and the respite from her sharp tongue had been a relief. The housekeeper also happened to be an illegal alien.

On the last day she was seen, Jonina Vandermay spent the morning being difficult, as usual, according to the housekeeper and maid. She had driven off at eleven A.M., as usual, in her champagne-color Jaguar, to visit her rental properties and oversee their management. Those visits were usually spent tormenting her tenants and employees. This time was different. She never came back.

The detectives were batting a thousand. Luck had smiled their way at last. The stunning news from ballistics excited them. This time, they hoped, the killer had made mistakes.

Jim knew he was right about them when he saw Rick and Dusty trying not to look at each other. "We finally got a break," he commented.

"Sure, but no thanks to me. I could kick myself," Dusty grumbled. "You know how every cop dreams of walking in on a big one in progress and doing the right thing? If you're lucky it might happen once in a lifetime. Well," she looked sheepish, "that was my chance, and I blew it by giving in to some self-indulgent, moody crap."

"Well, you seem to feel much better today," Jim said, smiling wryly. "Don't sweat it. If you'd been there you might've wished you weren't. Sometimes things happen for the best."

"Yeah." Rick rubbed his hands together and cut his eyes at Dusty. "When you get lucky, you get lucky." Her response was a look that could melt metal.

Jim pretended not to notice. Hot looks and heavy breathing in the office, it seemed like old times, before Laurel.

He and Rick hit the shopping center while Dusty pursued the Vandermay case.

To confirm the identification, Dr. Lansing planned to compare chest X rays of the corpse with the widow's medical records. A mere formality. The clothing and physical descriptions matched. So did the timing of her disappearance. Less than an hour after Dusty issued a countywide BOLO on the Jaguar, an alert motorcycle patrolman spotted it parked outside a Miami Beach apartment house owned by the victim.

As Dusty traced Jonina Vandermay's footsteps, Rick and Jim drove to the shopping center. Their stake in that investigation was now far greater than that of the local police in whose jurisdiction it had occurred.

Rick, Jim and two Miami robbery detectives canvassed the stores, listing the names and addresses, via sales receipts, of shoppers who had been there the night before, people who might have been witnesses. They had already debriefed the shaken security guard and the armored car crew. The results were disappointing. All three swore they had not seen the robber well enough to work with a police artist on a composite drawing. The detectives toyed with trying hypnosis to fish forgotten details from their subconscious minds. But it seemed fairly obvious that no such details existed. The lighting was poor and the events had been lightning-fast.

"Somebody else had to have seen him," Rick said as they parked. "He can't be that lucky. Good Christ, it's a goddamn shopping center. He had to have a car, he had to be somewhere before all the shit went down. He arrived, he left. Somebody saw that son of a bitch. Probably somebody who doesn't even realize who or what they saw. We're gonna find that witness."

The new developments energized them both. Frustrated by the Thorne case, they had, at last, a trail to follow. Jim even seemed to wheeze and sneeze less.

They canvassed the hotel fronts across the street and the help at the shopping center's outdoor cafés, with little luck.

"This guy is not invisible," Rick said angrily. "Somebody else saw him."

"This heat is gonna kill me," Jim said, mopping his face with a handkerchief. "You could fry your brains on the sidewalk. We got to come up with something soon."

Rick was determined. "What we've gotta do is come back at nine—with reinforcements. We need to see who is here at that precise time. We'll stop traffic going by, people on the sidewalk, employees who leave the center and the hotels, guys who pick up their wives from work the same time every night." The unyielding glint in his eyes was a sign of the persistence that made him more than a good detective. "If that doesn't work, we come back a week later, and do it all again on the same night, at the same time it went down. We're all creatures of habit. Maybe our witness eats here, or drops by once a week to window-shop."

"If there is a witness." Jim felt a trickle of perspiration worm its way down his back to puddle inside the line of his belt.

"There is," Rick said. "There has to be."

"I'm with you, bro."

*J*onina Vandermay's frightened housekeeper and maid were not suspects, Dusty decided. They were losers. Their employer's death had cost them their jobs. From talking briefly to the women and the accountant, Dusty formed a thumbnail sketch of the widow, a self-indulgent woman who spent lavishly on herself but was tightfisted with others. Dusty decided she would check the building where the Jaguar had been discovered, talk to the woman's lawyer to determine who would benefit most by her death and then compile a list at the courthouse of all the property the woman owned.

Her apartment buildings had live-in managers. The widow Vandermay gave them small discounts on the rent and a multitude of headaches. The job had a high turnover. Wearing three-hundred-fifty-dollar high heels and expensive designer fashions, perfectly coiffed and bejeweled, she visited her buildings almost daily to point a well-manicured finger at a leaky faucet or a burning light bulb that might cost her pennies, hedges that needed trimming or weeds that needed pulling—though she would prefer not to pay anyone to do it. When she had to pay, she preferred it to be below minimum wage, to an illegal alien pitifully eager to work and too afraid to complain when shortchanged.

The motorcycle cop who had spotted the Jaguar was standing by with the car, waiting for the crime lab. There was nothing obvious, no blood, no damage, to link the sleek machine to the crime. It was locked and legally parked. Some small change, mostly quarters, for tolls and parking meters was stacked on the console. A folded *Wall Street Journal* lay on the passenger seat along with a leather folder and what appeared to be an appointment book. Dusty would examine those after the lab techs got through. There seemed to be no sign of a struggle.

The twin two-story buildings were garden apartments constructed toward the end of the Art Deco era. They faced each other across a lawn mowed too short and singed yellow-brown by the sun. At one time, the grassy expanse had been graced by two stately coconut palms, one on each side. One still stood, tall and beautiful, its fronds chattering gently in the breeze. The dead stump of the other, probably a casualty of the blight, had never been removed. Nor had it been replaced. Its absence threw the symmetry of the twin buff-color buildings off balance.

Neatly trimmed Florida cherry hedges lined the brick-red sidewalk. Outside staircases with pink railings were located at each end of both buildings. The frames around the glass jalousie doors were painted the same salmon pink. Room air conditioners hummed beneath the front windows of each unit. A large square of twelve metal mailboxes was mounted on the wall next to the first apartment. Dusty knocked at apartment one. Moments later, the jalousies cracked open and an elderly woman peered out through the screen.

Dusty could hear TV news blaring in the background. She displayed her badge case and identified herself. "I know why you're here," the woman said. "I just saw it on TV. Is it really her?"

"Identification isn't positive yet, but it appears as though the victim is your landlady. Can I ask how long you've lived here?"

"It will be eighteen years on November first." The voice was flat, expressionless.

"Was she the owner when you moved in?"

"The place was sold to her about nine or ten years ago."

"Do you mind if we talk for a few minutes? We don't know much about her yet. I'm sure you could help us."

A safety chain rattled free, then the sounds of double dead bolts being released. Little good they would do with these jalousie windows, Dusty thought.

"It's hot out there, you can come in," the woman said. She was faded, with light, colorless eyes, a flowered cotton housecoat and a hair net around pink curlers. There were liver spots and a wedding band on her left hand, but no sign of a man in the immaculate apartment.

"I don't think there is anything I can tell you," she said, offering Dusty a seat on her yellow sofa. Curiosity colored the pale eyes. "Did they really cut off her head? Who would do a thing like that?"

"It's pretty much what you heard on the TV," Dusty said, nodding. "We're trying to find out. When did you last see Mrs. Vandermay?"

"A week ago tomorrow. She came and said I had to bring my spider plants in off the porch. Did you ever hear anything like that?" She shook her head slowly. "This is Florida. The word means full of flowers, and yet that woman doesn't want plants on the porch."

"Why was that?" Dusty looked up from her notebook.

"Just miserable, I guess. She said it's because she wants all the apartments to look alike." The woman leaned forward and spoke very slowly to emphasize her words. "This is Florida," she repeated. "Yet no plants—no plants, no pets. When something wore out, the former owner replaced it with a new one. With her, everything is used."

She leaned forward even further, her voice sharpening. "Every year she raises the rents, increases the deposit and won't pay interest on the money she holds. She's got it in an interest-bearing account, you can be sure, but she won't pay you interest. And I'll tell you something else: She will *never* give that deposit back. When people leave, she always finds a reason to keep their money. Mrs. Braverman, in the other building, died last year, a month after she signed a new lease. Mrs. Vandermay not only kept the deposit, guess what else she did?"

"What?" said Dusty, wondering who was doing the questioning in this interview.

"She sued the estate! To hold them to the lease and force them to pay for the whole year, even though she found a new tenant right away. You can ask anyone who knows me," she said, her hands fluttering around a plastic button at the neckline of her housecoat. "I don't talk about people, I don't say bad things about anybody, but that was not a nice woman. We never kept a good manager because of her. She drove them crazy."

"You didn't see her park her car outside on Tuesday?"

The woman thought, freckled fingers folded under her chin. "I'm not sure if it was Tuesday or last Thursday. I thought I heard her voice, those high heels, but it could have been anybody, I didn't look out. I try to avoid her, and with the air conditioner and *Geraldo* on the TV, you don't hear much from outside."

"Did she have any special friends here in the building?"

"She didn't have any friends that I know of."

"What about enemies? Did she have an argument with anybody here lately?"

The woman paused. "I don't know anybody she didn't argue with. She even snooped in apartments when the tenants weren't home. She said she had the right, that it was her property."

"Why do you think she came here that day?"

"No telling. She came by a lot, just to see what was going on or to meddle.

Money—money was always on her mind, if there was a way she could save it or cheat somebody out of it. Maybe to see if my spider plants were moved.

"She wasn't so bad before my husband died, but since then she's rude. You don't dare move because you know you won't get your deposit and security back unless you take her to court—and who can afford a lawyer?"

Dusty slid the cap back onto her pen and handed the woman her business card. "If you think of anything else that might help, anything you hear or forgot to tell me, please call."

The woman stopped her at the door. "If she really is dead, who's in charge of our building now?"

"I don't know if she had a will, or what it said if she did," Dusty said. "It'll probably be tied up in probate for a while."

"You think they'll raise the rents?" she asked, getting down to basics. "My lease is up in November."

*O*utside, Dusty stood in the sun, squinting at the building across the way. In some murder cases there are no immediate possibilities. In others, like this one, there are sometimes too many.

She felt buoyant, though she had had little sleep. Rick had to know now that Laurel was not right for him. Last night was proof that relationship was a mistake. It will end if it hasn't already, she thought, and I'll be there.

The woman had followed her out into the sun. She carried a wicker basket containing a large spider plant with long gracefully drooping leaves and several pups. She was humming.

Dusty smiled and turned to the mailbox to copy the names and apartment numbers of the eleven other tenants in the west building. She would come back in the evening to see the ones who were not at home. One name leaped off a mailbox marked apartment six: Terrance McGee. Could it be the same man? Of course, that's why the address had been faintly familiar.

Well, she thought, small world. I'll get to meet McGee in person. What a treat. He was probably not home. She remembered he worked at a library. But she decided to try his apartment anyway. Rick and Jim will love this. Number six was the last one on the first floor, a breezy southwest corner at the back of the building.

She knocked. Then knocked again. About to step away, she thought she heard a sound, or sensed a movement behind the opaque jalousies. "Mr. McGee, Terrance McGee?" she called. "It's Detective Dustin, Miami homicide. Remember me?"

The knob turned and the door swung wide open. He was barefoot, in rumpled shorts and a T-shirt that said COORS on the front. "You got my message!" he said, obviously pleased. "I didn't think you'd come in person."

He wore glasses with thick lenses, a two-day stubble of beard and a big grin. "Sit down," he said eagerly, greeting her like an old friend. "I don't have visitors too often." He showed her to the dining room, to a seat at a round oak table. The apartment was cleaner and better furnished than most bachelor pads she had seen. The thick carpet was beige, plush and soft.

"I wanted you to be the first to know," he said, "and I wasn't sure if you got the message. There are some things I want to show you," he said, bustling into what appeared to be the bedroom.

Dusty drank in the cool air. The apartment was comfortable. She hoped he would not ply her with his paranoid suspicions about his alleged poisonings when she wanted to ask questions about his late landlady. He emerged, as she had feared, with a fist full of newspaper clippings, letters, and what looked like legal documents and copies.

"It sure is warm out there," she said, sighing and pushing her thick hair back off her brow.

"Would you like something to drink?" he said quickly.

"I'd love it, if it's not too much trouble." She arranged her notepad and pen on the table in front of her.

"A beer? Or a Coke?"

"A Coke would be great."

He padded into the green-and-yellow kitchen behind her. She heard the whoosh of a flip-top can and the bubbly contents being poured into a glass. He emerged from the kitchen and set the half-full glass on the table in front of her, placing the can beside it.

He pulled up the chair to her right and sat down, smiling expectantly. "I'm surprised you're here," she said. "You're off today?"

"I had to take some sick time, to get this whole thing straightened out," he began. "You see, when your partners said the laboratory analysis showed no cyanide or any other poison in my sugar bowl, I knew the answer had to be one of two things—that somebody at the police department was in on it, or that it was an inside job."

Dusty sipped the Coke. It was warm. She put the glass down. "Actually, that's not the reason I'm here, Mr. McGee."

"Call me Terrance," he said. "You did on the telephone. I like that." His eyes looked huge, magnified by the thick lenses. His smile was thin and pale. He offered a cigarette from a pack of Marlboros, then lit one himself when she declined. His hands trembled slightly; she wondered if he was on medication.

Why is this the kind of Marlboro man I always meet, she thought ironically. Where is the stud in the tight pants, the one with the eye patch?

"I thought you'd be relieved that I solved my problems myself, without any help," Terrance was saying. He inhaled the cigarette smoke hungrily, flicking his pale lips with his tongue. "I guess I'll go back to work now that I'm no longer in jeopardy."

"I'm here about your landlady, Jonina Vandermay. I guess you're aware of what happened."

He nodded, somewhat casually, she thought, considering the subject matter. "Of course," he said, in matter-of-fact fashion.

"How long have you lived here, Terrance?" He was preoccupied, busily shuffling through his papers. Proof, in his mind, she assumed sadly, of the plots against him.

"The lease, where's the lease?" he frowned. He pushed his chair back, a struggle because of the thick rug. "Let me get it for you."

"Well, it's not really necess—" He had already disappeared into the bedroom.

She sighed, put down her pen and sipped her warm Coke. She stood up and carried her glass into the sunny kitchen. "Is it all right if I get some ice?" she called.

"Sure," he called back, apparently still foraging through papers in the bedroom, "but you better let me get it for—" He was too late. With her left hand she had already opened the freezer compartment of the refrigerator and was staring into the gelid eyes of Jonina Vandermay. Her eyelashes were frosted. So was her hair. Pink-tinged icicles hung from her nostrils.

The glass in Dusty's right hand crashed to the floor, the liquid inside splashed her shoes. Shards of glass and little bubbles clung to her stockings.

Dusty tore her eyes from those of the landlady. "Oh, Terrance," she said softly, shaking her head as if to deny what she was seeing. She shut the freezer door gently, as if closing a coffin.

He stood in the kitchen doorway, looking a bit embarrassed and almost shy. "I left word for you," he explained, "that I handled it myself. It had to be her," he said triumphantly. "I finally caught her at it."

A sudden chill crossed Dusty's shoulders.

"Don't say anything, Terrance. You don't have to talk to me."

"She left footprints, that was how I caught her," he said persistently.

"Footprints?" Dusty was gauging the distance between where she stood and the dining room table, wondering if she could make it if he became violent. Her purse sat on the carpet next to the chair she had occupied. Her gun and her handcuffs were inside.

"In the carpet," he said proudly. "I got this new carpet. It's so thick that you leave footprints. See?" He lifted his right foot to demonstrate. Sure enough, a perfect imprint was left in the soft pile, as clear as a footprint in wet sand. "I found hers. Her high heels. Only somebody with a key like she had would be able to come in and out and switch the sugar in the bowl without anybody noticing, before I could get it to the police. She was the one poisoning me all along."

His face glowed as though he was Perry Mason, center stage, explaining the identity of the real culprit to an enthralled audience.

Dusty could not help herself. "Why?" she whispered.

"She wanted my apartment," he said, as though the answer were elementary. "After I fixed it all up at my own expense, she wanted it, and she was too cheap to start eviction proceedings. If I died, she could rent it out for a lot more money and still get to keep my security deposit. She might even have tried to force my estate to pay the rent for the remainder of my lease. There was a widow who lived across the way, in the other building—"

"Mrs. Braverman. I know," Dusty said softly.

"You see!" he said. "I knew you would understand. Your partners wouldn't believe I had a problem."

"They will now," she promised.

*H*e was not violent, nor did he resist accompanying her to the station. In fact, he seemed quite eager to see Rick and Jim. "She owned a number of apartment houses," Terrance said earnestly. "Who knows how many tenants she poisoned? I even found a hair in my kitchen, light color, like hers, with a dark root. That's why"—he gestured toward the refrigerator—"I kept the proof."

The eyes behind the glasses shifted to Dusty's hair, as though he suddenly realized that hers too was light.

She knew what he was thinking and held up her hand. "I swear, Terrance, I'm blonde all over, believe it." They laughed. She even charmed him into wearing the handcuffs.

"I think they ought to check out what her husband died of, too," Terrance said. "That woman was dangerous."

"Some are," Dusty agreed.

TWENTY-SEVEN

*T*he street was lined with one-story, light-color tile-roofed South Florida homes. Small front lawns and short driveways, a tight little residential neighborhood, aloof from the glittery hotels, shopping center, high rises and tourist traffic of nearby Collins Avenue. The houses sat cooling in the evening hush, at the end of another day of sizzling ninety-five-degree heat. Nothing moved. Closed windows, central air conditioners and blaring TVs insulated those home owners in residence from the sights and sounds of the street.

Lights glowed in about half the houses. The odds of finding a witness in one of them did not seem favorable to Jim. He fought a desperate urge to pull off his shoes, knowing that if he did it would be impossible to work them back onto his swollen feet. They parked the unmarked at the corner. Rick checked his watch. "The time is right." He took a big breath and looked up and down the empty street. "Which side do you want?"

"This one," Jim said, and sighed. The fewer steps the better, he thought, settling for small favors.

Rick started across the street to begin canvassing at the stucco bungalow on the corner, then stopped. Someone was coming their way, an older woman with a small dog on a leash.

As they moved toward her, she hesitated, then bent to scoop the little dog into her arms. The light from a street lamp reflected off the lenses in her spectacles. Clutching the dog, she turned and scampered quickly in the direction from which she had come.

"Ma'am!" Rick hurried after her.

She glanced over her shoulder, gave them a quick once-over and broke into a trot.

Rick dug out his badge case as he sprinted after her, his long-legged stride easily covering the distance and leaving Jim hobbling along behind. "Police officers, ma'am. We'd like a word with you."

She cut her eyes at them again and reluctantly slowed her pace but kept moving. Rick caught her, danced a step ahead and flashed his winning, boyish smile. "Can we talk to you for a moment, please, ma'am? Can't blame you for being concerned. It's okay, we're police officers."

He exuded a wholesome, good-natured warmth, his strength in dealing with strangers, especially women. She responded with a small, guarded smile. Once certain there was no threat, the little dog began to yap furiously.

"Pookie," she chided. "Be a good boy, make nice." She placed the dog on the sidewalk, keeping him taut on a short leash.

"What a good little watchdog," Rick crooned while Pookie snuffled suspiciously at his shoes.

"He's a Lhasa apso." The owner beamed proudly, clutching her wrapper coyly around her, over what appeared to be a cotton nightgown.

The man does have a way with women, you have to hand him that, Jim thought, puffing up behind.

"Are you Bal Harbour policemen?"

"No ma'am, City of Miami detectives. We're interested in what happened last night at the shopping center."

She smiled, nodding with obvious relief and blinking behind her glasses. "I was afraid you were enforcing the new law."

When both men looked blank, she scrutinized them suspiciously, as though debating whether or not they were really police officers.

"The pooper-scooper ordinance. You have to carry scoops and little bags, to pick up the, uh, you know, doggie doo-doo."

"Doggie doo-doo?" Jim repeated, a look of wonder on his face. "You have police officers who actually enforce that?"

"Oh yes," she nodded. "It's a one-hundred-and-fifty-dollar fine for the first offense. If you get caught a second time, it's a five-hundred-dollar fine and a possible jail sentence. I *always* bring the scoop and carry Pookie's doo-doo home during the day," she assured them, her posture defensive, "but at night, in the dark, it's difficult, and Pookie usually does his . . . business in the morning anyway, after he has his breakfast."

The detectives nodded solemnly, in unison. "Sounds reasonable to me," Jim said.

"Makes sense," Rick said. "You were out here last night when it happened?"

"When what happened?" Her eyes were inquisitive behind her bifocal lenses.

"The shooting and the fire at the shopping center."

"Oh yes, we were out here, as usual. We always take our walk before the ten o'clock news. We never used to see strangers on the street here at night," she said, her expression apprehensive. "This neighborhood is changing."

She and Pookie continued their stroll as the detectives walked alongside.

Pookie paused to do something indelicate at the base of an umbrella tree. His owner looked concerned.

The men ignored it. "Did you see anything suspicious?" Rick asked.

"Well, I heard the excitement, the sirens and the fire engines. We walked up there for a look, to see what had happened."

"We?"

"Pookie and me. His real name is Prince Pook Song."

"Did you see any strangers or any strange cars in the neighborhood?"

"Just the one, walking away from the shopping center fast, all out of breath, parked right over here, I think," she said, stopping to squint at the curbside and then at Pookie, who was licking the sidewalk. She tugged at his leash.

"Did you get a good look at this stranger?"

"Well, we talked for a moment."

"What did the man look like?"

"Oh, no," she said, shaking her head, "it was a woman, a blond woman."

"A woman?" The detectives exchanged disappointed glances.

"What did she look like?" Jim asked, his voice weary.

"Almost like a man, from a distance. She was wearing jeans, some sort of windbreaker, blue, I think, and tennis shoes. She had a baseball cap under one arm and she was carrying a pair of glasses, sunglasses, I believe."

She opened a wooden gate and stepped into a small, well-kept yard. Rick wet his lips and reached out for her hand. "Ma'am, my name is Sergeant Barrish, and this is Detective Ransom. We'd like to talk to you some more, if it's all right with you. Do you mind if we come inside?"

Her hand was still in his. He did not look like a man who had been on the job for eleven hours or spent most of the night humping a fellow detective. Prince Charming had just found Cinderella. "Of course not," she said, gazing up at him. "I can fix us some iced tea. It'll just take a minute. Come on, Pookie," she said, and led them into the house.

TWENTY-EIGHT

T he suspicion struck like thunder during the drive home. Rick nearly swung into a U-turn toward Pigeon Plum, but decided against it. If what he suspected was true, seeing Dusty now would be the worst possible move. Crazy, he thought, crazy enough to be true. He might have already committed a major screwup. Furious at himself, he felt physically ill. He hoped Laurel would be asleep, but saw lights and heard the chatter of the police scanner as he opened the front door.

"Well, look who's here." The tone was almost confrontational.

"What the . . . " He did a double take. Laurel was parked in front of the TV. She had already turned her attention back to a wrestling match on one of the cable channels. She wore one of his T-shirts and was leaning forward, a can of beer in one hand, her forearms resting on the thighs of her blue jeans. The body language was tough, distinctly unfeminine. Her eyes glittered at the action on the screen. "Gotcha," Rick said. "Now I know who's been drinking my beer." He bleakly regarded the tag-team match in progress. "I didn't know you liked that stuff."

"What did you expect, soap operas at this hour?" Her voice was husky.

She leaned back suddenly, placing her hands on the armrests of her chair, her face softening. She looked up, eyes full of sleep. "Rick," she breathed, then glanced at the clock. "What time is it?" Her voice sounded mellow and befuddled.

He stared at her, then shook his head. "Late, babe. You really ought to get some sleep." He walked past her into the kitchen, realizing how little he really knew this woman who was sharing his life. He needed a drink.

She followed, looking down at the shirt and self-consciously tucking it into her jeans. "Is anything wrong?"

"I cut the night short because I have to get an early start tomorrow."

He took the bourbon from the kitchen cabinet, stared, puzzled, at the level in the bottle for a moment, then poured two fingers into a water glass and downed it grimly.

"What's wrong?" She looked big-eyed and scared, like a little girl.

"A case," he said. He shook his head and poured again.

"Rob's murder?"

"Yeah, partly."

"What about it?"

"It's all fucked up."

"Do you know who did it?"

"Maybe. No. I don't know."

She stepped close, hugged him around the waist, pressed her face against his chest and started to cry. "I'm scared," she said.

"Hey, I didn't mean to lay this on you," he said, brushing the blond hair from her forehead. "There's nothing for you to be upset about."

"I can't be alone at night anymore, Rick. You need to be here. Don't leave me alone again."

"Goddammit! Don't start in on that now. I need to think."

He pulled away, took his drink and marched out the back door into the warm night.

"Rick?" She stood at the door behind him.

"Get some sleep, will you? I need to be alone for awhile." He sat in a chair on the little wooden dock for a long time, nursing his guilt along with his drink and gazing across the water at the city skyline. Moonlight bathed the Centrust tower and the Metrorail bridge, a neon rainbow that straddled downtown. He loved the sight—it never failed to soothe him—until now. "How could something that feels so good be wrong?" The words echoed in his mind. He must be wrong. He had to be crazy. But it all fit—it all tied in. What if he was right?

He did not go inside until dawn began to lighten the sky. He was surprised that Laurel had not slept. She was busy, vigorously scrubbing something in the kitchen. He could smell bleach. She never looked up, and he went to bed—alone.

*R*ick was waiting at the city personnel office when it opened. He copied some information out of a file, went to headquarters and dialed the Jericho, Iowa, police department from his desk.

A woman answered, apparently the dispatcher. She sounded young and bored. The chief, she said, was out of town, gone to Sioux City to pick up a prisoner.

Rick identified himself and said he needed some information.

"I'm afraid only the chief can help you."

"It's about an officer who worked for your department a few years back."

"The chief will be back in a day or two."

"Her name is Mary Ellen Dustin."

There was a pause. "So that's where she is, Miami."

"You know her."

"I never met the woman, but I know *of* her. I guess everybody here does." The voice was now alive with interest and juicy malice.

"Well, maybe you can help me out," Rick said, turning on the charm. "I know it's tough working for a small-town department. Sounds like you're holding down the fort all by yourself there."

"You've got it," she said. "Everybody's out on the road."

"This is strictly a nonofficial inquiry at the moment," his voice dropped confidentially. "You know, sometimes you just need to know who you're dealing with."

"Sure thing."

"She must have been quite a policewoman out there if you recall the name so well without ever meeting her."

"Police work is not exactly what she was known for." She sounded cute and gossipy.

"So what is her claim to fame?"

"Well, I wasn't here when it all happened," she said slowly, "so you really have to talk to the chief"—the official disclaimer out of the way, her voice eagerly picked up speed—"but she ran around with a married man, with a family, you know, a love triangle and all that. Then they all wound up dead, and she got run out of town. Hasn't shown her face here since."

Rick closed his eyes, his fingers tightening around the telephone receiver. "What happened? Was it homicide? Did anybody go to jail?"

"A lot of folks thought somebody you know should have. But like I say, I wasn't here, and I've got to go now. Call back and talk to the chief."

He could hear a radio in the background, somebody repeating a request for her to send a tow truck. "When did you say he would be back?"

"Day or two, he didn't rightly say."

Dusty arrived from court a short time later. Smiling and confident, she wore a bright red blouse and a white wraparound skirt. The judge had ordered a psychiatric evaluation for Terrance McGee, who was being held without bond. When Rick saw her, he slipped the photos he had prepared into his top drawer.

"Jimbo," he whispered to the detective sitting across from him, "don't mention our witness or anything about the case to Dusty. Nothing."

"Why the hell not?" he growled under his breath. He looked surprised. He had been admiring the way Dusty's skirt showed off some leg as she swung by their desks.

"Hi, guys. Hear you found a witness. What's the scoop?"

Rick's head shot up from an FBI bulletin he was studying. "Who the hell told you that?"

"The grapevine, guys. I'm a detective. I work here, remember?"

"I hate it when other investigators mouth off about cases that don't belong to them." He glared accusingly around the huge room.

"What's the problem? Don't tell me it's gonna be one of those days. Woof! Somebody throw our sergeant some raw meat," she said to Jim, who was grinning.

She removed the fresh red hibiscus she wore in her lapel, put it stem down in a coffee cup, filled it at the water cooler and came back humming. "You look like hell," she commented, passing by Rick's desk. He did not answer.

"Can't say the same for you," Jim said. "You look terrific."

"I feel terrific." She glanced at Rick, who did not look up. "I cleared my case pretty fast, you must admit."

She sat down, crossed her legs and removed some legal papers from her briefcase.

"I need to talk to you about that," Rick said abruptly.

"Yes, Sergeant." Dusty smiled expectantly.

"That must have been quite a shock, finding the woman's head in the damn freezer."

"Well, I must admit, I will never look at my Kenmore in quite the same way again. Let's just say it was one of those unforgettable moments that occur from time to time in this business." She tilted her head and studied Rick's face. "Didn't you get any sleep?" Her eyes began to mirror his grave expression.

"It had to be a helluva shock," he said, ignoring her question. "I want you to see Doc Feigleman to help you through it. Set up an appointment—and go on home now, take the rest of the day off, comp time. I already cleared it with the lieutenant."

"I don't need it, Rick. I've got tons of paperwork. I also got the warrant and want to go through Terrance's apartment with the lab. He sends you both his best, by the way, though he is beginning to regret not making use of the city's landlord-tenant dispute hotline."

Rick shook his head. "I'm serious, Dusty. Go home, chill out. Hit the beach, work on your tan, whatever. And go see the shrink ASAP."

She looked from Rick to Jim, who shrugged, grimaced and rolled his eyes simultaneously. "I'm a professional," she said quietly. "It is nice of you to be concerned, but I go to autopsies all the time. I've seen lots of dead bodies, admittedly never between the Mrs. Paul's fish sticks and the turkey TV dinners, but I am fine. In fact I feel terrific because we wrapped this one so quickly."

"It's an order." His voice held the ring of finality. He looked impatient. "Taking some time off and seeing the doc is mandatory, SOP when a police officer is involved in a shooting or injury incident, and I think the shock you experienced yesterday is as traumatic in many ways."

"May I speak to you in private, Sergeant?"

"I see no reason for it. Nobody else is in earshot. The three of us have no secrets. Do we?"

Jim shuffled papers, suddenly pretending to be busy.

"What's wrong, Rick?" Her voice was low and personal.

He shook his head, his face closed, his eyes focused somewhere behind her.

"Is this some chauvinistic, paternalistic bullshit?" she demanded. Suspicion and anger were fast replacing bewilderment. "I am no sissy and no pantywaist. If I had to run to a shrink everytime I stepped in a little gore, I couldn't hack this job. And I damn well can. We all know that. What *is* this? Whose idea is this?"

"I'm doing you a favor. Take off. Now."

"Can I go too?" Jim said hopefully, trying to break the tension.

"No," Rick said. "You stay."

"You're trying to get rid of me."

Rick did not answer.

Quietly, without another word, she gathered up her belongings and slammed her briefcase shut.

The minute she was gone, Jim parked himself on Rick's desk. "Now she's really on her high horse. What the *hell* are you doing?"

Rick opened his mouth, but the telephone interrupted and he picked it up. It was the front desk. "Shit," he muttered to Jim, "she's downstairs already."

Ten minutes later a public service aide, a black youth in a blue uniform shirt, escorted Ms. Viola Sneath into the fifth-floor homicide office. She wore a paisley print dress, clutched a handbag the size of a satchel and carried a sweater. Miami natives carry sweaters or jackets on the summer's hottest days because of the uncontrollably frigid air conditioning inside most public buildings.

"Oohh," Jim murmured to Rick in mock disappointment, "she didn't bring Pookie."

Viola Sneath peered alertly from behind the smoke-tinted lenses of her eyeglasses and focused on Rick as he rose to greet her. "So this is where you work."

"This is it," Rick smiled. "Would you like some coffee?"

"I think so," she said. "It's so chilly in here."

Rick held her sweater as she struggled into it. "Cream and sugar?"

"Both," she said pleasantly. "Your young man came for me promptly at nine, but he was driving a patrol car. Pookie barked and barked." She giggled girlishly. "I don't know what the neighbors think."

*I*n the interview room, Ms. Sneath fretted and plucked at the threads on her sweater. "I told you boys last night, I probably won't be much help. It was very dark, with just the streetlight. My bifocals are new, I'm not quite used to them and there was all that excitement at the shopping center."

"All we ask is that you do the best you can," Rick said. "Often people remember more than they think. Sometimes a face will jog their memory. You don't see many strangers in your neighborhood, you're an alert and perceptive person. You may remember this individual better than you realize. Just go slow and look at each one carefully."

She solemnly placed both hands on the table, as if for a seance.

Rick spread out a set of six pictures.

Ms. Sneath scrutinized each one, carefully examining both the full-front mug shot and the profile. "No," she said slowly, "that one's too heavy, and the hair on this one is all wrong."

"Keep in mind," Jim said, "people, especially women, can change their hairstyle, change the color, even alter their looks with makeup. Try, if you can, to zero in more on their features."

She nodded, pursing her lips in concentration. "This one is . . . oh my, is that a tattoo?" she said, peering closely at another. "Does that really say—"

"Yeah," Jim said bleakly.

She finally leaned back in her chair and shook her head. "She's not here."

"Okay," Rick said patiently. "How about these?" He dealt out a second set of pictures, one by one, like playing cards. The muscles in his jaw worked.

The first batch had included a few female robbers and the wives and girlfriends of known holdup men. The second was a mixed bag. One was long dead, a firebug who had loved to call and taunt firefighters after torching hotels. Another would soon be dead, a much-arrested prostitute suffering from AIDS. Then there was a woman who had thrown her children off the roof of a Miami apartment house, another who had murdered her brutal husband in his sleep, a fifth who robbed banks, and Miami homicide detective Mary Ellen Dustin.

Jim's eyes widened when he recognized Dusty's picture, shot a few years earlier for her detective ID card, but he said nothing. Viola Sneath hesitated, then picked it up for closer study.

"This one looks familiar," she said.

"Is that the woman?" Rick asked softly.

"I told you I can't be sure. But she certainly looks familiar. The hair was similar, quite blonde. It could be someone like this."

Jim and Rick stared at each other across the table.

"I couldn't say for sure. I told you, it was dark, there were sirens, my glasses. . . . But she sort of looked like that, on that order. I think I've seen that face."

"You think if you saw a live lineup, with real people, that you might be more positive?" Rick asked.

Viola Sneath sighed, pulling her sweater more tightly around her. "I really don't know," she said quite honestly.

Rick took her hand. "Thanks for all you've done. You'll hear from us."

*W*haddayou, crazy?" Jim raged once she was gone. "What the fuck is going on, and why didn't you tell me?"

"I didn't have time and I wasn't sure myself."

"She's a pro, she's a cop! You're saying . . ." Jim could not bring himself to say the words. He looked around the office as if the whole world had gone mad.

"I feel the same way you do, but it all fits. There is something wrong, she's always been secretive. She goes off to the shopping center and never arrives, but the robber does."

"But that means—whoever was at the shopping center killed the Thorne kid and the convenience-store clerk."

"Yeah. She just happened to be the first at the scene when Rob Thorne was shot. She was off when the clerk bought it. The opportunity was there every time. And whoever did it used a .38 detective special."

"That don't prove nothing. Half of Miami owns .38s. Why? What motive? Why would she—?"

"Maybe she was after somebody else the night Rob Thorne got killed."

"Who, for Christ's sake?" They stared at each other. "No." Jim was shaking his head. "No way."

"Laurel could have been the target. I started thinking last night about how secretive Dusty has always been about her past. Every time the subject of her life in Iowa comes up, she gets hinky and snaps shut like a clam. I called out there this morning. It looks like she is hiding something, something serious. She might be really screwed up, Jim. Remember that note, that obscene note that Laurel got? I think Dusty wrote it. I think she's got problems."

"Not the least of which is you. You're saying the motive is jealousy, that all this might have happened because you dropped her for another woman? What makes you think you're such a . . ."

"Back in Jericho, Iowa, she got into a love triangle and some people supposedly got killed. Evidently that's why she left town and came here."

"What exactly happened?"

"I won't know until I talk to the chief, and he's out of town."

"I ain't buying it," Jim said flatly. "Did you happen to compare Laurel's handwriting to that note?"

"What the hell do you mean?"

"Come on, I never mentioned it 'cause I thought you'd figure it out all by yourself. She's pissed 'cause you're working midnights, especially with Dusty. She's lonesome. Little girls crave attention. They get lonely. We see fake rape reports all the time. Lonely little girls who want attention. Sometimes lonely little girls even report phony threats."

"Bullshit! Not Laurel."

"She wants you to rush home and hold her hand."

"Give me a break, Jim. I know what her handwriting looks like. It wasn't hers."

"You sure? You know how cops all have a blind spot when it comes to people we're close to."

"Son of a bitch. You're the one who's blind. She was scared as hell. Laurel may be young and somewhat spacy. Sometimes I don't even know who she is. I don't think she knows herself. But that kind of crap, it's beyond her. She wouldn't do a thing like that in a million years."

"Sure. She's such a perfect angel that you decided to camp out at Pigeon Plum the other night."

"Now, that's really your problem, isn't it, Jim?" He jabbed his index finger fiercely. "You're jealous. You've always wanted to ball Dusty yourself, haven't you? I admit I got carried away the other night . . ." He gestured helplessly. "Because of it, I could be in deep shit right now."

Jim glared straight into his eyes. "Exactly where you belong in my book, pal."

"It's time we hand it off to internal affairs."

"What? Without even talking to her, giving her a chance?" Jim was incredulous.

"We can't compromise the cases. Christ, two people are dead, Laurel could be in danger, and the suspect is our partner."

"Damn straight she's our partner!"

"Jim, I care about her too. Too damn much, in fact. But something's not right. It could be real wrong. We have to report it to IA so if she is in trouble she can get help, so nobody else gets hurt and so we all don't go down with her. I'm going to catch heat anyway, once they find out about the other night. Jesus, what a mistake."

"So you're gonna blow the whistle? Listen to me. Whad I tell ya about cops and sex? Think about it." Furious, he lowered his voice as Mack Thomas and another detective passed by, looking curious about their heated discussion. "You're so ready to run to IA, but what have you got? You'll make us look like damn assholes. We've got nothing but your own guilty conscience which brought on this stroke of genius. You know the first thing they'll do when they start investigating her is find out if she's been screwing around with any other cops who might be involved. You'll blow the whistle on yourself. This thing could backfire."

He stared grimly at Rick, letting the words sink in. "If I thought for a minute that Dusty was guilty of murder and robbery, I'd put her ass in jail myself, in a heartbeat." He glowered at Mack Thomas, now talking into a telephone across the room. "You know anybody who hates bad cops more than me? Let's talk about this rationally and see what we got."

"The witness, Mrs. Sneath . . ."

"Who says 'looks familiar, can't be sure, new glasses, it was dark, the fire . . .' Christ, the woman's bifocals are as thick as the lenses in Mount Palomar."

"Jim, I tell you again, you're the one who's blind. You want to protect Dusty, you care about her. You'd sell your soul for a night in the sack with her. But she's hiding something, always has been, about her past. You know yourself that some people who become cops shouldn't, that there are behavior patterns, skeletons—"

"No problem," Jim said. "I'll find out the particulars, like you should do before making accusations. If you're right, I'll be the first to admit it, but I think there is some explanation for all this, and I think your imagination has run off half-cocked because of your screwed-up sex life."

Rick opened his mouth to protest, but Jim stopped him. "I know all about your gut feelings, but this one ain't right, Rick. It ain't right."

"Nonetheless, while she's not here, we've got to start drafting a memo to IA, just in case we have to move fast and send it upstairs to cover our own asses."

"It's your decision, but don't be too quick to put your foot in it. She ain't going anywhere. She loves this job, she loves Miami. And she's nuts about you."

"Thanks a lot, partner," Rick winced. "I really needed to be reminded of that."

Jim's reply was scathing. "A helluva lot better men than you would consider themselves damn fortunate."

TWENTY-NINE

*D*usty did as always when troubled. She pulled on a T-shirt and shorts and drove to the beach. The weather wavered between beautiful and threatening, a kaleidoscope, sharp bursts of blue sky and green water, changing form and color into gray sky and slate sea. The day mirrored her life lately, bright moments of passion and exhilaration evolving swiftly into dull heartache and frustration.

Her spirits had soared, knowing it was not over forever with Rick after all, pleasure heightened by the quick solution of the Vandermay case, one of those puzzles that starts out complex, then suddenly fits together with ease, click, click, click. She should have known such a roll could not continue. Winning streaks never last. But what the hell was happening now? She was baffled. After their night together, she was certain Rick would go on wanting her. At least for as long as they were in close proximity, working together. Dusty was a realist. She knew that if her job was in jeopardy, the relationship could be too. They were perfect together, but out of sight is out of mind. What was wrong? Was it something she had done? Or not done? Was he was having a case of the guilties? Or trouble with Laurel? She had been totally unable to read him. Jim seemed just as puzzled, although by now he must know what the hell is going on.

She could not resist. She parked her red Datsun near the boardwalk, dropped a quarter into a pay phone and dialed homicide, willing Jim to answer. If anyone else did, she would hang up. She did not want her voice recognized and her name called out within Rick's hearing. She hated callers who hang up. She hated herself.

Jim did answer. "It's me," she said miserably. "Can you talk?"

"Not exactly," he said.

"Rick's there?"

"You bet."

"Am I in some kind of trouble?"

"Could be, but no sweat," he said, not unkindly.

"Whatever it be, I isn't guilty," she wailed in a mock lament.

His only reaction was a grunt. The situation must be worse than she thought.

"Well," she said briskly. "Whatever it is, put in a good word for me. You still are my buddy, aren't you?"

"Count on it."

"I'm off to the beach," she said with false gaiety, and hung up.

She wanted to cry. Instead she took a deep breath. She would use the energy to burn calories, give her heart and lungs a good workout and refuse to think about it, she decided, sniffling a bit. Son of a bitch, she thought. Whatever it was, she would know soon enough. What was that old prayer AA uses? "Grant me the serenity to accept the things I cannot change, the courage to change the things I can, and the wisdom to know the difference." Later, she decided, she would pamper herself with a long hot bath and a good dinner, maybe even cheesecake, without guilt, if she worked out hard enough. Hell, it's a day off, she thought and vowed to enjoy it, no matter what. Pressing her hands against the seawall, she leaned into it, stretching her hamstring muscles, then trotted down onto the sand.

It was a Winslow Homer sort of day, she thought, brilliant blues, muted greens and a wash of gray along the shoreline. Running on the beach always instilled in her a sense of freedom and well-being. A gusty northeast wind kicked up low clouds of gritty sand that discouraged sunbathers, so the beach was almost all hers. She watched the surf evolve to a phosphate green. A wall of white fleecy clouds tumbled together on the endless eastern horizon.

She began to run south, barefoot in the wet sand, the wind at her back. A cruise ship, probably the *Emerald Seas,* was sailing out the channel into open ocean from the port of Miami, bound for fun and frolic in the Bahamas. She smiled wistfully. Once she and Rick had talked about escaping for a weekend in the islands. Someplace remote and lazy with white sugar beaches and no telephones, where they would not have to see anyone or dress up, a hideaway for swimming in crystal-clear water, basking in the tropical sun and making love. What had gone wrong?

She let the wind and the salt air sweep the clutter of the past few days from her mind and concentrated on the slap of her feet on the hard wet sand, her breathing and the sound of the wind in her ears.

Her hair whipped against her face. The pink Art Deco tower of South Pointe rose in the distance. She fought intrusive thoughts of Rick and headquarters by counting the freighters and fishing boats and the occasional sail rising where the sea meets the sky.

The light changed in an instant, scattering seabirds before it. Stormclouds, dark and ominous, were boiling up in the west, moving swiftly, spirited squalls heralding their arrival. The few sunbathers fled, their beach towels and blankets flapping uncontrollably in the gathering storm. Summer lightning pirouetted crazily across the western sky. The wind and the dropping temperature made running and breathing easier. She was able to pick up speed, pumping hard.

She welcomed the storm without fear, in no mood for caution. Lightning lit up the west again, closer now, over Miami. It will strike in the same place twice—or more, she thought, remembering the man struck by lightning more often than anyone else who ever lived. A park ranger, he had drawn lightning to him like a magnet. He had survived seven strikes before committing suicide.

Fatal lightning strikes more often in Florida than any other state, but she knew that in Miami people stand a far greater chance of being murdered. She had handled several lightning deaths during her police career. Life can be so deadly and so unpredictable, she thought, like this city she loved. What was it Jim always said about death? It's the last thing you do, when it's the last thing you want to do. She remembered the men caught on the golf course by a storm. Nine people or so. Only one hit. The small change in his pocket was blackened by the electrical charge. The worst, she thought, was near the Japanese Garden on the MacArthur Causeway. Tourists and their six-year-old son walking, snapping pictures. The boy ran ahead, chasing a squirrel. The sky was still postcard-perfect blue, although a summer storm stalked the horizon. The boy was hit, the parents spared. He died after weeks in a coma. She remembered the others, ticking them off in her mind. The teenager carrying a boom box that apparently lured the fatal strike. The old man fishing from his small boat. The lightning that killed him danced right up the fishing line and the pole he was using.

Shaken survivors had described to her the tingling, the hair on their arms and the backs of their necks standing on end in the split second before the fatal strike. It is not the voltage but the amperage that kills. A quarter of an amp at precisely the right moment will stop your heart.

She had read all the police brochures and booklets advising Miamians how to protect themselves against a welter of perils, including the murderous side of Mother Nature. One dealt with lightning, sternly warning those caught out in the open not to seek shelter beneath a tree during a storm but to lie facedown in a ditch. Dusty had never met anyone who had done so. She imagined a golfer shouting to his partners, "Hey, guys, looks like a storm, let's go lie facedown in a ditch."

The thought made her smile. Another flash, closer now, over the bay. Out of control, she thought. That was why she was so upset. Her life seemed out of control. She was accustomed to being in charge. After what had happened back in Jericho she had sworn that her life would never slip out of control again.

Turning at South Pointe, she plunged headlong into the wind without stopping, retracing her steps north. Salt air stung her face, along with tears, and she felt chilled despite the exertion. Roiling clouds were dumping their rain at sea in a solid gray wall visible from the shore. The sun suddenly broke through as the fickle storm briefly battered the beach with high winds again, then sailed swiftly to the southwest. Breathing hard, she saw a brilliant green-yellow-pink rainbow appear in a wide arc over the eastern horizon, across a bottle-green sea that faded to pale jade at the water's edge.

She slowed her pace to absorb the colors and the beauty. A light rain was falling, as soft and sweet as a baby's kiss. It felt cleansing and warm on her skin. As she gazed up in awe, the rainbow doubled into a second, wider arc sweeping across the entire horizon in breathtaking splendor.

Miami, with its stunning rainbows, storms and summer sunsets, this is where I belong, she thought. I belong with Rick too. The double rainbow was an omen. She had ridden out the storm and was still strong, still on her feet. Things can't be all that bad, she told herself. It will be all right. It will.

She carried that thought with her.

THIRTY

usty reluctantly kept the appointment with Dr. Feigleman. She dreaded and resented it. Seeing a shrink was, to her, a sign of weakness. On the farm where she'd grown up, back in Jericho, you did not whine, or cry, or run for help when things went wrong. You worked through it, you carried on. Strong and self-disciplined, she kept her secret hurts to herself.

She hoped all the people she worked with would not learn about her session with the shrink. Feigleman was not famous for keeping secrets. Though in private practice, he was also consultant to the department. His quotes about the problems of police officers appeared regularly in the newspapers, and he often granted radio and television interviews. He never mentioned names, but everybody always seemed to know who he was talking about and who was seeing him. Dusty did not want to become a case study for one of the many articles he wrote for police and FBI journals.

Feigleman did not see officers at headquarters, in order to preserve their privacy. His office was located in a medical building, but it was near the justice complex, and there is no more fertile ground for gossip than the police community. Talk about little old ladies, Dusty thought, cops are the worst of all.

She cringed inwardly at the touch of Feigleman's cool but clammy skin as they shook hands. His mustache was neatly combed, and his face over the bowtie was attentive and almost too eager. She made it clear that the session was not voluntary on her part and that she considered it unnecessary.

"The first step to solving our problems," he said cheerfully, "is to confront them."

She did not answer, and he began to discuss stress management, stress overload, conflict management, chronic tension and burnout.

"People change when they become police officers," he concluded, folding his hands in front of him. "You become tough and hard and cynical, because you must. It helps you to survive, but sometimes you find yourself behaving that way all the time and it becomes a problem."

"But if you became emotionally involved with all the things you see on the job, you'd wind up in a padded cell."

"Are you ever afraid?"

"Of course. Anybody who's not afraid is a fool. It's cops who are not afraid, who think they will live forever or who become complacent and fatalistic, who get hurt or killed. Fear is your best friend. The trick is that you can never show it."

"Any job-related personal difficulties?"

"I like to handle my own problems." She knew as she spoke the words that she'd said them too quickly, too sharply. He seemed pleased and waggled a warning index finger at her.

"That is typical of the subculture police officers belong to. Emotional problems are seen as weaknesses, and therefore a threat to your macho image as 'the crime fighter.' "

"I like to think of it as being grown up," she said sweetly.

"Any problems with alcohol?"

"I drink socially, but no problem."

"How much do you drink?"

"Wine, with dinner."

"How much wine?" He was trying to appear casual.

"Doctor, there is no problem there, I can assure you."

"Are there ever mornings after when you can't remember what happened the night before?"

"Good God, no. Maybe sometimes I wish I *could* forget." She could not resist that little self-deprecatory remark, though she knew she should have. He scribbled something on a yellow pad in front of him.

"Sex problems?"

"Only lack of. I'm single, doctor, with no immediate prospects."

"Do you have a problem relating to men?"

"Not as much a problem as most men have relating to a woman who carries a badge and a gun and can put them in jail."

The way he fidgeted and rubbed his smooth hands together while discussing her sex life made her uncomfortable. He was obviously eager for something kinky, something to write about in his next article.

"How's your relationship with your father?"

"It was fine."

"He's no longer with us?"

"He lives in Iowa, still operates the farm where I grew up. I haven't been back there for some time."

"Is there some reason?"

She hesitated. "Yes," she said. "I love Miami."

"It isn't much like Iowa, is it? Working in homicide, how do you manage to cope with the horrors you encounter daily, such as opening the freezer in that suspect's apartment the other day?"

She suddenly realized that her arms were tightly folded in front of her, body language that must make her look defensive, like a suspect, for God's sake. She quickly unfolded them and for a split second was not sure what to do with them. She wished she had accepted the coffee he had offered when she arrived. A cup would have been something to hold on to. She placed her hands demurely in her lap. "As a professional," she said carefully, "you can't express emotion, disgust or anger, but as a human being, you do have feelings. I try to convert that energy into motivation, to get the job done, to solve the case, to seek justice for the victim. And I try to work off the physical stress with exercise. Want to see my bicep?"

He smiled, his long fingers forming a pyramid in front of him. "Am I that intimidating? You're acting like a little girl sent to the principal's office."

"Maybe I feel like the little girl sent to the principal's office for no good reason."

"Do you like your life? Is it good?"

"Almost," she said, and smiled wistfully. "Only one thing missing, and I'm working on it."

After she left his office, he glanced at what he had scribbled on his notepad: "Needs to get laid." Chuckling, he tore off the page, crumpled it and tossed it into the wastebasket.

$\mathcal{D}$usty strode into homicide, relieved that the session was over. A message was waiting.

J.L. had called, wanting her to meet him "in the garden with the Fat Man."

"Can you make any sense of that?" asked the puzzled secretary who took the message.

"Yeah." Dusty smiled. "When did this come in?"

"Ten, fifteen minutes ago."

$\mathcal{I}$t was a short drive to the Japanese Garden on Watson Island, just off the MacArthur Causeway. Donated to the people of Miami by a friendly Japanese industrialist years ago, the garden is just minutes from downtown. The perfect place to meet a confidential informant, centrally located and safe. The only other visitors are strangers. Out-of-towners. Local people almost never visit their own tourist attractions.

A small, open-sided teahouse and a pagoda grace the garden, but the centerpiece is a giant stone statue of Hotei, the incarnation of happiness. The Fat Man. Rub his big round belly, so goes the tradition, and good fortune will find you.

The garden was one of J. L. Sly's favorite haunts. He was practicing his kung fu moves at the edge of the reflecting pool.

"Miss Dustin, or should I say Miz Dustin, or perhaps Detective Dustin?" Loquacious as usual, he wore a white shirt open at the throat and white trousers.

"Just Dusty," she sighed. "We've known each other long enough, J.L. Once you read somebody their rights and put them in jail, I guess you're on a first-name basis."

"Dwelling upon the flaws in the universe can lead to bad karma."

"I'd glad it's behind us," she said. "No hard feelings?"

"It was but a moment in infinity." They strolled together over the small wooden bridge. "But something is troubling you."

"Is it that obvious?"

"You may hide something from the world but nothing from a true friend of the spirit."

She sighed aloud. "It's a long story that neither you nor the spirits want to hear." They sat on a stone bench shaded by a silver buttonwood.

"Perhaps I can brighten the day of one so beautiful."

"Try me."

"At the occasion of our last meeting, after the unpleasantries we have all put to rest, I recall your partner referring to two gentlemen of the Colombian persuasion, one of whom might have certain characteristics about his countenance."

"You mean a singed face." Dusty was suddenly all attention.

"You are full of wisdom, as well as beautiful."

"You have a line on where they are?"

"Indirectly. A certain lady of their acquaintance has come to my attention."

"Where can we find her?"

"In business at the Jolly Roger Motel and Dream Bar on Biscayne Boulevard. The name is Little Bit. She has been heard to discuss a number of encounters with the two gentlemen in question, both before and after one of them lost all the hair on his face in an unfortunate mishap. She entertained them at a location shared by a brief acquaintance of mine. He was extremely uncommunicative. He wore a tag on his toe."

"Bingo! Thank you, J.L.," she said fervently.

"And now, tell me what dark cloud has cast its shadow across your countenance? Is there some dragon I can slay, some wrong I can right, in order to restore your smile?"

"No, this information sounds good. It really helps. The rest I have to take care of myself. But thank you."

"If happiness be your destiny," he told her, "you need not be in a hurry."

She brightened. "You know, you're beginning to make sense, J.L. That probably should worry me."

She fought the ridiculous impulse to hug him. His words, she thought, are the second good omen in twenty-four hours. Everything will be all right, she told herself. She rubbed the big belly of the grinning stone statue for luck and left the garden.

*7*hey picked up Little Bit not long after dark. She was flagging cars on the Boulevard. Business must have been slow at the Dream Bar, an intriguing establishment with only twenty stools but at least eighteen "waitresses" usually on the premises.

A thin dishwater blonde with a ruddy complexion, Little Bit smoked crack and spoke a smattering of both Spanish and Creole, just enough for basic communication with her clientele. She was wearing cutoff blue jeans and a halter top. More provocative attire was currently unfashionable among the Boulevard hookers because of recent vice squad crackdowns. In more modest dress, the girls could insist that they were not loitering for purposes of prostitution but simply on the way to the store. Which is exactly where Little Bit maintained she was going when their unmarked car pulled up and spooked the middle-aged motorist with whom she was conversing. He drove off in a hurry.

She was smart and streetwise and all of nineteen. "What is this fucking shit!" she screeched. "I was just going to the store for a quart of milk and some bread! The guy was asking directions. I'm a taxpayer! You've got no right to stop me, you, you're not even vice cops," she howled.

"Aha, bound for the supermarket with no money, no ID, no underwear and a pocket full of condoms," Dusty said, as she searched the pint-sized prostitute. "And, oh, look at this neat little device." She removed a box opener the size of a pocket comb, with a razor-sharp blade, from Little Bit's waistband and passed it to Jim. "The perfect accessory to wear for shopping."

"Ya never know what you'll encounter in the checkout line," Jim said reasonably.

"It looks like she was obstructing traffic, soliciting for prostitution and carrying a concealed weapon," Rick said.

"And she seemed like such a nice girl," Jim said. "Too bad we have to put her in jail."

"You can't get away with this!"

"Maybe we won't have to," Rick said.

Little Bit was hyper, red in the face, and watery-eyed with anger. "What do you assholes want with me?"

"Just a little information."

"Go fuck yourself!"

"Tch, tch," Jim said. "Add public profanity and disorderly conduct."

"We're looking for two friends of ours," Dusty said. "Latinos. One had a little accident, burned his face."

"Those assholes?" Little Bit looked repulsed at the very thought of them.

"I see you're acquainted."

"I ain't saying nothin'. They're crazy."

"We know," Rick said. "Just tell us what make of car they're driving, where they're staying, their names."

She opened her mouth, then her too-bright eyes flickered for a moment as though recalling something unpleasant, and she thought better of it. "I ain't saying nothin'." Little Bit had apparently come to the conclusion that she was better off in jail than risking the wrath of the Colombians.

"Okay, fuck you, lady!" Jim said. "You're going to jail."

Little Bit shrugged her skinny shoulders and looked unconcerned. "Not only that," he growled, "I'm gonna put your ass in jail every time I drive down the Boulevard. Your days of live and let live with the policemen on the beat are all over, because I'm gonna bad-mouth you to them, and they're gonna put you in jail too. You're not only gonna go to jail whenever I'm working, you're gonna go to jail everytime you stick your little fart face out the door."

"Come on, Jim, don't be so tough." Rick turned to Little Bit and flashed his boyish smile. "Just tell us what we need to know and you can be on your way, sweetheart."

"I'm not your sweetheart," she glowered.

"Add accessory to armed robbery and illegal transportation of a dead body," Jim said, ticking more charges on his fingers.

Little Bit was becoming unnerved, not by their threats, but by the scrutiny of other street people across the Boulevard. "It's gonna cause me problems, being seen talking to you pigs. Arrest me. Hurry up," she said. "I don't want to be seen standing here with you."

*L*oved your good guy, bad guy act," Dusty teased after Little Bit was booked at the women's detention center. "Too bad it didn't work."

"It will," Rick said. "We'll ask the judge for ninety days and then have another little chat with her."

"I wonder if she's had an AIDS test lately," Dusty said. "The poor little thing really should have a checkup. Did you see how pale she is? I wonder how long she's been on the street?"

"You could always post her bond, take her home with you and play big sister," Jim said.

"I have enough problem people in my life already," Dusty said playfully, cutting her eyes at Rick, who had been deliberately distant all evening. "But thanks anyway."

THIRTY-ONE

ittle Benjie from next door was visiting and Jennifer was giddy with excitement. They jumped up and down on the bed, hurled pillows and screamed with laughter. They ate cake and ice cream and colored with Benjie's Crayolas. Jennifer was quite pleased that she stayed inside the lines better than he did.

aurel was afraid of being alone. She usually welcomed company, even a three-year-old, but this time she had been reluctant to baby-sit. She could not trust herself to be responsible for a child. She was too upset, too much was happening. She was even afraid to go to the fitness center to exercise, because of violent, terrifying dreams about Barry, the aerobics instructor. Another new torment was the magazines. She had to reach the mailbox every day before Rick so she could hide them. She had ordered the *Reader's Digest* from an advertising brochure that offered a selection. She had mentioned it, and Rick had no objection, but now she was besieged—bombarded. A dozen others kept arriving, as well as some packages, such as a pink plastic squeeze device with springs, intended for enlarging one's breasts. The bust enhancer arrived in a plain brown wrapper. So did the leather G-string. She hoped at first that Rick was playing some tasteless joke, but she did not tell him, because deep down, she knew: He was not responsible. They all came addressed to her. So did the bills. She must have ordered them. She was missing more and more time, and she was terrified that she was losing her mind.

She had wanted to make excuses to Beth, but there was no way out. Beth's pregnant sister in Kendall had gone into premature labor after a minor auto accident. Her insurance executive husband was out of town on business.

Without warning, Beth had appeared at the door, Benjie holding her hand. He was already in his pajamas, carrying his coloring book and crayons. "Would you mind?" She said it was a family emergency. "I have to go to the hospital to be with Sue. I can't take Benjie, and Ben has got to go find out where her car has been towed to and what the damage is." She did not wait for an answer. "Honestly, Laurel, I don't know what I did before you moved in here." She hugged Benjie and told him to be good. He nodded solemnly.

"No tears. He *loves* to come here," Beth whispered to Laurel. "I'll call you in a couple of hours. He should be sleepy, he only had a short nap this afternoon."

Benjie waved at his mother's car from a front window, then turned expectantly. She was already waiting, impatiently shifting her weight from one foot to the other. "Hi, Benjie," she whispered. "Laurel isn't here anymore. I'm Jennifer!" He whooped with delight and they ran, giggling, to play trampoline on the bed.

W anna play policeman?" Jennifer asked. They were smeared with chocolate ice cream and tired of coloring.

"Yeah, policemans," Benjie said.

Jennifer knew where to find Rick's old uniforms. Some of the shirts still bore the lightning-bolt insignia of the motor squad. The shiny boots were in the closet beneath them. Benjie put on Rick's visored police hat. It nearly covered his face. Pushing it up, he aimed a pudgy forefinger at Jennifer. "Bang! You're dead!" Jennifer clutched her chest dramatically and fell. They shrieked with glee.

"Want to see something?"

"Yeah," said Benjie, game for anything.

"Come on," she whispered.

"Okay," he whispered back.

He tiptoed behind Jennifer to the night table on Rick's side of the bed. She slid open the drawer and lifted some folded T-shirts.

"It's Rick's," she said proudly.

"Ohhhhh," Benjie breathed in admiration.

The gun did look impressive, bright stainless steel with a short barrel.

"It's real," he whispered. "Can I hold it?"

"Okay," said Jennifer, "but now it's my turn to wear the hat." He gave up the cap with little reluctance, enthralled by the shiny new toy.

Benjie's small hands could barely manage the weight of Rick's off-duty gun, a snub-nosed .38-caliber Smith and Wesson detective special. The weapon flopped heavily to one side. "Bang, bang," he shouted, jerking the gun at Jennifer.

Then he turned it toward his face and peered gravely down the barrel.

Pointing it again at Jennifer, he held it like a cowboy he'd seen on TV. Two little thumbs straining, he pulled back the hammer and cocked it.

"Jesus Christ!" Alex had emerged, hurling Jennifer against the wall, out of the line of fire. Lunging at Benjie, he snatched the gun away. Knocked off balance, Benjie sat down hard and began to wail.

"You could've killed somebody! This is not a toy for kids to play with," Alex said. "Christ!" He held the hammer with his thumb, squeezing the trigger and letting the hammer down slowly. He flipped open the chamber, dropped the load, five hollow-point bullets, into his hand and stared down sternly. "Real guns are only for big people like me who know how to use them." His voice was husky. "That's what the hell is wrong in this town. Nobody has any respect for guns. Got me, kid?"

Whimpering, Benjie nodded.

"Jennifer's been a bad girl," Alex said. "She knows better. Shoot her and we're all in deep shit. You want to play with her some more?"

Benjie nodded, tears still glistening on his cheeks.

"Only if you promise to leave the gun alone."

"I promise."

Jennifer again emerged. Badly frightened when Alex had thrown her against the wall, she was crying too. She wiped her tears with a balled fist. "We can't play policeman anymore."

Benjie nodded and then looked puzzled. "What was his name?"

"Alex," she said, pouting. "He's a bad man."

"Wanna watch cartoons?"

"There are no cartoons on now," Jennifer said contemptuously. "It's too late." She thought for a moment, then brightened. "I know another game, a kissing game."

Benjie looked guarded. "Okay," he said uncertainly.

"Good," she said, unbuttoning her clothes. "Take off your pajamas, and I'll get Teddy."

THIRTY-TWO

*L*ittle Bit could not believe her good fortune. The social worker trying to recruit her to participate not only in AIDS testing but in a job-training program had slammed out in a snit. *It must have been something I said,* she thought gleefully. Now she was alone in the interview room at the women's detention center.

The setting was not bleak, grim and institutional. There were no bars, in fact. The walls were painted yellow, with brightly colored murals. This was a cheerful place where inmates, called "residents" by the guards, could visit in comfort with their lawyers, their bail bondsmen, their families and even their children. There was lilting piped-in music, color TV in every room and even a fully equipped, inmate-operated beauty salon, where prisoners could have their hair done and their fingernails manicured before receiving visitors or making personal appearances in court. All in all, it was not a bad place. Even the food was good, prepared by inmates undergoing job training in the culinary sciences.

What Little Bit liked best about this new state-of-the-art jail, however, was the high window in the first-floor interview room where she sat, without restraints, waiting interminably for a matron to escort her back to her room. The window looked easy to open. It unlatched, to swing down during months when air-conditioning was not necessary and provide ventilation in a room where the inmates and their visitors often smoked.

Little Bit dragged the wooden table over to the wall. She placed her chair atop it, then climbed up onto the table. Standing on the chair, she could easily work on the window latch. "No problem," she murmured.

In her crack cocaine–induced hyper state, from which she knew she all too soon would crash, she began to wonder if this was too easy. Maybe those asshole cops who busted her were setting her up for an attempted escape rap.

She was just paranoid, she decided. The people who ran this user-friendly jail would not be party to any such setup. That would be entrapment and a violation of her rights.

The window came down with a creak and a fine scatter of dust. Then it was just a matter of getting a good grip on the top frame, hoisting herself up and throwing one leg over. The screen did not appear to be attached to any alarm. At least she could not see one. She hesitated, then heard a step in the corridor outside the room below. Now or never. Planting the sole of her foot firmly on the screen, she kicked it out. No alarm. Not an audible one, anyway. The screen made no clatter when it fell. What a break, she thought, the sidewalk below did not extend to the wall of the building. Instead, there was fucking grass and flowers. Landscaping. What a great jail! She would not have minded a longer stay, had it not been for two outside attractions, crack cocaine and her man, Jake the Snake.

The drop was no sweat, about twelve feet, onto soft dirt and grass. She clung to the lower frame of the window, stretched out her legs and let go, landing soundlessly, in a crouched position. Little Bit trotted across the street, stuck out her thumb and hitched a ride to the Boulevard with a friendly postal employee on his way home from work.

THIRTY-THREE

*A*fter Benjie and Jennifer fell asleep, Harriet climbed out of bed to clean up the mess. She was furious. That little bastard, she thought, fuming. Red crayon ground into the rug. Ice cream stains on her crocheted tablecloth. The bedclothes were a tangled mess, and the guest towels lay crumpled and sodden on the bathroom floor. The toilet had not been flushed, .and the seat was wet. That was the last straw.

She stalked into the kitchen and drew the seven-inch butcher knife from the block on the counter. Pondering it for a moment, she slid it back into place and reached for the meat cleaver instead. She smiled at her reflection in its stainless steel surface and admired the curved easy-grip handle. Handcrafted in Germany, it was her favorite piece of cutlery. The cleaver never needed sharpening, but she liked to sharpen it anyway. She carried it to the bedroom and gently pushed open the door. Benjie was curled up in the middle of the bed, all rosy and angelic. His thumb was in his mouth and his eyes were closed.

Fury coursed through her as she watched him drooling onto her quilted bedspread. Her fingers tightened around the handle of the cleaver, then her shoulders sagged as she sighed audibly. The timing was not right.

It just would not do when they were so close to having it all. Action now, no matter how justifiable, would surely upset the others. Alex seemed to tolerate the little brat surprisingly well and Jennifer would be inconsolable at the loss of her only playmate. Marilyn was already furious because of what happened to Barry and because Laurel had tried to send back her breast enlarger. Laurel had rewrapped the package, addressed it and put it in her bag. Marilyn had emerged to unwrap and hide the thing. She used it faithfully for an hour every night, squeezing it between the palms of her hands, trying to build up those chest muscles. Afterward, she would strip in front of a mirror, examining her breasts from all angles, trying to discern an increase in her measurements.

Disposing of Benjie right now could create enough excitement to push Laurel over the edge. No telling what she might do. She was already shaky—especially since the scene at the post office, when she had emptied her bag searching for the parcel she intended to return to sender. Harriet could sense her mounting hysteria, particularly after she discovered the new black dress, appropriate for a funeral, hanging in the closet. The magazines had rattled her, too, because of the bills. How could she pay them? Well, that's her problem, Harriet thought. I am certainly entitled to Good Housekeeping *and* Home and Garden *and* Gourmet. *Alex had demanded* Sports Illustrated, True Detective, Popular Mechanics *and* Penthouse. *So it seemed only fair that Marilyn should have* Playgirl, Cosmo *and* The National Enquirer. *And poor little Jennifer, all she wanted were subscriptions to* Jack and Jill *and some magazine about raccoons and woodchucks. It did not seem like too much to ask, so Harriet had helped her fill out the proper forms.*

Reluctantly, she replaced the cleaver in her kitchen and finished cleaning up the mess. Soon she would have time to sit down for a cup of coffee and a few telephone calls. She and Alex had alternated lately, dialing Tawny Marie at four A.M. *If not for Benjie and the chance that Beth might call or pop in at any time, they could have driven over to Pigeon Plum Circle to see if Rick and Dusty were at it again. Let them fuck around while they still can, she thought malevolently. She took out a notebook and began to sketch plans for converting Rick's study into a sewing room. Harriet was looking forward to getting married and becoming a police widow.*

Then she could have the place all to herself.

THIRTY-FOUR

*R*ick stood in the doorway, gazing at Benjie and Laurel curled up together in peaceful slumber. The scene was touching after a tense tour of duty. The memo to internal affairs was written but not yet sent. It all seemed too impossible to believe, but stranger things happen all the time in Miami. He hated uncertainty. His usual unerring instinct for guilt was skewed. He was too close. Too much guilt of his own was involved. Dealing with strangers is so much easier.

The telephone rang, and he hurried to take it in the kitchen.

"What? Are you sure? Goddamn son of a bitch! How the hell? I don't believe this. Have uniforms hit the Jolly Roger Dream Bar and the Boulevard from Twenty-sixth Street to Seventy-ninth. Maybe I'll come back in for a while to see if we can pick her up fast. Shit! That broils my butt. We needed her."

Laurel and Benjie trooped into the kitchen now, sleepy-eyed and curious. She was pulling on a terrycloth robe. Rick put the telephone down. "I'm sorry it woke you," he muttered.

"What time is it?" She was apprehensively studying the wall clock. "Did you say you're going back to work?"

"Just for a little while," he said, angrily pacing the kitchen and rubbing the back of his neck. "They lost a prisoner on us. Let her escape. Damn!"

"Coffee?"

"Yeah." He saw Benjie staring wide-eyed. "Take my advice, Ben, don't grow up to be a policeman. It's too frustrating."

"I like policemens," Benjie said, looking hopefully at a tin of fresh-baked brownies on the sideboard.

Laurel poured two cups of coffee and a glass of milk. She wanted to tell Rick about the clothes, the magazines, all the lost hours and the inexplicable events that were frightening her, but this was not the time.

"It's that country club of a jail," he was saying, "the women's detention center. What the hell kind of operation are they running over there anyhow? We put this . . . woman," he said, glancing at Benjie who sat at rapt attention, "that we're trying to flip in there last night to chill out. Apparently they go off and leave her in an interview room with some social worker who takes off. Before they send somebody to escort our prisoner back to her—her suite—she drags the conference table over to the window, puts a chair on top of it, climbs up, opens it, kicks out the screen and out she goes. By the time those cretins noticed she was missing she was probably . . . having a beer in Opa-Locka."

"You mean she *jumped* out the window?" Laurel, like Benjie, was all eyes. "Did she get hurt?"

"It's no big deal. It was probably only ten, twelve feet, onto grass. And she was motivated. Wait till Dusty hears this. She's gonna be PO'ed."

Laurel poured cereal into a bowl for Benjie, who looked disappointed, his big eyes still caressing the brownies. She watched Rick, hoping that when he calmed down, they could talk. Maybe after Benjie goes home, she thought hopefully.

He got up from the table, paced the length of the kitchen twice more, then gulped the rest of his coffee. "I'm gonna run back out and see if I can spot her in her usual haunts before she relocates."

He ruffled Benjie's hair in passing, then slammed out the door. She winced at the sound of gravel flying as he backed too fast out of the driveway.

Two hours later he was back, empty-handed, frustrated and still raging about sloppy security at the women's detention center.

THIRTY-FIVE

Jim squinted painfully in the sunlight that streamed into the fifth-floor homicide office. He was using the WATS line before going home.

A woman dispatcher had answered his first call to the Jericho police department. The chief was back in town but out on patrol, she said. Chief Quincy Berke returned his call forty minutes later. The first thing he asked about was Miami's weather.

"It's hot, muggy, miserable and the natives are restless," Jim said. "Business as usual."

"Miami must be quite a place. Never been there. Always thought I'd like to take a trip down sometime. But with all the stuff I read about in the newspapers, I'm not so sure." The voice was jovial.

"One of your people did a few years back. She stayed."

"You must mean Mary Ellen." The chief sounded enthusiastic. "Is she working for you?"

"You mean Detective Dustin?"

"Detective. How do you like that? It had to be six years or so ago, I got a call and a reference form to fill out for a preemployment background investigation by Miami PD. Never got any more requests for references, so I figured she got herself the job. She is a sharp girl. Is she okay?"

"She's been doing a helluva job, homicide detective now."

"Homicide. Knew that girl'd go places. She don't keep in touch."

"So, she worked out on your department?"

"Sure. She was the first woman we ever hired. Had a few since—none as good-looking as her. She still a head turner?"

"For sure, chief. Her folks lived out there, didn't they?"

"Still do, Tom and Claire farm a place about thirty miles out of town."

"Why'd she leave?"

Jim heard the breath go out of the police chief in a whoosh, like a balloon deflating.

"Wanted to see the big city, I guess." The words were flat, did not ring true.

"There was another reason . . ."

He was fishing. The chief bit.

"Is Mary Ellen in some kinda trouble?"

"Did she have trouble there?"

"There was a ruckus."

"You never mentioned it in the background investigation."

"It didn't seem proper—or fair. It was a personal thing, didn't directly relate to the job she did out here."

"What happened?"

"Well, now, Detective, that's all water under the dam. No sense dredging up the past. She's a nice girl, got a whole new life down there. I'm shore she wouldn't appreciate it."

"Guess it was her love life, huh?"

"You got it. The scandal's died down. People don't hardly mention it anymore."

"What happened?"

"The man was my lieutenant, a good man, but married too young—shotgun wedding. She had the baby five months later. Was always high-strung, a jealous type. They had their problems. Next thing you know, they was separated. Well, he and Mary Ellen were working together, and you know how that is."

"Yeah, tell me about it," Jim muttered.

"The next thing you know, they had something going, hot and heavy. It just drove the wife wild. I don't blame Mary Ellen, she was young and he was separated, living by hisself in a trailer. He kept saying he was getting a divorce but never really started the paperwork. He'd go by to see the baby, guess it would get his wife's hopes up. She was always pestering him at work, I guess it was the one place she knew to find him. Even slashed the tires on his patrol car once right outside a the station." The chief chuckled at the recollection.

"She was always threatening suicide to get his attention. She called the station one night, and he went by there. To stop her from doing anything, I guess. Looked like she got him into the bedroom, and they was getting real friendly again. Hell, they *were* married. Looked like when he was all relaxed and dozing, off guard, she picked up his gun and shot him right in the temple. Then she killed the baby and took her own life. Found her lying across his body, the gun right there."

Jim winced. "No question it was murder-suicide?"

The chief hesitated. "Not to my mind. There was some talk, malicious gossip."

"That Dusty was involved?"

"Yep. The wife was crazy as hell. Before she pulled the trigger on herself, she called the station and said Mary Ellen had threatened her and her family. But hell, Mary Ellen was working that night, helping the troopers handle a bad wreck up on the interstate. Wasn't even near the place. Forensics confirmed the murder-suicide.

"The other police wives had been giving Mary Ellen the cold shoulder all along. You can imagine what they were like after the bodies were found. There was no living here for her anymore.

"Mary Ellen loved the job, but this is a small town and the women here just didn't want her working with their husbands, plain and simple. They gave her all kinds of grief. So did some of the church people. Her parents had never approved of her seeing a married man. They were hard on her too."

"That's it? Nothing else?"

"Hell, ain't it enough? It was king-sized scandal in this here town. I guess that's why she decided to lose herself in the big city. Jericho ain't no Miami, and I'm glad for that."

"Me too," Jim said.

"Is she all right?"

"Terrific," Jim said. "She's just great."

"Married?"

"Nope."

"Well, if you should mention that we talked, tell her I was asking for her and wish her all the best."

"Sure will, Chief." Jim sat at his desk and smiled. The truth about the deep dark secret in the past of Mary Ellen Dustin was tragic, but nothing for Rick to panic about. The rest of Rick's suspicions could probably be laid to rest as easily. Struck by a sudden hunch, he reached for the telephone again.

Prescott Williams strolled into homicide five minutes later with the loose-limbed undulating saunter native to his Overtown neighborhood. His shoulders tilted and his hips swayed as though keeping time to a rap beat that only he heard. This was a subdued version of his usual shuffle. He tried to maintain a low profile at the station so as not to offend high-ranking nonblacks who might take exception to his image. A street-grown boy who had somehow stayed out of trouble, he had become a blue-shirted public service aide at eighteen and hoped to attend the police academy when he was twenty-one. He smiled happily at Jim, who groaned inwardly and hoped fervently to be long retired before anybody ever gave Prescott Williams a badge and a gun.

Jim waved him toward a chair. "Sit down, Prescott."

Prescott sat, expression placid.

"Remember the day last week that you brought the lady witness in here from Bal Harbour?"

"Yeah, the old lady with her own little K-9 dawg," he grinned.

"You met Pookie."

"Yeah, yeah, that's what she say his name was, I think. He come right at me, all tooth, until she called him off my ass."

"Yeah, this life is full of peril, Prescott. Now what happened when you brought her to the station?"

"Nothin'." Prescott looked apprehensive. "What she say? I brought her up here, just like you said." He fidgeted uncomfortably in his seat.

"She didn't say anything. You did everything right. No problem, Prescott. Listen to me, it's important. I want to test your skills as an investigator, as an observer. Tell me everything that happened after you pulled into the parking garage."

Prescott studied Jim from under heavy lids at half-mast. Crossing one long leg over the other, he leaned back and stared at the ceiling, contemplating the challenge, his lips tight together. Then he leaned forward, both feet on the floor.

"We pulls into the parking lot, see, and I drop the old lady by the elevator 'cause there was no spaces close by. Those guys from SWAT always grab all the visitor parking," he said, his expression indignant. "They know they not supposed to park there, but they do it anyways 'cause it by the elevator." Prescott stared again at the ceiling, brow furrowed, for a good twenty seconds. "I park the car, then I go meet the lady by the elevator which we jump to go to the lobby." He looked for approval to Jim, who nodded pleasantly.

"Den we git to the lobby, and me and the lady signs in. The old lady had to give the sergeant a piece of ID, and he give her a pass to clip it on her dress. I calls upstairs to the sergeant, you know, who sent me to git the lady—to announce our arrival."

"What then? Remember now, every detail, who you saw, who you talked to, what happened."

"Well, den we had a little problem." Prescott looked sheepish. "Nothin' serious. I temporarily mislaid my key card for the lobby elevator to homicide. Lef it back in the car. But we already called upstairs to say we coming up, and I know the sergeant, he don't like to wait. So I look around the lobby for anybody with a key card. The elevator opens and out come the big blond lady detective, you know. The bad one with the big . . ." he gestured. "She in a big hurry, she look pissed off at somethin', stomping acrost the lobby. But I ast her if she would just let us use her key card to jog the elevator into taking us upstairs. So she look at me and the old lady, turn around, and we go back to the elevator, you know, she put in her key card, I punch the button and we go, me and the old lady."

"Did they talk?"

Prescott looked blank.

"The old lady and the blond detective, did they talk to each other?"

"No." Prescott shrugged. "I think the old lady say 'Thank you,' or some such, she was po-lite, but the detective, Dustin, that's her name, that's it, just say 'Welcome,' and take off. She looked put out about somethin', in a big hurry."

"You sure it was Detective Dustin?"

"Sure man, I *know* her. She drop me off to home one night when I first started, didn't have a ride. Nice lady. Nice legs."

"You're gonna make a great cop someday, Prescott." Jim even pumped his hand. Prescott strolled out of the office doing an exaggerated version of his Overtown shuffle.

But not while I'm alive, I hope, Jim told himself. He leaned back in his chair. "Suspect eliminated," he said aloud.

The killer was still unidentified and at large, but at least Rick had not made a fool of himself by running to IA half-cocked. He checked his watch. Rick had gone home after one more fruitless search of the Boulevard for Little Bit. Jim dialed his number.

"He's asleep already," Laurel said. "Should I wake him?"

"No, no emergency. I'll see him tonight."

THIRTY-SIX

$\mathcal{E}$dgy and full of nervous energy, Dusty was unable to sleep. The only way to impress Rick now, she decided, pacing back and forth, is with strictly professional conduct. If nothing else, it would restore her dignity. If she could not have his love—and that prospect was painful—she would damn well have his respect. She would show him she was one helluva detective. She still had some pride. She got dressed, drove to the fitness center and took Tawny Marie's grueling ninety-minute aerobics class with hand weights. Tawny Marie seemed to lack her usual luster. She looked positively hollow-eyed. Dusty learned why after class.

"Barry has not shown up for two days—doesn't even answer his telephone— so I'm handling his classes, and some sicko is calling me all night," Tawny Marie told her.

"Obscene calls?"

"Yeah, weird ones. First it was just hangups, like somebody had a wrong number, but now it's whispers, scary, dirty stuff."

"I seem to be the only one ignored around here." Dusty faked a pout. "I should feel slighted."

"It's not funny." Tawny Marie looked close to tears. "I hate leaving the phone off the hook, but I've got to get some sleep. It's spooky at four A.M., when you're alone and you have no idea who this weirdo is. I heard noises on my patio late the other night. When I put on the light, somebody ran."

"I'm sorry. I didn't mean to make light of it, Tawny. Defensive mechanism, I guess."

"You think it could be connected to the center? Maybe the same person who sent Rick's girl that ugly note?"

"Dunno. Tawny"—Dusty looked thoughtful, as though groping for something elusive—"did you ever date Rick?"

"Yeah, sure, a long time ago. He was real sweet. You too?"

"Yeah. He gets around. I guess we're just pushovers for a pretty face. Think Laurel knows it?"

"I don't know why she would, unless Rick told her."

"Yeah, unlikely."

"You think there's some connection?"

"I don't know. Maybe. Did you try the phone company? Maybe they can zero in on your caller."

"I don't want to make a big deal out of it. I just want it to stop."

"I think I'll go in early today. I have some work to catch up on. I'll talk to the department's contact at the phone company and find out what can be done. Where do you think Barry is?"

"Not a clue. It's not like him to just not show up. Nobody's heard from him. He better have a good excuse."

*T*he station was Saturday afternoon quiet. Dusty intended to finish the paper work in the Vandermay case and review the files on Rob Thorne and the convenience-store clerk. A notice on her desk called for volunteers to work security at two big Labor Day political rallies. The chief wanted minorities to be well represented because of the expected news coverage.

Unenthusiastic about the prospect, she wondered if Rick and Jim were also being recruited to take part. If they did it, she would. She checked Rick's desk to see if there was a notice in his basket. Riffling through a sheaf of papers, her own name, typewritten, jumped out at her. She slid it from the stack. The yellow carbon of an official memo to internal affairs, re Detective M. E. Dustin. She felt her heart beat in her throat. Her knees went weak as she read and reread it in disbelief. Words and phrases sprang off the page: "a possibility that this detective is a suspect in two homicide cases as well as armed robbery and attempted murder . . . witness . . . photo lineup."

How crazy, insane. That explained Rick's behavior. But how could he suspect her? He knew her, she loved him, they shared so much. She wanted to scream and pound the walls with her fists. He actually thought she was capable . . . of all this. She wanted to trash his desk and fling reports and papers everywhere. Trembling, she sat down in Rick's chair and read it again more carefully. This was no joke. Why hadn't Jim told her? They've been busy investigating me, she thought.

She had to talk to Rick. She reached for the phone, then hesitated, mind racing, panic rising. She had to get out of here, she thought, glancing around the big room to see who was there. Internal affairs would suspend her, pending the results of their investigation. That was routine procedure. The department had weathered the recent trauma of cocaine-linked cops suspended and arrested, fired and indicted for crimes ranging from narcotics trafficking to robbery to murder. Suspension was official action and therefore public record. Somebody always leaked it to the press. There would be a story, a picture, a pointed finger that would haunt her career and reputation. You never live it down, she thought, even if you're cleared. She could not walk away and start over somewhere else. She could not begin again. Where would she go? What would she do? With this suspicion, this taint, she would never be able to work as a police officer. Anywhere. She looked around fearfully. She had to get out of there. Automatically, without thinking, she rolled a form into the typewriter. Her hands trembled on the keyboard as she filled in an official request for several days' leave due to a family emergency.

Heart pounding, she left a copy in Rick's mailbox. Another went to their lieutenant. She felt like a thief in the night. The front desk officer who waved when she walked in might have had instructions to notify IA when she arrived. Somebody could be on the way right now to serve her with suspension papers. She nearly ran, took the elevator to the lower level, avoided the central lobby and front desk and walked shakily to her car, all senses tingling, stomach knotted in panic. Security cameras were mounted everywhere, monitored at a console in communications. Somebody might be watching. She had to control herself and think clearly. Go home, pick up a few things and check into a motel. From there she would figure out what to do.

Images of arrested officers flashed through her mind. Each arrest a major news event. Crowds of reporters eager for footage of a cop in handcuffs being led away by former colleagues, photographed, fingerprinted, jailed.

She drove out of the parking garage, checking her rearview mirror uneasily. She had to think rationally. There had never been any clue that she knew of, any hint that the killer was a woman. Hell, how could she pass for a man? Rick and Jim had found a witness after the shopping center caper. Now she knew why Rick had become cold and evasive. That was when it started. All because she did not go to the shopping center, driving around instead, feeling sorry for herself and listening to blues songs on her Walkman instead of the damn police radio, mooning over Rick because he was almost killed and then talked about marrying Laurel and making babies.

Would she ever learn? What was wrong with her? Other women fall in love and live happily ever after. Here she was, almost thirty, in love only twice and both were disasters.

Rick is not a bad man, she thought. He may be spoiled when it comes to women, but he is fair. She was sure she could convince him she was no criminal, explain away his doubts. Murder Rob Thorne? Christ, that adorable young kid. That Rick and Jim could consider it even for a moment was inconceivable.

She loved those guys. Rick and Jim were family, as much family as she had any more. But now she felt her family turning on her, accusing her. It was déjà vu. It had happened before, in Jericho. God, what was lacking in her that she could not inspire love, trust or loyalty in those she cared about most?

She turned off the expressway exit toward Pigeon Plum Circle. She would drive by first to see if anybody was waiting. Maybe IA was delaying action until Monday, but she doubted it. Not with allegations this serious. Damn, her red car was a dead giveaway. She bit her lip in anger. They can't do this to me, she thought bitterly. I won't let them.

THIRTY-SEVEN

*H*ow could I be so wrong?" Rick shook his head in disbelief. "No doubt in your mind?"

"Of course not," Jim said.

"And the guy in Iowa, he was a cop she worked with?"

"Yep. No wonder she never talked about it."

"Shit, the wife and kid. . . . The poor bastard. He must have been a jerk."

"Looks like her taste in men never did improve."

"Where the hell is she anyway?" Rick shuffled through his mail. "She's late. Uh-oh. Look at this." He leaned back in his chair, reading a document he held in his hands. "From Dusty, requesting emergency time off, as of now."

"Oh, no!" Jim said. "You know how she always shows up early on weekends. Where's that memo you were gonna send to IA?"

"The original is locked in my desk, but I think I left a copy in the basket here with some other stuff." He began to fumble through a stack of reports and memos.

Jim looked pained. "What do you wanna bet that *if* you find it, it's got her pawprints all over it."

"It's not here."

"Christ, call her right now. Ya never shoulda left that lying around."

"Dusty, if you're there, pick it up," Rick told her answering machine. "Call me. ASAP. At the office."

"Damn," he said to Jim. "That woman will never trust me again."

"Forget trust, try begging for mercy."

"This also puts us back at square one in the case, though I'm sure not sorry. At least we know that our man *may be* a woman. If our only witness is so suggestible that she picks somebody out of a lineup because she saw them downstairs twenty minutes ago, we have to seriously doubt her credibility."

"Not necessarily. I'm betting she saw what she saw. A woman or maybe a transvestite. I think it was a blonde. Some other blonde."

"We gotta make this up to Dusty, Jim."

"Whaddaya mean *we*? I told ya you were full of it."

7 he shift was typical Miami Saturday night; two critical bar shootings, a natural and a suicide by hanging. Both men tried Dusty's number whenever they had a break, the last time was just before dawn. Only the machine answered.

"You don't think she'd take this so seriously that . . . she'd do anything, do you?"

"No, she's cool," Rick said, but he swung by Pigeon Plum Circle before going home. Nobody there. No sign of her car. He scrawled "Call me" on the back of his card and left it on her front door. He also checked the Southwind and the parking lot at the fitness center. Maybe there really was a family emergency and she'd gone home to Iowa for a couple of days. But he doubted it.

Rick found Laurel crushing mint leaves between her palms, so that the warmth of her skin would enhance the scent.

She wore a gingham apron and oven mitts and her face was flushed from peering into the oven. Something smelled heavenly. "Leg of lamb," she announced. "I'll serve it cold later. It's a classic recipe." She smiled proudly. "It's all crusty and the juices stay sealed in until you slice it."

"Sounds great." He pecked her cheek and wandered toward the bedroom. "Dusty hasn't called, has she?"

Laurel straightened, staring after him. "No, Rick," she answered. "Haven't heard from her. Didn't she work last night?"

"No, she took some time off. There was a misunderstanding, and she may think she's in trouble at work." He yawned. "I'm gonna get some sleep, but if she calls, wake me. I need to talk to her."

Laurel appeared in the bedroom doorway. She looked concerned. "It's nothing serious, this trouble, is it?"

Rick looked sheepish. "No, but she might think it is. It's all my fault. That's why I need to talk to her. She may be upset. So wake me up."

"Of course," she said.

He removed his shirt and peeled off his undershirt. She watched the muscles ripple in his back. "I could stay awake for a while," he said smiling, his eyes tentative. "If you want to stay and entertain me."

She seemed taken aback by the suggestion. "I have something on the stove, it needs watching," she replied briskly, and bustled a retreat to the kitchen.

Moments later Marilyn took over from Harriet. She stripped, leaving her clothes scattered on the kitchen floor, all except for the gingham apron. She tied it around her waist, slipped on her stiletto heels, took the can of Reddi Wip from the refrigerator and sashayed into the bedroom. Almost dozing, Rick was thinking about Dusty when he heard the hiss of the spray can and felt the cool sensation on the most private parts of his body. He forgot Dusty as he helped the sensuous woman with the apple-green eyes remove her apron.

He dreamed later that he was in paradise and it was full of fluffy white clouds and yellow-haired angels with flocculent sweet-tasting wings.

*H*arriet was in the kitchen when Dusty called at about four P.M. "I hate to bother you, Laurel, but is Rick there? I need to talk to him."

Her voice was serious, with a sense of urgency.

"Gee, Dusty, he's asleep and he left strict orders. I'm not to wake him up for the pope." Her voice was apologetic.

Dusty sighed. "It's kind of important."

"I know, he said you had a problem. Sounds serious."

There was an embarrassed silence. "It's police business, Laurel." She sounded a bit testy.

"Well, you know Rick," she said cheerfully. "He tells me everything. He did say he needs to see you—in person."

"When will he be awake?" Dusty sounded hopeful.

"Oh, he didn't mean tonight. He said not to call him at the station. He wants you to come here. Tomorrow. Tomorrow evening about seven."

"Will he . . . be the only one there from the department?"

"I think so. That's why he wants to meet here."

"Okay." Dusty sounded uncertain. "I'll see you at seven tomorrow. I'd appreciate it, Laurel, if all this stays just between us."

"Of course," she said warmly. "Do you like Key lime pie?"

"What?" Dusty sounded distracted.

"Homemade Key lime pie? I think I'll make one for the occasion, or maybe pecan. I haven't done pecan pie for ages."

"Please, please don't go to any trouble for me, I'm not much on sweets. Just don't forget to tell Rick I'll be there."

"We won't forget. How could we forget you?"

*R*ick awoke at eight and asked if Dusty had called.

Laurel said she had not, her eyes startled. "Why, was she supposed to?"

Rick glanced at her sharply. "Remember, I told you I need to talk to her."

Laurel looked vacant until she caught Rick's puzzled look. "Oh, that's right," she nodded. "But she hasn't called."

"Still sure you don't want to ride along with me and Jim tomorrow?" he said, pouring himself a cup of coffee. "We won't be back until late."

"Tomorrow?" She looked uneasy.

"When we go to Key Largo to bring his neighbor's boat back."

"When?"

He became impatient. "Jesus, do you ever listen to a thing I say? Tomorrow afternoon. Remember? I asked you yesterday if you wanted to come with us, but you said you had work to do in the garden. Come on, girl, get with it."

"I'm sorry, I can't help it," she cried, and burst into tears. "Oh God, Rick. Something is wrong with me!"

"Hey babe, no sweat. There's nothing wrong with you," he said kindly, and hugged her. "You're too sensitive. I just get a little tired sometimes of living with the absentminded professor."

He swung by Pigeon Plum Circle later, on the way to the station. His card was still in the door.

THIRTY-EIGHT

The yard was a multishaded green tapestry against a stained-glass sky. A royal poinciana erupted in molten metal-red blossoms next to a golden shower that cascaded petals in the afternoon breeze. Harriet wore pigskin garden gloves and a wide-brimmed Panama sun hat to shade her eyes from the glare off the water. She was the one who had declined Rick's invitation, and was relieved now that he was gone. She had vowed not to tolerate any tree or plant that did not produce fruit or flowers. But when she had explained her intentions to Rick, he had objected to removal of his mother's ferns. Apparently the woman had doted on the stupid things. Well, the mother was in St. Petersburg, the son was on his way to Key Largo, and she was in charge. She hummed as she poured weed killer on all the feathery ferns around the rock garden, then sighed contentedly. A weed, she told herself, is simply a plant out of place. If an orchid blooms where you intend to grow cabbages, it is a weed.

Poor Laurel. She would be shocked when the ferns died. She had even called Rick's mother for advice on their care. She would blame herself, as usual. Probably think she overdid the fertilizer. Well, who cares what she thinks. The metal garden shears sang as she trimmed the Ixora. There was so much to do. The mango leaves seemed to bear traces of fungus. The tree needed to be sprayed with copper. She should probably spray the avocado too.

She had discovered why the otherwise healthy avocado had not borne fruit. The trees have both male and female flowers. On some, like this one, the male flowers open only in the morning while the female flowers open to the afternoon sun. In order to fruit, there must be another tree nearby with flowers of the correct gender open at the right time. The fruit tree's mixed-up sex life made her smile. It's as confusing as ours, she told herself and the others. She stopped working for a moment and gazed fondly at the house. When Rick was dead, she decided, she would have a carpenter build window boxes.

She snipped cuttings from a Surinam cherry bush, to root for planting in the sunny north-side yard. On the Singer side she planned something with thorns, perhaps something poisonous, to keep out Benjie, that little marauder.

Her stainless-steel trowel caught the light as she worked amid the beds of pink and white impatiens and shiny-leafed begonias. The shadows were lengthening. She should finish up, she thought. The most arduous task was still to be done. Several bromeliads in big red clay pots needed to be moved from the front to the back of the house. Currently in bloom, their radiant bracts and masses of flowers were breathtaking. The Spanish considered them symbols of hospitality, which might explain why they had been placed out front. But in back, down by the water, their blooms could be viewed from both the patio and the breakfast nook. The clay pots were far too heavy and cumbersome for Harriet to lift. So Alex emerged to do the job.

He hoisted a pot to his shoulder and strode around the side of the house as if it weighed nothing. "Hey, there."

Benjie peeked through the hedge, then stepped into the yard. He wore a blue sunsuit and carried a pail.

"Not planning to dig over here, are you, Ben?"

"Looking for my shovel."

"I don't think it's here." Alex put the pot down. "You being a good boy these days?"

He nodded gravely. "No playing policemens. Where's Jennifer?"

"She can't come out right now. Too much work to do. We've got a big evening ahead. Play nice, kid." Lifting the pot back onto his shoulder, he carried it down to the water as Benjie ducked back through the hedge.

*L*aurel thought she heard laughter but did not know where the sounds came from. She looked around but saw no one. She felt hot and thirsty. No wonder, she thought, seeing all the work she had done. The heat from the sun made her feel a little woozy. She could not even remember coming out here. She would have to clean up the clippings before going back inside to shower and rest.

She twisted the outside faucet, ran the garden hose over her wrists and patted her face with cool water. A movement in the bushes startled her. Her heart pounded. "Benjie!"

His eyes were big, blue and uncertain. She smiled weakly. "How are you, my big boy?" The tot looked up, studied Laurel's face intently, then turned toward the bay with a puzzled squint. After a moment, he looked back at Laurel and frowned. "What is it, Benjie?" She hoped she and Rick might have a little boy like him someday. Maybe they could borrow Benjie for a trip to the zoo on Rick's next day off. She tried to remember when that would be, and scowled. What day is today? she wondered. Her memory seemed scrambled.

"Want to come in for a cold drink? How about a glass of milk or some orange juice?"

He ignored the question and turned again toward the water, where shadows were deepening as the red sun began to sink toward the horizon.

"What's the matter, son?"

"The man," he said gravely, his smooth little brow creased.

"What man?" Her eyes followed his stare down toward the thick sea grapes and the Phoenix palms along the water.

He turned back toward her abruptly, staring. "The man," he said, lifting his chubby hand and pointing. She saw nothing but the shadows among the trees and the dazzle of sunlight sparkling on the water. The bromeliads. How did they get down there? She experienced a curious sensation as a chill prickled her skin, though the temperature still hovered at 85 degrees.

"What man, Benjie? What man? Rick?"

He lifted his eyes, looking precocious. "No." He pursed his lips. "The bad man. Alex."

Alex. A., as in the scrawled signature. Had she locked the back door? She could not remember. Rick had warned her, especially after that frightening note, that even when gardening or visiting a neighbor, she must always lock the door and carry a key. She explored her pockets—no key. The words from the obscene note echoed, as though spoken, in her mind. *I am going to kill you.* She shuddered in the sunlight.

"Benjie." She stooped down to his level, resting her hands lightly on his shoulders. "Did you really see a man?"

He giggled nervously, shook free and danced back a pace, eyes darting down to the water and back again to her. His round, obstinate face wore a look both sly and smug, as though they shared some secret.

"Where's Jennifer?" he demanded.

"Who's Jennifer? Benjie, are you just making up stories?" She pushed back a straggly lock of wet hair from her face. "Where did you see the man, Benjie?" Perspiration dripped from her forehead, though the backs of her knees felt like ice. Something roared in her ears. "Where did you see the man, Benjie?" Her voice was too loud, too high-pitched, she realized. She no longer cared.

The little mouth opened, each baby tooth gleaming like a perfect kernel of white corn. He watched her, and waited.

"Answer me, Benjie!" Laurel tried to grasp his wrist but her palms were moist and he struggled free, scampering backward, just out of reach, his face frightened for the first time. A shadow fell across them both, blocking the late afternoon light.

"Benjie? Stop annoying Laurel while she's working."

Beth was speaking to the child, but her eyes were on Laurel, her expression odd.

Laurel scrambled to her feet, ashamed and embarrassed at how disheveled and sweaty she must look. Beth scooped Benjie up in her arms. "It's time for your dinner, young man. Laurel," she said softly, "you're working too hard, don't push yourself so much. Take a break and leave that stuff for the yard man. It's his job."

She turned and walked into her house, still carrying Benjie, who stared sullenly over her shoulder.

Laurel sank to her knees and gathered the garden tools. The odors around her were pungent and earthy. The maidenhair ferns looked wilted and dead. My God, what was happening to her? She sprang to her feet, ran into the house and with trembling fingers dialed long distance.

"Mother," she said, weeping. "I thought you were coming. It's happening again. I need help, please."

Her mother's voice was sad and resigned. "Your father and I are on the way."

"Thank God." Laurel slid to the kitchen floor, and sat hugging her knees.

A few minutes later Harriet stood, straightened her clothes and dialed the same number. "Everything is fine," she said crisply. "Don't listen to her and don't bother making the trip all the way down here. We'll call you in a few days."

*7*he doorbell rang at precisely seven.

Laurel looked surprised. "Dusty! How are you?"

"Did Rick forget our appointment?" Dusty looked pale and drawn. "I didn't see his car in the driveway."

"I'm sure that if you have an appointment, he'll be here. Come in and sit down."

Dusty appeared confused and uncomfortable. She chose a straight-backed chair near the front window.

"Can I get you anything, coffee, a glass of wine?"

"No, thanks."

Laurel walked toward the kitchen, then stopped for a moment. When she turned back into the room, her eyes and the tilt of her head were decidedly different.

"Dusty, have you seen my kitchen?"

"Not really, Laurel."

"Come on, you must." She beckoned.

Dusty cast a desperate glance out the window, hoping to see Rick's car, then reluctantly followed. She left her purse on the floor.

"This is the most efficient kitchen I have ever seen," her hostess said proudly. "Did you know it was custom-designed? See how the colors are bathed in a warm glow? That's because several tiers of lighting were installed above and beneath the soffit and under the cabinets to illuminate the counter-tops."

Dusty nodded politely.

"And the appliances are all top of the line. A subzero refrigerator," she swung it open, like Betty Furness on TV, "a regular oven, as well as a microwave. And look at all this storage space." She displayed the slide-out shelves for pots and pans.

"It's lovely, Laurel." Dusty seemed impatient. "Do you think Rick will be here soon?"

"Of course not."

Dusty looked startled and cocked her head to one side, as if she had heard wrong.

"As I was saying, when you see this home, this kitchen, you have to understand why I will allow none of it to be compromised or put in jeopardy. We've all discussed it, and we all agree," she said, drawing the filet knife from the block on the counter and turning to Dusty, her hand low, the blade gleaming, "that you will no longer be tolerated."

The knife caught Dusty in the midsection, below the rib cage. "Oh my God. Laurel!" She felt no pain until it was pulled out. She dropped to one knee, staring in disbelief at the blood on her hand and her clothing. Harriet had retreated. Dusty pulled herself up, wincing in pain. She swallowed hard and moved fast toward the door. But Alex blocked her way. He had a gun in his hand and a grin on his face.

*B*eth thought she heard a loud bang about half an hour later. She stopped and listened but heard nothing else for several minutes. Then a car roared out of the driveway next door at high speed, tires spinning on the gravel, then burning rubber on the blacktop. Her mouth tightened in indignation. What a reckless and dangerous way to drive in a residential neighborhood where small children play. The car was red, the same car she'd seen arrive earlier. She dialed Laurel's number, but it was busy. She looked next door and saw the front door ajar. Stepping out into the cool dusk, she crossed the lush green lawn and pushed open the door. "Laurel? Are you there?" Nothing. She stepped further inside and saw blood spilled on the carpet, spattered on the walls and staining the pale flowered sofa. Lamps had been knocked over and the coffee table and a chair upended. She began a low keening when she saw Chuckles, the Siamese cat, blood-soaked and crumpled in a corner. For a wild instant she believed, she hoped, that all the blood she saw came from the dead animal.

"Laurel?" As though mesmerized, eyes huge and haunted, she silently followed the crimson trail, padding down the carpeted hallway to the master bedroom, then looked inside.

Her screams bounced off walls as she ran headlong through the house and out onto the lawn where she dropped to her knees, retching and sobbing.

THIRTY-NINE

*I*t had been a good day, like old times. Rick was relieved that Laurel had not joined them. He needed this. Jim never even complained about being out on the water. They drank beer, talked cases, and as they climbed back into his car at the marina, Rick invited Jim home for dinner.

They swung by Pigeon Plum Circle on the way. Rick's card was still in the door. "Wonder where the hell that woman is?"

"It's not like her to go off and sulk without letting us know where she's at."

"Maybe she left word at the station," Rick said.

A police crime-scene truck whizzed by as they drove leisurely across the causeway. "Wonder where they're headed in such a hurry?" Jim said. They saw the answer when Rick turned onto the island minutes later. The scene seemed a replay of the night Rob Thorne died, the eerie rhythm of flashing lights, the morgue wagon, men in uniform measuring out yellow crime-scene tape. Even a distraught woman in the arms of her husband. The woman this time was Beth Singer. Rick's first thought was that something had happened to Benjie. Then he realized that the tape was being strung around his house and his lieutenant was striding toward the car, his face strained and solemn.

Beth ran toward them. "Rick! It's Laurel! It's Laurel!"

"What the hell happened?" Rick stepped from the car, his mouth suddenly dry.

"Christ," Jim was saying behind him.

Beth's husband caught her and she turned, weeping into his shoulder. "What is happening here?" she wailed. "My baby! I don't want my baby to grow up here."

"I'm sorry, Rick," the lieutenant shook his head. "You can't go in there."

Rick ignored him and bolted for the front door. "Laurel! Laurel!"

Two uniforms, men he knew, barred his way, looking back uncertainly to the lieutenant for instruction. "This is *my* house! I'm going in there."

"Sorry, Sergeant."

"Then you're gonna have to arrest me! It's my fucking house!" He tried to push past them.

"Christ, Lieutenant, ya gotta let him in there for just a few minutes."

"It won't give him any piece of mind, Jim." The thin, sallow-skinned lieutenant ran a hand through his thinning hair and relented. "Go with him, don't let him touch anything. In and out. Taggerty and Dominguez have the case."

The uniforms stepped aside. "The bedroom," the lieutenant said, and turned away.

"Hang in there and be cool," Jim muttered. He held Rick's elbow tight as they stepped carefully. The bed was bloodstained. The body lay on the floor, covered by bedclothes and a gingham apron. A bare, blood-smeared leg was visible, and a sweep of blonde hair. Brain matter clung to the ruffled bed skirt.

Rick moved no closer. "Get me out of here," he whispered, paler than Jim had ever seen him.

Steered out the front door, Rick sank down onto the stone bench where he had found Laurel the night of Rob Thorne's murder. Jim left him there, elbows on his knees, face buried in his hands.

He was in the same position when Jim returned from conferring with the lieutenant. "Beth, your neighbor, heard a shot and saw a red Datsun take off. She found the body."

Rick raised his face from his hands. His eyes were a luminous glimmer.

"Lotsa red cars in the world," Jim said. "We have to go down to the station, give statements."

"Us?"

"Routine. They wanna know about the threat she got, the note. Where we were today, whatever leads you can offer."

Rick got to his feet slowly, like a man numbed by novocaine. Jim guided him to a patrol car. "No." Rick shook him off. "I can drive."

The lieutenant moved to intervene, and Jim stopped him. "I'll go with him. We'll meet you there."

Jim drove. Rick spoke only once. "She was so young. I didn't even say good-bye. She was still asleep when I left this morning."

"We got an early start," Jim said.

*D*r. Feigleman was impatiently pacing the detective bureau. He had responded quickly to the call of a bereavement. This was a unique case. Since his association with the department, he had counseled only two other officers who had lost loved ones to murder. Both were patrolmen. Robbers had killed the young brother-in-law of one, and the sister of another had been shot by an obsessed would-be lover. There had been nothing like this, the young sweetheart of a detective who investigates murders, slain in the home they shared. He double-checked before leaving the house, to be sure that the detective himself was not a suspect. A domestic dispute would not be nearly so desirable a case from his point of view. The department had already confirmed the man's presence on a boat, at a marina, in the company of another detective at the time of the slaying. This would be an extremely interesting case study.

The department chaplain was also waiting at headquarters, clutching a leather-bound Bible and looking soulful. His presence annoyed Feigleman. If Sergeant Barrish wanted a clergyman present, he could call in his own, if he had one. The two men did not speak as they waited. They had never been on the best of terms.

As Rick emerged from the elevator, still clad in a pullover shirt, blue jeans and boat shoes, both men lunged out of their seats and rushed toward him.

"My son," the chaplain said.

"Sergeant," Feigleman said, "it's important to sort out—" Jim brushed them to one side with a sweep of his big hand and a cold stare that meant business.

He steered Rick by them, speaking bitterly from between clenched teeth. "Goddammit! This man has just lost somebody close to him."

"Precisely. Which is why I am here," Feigleman said. "To do everything I can for him."

"He needs words of solace and assurance," the chaplain said. "We can pray together."

"Maybe later," Jim said brusquely.

"The press is already calling," a harried-looking civilian clerk told him.

"No calls," Jim said, "no reporters. Refer them to public information."

A man in uniform escorted a well-dressed elderly couple into the detective bureau. The woman was weeping. The man walked with difficulty, using a cane. Rick swept them into his arms. "How did you get here so fast?"

The woman clung to the front of his shirt as if she was drowning and he was a life preserver.

"Laurel called her mother again earlier today and said she needed help. We started the drive down an hour later. When we got to the house, they told us . . ."

"She called for help?" Rick looked bewildered.

"They want to take a statement from us," the old man said, his eyes swimming. "What happened?"

"We don't know yet," Jim said. He grasped Rick's right shoulder and spoke into his ear. "The ME needs somebody to make the official ID. I'll go. You stay here with her folks. I'll be back."

Rick nodded.

Feigleman and the chaplain still hovered nearby, like birds of prey. Feigleman was scribbling in a small notebook.

FORTY

Miriam manned the front desk at the medical examiner's office. "This is a tough one," she said sympathetically.

"Life sucks," Jim said.

"How is Rick?"

"Not good," Jim said. "They were living together. I don't know what their plans were. He wasn't ready to lose her."

"Not like this," Dr. Lansing said. He had stepped out of the morgue to join them. "From what I can see, there was a hell of a fight. She was sexually molested with a foreign object, looks like a can of hair spray. We'll know better in a little while. They're cleaning the body up right now."

"Let's fill these out," Miriam said briskly, reading aloud as she filled in the blanks on the official forms in front of her. "I, James Ransom, do hereby assert that I have viewed the body and identified the deceased as Laurel Trevelyn, whom I have known for a period of"—she looked up at Jim—"how long did you know the deceased?"

This is all it comes down to, he thought, looking into her bright, questioning eyes: How long did you know the deceased?

"About eight months, but I helped them move her things into Rick's house." Images of that day flickered through his mind like an old home movie. He quickly blocked them out—forever.

"Before you leave, you can sign, and I'll witness the signature," Miriam told him. She patted his hand like a grandmother about to serve cookies and milk.

She's a mess," Lansing said as they entered the morgue. "Shot in the face. It's good that you came by instead of Rick or some family member.

"We took the initial photos, and the guys from the lab were here. They did laser printing of the body. God, that machine is a pain in the ass. She was lying partially on a sheet pulled from the bed, so we wrapped her in that so there would be no contamination and we would be sure to bring everything in with her.

"It was a contact wound to the forehead, the muzzle right against the bone, almost between the eyes. Pulverized the inside of the skull. You can see the result."

She lay on a stainless-steel tray with raised sides locked over the end of a large sink. There was the smell of blood, disinfectant and oily peppermint from the polish cleaner used on the trays. The only sound was the gentle whoosh of water running from two clear rubber hoses. The water circulated around the edge of the tray and emptied into the sink through a hole at the foot.

Her head was raised on a Formica-covered wooden block about four inches high to prevent blood from settling in the brain. Little shape was left to the face, which had collapsed in on itself like a Halloween pumpkin left too long in the sun. Lester, the morgue attendant, had picked up the larger of the two hoses and a fat sponge and was gently washing away the blood. It swirled red, then pink, and eddied away in the constant flow of water.

Jim watched with a clinical curiosity as the routine cleansing revealed the damage. The bullet had taken the left eye, leaving an empty socket. The right eye remained, big and blue. Blue. *Blue.* Jim rocked back on his heels.

"What's the height and weight?" He sounded normal, but his face betrayed him, eyes moving over the long legs, narrow hips, well-developed breasts, the blond hair.

Lester put down the bubbling hose and reached for the chart. "She weighed in at 129 pounds, five feet six and a half inches."

"Doc, tell Miriam to tear up the ID form that says this is Laurel Trevelyn." Jim's fists were clenched. "It ain't her."

Lansing looked startled.

"Take a better look, Doc. You know this lady."

Jim left the morgue quickly. Lansing walked around the tray for a better view. "Oh, my Lord," he said softly.

Jim drove fast, back to the station. "Oh shit! Oh shit! Oh shit!"—he slammed the steering wheel—"Dusty! You were right!" Tears streamed down his face.

FORTY-ONE

*T*he clerk timidly intruded. "I know you're not taking calls, Sergeant, but it's a family member."

Rick nodded, stepped back to his desk and picked up the telephone. His hunched shoulders dropped, and his spine slowly straightened as he listened. He spoke in a voice too low for others to hear, but the tone sounded urgent. A secretary walking by heard the end of the conversation as he pleaded with the caller, "Please, wait right there."

He cradled the phone and walked out of the detective bureau. No one thought to stop him.

*J*im walked into homicide, his face gray. "Where's Rick?"

"That's just what the fuck I was going to ask you," Dominguez said. The short, muscular detective was furious. "We never got his statement. He takes a call, we turn around and he's gone. The guy at the front desk says he took off outta the parking lot like a bat outta hell. What the fuck is going on?"

"I guess he found out what I was just gonna tell him. The body at the morgue, it's not Laurel."

"Whattaya—?"

"Laurel's alive?" her mother asked weakly, clutching at a chair for support.

"Yeah. It looks that way."

"Who the hell is the victim?" Dominguez said.

"It's Dusty."

"You're shitting me. Oh, my God," the short detective said.

Laurel's mother gazed at her husband, her head wobbling back and forth in an expression of denial. "We should have known. We should have known . . ."

"What does that mean?" Jim said.

"Laurel, has always had . . . problems." The father said the word precisely, infused with meaning beyond its definition.

"What kinda problems?"

"You know she is our adopted daughter?"

Jim nodded. "No secret."

"We adopted her late in our lives. She was six years old, a severely abused child. We were in our fifties, foolish and idealistic. We thought we could make up for all that had happened to her by giving her love and the things money could buy. It never worked out. There was always trouble. She was under care. . . . But she seemed to be doing so well that we thought that with a man like Rick . . ." his voice trailed off.

"In other words, you handed your problem off to Rick and blew town." Jim's words were controlled, his eyes accusing.

"It's been very hard for us," the woman said. "We're not young . . ."

"Where the hell is he?" Jim roared to the other detectives. "Did he have a radio with him? His walkie was in the car. Try to raise him," he told Dominguez. He turned away from Dusty's desk and the shriveled flower in her coffee cup. "Who was it that called him?"

"Somebody named Alex," the clerk said.

The parents reacted. "That is a name that Laurel sometimes used," the father said, raising his hand in a feeble gesture.

"I'm going by the house, in case he went back there," Jim told Dominguez, and lumbered toward the door. "Put out a BOLO for both of them."

Feigleman, still hovering, looked spellbound as he joined the parents.

FORTY-TWO

*A*lex wished he could have seen Rick's face when he took the call. That dumb shit would have trouble finding an elephant in a telephone booth. He regretted the mess he had left at the house, but he had waited a long time for Dusty and got carried away. He would make it up to Harriet by getting rid of Rick.

The Japanese Garden was quiet and almost deserted on its windswept causeway island. The only person he had seen since using the pay phone was some spacy black dude practicing kung fu moves down by the reflecting pool. His battle cries sounded to Alex like those of a bleating goat.

He backed Dusty's red car into a space against the fence out front so no cop on patrol would spot the tag. Most are too lazy to step outside their cars, especially in the summer heat. Rick had promised to come alone. No mention of Dusty on the telephone, but presumably Rick had figured it out by now. Sex and death—Rick and Dusty.

Alex paced back and forth over the wooden footbridge, the small stone bridge, through the pagoda, skirting the lanterns and the statues, seeking the best position. He stopped to gaze at the serene and placid smile of the big-bellied Hotei, a deity of good fortune. Perfect, he thought. A metal plaque beneath the statue called it the "Incarnation of Happiness." How appropriate. This would be the birthplace of his own incarnation as the one in control.

The bulk and weight of the gun at his waist gave him strength. The same breeze that rustled through the branches of the silver buttonwoods clanked the halyards of the sailboats moored at the Miami Yacht Club nearby. Alex listened to the bell-like chimes and reveled in the thrill of anticipation. No warrior, he thought, was ever more ready or eager for battle. Everything else that had happened was simply preparation for this night. He would show that damn cop.

He heard a car, saw the headlights. It was coming. The Hotei smiled. Alex smiled back.

A car door slammed. Just one, that was good. He came alone, as promised. For Laurel, that pasty-faced little puke? We'll soon see the last of her, too, he thought. He knew he was powerful enough now.

Alex heard the thud of cushioned footfalls, somebody running across the wooden bridge. So eager.

He drew the gun and held it in both hands behind him.

*R*ick ran into the garden. He was unarmed, carrying only the walkie which had been in the car. Seeing no one at first, he moved toward the Hotei, the meeting place at the end of a twisting path.

The shadows were warm and fragrant with oriental blossoms, jasmine, feather ginger and pomegranate. A galaxy of stars glittered overhead. The rotor blades of a sightseeing helicopter beat the air on the far, south side of the causeway. Miami's downtown sparkled gold and silver, the Centrust tower bathed in turquoise blue on this azure night. A night for lovers, he thought.

He still saw no one. Then there she was. Standing oddly, legs apart, chin up, hands behind her back, looking somehow fearless and boyish in the night, directly in front of the towering Buddhalike Hotei. She was smiling. My God, after all that has happened, he thought.

He reached out his hand as he approached. "Oh, babe."

She brought the gun from behind her back and dropped into a shooter's stance, the weapon extended in both hands in front of her.

He hesitated for only an instant, shook his head and kept approaching. "You can't shoot me. Everything is gonna be all right. You're sick, but I'm going to take of you and everything will be all right. I promise you."

The gun moved slightly to aim dead center at his chest.

"I'm not armed. I could never hurt you. Look."

He slowly bent to place the walkie on the ground, then straightened, his open hands empty and outstretched. "You can't shoot me," he said again. He shook his head and flashed his winning, boyish smile, "Hell, I'm the guy who taught you how to shoot. You love me, baby." He walked toward her without fear.

He was five feet away when Alex squeezed the trigger.

Rick saw an enormous flash of light and a puff of smoke that hung on the air. He never heard the shot that hit him. It went through the tip of his right thumb, shattering bone and halving the nail, slammed into the right side of his chest and continued out his back. The impact knocked him down. At first he thought he'd been hit only in the hand, which seemed to explode in pain, but as he rolled, seeking cover, a burning sensation snatched his breath away. He felt as though someone had rammed a red-hot poker through his chest.

The muzzle of the gun came closer. He saw nothing else until J. L. Sly appeared, out of nowhere, running toward the gun, eyes wide, terrified, shouting, "No! No!"

Cursing in surprise, Alex swung the gun toward him and fired twice, as J.L. dived behind the wooden bridge over the dry riverbed.

Rick's punctured right lung had collapsed. He realized what was happening. He could not breathe and in his struggle for air saw he was bleeding from the mouth.

Alex glanced briefly at him, then ran. J. L. Sly scrambled out of the dry riverbed and rushed to Rick, breathing heavily. "Son of a bitch! You got shot. You got shot."

"I'm gonna die," Rick gasped. "I'm dying."

"No!" Sly yelled again. "What should I do?"

Rick writhed in pain, gasping and unable to answer. Sly spied the walkie on the ground and dived on it.

"Mayday! Mayday!" he shouted, fumbling with the buttons. "We got an officer shot here. Mayday! Mayday!"

The dispatcher's voice was cool. "All other units stand by. Will the unit broadcasting identify himself."

"Mayday! Send an ambulance!"

"Are you a civilian?"

"Yeah, J. L. Sly."

"You say you have an injured officer?"

"Rick. Sergeant Rick Barrish. Somebody shot 'im. Hurry."

"What is your location?" The dispatcher's cool voice gave no hint of the grim-faced personnel in a growing cluster around her console.

"The Japanese Garden, on the causeway. By the big Buddha. Please hurry. He's choking! He can't breathe."

Jim made a screeching U-turn on the nearby Venetian Causeway at the first radio transmission, slapped the blue light onto the dashboard and opened up the siren.

"We have units en route," the dispatcher said. "Is the person with the gun still at the scene?"

J.L. scrambled around in the dirt, his eyes big and scared.

"No, I don't think so."

"Where is the officer hit?"

"What is this shit? Get an ambulance. Mayday!" he screamed.

"The squad is en route."

Another voice broke in. "J.L., this is Jim Ransom. I'm on the way. I'm not far, you can hear my siren coming. Where is he hit?"

"There's a hole in his chest, man, he's bleeding all over the place! He's spitting blood."

"Put the radio down, J.L. Take off your shirt. Fold it over four times and press it over the hole to stop the bleeding."

"I don't know first aid, man," he wailed. "I'm no medic."

"Do it. You can do it, J.L. Everybody has to be a hero sometime."

J.L. ripped off his shirt with both hands, buttons flying. He heard the sirens approaching as though from all directions. He was still holding the compress and whimpering, "Please, please," to Rick as they surrounded him and took over.

Jim rode in the rescue van with Rick, who stayed conscious, in excruciating pain as they hurtled across the expressway toward the hospital, sirens wailing, a police escort in the lead. Rick fought the oxygen, determined to talk. "I'm scared, Jim. She shot me—Laurel did it. You should've seen her. Like a stranger. Somebody I don't know." He gasped. "It's my fault. She's sick, and I'm gonna die. Don't let anybody hurt her." A wave of shock swept over him.

"Hang on," Jim said. "You're gonna be okay. I shudda been there. I shudda realized she knew about meeting in front of the fat man. She knows everything."

IVs in his arm, an oxygen mask over his face, deep inside his pain and shock, Rick experienced a strange sense of déjà vu as they rushed him into the hospital. He had seen all this before, from a patient's point of view. Doors crashing open, ceiling lights rushing by one after the other, rolling down the hallway at top speed. He had seen this a hundred times on television. This time he was the camera. He hated to die thinking about TV.

His welcoming committee impressed him. The entire trauma team was waiting, three or four nurses, four or five doctors, Aileen, looking totally professional and teary-eyed all at once. He tried to manage a smile.

Even the smooth move onto an examining table was excruciating. A doctor stood behind his head, reaching over in his surgical gloves, counting his ribs from the top down to find the spot. The hands disappeared. The next time Rick saw them, one held a scalpel. "Hold on," the doctor said. "I can't give you anything for pain because you're in shock."

He cut an inch-and-a-half incision and inserted a chest tube. Once the tube was in, the collapsed lung began to inflate and Rick was able to breathe. His chest still hurt, his split thumb throbbed, but for the first time since the huge flash of light, he began to think that perhaps he was not going to die.

He hurt bad every time they moved him and now they were taking him to X ray. "Find her, Jim," he whispered. "Don't let them hurt her. But watch yourself. She'll try to kill you. She's an escape artist, can slip outta the cuffs."

"Will you stay with him, Aileen?"

"Don't I always?"

*J*im only knew one place to look, the house on San Remo. The red car sat out front, the hood still warm. The yellow crime-scene seal on the front door was broken. Somebody was inside.

Gun drawn, he tried the front door. It was open. She was on her hands and knees with a sponge and paper towels, trying to clean a bloodstain off the living room rug. She looked up, small and vulnerable. "Jim. Do you know what happened here?" The amber eyes looked dull, like those of a corpse. Her voice dropped to an urgent whisper. "Where's Rick? Has something happened to Rick?"

Jim nodded. "He's hurt. He sent me to get you."

"Oh my God, is it serious?" Her stricken face was pale, smooth skin taut over luminous cheekbones. "I could see," she said, gesturing vacantly at the room around her, "that something terrible happened. I was working in the garden," she said slowly, as if struggling to remember. "Then Dusty came by . . ."

"I'll take you to the hospital. What have you got there?"

She was on her feet now, standing next to an open drawer in the sideboard. "I was looking for something and I found all these . . . things. I don't know who put them here."

Stacks of starched linen napkins and tablecloths had been pushed aside, exposing a visored cap, a ski mask, a man's dark glasses, a sheathed hunting knife, a handful of lottery tickets, some cash, a cameo brooch and a pair of gold earrings.

"They're not yours?"

"No, I never saw them before." She moved her fingers across half-closed eyes and cocked her head, as if listening for something only she could hear. "I don't think I have."

"What about that?" The gun lay in plain sight on the dining room table.

She stared. "Oh, that. Rick's off-duty gun. I don't know why he left it there. We should put it away. It's not safe. Benjie, the little boy next door, visits sometimes."

"I'll take care of it." Jim had holstered his own gun. "Let's go."

"To the hospital?"

"Yeah."

FORTY-THREE

*L*aurel waited quietly in a small interview room, staring timidly at the floor.

Dominguez joined them.

"When will I get to see Rick?" she asked.

"Later," the detective said.

She sipped coffee, showed little reaction when read her rights and willingly waived the presence of an attorney.

"Tell us what happened today," Jim said.

She looked confused. "You and Rick went to Key Largo."

"That's right. What did you do?"

"I worked in the yard. Then I was frightened because Benjie saw a man. I've been threatened," she said, leaning forward. "Somebody who hates me keeps doing things."

"What kind of things?"

"Threats, scaring me, stealing time from me."

The detectives exchanged glances.

"What time was it when you went out to work in the yard?"

"I—I'm not good on time. Rick can tell you that. I've always had that problem. It's been worse lately."

"Jesus Christ," Jim said. He and Dominguez conferred in the hallway during a break. "She's already pulling that incompetent crap."

"Maybe she really don't know what the hell day it is half the time."

"She's not nuts," Jim said. "It was jealousy, pure and simple. Now she's thinking about a legal defense."

"But what about the other stuff, the neighbor kid, the convenience-store . . ."

"Let's find out." They went back inside.

"Why did you kill Dusty?" Jim asked, point-blank.

"Dusty is dead?" The voice was a shocked whisper. She shook her head almost imperceptibly, eyes narrowing. "I don't believe it."

"You were jealous, weren't you?"

"Of Dusty? I don't like her, but I wouldn't hurt her."

"You killed her, then you tried to kill Rick. Why?"

"Try to kill Rick? That's insane. I love him. He's the only person in the world I feel safe with."

"Well, he sure ain't safe with *you,* lady."

Huddled pitifully in her chair, she was weeping now, her slim fingers covering her eyes. Jim almost felt sorry for her.

"We know you did it." He leaned forward in his chair, his big face close to hers. "Ballistics just came back. Dusty, Rick, Rob Thorne and some poor slob of a convenience-store clerk, an immigrant with three kids, just trying to make a living, they all got shot with the same gun. Rick's off-duty gun, the one he left home with you while he was working, the gun that magically turned up on your dining room table tonight, with your prints on it. The tooth fairy didn't put it there."

"No! No!" Her eyes went wild with terror, but only for a moment. Suddenly she relaxed and slumped back in the chair, head to one side, looking cocky and in command. The elbows, which had been rigid at her sides, found the armrests. She placed her left ankle on her right knee.

The sharp cheekbones seemed to melt into the flesh around them until the small face looked fuller. The eyes darkened into narrow slits. "I ain't gonna take any of this bullshit." The voice was husky and low. The lips curled as an angry index finger jabbed the air. "I don't have to talk to no goddamn cops. I'm up to here with cops," the finger slashed across the throat. "I want my lawyer."

"I thought you waived your right to have an attorney present," Dominguez said.

"Not me, asshole." The dark eyes stared arrogantly at Dominguez, then sneered at Jim. "Got yourself a new partner, I see. You keep losing them, huh?"

"Thanks to you."

"Well, we ain't admitting to nothing, but those fuckers deserved what they got. If Rick is still alive, I hope the hell he dies, squealing like a pig, just like she did."

Jim half rose from his seat, restrained by Dominguez.

"Let's talk outside, Jim."

"Did you see the change in her?" Dominguez muttered out in the hallway. "The eyes? I could've sworn we was talking to a different person."

A patrolman interrupted. "Her parents are here. They want Feigleman to sit in on any questioning."

"Oh, shit," Dominguez said.

"Maybe that's not such a bad idea," Jim said. "I don't like that sumbitch any more than you do, but he'll probably see through this bullshit. If nothing else, he'll see we're protecting her rights."

Feigleman joined them, looking intent. "She must be very frightened," he said.

"So frightened that she's cussing like a con and saying she hopes Rick dies," Jim said, raising his eyebrows.

"This is one tough cookie," Dominguez warned.

When they ushered the doctor inside, Laurel's chair was empty. Crouched on the floor in the farthest corner, she was whimpering softly, her right thumb in her mouth. The eyes under the tumbled bangs were terrified. "I wanna go home," she wailed in a baby voice, heels stomping in a full-blown tantrum. "Want my blankie!"

"Christ almighty," Jim said in disgust. "Whad I tell ya? Look at this act, Doc."

Feigleman placed a small tape recorder on the table and pushed the "record" button. "I'm here to help you," he said pleasantly. "Your parents sent me."

He smiled. "Don't cry. Why don't you come sit here and have a talk with us? Everything is going to be all right."

Jim watched the self-assured, unruffled doctor. How can anything ever be all right again? he thought. He turned his back for a moment to compose himself, then rejoined the charade.

Feigleman gently offered her his hand and coaxed. She had stopped wailing but was still snuffling and hiccupping. Shyly she took his hand, got to her feet and he led her to a seat.

"Comfy?" Feigleman said.

Jim wanted to throw up.

She nodded. "I wanna Coke." Her eyes were round and looked soft green.

Feigleman turned expectantly to the detectives. Dominguez went to fetch the soda.

When he placed the Coke before her, she stared at it in disdain and said she never drank soft drinks. Sitting up straight and looking for all the world like a suburban housewife, she said she would like a cup of coffee. When it was placed before her, she tasted it, closed gray eyes, wrinkled her nose and pronounced it terrible.

"Doesn't anyone around here know the proper way to brew coffee? This place is disgusting," she announced, emptying the ashtray into a wastepaper basket. She wiped it out compulsively with a tissue as the stony-faced detectives and the absorbed doctor watched. "And that light fixture hasn't been dusted in years," she said indignantly.

It was a long night.

At dawn they booked her into the women's detention center on charges of murder and attempted murder.

*F*rancis Albert Feigleman considered himself extremely fortunate. He had talked at some length to the adoptive parents, but the growing suspicion that now excited him had never even crossed his mind until witnessing the woman's sudden, split-second shifts of personality and demeanor. Even her eye color and physical appearance seemed to change.

Though he had gone without sleep, he felt too energized to go home. He returned to his office, brewed a pot of coffee and sat down to review his notes and the tapes he had recorded during the night.

What the Trevelyns knew about Laurel's early life was that it had been hideous. When she was three years old, her mother committed suicide. When Laurel was five, her father was arrested on sex charges. She was the victim. He went to prison, and Laurel went to the paternal grandparents who blamed her for their son's trouble. When he died in prison, killed by another inmate, they gave her up to the state.

The adoptive father owned and operated a successful furniture store. He and his wife were childless and lavished love on the forlorn little girl. Parenthood was not easy for them, however, and became increasingly more difficult because Laurel was a strange and erratic child.

"She seemed to have a mean streak that would come on for no reason at all," the mother told Feigleman. Though Laurel was highly intelligent, even scoring 146 on one IQ test, she had problems at school and often wandered off in a daze. At the start of one fall semester she reported to the fifth-grade classroom, insisting she belonged there, even though she had successfully completed fifth grade the prior spring. She frequently forgot people she knew and suffered bouts of apparent amnesia, depression and childish behavior far below her age level and abilities. At other times she was bright, efficient and cheerful, an athletic tomboy.

Hospitalized for three months when she was twelve, she was tested for epilepsy and treated with drugs and psychotherapy to deal with her mood swings. She returned home "cured," but the old patterns quickly reestablished themselves. The occasional mean streak commingled with promiscuous escapades as she blossomed into stunning adolescence.

Police had arrested her twice as a teenager. She was caught shoplifting in a Bal Harbour store, stealing items she had no need for, men's underwear, in fact. The second arrest was more serious, behind the wheel of a stolen car after a police chase. The car belonged to a neighbor. Luckily, Laurel was a juvenile at the time and did not incur a permanent police record. "She always lied," the mother said. "Even when she was caught red-handed she always claimed that it wasn't her, that somebody else did it." When she was younger her parents assumed she had "imaginary playmates." As she grew older, they concluded that she was a chronic liar.

After years of trying failed, after spending thousands of dollars on counselors, therapists and tests, the Trevelyns, in desperation, tried to solve their problem by throwing money at it, the theory being, give her what she wants so she won't get into trouble. They bought her a car so she would not steal one. They gave her money and credit cards. They continued to pour their resources into the maw of the monster, who still waxed erratic and unhappy. In their late sixties now, they were tired of trouble and at their wits' end, when she seemed to settle down a bit. They were aware of no unusual episodes for several months, then Rick entered the picture and their prayers were answered.

They held their breath until the couple moved in together. It had worked out. They decided their daughter's problems were all just phases she went through after all. Safely living with a man certainly capable of handling her, she even seemed happy, so they sighed with relief and moved to Orlando. There they could lounge around the pool with new friends, enjoying their retirement, talking about their daughter in Miami and waiting for a wedding and perhaps grandchildren to spoil, from a safe distance. "We did everything we could. Didn't we, Doctor?" the father asked plaintively.

Feigleman listened to the tapes over and over, stopping and replaying sections. She sounded like different people talking. He was barely able to contain his excitement. He would videotape the next session, to capture those physical transformations on tape. The parents, shaken and weary, had checked into a hotel. He looked at the time and wondered if it was still too early to call them. He would invite them to brunch or lunch. He had to make certain that they trusted him and hired no one else. This case had to be his exclusively. He was increasingly convinced that he had encountered a case so rare that it was the stuff of dreams, a patient to build a career on.

FORTY-FOUR

Rick was sitting up in bed, his color good. "You look a helluva lot better," Jim said.

"You wouldn't say that if you had been here when they took out the chest tube. I thought they were pulling my whole lung out of that little hole."

"You'll be back to work in no time."

"Who are you kidding, Jim? You know I can never come back."

"Whaddaya mean? You'll be going home in a day or two, the doc says you'll be a hundred percent in a couple a weeks."

"The department says my injury is not service related. The chief hasn't been by to see me. You know what that means. Christ, every cop who stubs his big toe gets a hospital visit from the chief. They're treating what happened to Dusty and me as a love triangle, a domestic. I'm an embarrassment to the department."

"Hell, all you have to do to embarrass this department is hand the chief a microphone."

"The handwriting is on the wall."

"It ain't fair," Jim said bitterly. "The whole fucking thing is just not fair. There's something else. Another body."

"What do you mean? Who?"

"Barry, that aerobics instructor from the fitness center. The guy with the ponytail. Tawny Marie found him. Mutilated. Went by and got his landlady to open the door."

"You don't think . . ."

"Yup. Ballistics isn't finished, but it was a .38 and I'm betting it was from your off-duty gun. The last visitor his neighbors saw sounds like little Laurel. Wearing a leather miniskirt. We found one in a closet at your place."

"What happened?"

"He'd been dead more than a week. It was bad. Looks like they were partying and things got out of hand. Somebody used a really sharp blade to take off his three-piece set. Haven't found it yet."

"Christ almighty."

"You should consider yourself lucky that all you took was a bullet in the chest. Watch," he said grimly. "She'll get kid-glove treatment in jail and probably wind up in a hospital. Mark my words. Meanwhile, Dusty's stuff was boxed and sent back to Iowa. So was she. The department didn't even send anybody to the funeral. Just like that, it's all over. We lose two of the best cops on the department . . ." He shook his head. "Something's wrong." He blinked and looked away. "I should've quit a long time ago."

"Hey, partner." Rick tried to sound cheerful, but his voice was hollow. "Don't look so grim. I'm not dead. I'll still be around."

"What are you going to do?"

"I don't know. I'll still thinking about that. Maybe PI, or I could sell insurance."

"Oh, sure." Jim's voice was derisive. "You oughta fight for your goddamn job. The Fraternal Order of Police would back you."

Rick shook his head. "Seven years to go, to qualify for a pension, and I blew it. Boy, did I blow it."

"All the women in the world and you find that one. What are you gonna do about her?"

"I've talked to her folks. They're gonna hire Sloat to represent her."

"Sloat? That son of a bitch?"

"I told them he was the best."

"You sure you didn't get shot in the head? I hope that's just your pain pills talking."

"Feigleman says she's sick."

"There's another sumbitch. He's already playing footsie with her family. He sees a high-profile case, his name in the newspaper. And her folks, after all they dumped on you. . . . What about Dusty?" he asked angrily.

"I won't ever forgive myself, Jim." Rick sank back on the pillows and looked away, staring out the window. "I can't believe she's gone. I feel so goddamn guilty. She was a good woman, a fair person. She'd understand. Help me through this, will you, partner?"

"Sure," Jim said morosely.

*J*im stopped by the church later. Just to think, he told himself. It was empty, a weekday afternoon. He sat for a long time.

As he walked through the courtyard garden toward the street, the young pastor called out to him. "Did you get my messages, Jim? Are you all right? You don't look well. Your partners . . . It must be difficult."

Jim did not answer. The pastor walked with him.

"It's so damn unfair, and there is no justice," Jim finally said. "All my life I've been part of the system—part of the problem. It's broken down, it doesn't work. I wasted all those years on something that's a piece a shit."

"Nobody promised that life would be fair, Jim. But there is justice, if not here, then a higher justice." Concern etched the clergyman's broad, sincere face.

They stood together in the shadow of the tall iron gate between the rectory and the street. "Some people don't like to wait that long. What if this is all we ever have?"

"You can't think that way, Jim, not if you believe in God."

Jim's brief smile was sardonic as he lifted his eyes. "If there is a God, he must be out for a beer." He turned on his heel and left.

*L*aurel was moved into a solitary cell at the women's detention center. There were several reasons, including alleged sexual overtures to other inmates. She was already on a suicide watch because when not compulsively cleaning her quarters, cursing the guards or stalking other prisoners, she was sobbing hysterically, like a child.

Sloat agreed to represent her after a conference with Feigleman and the parents. The lawyer met Laurel for the first time in an interview room at the center. Feigleman was also present.

When they emerged from the interview, the faces of the two men were as radiant as those of little boys on Christmas morning.

FORTY-FIVE

The psychiatrist and the defense attorney wore pinstripes to the arraignment and pale blue shirts that would photograph well on TV. Sloat had informed Laurel's parents that he would request a psychiatric evaluation. He elaborated no further, thus avoiding the risk of being challenged on some point. Once the juggernaut of publicity began, it would be impossible to stop.

Sloat rubbed his palms together and scanned the courtroom. Exactly the way he liked it, standing room only. The press section was packed. The usual court observers, mostly older folks sick of TV soap operas, were out in force, as well as a number of off-duty police officers.

Laurel's entrance created a stir among the murmuring spectators. The jailhouse beauticians had outdone themselves. Nicely manicured, perfectly made up, she wore a new hairdo, a short, boyish cut, and she wore it well. Sloat had suggested that she dress simply and demurely and she and her mother had selected a soft pink dress with a lacy collar. She looked like a schoolgirl.

Jim stood watching just inside the courtroom door.

The proceeding was routine. The plea was not guilty. Sloat moved that Laurel be transferred to a private psychiatric hospital for evaluation and treatment, if necessary. Instead of the usual thirty to ninety days, the lawyer requested an unspecified length of time.

The judge raised his eyebrows. Sloat dropped his bombshell.

"This is an unusual situation, your honor. We all have read such true stories as *The Three Faces of Eve* and *Sybil.*" Total silence reigned as Sloat turned theatrically to his client, pinky ring flashing. "You see such a case standing before you now, your honor. Dr. Feigleman has conducted some preliminary interviews, and he is convinced, as I am, that my client is a victim of multiple personality disorder.

"We have reason to believe"—he paused for effect—"that at least five different and distinct personalities occupy the body of this young woman."

"Most likely the result of unbearable abuse she suffered as a child," volunteered Feigleman, unable to contain himself any longer.

"As to whether any of *them* are guilty of a crime remains to be seen. *She* is not," Sloat said. "She has no knowledge whatever of any of the crimes with which she is charged."

"It is an illness," Feigleman added. "A disorder that can be cured." He continued, his Adam's apple bobbing behind his bowtie. "In the past, multiple personality disorder may have been confused with schizophrenia. But that's wrong. It is definitely not schizophrenia. It is something far more rare. What she suffers from is a multitude of personalities warring inside the same body, grappling for control, emerging, submerging and reemerging in sudden unpredictable bursts."

The judge appeared skeptical. "What did you say would cause this disorder?"

"Repeated abuse as a child, probably sexual abuse. A little child trapped in a painful and abusive situation copes by withdrawing, and part of the personality is shut off to deal with the horror and pain. Another part of that child goes on as if nothing happened.

"If the trauma continues through important stages of development, it happens again and again. That explains her lack of knowledge about what occurred when one of them was in control. The transitions can be triggered by stress."

"The good news," Sloat said, nodding his head sagely, "is that it is curable."

"Are you positive?"

"Yes," Feigleman said emphatically. "The treatment is called fusion therapy. I'd like to begin as soon as possible."

The judge ordered the evaluation but refused to leave it open-ended. He instructed Sloat and Feigleman to report on their progress in ninety days and left the bench.

The press moved in one motion, like a great wave, toward the door.

The pressroom stood open to accommodate the crowd that spilled out into the hall along with the glare of high-intensity camera lights. Sloat and Feigleman presided, their faces aglow. Laurel, looking bewildered, had been returned to the women's detention center. Her parents were present, however, a bit dazzled by all the attention, but eager to assist in her cause and to make it clear to reporters that the abuse suffered by their daughter had taken place long before they ever saw her.

Jim lingered to watch the spectacle on a TV monitor set up in a hallway by one of the local affiliates. He had not slept, had not eaten. Who could? he thought.

Sloat was describing Laurel's condition as "a form of posttraumatic stress disorder, such as afflicts some Vietnam War veterans."

Feigleman offered that "Laurel Trevelyn, the core personality, remembers none of the abuse she suffered as a toddler and a young child. But the others do, and it fills them with rage and anger, accounting for her behavioral problems over the years."

He shifted his eyes to the parents for affirmation. They nodded vigorously.

"As a small child, she was sexually abused by her natural father. The records we have been able to find indicate that the man dominated and terrorized her mother. Laurel discovered her mother's body—in a sea of blood—in a bathtub, her wrists slashed. This little child became convinced that somehow she was to blame for her mother's death. The child's physician later reported her sexual abuse, and she testified against her own father. When he went to jail, our juvenile authorities, acting with their usual wisdom, released this already traumatized little girl to her parental grandparents, who then"—the doctor's voice rose—"blamed her for his incarceration and subsequent death in prison."

"When this child was given up for adoption, these good people," Sloat said, his gesture sweeping, "came into the picture, gave her a loving home and did what they could, but it was too late. The damage had been done."

"Doctor, how does an abused child become a multiple personality?" The questioner, a young black woman, held a radio microphone bearing the call letters of a local station.

"Personalities begin to split off the core in self-defense to maintain safety and sanity. Painful experiences are broken into parts with which each personality can deal. Each personality has different and consistent traits. They usually emerge when the victim is angry or under stress."

"Doctor, isn't it a conflict of interest for you, the police psychiatrist, to represent a defendant accused of shooting two police officers?" The thin, intense young man in horn-rimmed glasses was an investigative reporter for the morning paper. Always looking for something to expose, Feigleman thought furiously, instead of paying attention to the real story.

"Not at all," Feigleman answered, removing his eyeglasses in an effort to appear more earnest. "I am in private practice and merely a part-time consultant to the department. An important aspect of that job is counseling, not only police officers but their loved ones. Laurel certainly fits that criteria, but in order that there be no question, I will be resigning my post as of this afternoon to devote more of my time and energy to this case."

"Who are these other personalities, what are they like?" a sleek, honey-blond anchorwoman wanted to know.

"We know of four, in addition to Laurel," Feigleman said enthusiastically, relieved to see the questioning back on track. "That is not to say that no others exist. Some MPD victims have had as many as ninety-nine different personalities, each with distinctly separate identities, physical characteristics, attitudes, speech, handwriting and values. They can be different ages and sexes, with varying degrees of intelligence. In this case one of them, a male personality named Alex, appears to be antisocial and the root of many of the patient's problems."

"I have met a frightened little girl named Jennifer and a flirtatious young woman who calls herself Marilyn," Sloat said, seizing the spotlight. "As well as Harriet, a woman who is apparently the housekeeper among them, adept at cooking and cleaning and homemaking."

Jim's incredulous expression caught the eye of one of the reporters log-jammed outside the door. "What do you think, Detective?"

"It's all bullshit. Do they get an Academy Award now or later? This is nothing but a circus, a fucking three-ring circus. Lookit those guys," he said angrily, staring at the screen where Sloat and Feigleman were now talking in tandem.

*I*t was the night of the full moon over Miami. The shooting started early.

Irate shopkeepers, employees and customers armed with soda bottles, guns and CB radios won a bloody gun battle with two armed robbers. The manager of a produce market was beaten to death in a fight over who would unload a truckload of onions from Texas. An enraged auto repairman shot down a dissatisfied customer who had stopped payment on a check. And a troubled Vietnam veteran held his landlady hostage at rifle point in a rundown hotel for hours, demanding to talk to the president. Cuban gangs stomped Puerto Ricans, American blacks fought Haitians and Anglo rednecks warred with blacks and Latins.

The afternoon shift went on overtime, and the midnight crew was called in early. The story of Laurel's courtroom appearance and the press conference that followed was stripped across page one in the afternoon paper. When Jim arrived at the office, a copy folded under his arm, he found an apologetic secretary cleaning out Rick's desk. "The lieutenant says we need the room. We have to have some place to put your new sergeant."

Among his messages was one from Sloat. Jim crumpled and tossed it. The lawyer called again five minutes later.

"Sorry to bother you, Detective, but we plan to confer with my client this evening, prior to her transfer to the hospital in the morning. The parents will not be present. They're exhausted. It's been quite a day.

"The judge has suggested that, in the interests of propriety, someone from your department sit in on this meeting. We have no objection. We want it made clear that there is no coaching involved, no prompting of the defendant on our part." He paused. "I know the revelations today may have been a surprise."

"Yeah," Jim said, "and I don't like surprises. Neither does Rick. He's been released from the hospital and saw the news this afternoon. He talked to the parents last night. They didn't mention this multiple personality business."

"It was a surprise to them too. Everything has been happening so fast that Dr. Feigleman and I haven't had much opportunity to report to the family first. If you're busy," Sloat said, almost too accommodatingly, "we understand. But we wanted to extend the invitation, per the judge's suggestion."

Jim sighed and picked up a pencil. "Gimme the time and place." He called Rick, filled him in, grabbed a slice of pizza, his first food of the day, then took his next call, a routine DOA. Full moon, he thought, as he drove there alone, with all hell breaking out in the city and they give a routine case to the most experienced man in homicide. Another demonstration of the brainpower in charge. The department was like a freight train roaring downhill at top speed with nobody at the helm. He, Dusty and Rick had been a terrific team, the cases they had solved, the hours they had worked. The years. They should have been bringing us gifts of frankincense and myrrh, he thought. Instead they don't give a shit what happens to any of us.

His mind was made up by the time he reached the scene. When he got back to the office he would find the forms and fill out his retirement papers. The bastards! Dumping Rick, treating Dusty like her life didn't matter—no reason to hang around now. He was eligible for retirement, and he would take it—make it effective in thirty days. With the vacation time he had coming, he could leave next week. He had no plans beyond that. In the old days he and Molly used to talk about what they would do when he retired. Too bad it was too late. Twenty-seven years and what did he have to show for it. Time to walk away. Should've done it a long time ago, he thought.

The call was at an old house, fallen into disrepair, in a changing neighborhood. The man who lived there for fifty years had died there, slumped on the bathroom floor. Elderly people who die of natural causes generate routine paperwork, distasteful tasks, and they remind detectives of their own mortality. They offer no challenge to investigative skills, and because so many older people live and die alone and their corpses often lie undiscovered for days, dealing with them is decidedly unpleasant. That was the case on this call. Flies had led the uniforms to the dead man after they broke in through a front window.

A neighbor had become suspicious and called it in just before dark. She had not seen the old man for days and his porch light had been burning constantly.

She was concerned. A frugal man who just got by, he was never one to waste electricity. He tried to keep expenses down. His budget was too tight to take a newspaper or even own a telephone. Death appeared to be from natural causes.

In the bedroom Jim found a locked metal file box. The likely place for burial instructions and personal papers with the names of the next of kin. Sure enough, the key was taped to the bottom, probably so it would not be mislaid. So many of the elderly who lived alone were forgetful. Jim opened the box and found a scrapbook of faded family photos that appeared to have been taken in pre–World War II Europe. Beneath the scrapbook was what made him gasp. Stacks and stacks and stacks of bills, hundreds and fifties, almost all old-time silver certificates, worth more than face value now. Thousands and thousands of dollars, and a smaller metal box with gold jewelry and coins, old silver dollars in mint condition and an antique gold pocket watch. Another survivor of the Depression, Jim thought. Many go to their graves still distrusting banks, hoarding away life savings in shoe boxes or coat linings or mattresses.

Jim turned to summon one of the young uniforms to witness and help inventory the find, then hesitated. Why should the man's uncaring relatives cash in? This kind of money could set him and Rick up in any sort of business they chose. Neither had ever taken a dime, and look where it had gotten them, he thought bitterly.

He strolled into the kitchen, found a big brown, double grocery bag and carried it folded, at his side, into the bedroom. A lanky uniform cop stood a few feet inside the front door, his nose wrinkled in distaste at the odor. "Do me a favor, will ya," Jim said. "I think the medical examiner's wagon must be lost. They should've been here by now. The driver is probably having a problem with the address. Go down to the corner and see if they're looking for us on Sixty-seventh Terrace instead of Sixty-seventh Street."

"I thought you just called them."

"Nah, they should've been here already."

The officer shrugged and stepped out onto the porch.

His heart thudding painfully in his chest, hands shaking, Jim filled the big brown bag with the stacks of bills and the smaller metal box. He moved fast. There was *so* much. He stuffed old receipts and bills from a bureau into the top of the grocery bag along with some newspapers to camouflage the contents. He dropped all of the old man's unopened mail, old papers and letters into the file box. He would conspicuously examine it in front of witnesses at the station, in case someone asked questions later.

He carried the grocery bag out the door, past two young patrolmen, and set it on the front seat of his unmarked Plymouth. "Give me a hand, will ya, and bring out the file box in there."

An officer carried the box out onto the porch. "I haven't looked in here yet," Jim announced, "but there may be some clue to next of kin. Open it up." He lifted the scrapbook and stirred all the papers he had shoved beneath it. "Yeah, there must be a name to contact in here. Somebody's got to foot the funeral bill," he said. "We don't want to stick the taxpayers with it. Put this in the trunk for me, I'll go through it back at the station along with that other stuff in the bag."

The young cop nodded, closed the box and placed it in the trunk of Jim's car.

"Jesus, that damn pizza." Jim winced and pressed his fist into his chest to relieve the heartburn. No more lousy rubbery pizza for me, he thought, sliding heavily behind the wheel. This is it. Time to retire. Thank God for the call from the neighbor across the street. The treasure trove he had found was a crack monster's dream. Had one of them broken in, there would have been nothing left.

He wondered what the gold coins and silver dollars were worth. The dead man had held them for decades. He would call Rick after the meeting at the detention center. He would just tell him, at first, that he was putting in his papers. It was over. Never again would he see or smell another dead body. He was never again going to have to look at maggots, wipe gore off his shoes or be stared at by the empty eyes of some corpse.

He wondered why the old man had never moved out of that crummy house and this stinking neighborhood. He could have had the best. Sometimes, Jim thought, we cling too long to familiar things. This neighborhood was one of the worst. He shook his head as he drove past rows of dilapidated homes and run-down apartment buildings. This guy was lucky he didn't get ripped off a long time ago. Probably because he looked like he had nothing to steal. He obviously did not whip out his gold pocket watch to check the time in this neighborhood. In the thirties and forties, it had been top drawer. But that was long ago. The corner he was passing now was where the 1980 riots had begun, a bad neighborhood.

His career was at an end. Fuck the police department. Fuck all the dead bodies. He almost said it aloud, thinking for a moment that Rick was beside him. They had been partners for so long they could almost read each other's thoughts. He knew what Rick would say about what he was doing. He could hear his voice: "It makes you as bad as they are."

He remembered the pastor. "There is justice . . . a higher justice."

Shit, he hated the pricks, the connivers, the thieves on both sides of the badge. He sighed aloud, knowing suddenly that he could never be one of them. No matter how justified or providential it might seem, he thought, this just ain't right.

He sighed again. Some damn relative, who probably never gave a hoot about the old man, is about to come into a nice inheritance. He had joined the department an honest man, and that was the way he would leave it. At least he would have that. He shook his head and almost smiled. Once a chump, always a chump.

The squeezing sensation in his chest intensified—heartburn city. He rolled the window down for some air and breathed deeply. The pain struck with such cataclysmic intensity that his knees jerked up and cracked against the steering wheel. He knew what it was. But it can't be, he thought. Not now. *Not now.* The pain was agonizing. His clenched hands gripped the wheel as the car mounted the sidewalk and thudded to rest against a telephone pole.

A fucking heart attack. He hoped the pain would ease up long enough for him to use the radio. Faces—he saw faces in the shadows out on the street. They had seen the car mount the sidewalk and roll into the pole. He reached for the walkie, next to the paper bag on the seat next to him. But the radio slipped from his trembling grasp and fell to the floor as pain convulsed his entire body. He needed help. Groping blindly for the door handle, he pushed it hard, with all the strength he had left. It fell open, swinging wide. He would have fallen with it, but his seat belt held him securely in place. He saw the faces. Closer now, wary and curious at first, now more confident. Help—they would get him help. The first was a scrawny, swaggering teenager, a street thug, the local purse snatcher, Jim thought. But he was a cop, and he needed help. "Help me, call the squad," he gasped. "Police."

The thin young face with crafty, soulless eyes was close to him now. "Police," he repeated. He was grinning and unfastening Jim's watch. The detective saw a glint of gold tooth as the still grinning youth reached across him for the police radio. Other faces moved in closer, bolder. The car doors were all open now. Jim felt hands on his body. His gun, his wallet, his badge case. The big brown bag disappeared from the seat beside him, passed from hand to hand with inquisitive murmurs until there was a sound like a sigh and then scrambling noises among the scavengers that surrounded the car.

No! No! he thought, gasping for breath. Not like this. This isn't fair. Molly! Oh, Molly! Pain exploded in his chest. He listened to his own moans and could not move. His last conscious thought was about his shoes. They were taking his goddamn shoes.

*7*he medical examiner's wagon arrived ninety minutes after Jim had left the dead man's house. Twenty minutes later, after the body was removed, the waiting uniforms checked back into service, or tried to. Their radio transmissions to the dispatcher were disrupted by playful citizens. Hoots and hollers.

"Hey, we got your radio!" Loud laughter and music. A police radio had obviously fallen into the wrong hands. It happens. Forgetful officers occasionally leave them in restaurants or on the roofs of their cars. Sometimes they are stolen, or dropped during a foot chase. Strange voices intruding on police frequencies could also mean the officer that radio was assigned to is in trouble and needs help.

Between the curses and insults broadcast over the wayward walkie, the dispatcher conducted an on-the-air roll call. Every man and woman on duty responded, except one. Jim Ransom. The location of his last call was broadcast and a manhunt launched.

*R*ick heard the news when he went to the station to pick up his belongings and wait for Jim to come back from the conference at the women's detention center. He joined Dominguez and Mack Thomas. "Jesus, will you look at that moon," Dominguez said, as they drove toward the address of Jim's last call. The huge yellow disk hung low over the city. "We are in for it tonight."

"Never fails," Mack said.

They passed the corner where the 1980 riots had started.

"Something's wrong," Rick said. "It's too damn quiet."

"Yeah," Dominguez said. "Where is everybody? Nobody's out on the street."

"If this neighborhood had birds they wouldn't be singing. This must be how the settlers felt just before the Indian attack," Mack said, scrutinizing the oddly deserted streets and alleyways.

Rick saw it first. "Is that . . . that *can't* be one of our cars. It is!"

"Oh, shit!" Dominguez said, screeching to a stop. Jim's unmarked was difficult to recognize. The hood and the trunk lid were up, the battery was missing and the city tag was gone. So were the tires and the wheels. Pale bare feet hung out the open passenger side door. The dead driver was sprawled naked across the front seat.

*R*ick called the married daughter in Orlando from Jim's desk at the station. He asked her to call Molly. He sat there alone for some time. The office was nearly empty. Everybody was out on the street.

A clerk switched on a TV news report. The police chief expressed his outrage. The mayor delivered an emotional speech. "What has this city become," he asked, "when scavengers rob the dead? When a dedicated public servant, a law enforcement officer who devoted his entire life to the city of

Miami, is picked clean by human vultures and left to die like an animal in the street?"

Had he been with Jim, Rick thought, he might have saved him. He knew he could have prevented what happened after. What was it Jim had always said? Even the dead aren't safe in Miami. Jim was right. He shouldn't have died alone. He wouldn't have—I would have been with him, he thought, had it not been for Laurel. Dusty would have been with him, if not for Laurel. He remembered what Jim had said about Laurel. In the rescue van, after the shooting at the Japanese Garden, when Rick thought he was dying. Jim had held his hand, raging, "I shudda been there. I shudda realized . . . she knows everything."

She knows everything. Everything. He checked his watch. The session at the women's detention center was already under way.

*7*hough the doctor and lawyer could scarcely conceal their elation, Laurel appeared nervous, gnawing at her lip. She faced them across the wooden table in the interview room. They were somewhat relieved that no one from the department had joined them after all. They could speak more freely.

"I thought I was going to the hospital right away," Laurel said, her voice tense. "I don't want to stay here another night."

"The admittance had to be arranged," Sloat said. "First thing in the morning—you're outta here. Don't worry. Things could not be progressing better."

"You would not believe the interest your case has already generated," Feigleman said.

"We've already had inquiries about book rights and at least one call from a major Hollywood studio. Once we sort out all the offers, we can negotiate a deal," the lawyer said.

Laurel acted as though she had not heard. "What will it be like?"

"What?"

"Tomorrow, the hospital."

"It's a private hospital," Feigleman said soothingly. "You have your own room, your own color TV, arts and crafts if you care to participate, and I'll see you there every day."

"I don't want to go to prison." Her voice had dropped to a whisper, and she looked stricken.

"You won't." Sloat's words rang with confidence. "*Never* happen. Tomorrow you kiss this place good-bye for good."

"How can you be so sure?"

He leaned forward, his smile almost a leer. "The treatment for multiple personality disorder is psychotherapy, individual analysis for each of the personalities, with fusion the ultimate goal."

She still looked confused.

"Do you realize how long that will take?" Feigleman said. "Years and years."

"During that time," the lawyer continued, "you will be incompetent to stand trial. Under Florida law, when a defendant is not declared competent after five years, all charges are dismissed—forever. That's not all." His shiny fingernails tapped a burnished leather folder. "I've done my homework. Should you go to trial, you stand an excellent chance of acquittal. There are precedents. An Ohio man with twenty-four personalities was found innocent, by reason of insanity, of kidnapping, raping, and robbing three women. In another case, a California man was acquitted of killing his wife after his doctors convinced the jury that the crime was committed by one of the husband's separate identities, not him."

"Young lady," Feigleman said, "you don't have a worry in the world."

"Except," Sloat said, "maybe, who plays you in the movie. You're going to be a celebrity."

Both men laughed, caught up in their own excitement.

Laurel stared at the floor.

Her eyes darkened as she raised her head. Her elbow found the table, her fist balled under her chin. The other hand was open and on her hip.

"What happens to us if this fusion therapy works?" the husky voice asked.

The two men exchanged glances, and Feigleman hesitated a moment. "After the problems of each personality are solved in analysis, all are eventually absorbed into a single well-rounded individual."

"Who is the one who survives and keeps control?"

"I think the answer to that will come later, during therapy," the doctor said uneasily.

"Remember," Sloat said quickly, "the course we are taking means treatment and hospitalization rather than prosecution and imprisonment."

His client nodded. "One more thing." Doctor and lawyer sat at attention. "Jennifer wants her Teddy and her blankie. She says she can't sleep without them."

"Teddy and blankie," the lawyer repeated solemnly, jotting it down in a notebook. When he looked up again, his client's body language had assumed a straight-backed, prim posture. Staring with distaste at a rude word some other inmate had scrawled in pencil on the smooth tabletop, she tried to rub it clean with her handkerchief, then stared at the two men.

"What about my right to the house? That is my home."

The lawyer nodded and scribbled another note. "That may be a touchy matter since you were not married and the relationship was of relatively short duration."

"The man made me promises," she snapped. "We were living as man and wife."

"I have an associate whose speciality is domestic litigation, and I'll have him check into it. We'll make sure that any interests you have are protected."

"I think that about does it," Feigleman said cheerfully.

Sloat nodded and snapped his briefcase shut. "It's been a long day."

The two men pushed back their chairs. Laurel stared in panic, then looked wildly around her at the colorful cartoon-character murals on every wall.

"Please don't leave me alone here. I'm scared," she said.

"This time tomorrow, you will be in your own room with all the comforts of home," Feigleman said. He spoke the words slowly and soothingly.

"It's max security of course," Sloat added. "Otherwise the judge never would have agreed, but it's comfortable."

"Comfy," Feigleman said, his pink skin flushed above the bowtie.

"Don't go," she pleaded, half rising and reaching out to them.

"Everything will be fine," Sloat said. "Compared to what most cop killers face, you are going to come out way ahead of the game."

"I'm not a cop killer!" She shook her head and slumped back into her chair.

"Of course not," Feigleman said gently.

"You couldn't help yourself," Sloat crooned.

"I'll look in on you tomorrow after you're settled at the hospital," the doctor said.

She did not answer. She huddled in the chair, weeping like a brokenhearted child. The two men moved to the door, and Sloat punched the buzzer. "Shall we stop somewhere for a drink?" the lawyer asked.

"By all means. I think the occasion calls for one."

A corrections officer let them out of the locked interview room, removed his handcuffs from his belt and manacled Laurel's left wrist to the arm of her chair. "A matron will be back for you in a minute," he told her.

Alone in the room, Laurel wept aloud, venting her misery and hopelessness. Eventually the tears subsided and the room grew quiet.

7he slumped figure straightened and stretched. The right foot tapped speculatively. Jangly metallic sounds, as the handcuffs fell away from an arched wrist. Pacing the room now. No one coming.

The table made a scraping sound when dragged over to the window. The chair on top. The latch. The screen screeched slightly as it was pushed out of place.

Alex swung his legs out the window, clung for a moment to the dusty sill and then dropped easily to the wet grass. He landed in a crouch. Free again, in the warm and moonlit night. The smells of mowed grass and rain were in the air. He breathed deeply, drinking it in, almost greedily. He stood and wiped his hands on his jeans. No one in sight. Did they think he was stupid? He knew what fusion therapy meant. That doctor wants to kill me, he thought.

But he won't get the chance. Alex listened again to the endless whispering in the palm trees. Darkness always gave him a sense of freedom, especially on this night. Breaking out of a place is almost as exhilarating as breaking in, he thought. He felt no remorse. They were all so stupid.

Alex smiled at the thought. He trotted down the small landscaped slope toward the street, then froze like a shadow, his skin prickling. Smile gone, his eyes probed the darkness. He raised his head and sniffed the air like some wary nocturnal animal seeking the source of danger. Something stirred in the bushes between him and the street. A familiar figure slowly straightened to full height and brought up the long gun from behind dense shrubbery.

Oh shit, Alex thought, bushwhacked. He was waiting for me. Sharp sounds of metal on metal, as Rick pumped a round into the chamber, the sliding action of a Remington twelve-gauge shotgun, police issue. Nowhere to run. Alex shook his head slowly.

"Wait!" he shouted. .

Unforgiving eyes never wavered.

They all screamed, as the night dissolved into a deadly burst of light.

ABOUT THE AUTHOR

Edna Buchanan's police-beat stories won her a 1986 Pulitzer Prize in journalism. *Nobody Lives Forever* is her third book and first novel. As crime reporter for *The Miami Herald* she has covered over five thousand violent deaths, three thousand of them murders. She lives in Miami Beach with her dog, Rocky Rowf, and her five cats, Misty Blue Eyes, Flossie, Baby Dear, Sharky and Kim.